"Crafting characters rich with emotion, Amanda Cabot pens a compelling story of devastation and loss, of healing and second chances—but most of all, of transcending faith."

Tamera Alexander, bestselling author, *From a Distance*, *Beyond This Moment*, and *The Inheritance* (Women of Faith Fiction)

"*Scattered Petals* combines memorable imagery and likable characters in a story that illustrates both the redemptive power of forgiveness and the beauty of unselfish love in ways readers will not soon forget."

Stephanie Grace Whitson, author, *A Claim of Her Own*

"A wonderful novel with heartrending depth of raw, human emotions, *Scattered Petals* brings the reader face to face with unspeakable tragedy. Amanda Cabot's gifted pen tells a beautiful story of sorrow, pain, and forgiveness with the hope of unconditional love set amidst the backdrop of the 1856 Texas frontier. Don't miss this second book in the Texas Dreams series!"

Maggie Brendan, author, Heart of the West series

"*Scattered Petals* is an exceptional book! Insight into situations that sometimes appear unfathomable, the healing power of God's love, and the consolation he provides so magnificently are written with heartfelt emotion that brings the characters' romantic love to life. Do not miss *Scattered Petals*. Reading it is an experience that fills the heart with joy."

"In *Scattered Petals*, Amanda Cabot crafts a compelling story of lives shattered by cowardice and greed, of bearing unspeakable pain and sorrow and regret—all redeemed and restored through faith and trust in a steadfast Lord. From the deepest of tragedies comes the sweetest love. A wonderful sense of community and an endearing core cast have me eagerly awaiting the next book in the Texas Dreams series. Bravo, Ms. Cabot!"

"Amanda Cabot tugs hard at the heartstrings in *Scattered Petals*, the deeply emotional story of a resilient woman who faces unimaginable tragedy and a selfless man who gives all to see her spirit restored. I highly recommend this poignant novel."

"In *Scattered Petals*, Amanda Cabot creates wonderful, believable characters that capture your heart. Both hero and heroine have deep wounds that make them say 'never again.' But with a strong story and a skillful touch, Cabot turns their 'never again' into 'forever after.'"

Scattered
Petals

SCATTERED PETALS

A NOVEL

TEXAS DREAMS • 2

Amanda Cabot

Revell

a division of Baker Publishing Group
Grand Rapids, Michigan

Published by Revell
a division of Baker Publishing Group
P.O. Box 6287, Grand Rapids, MI 49516-6287
www.revellbooks.com

Printed in the United States of America

Library of Congress Cataloging-in-Publication Data
Cabot, Amanda, 1948–
    Scattered petals : a novel / Amanda Cabot.
        p.   cm. — (Texas dreams ; bk. 2)
    ISBN 978-0-8007-3325-4 (pbk.)
    1. Orphans—Fiction. 2. Cowboys—Fiction. 3. Texas Hill Country (Tex.)—
Fiction. 4. Texas—History—1846–1950—Fiction. I. Title.
PS3603.A35S33 2010
813′.6—dc22   2009044969

10   11   12   13   14   15   16   7   6   5   4   3   2   1

In memory of my grandmothers, Augustina Sempert Harte and Charlotte Preble Bailey. Though they were two very different women, their deep faith and love of the Bible helped shape my childhood.

1

November 1856

"How much longer?"

Priscilla Morton tried to smile at the woman on the opposite side of the stagecoach. Now that Papa was asleep, Mama's normally quiet voice had turned querulous, sending waves of regret through her daughter as her words reminded Priscilla for what seemed like the thousandth time that this was her fault. She was the one who'd insisted they come.

"Soon." Priscilla reached across to pat her mother's hand, her smile wry when she recalled Mama warning her to be careful what she wished for. Priscilla had wished for adventure, never dreaming that the adventure would involve comforting her mother as if Mama were the child.

When they'd received Clay's letter inviting the family to his wedding, Priscilla had realized this was the opportunity she had sought for so long and had convinced Mama and Papa they should go to Texas. Though she'd relished the idea of leaving Massachusetts and venturing into parts of the country that her sister had described as wild and foreign, she had been careful in phrasing her arguments. While her parents would not willingly seek adventure, they loved Clay, and so it had taken little persuasion for them to agree that Clay deserved to have family with him at his wedding, even if the family was only his by marriage.

At home in Boston, it had seemed a fine plan. But the journey had been more difficult than Priscilla had expected. Though Mama had been stoic on the train, once they'd left its relative comfort for the bone-jarring stagecoaches, her mood had deteriorated, and the days had turned into litanies of complaints. Dust, mud, insects, the rutted roads, even the scenery, which Priscilla had found beautiful, had bothered Mama, and now that the other passengers had left the coach, she saw no need to mute her laments. This was not the adventure Priscilla had sought.

"We'll reach San Antonio tomorrow." Priscilla gave her mother the same response she'd provided only ten minutes earlier. "Clay will be waiting to take us to Ladreville." The small town, he had told Priscilla, was a half-day's journey northwest of San Antonio, located on what he had described as a particularly beautiful stretch of the Medina River. Mama didn't care about that now. What she needed was reassurance that she would survive the stagecoach's jolting. Priscilla gestured toward her mother's Bible. "Would you like me to read to you?" Most days, the Psalms comforted Mama, although recently she had insisted on Job, claiming she was suffering as much as he had.

Mama shook her head. "Not now. My head hurts." Poor Mama. She was like a hothouse flower, wilting in the Texas sun. She twisted her rings, a sure sign that she was distraught. "I certainly hope Clay has a hot bath waiting for me when we reach that ranch of his."

"He will." In all likelihood it would be Sarah, his bride-to-be, who would provide the amenities Mama expected, but Priscilla knew better than to mention that. At first she had attributed her mother's complaints to the rigors of travel, but as the journey had progressed, Priscilla had discovered the causes were not simply physical. Mama was deeply disturbed that Clay was remarrying. Though Patience had died more than a year ago, Mama seemed to believe he should spend the rest of his life mourning the loss of his wife, Mama's firstborn daughter.

"Isn't the countryside beautiful?" Priscilla pointed to the window. This part of Texas boasted gently rolling hills and valleys dotted with small ponds. Clusters of trees, some of them dripping with what she had learned was Spanish moss, lined the banks of narrow streams. With the greenish gold grass and the vibrantly blue sky, Priscilla found it a scene of pastoral beauty. Though she doubted Mama would agree, this was a safer topic of conversation than her mother's former son-in-law.

Mama stared outside for a moment. "I suppose some might like it," she conceded, "but I cannot picture Patience here."

Neither could Priscilla. Her sister had been a lot like Mama, content with her life in Boston, uncomfortable in Texas. When Patience and Clay had returned to his birthplace, it was supposed to be for only a few months. For Patience, those few months had been the last of her life on Earth, and now, though no one would have expected it, Clay had decided to make the small town of Ladreville his home.

The coach gave a sudden lurch, knocking Papa's head against the side, destroying his hope of sleep. "What was that?" he asked, his voice groggy.

"Just a rut, Papa."

"That's all this road is," Mama grumbled. "One rut after another."

Now fully awake, Papa took her hand between both of his. "I'm proud of you, my dear, coming all this distance to be with Clay on his wedding day. You were the one who recognized how important it was to him."

Priscilla bit back a smile at the way Papa changed history to make Mama happy. Not for the first time, she marveled at how different her parents were, and how well those differences suited them. It wasn't simply their physical differences. Papa was tall and lanky, characteristics he'd bestowed on Priscilla, with graying brown hair and eyes. Though no one would call him handsome, Mama was an undisputed beauty with deep auburn hair, green eyes, and what she described as a pleasingly plump figure. Despite Mama's claims to the contrary, Priscilla knew she'd inherited little more than her mother's green eyes. Even her hair was a pale imitation of Mama's, and she lacked her mother's eye-catching beauty. Mama was as spectacular as an orchid. If her mother was a hothouse flower, Papa was a dandelion, able to thrive anywhere, and just as dandelion greens served as a spring tonic, so did Papa heal others. While it was true he was a renowned physician, in Priscilla's estimation, his greatest feats of healing were reserved for his wife.

Mama's face softened into a smile. "You're right, Daniel. Just think of the stories I'll be able to recount for our friends."

"I assure you, none of them has ever had an adventure like this." The kiss Papa pressed on Mama's hand broadened her smile. "You'll be the talk of the town."

Leaning back, Priscilla felt her own tension begin to ebb. In less than two days, they'd be in Ladreville, reunited with Clay. He and Papa would talk about patients, Mama would have her bath, and Priscilla would meet Sarah. Though it seemed vaguely disloyal to her sister, Priscilla was looking forward to getting to know the woman Clay loved.

Perhaps she dozed. Afterwards, she was never certain. All she knew was that two gunshots rang out.

"Stop or I'll shoot!" The voice was harsh and filled with menace.

As Mama gasped, Priscilla leaned forward to peer out the window, blood draining from her face at the sight of three men, their faces partially hidden by bandanas, their shotguns pointed at the coach. Surely she was dreaming. This must be a nightmare. A moment later, as the coach lurched to a stop, one of the bandits slid off his horse and wrenched the door open. When the stench of his unwashed body assailed her, Priscilla knew this was no dream.

A second bandit rode toward the front of the coach while the third remained on horseback, his gun fixed on the open door, as if protecting the man who was glaring at Priscilla's family.

"Git out!" that man ordered. "Keep your hands up. Don't try nothin' tricky." Though her mouth was dry with fear, Priscilla's mind registered odd details. The man who threatened them was tall, probably over six feet, with hair so dark it was nearly black and the meanest blue eyes she'd ever seen. Though there was no doubting the strength in those arms and shoulders, the greatest menace was what his index finger could do if he pulled the trigger.

"What's happening?" Mama whispered.

Papa slid an arm around her shoulders and drew her closer. "I believe we're about to be robbed."

"You got that right." The dark-haired man reached into the coach and grabbed Mama's arm, yanking her from the seat. "Git out!" As he looked around, his eyes lit on Priscilla, and the greed she'd seen radiating from them changed to something else, something she did not want to identify. "Hey, Jake," he yelled to the man who remained behind him. "There's a right purty gal here."

"You ain't got no time for that, Zeke." The man named Jake kept his gun pointed at Mama as she descended to the ground. His hair and eyes were the same color as Zeke's, but his voice was firmer, as if he were accustomed to being in charge. "Git the others out, then git their valuables. Chet, you git the payroll."

"All right, old man. You're next." Zeke gestured toward the door.

Priscilla willed her hands to stop trembling. Somehow she had to find a way out of this situation. It was her fault. Thanks to her desire for adventure, her parents had endured weeks of discomfort. Now they were about to be robbed. Priscilla's lips tightened with resolve when she saw her mother's reticule. Hoping no one noticed what she was doing, she stuffed it behind the seat. The thieves wouldn't get everything.

She looked down and saw a flash of gold. They wouldn't get this, either. The bandits could take her earbobs, but they wouldn't get the locket with the miniatures of her parents and

Patience. While Zeke's attention was focused on her parents, Priscilla tucked the necklace inside her collar.

"You're next, little gal." Zeke punctuated his words with a laugh that made Priscilla's stomach turn.

Refusing to look at the man whose voice raised such loathing, she kept her head averted as she descended from the coach, and as she did, she saw the third bandit, the one they'd called Chet, gesture toward the stagecoach driver. "Gimme the payroll," Chet demanded.

"You can't take that." Priscilla heard the driver's voice waver.

"Can't I?" As calmly as if he were swatting a fly, Chet shot him.

Priscilla gasped, and her legs threatened to buckle at the bandit's casual disregard for human life.

"Oh, Daniel." Mama buried her head against Papa's chest and began to moan. Though Papa's face was unnaturally pale, he murmured comforting words. Only the bandits were unaffected by the driver's death. Jake and Chet climbed onto the coach, tossed the driver's body onto the ground, then pulled a wooden box from under the seat, while Zeke kept his gun aimed at Priscilla and her parents.

"Looks like we got ourselves some rich ones," Zeke told his partners. There was no answer, for the other men had moved to the back of the coach and were dragging out trunks. Zeke nodded at Mama's left hand, splayed across the front of Papa's coat. The day had been so warm that she'd removed her gloves. "That's a right purty sparklie you got there, ma'am. Give it to me."

"No!" Mama shrieked, as if her refusal would dissuade the bandits. Priscilla knew better. "Daniel, tell him he cannot have my ring." Mama was acting as if Papa had any control. Had she forgotten what had happened to the driver when he'd refused?

Papa reached for Mama's hand. "I'm sorry, my dear, but we need to do as he says." He slid the diamond ring from her finger.

"Yer man's right. You ain't got no choice. Now, hand it over." Once the ring was deposited in a cloth sack, Zeke turned his attention to Papa. "Gimme your watch." Papa complied. "Okay, little gal, you're next. I'll take those earbobs."

Thankful she'd hidden her locket, Priscilla unclipped the earrings and dropped them into Zeke's hand. Maybe now that the bandits had what they'd sought, they'd leave them alone.

Clearly unhappy, Zeke glared at her. "Where'd you hide it?"

"I beg your pardon."

"You cain't fool me. I saw gold around yer neck. Give it to me, or I'll take it."

"Priscilla, we can't fight them." Though soft, Papa's words were tinged with resignation. "Give him your locket. It's not worth your life."

He was right. Priscilla unclasped the chain and flung it at the bandit. She had hoped he would fumble and would have to pick it up off the ground, but Zeke caught the necklace with ease.

"That's a good gal." He darted a glance at his partners, who'd unhitched the stagecoach horses and were searching the luggage. "You ready?"

Jake nodded. "There ain't much here. Chet, you take care of the rest. Zeke, let's go."

Zeke tossed the bag that held the Morton family's jewelry from one hand to the other. "I got me one more piece of business," he told his brother. "I'll catch up with you."

"Don't take long."

"Don't worry. I won't."

Jake mounted his horse. "C'mon, Chet. Do what I told you. I ain't got all day."

The man shrugged, then picked up his rifle. Before Priscilla realized what he intended, he'd fired two shots. Mama and Papa slumped to the ground.

"No!" The word echoed in her brain along with the sound of gunfire. And then there was silence. The horse pawed the ground, but she heard nothing. The bandit's mouth flapped, but no sound came out. Priscilla stood, unable to move, unable to hear, unable to do anything but feel. *No! This can't be happening.* Terror ripped through her, squeezing her heart until she thought it would burst. There was blood, so much blood. As the sickening smell reached Priscilla's nostrils, her senses returned, and she heard the men behind her, chuckling as if something had amused them.

"No!" She stared at her parents. It couldn't be true. God wouldn't have let these evil men kill them. Priscilla fell to her knees. "Talk to me, Mama," she pleaded. But her mother's eyes were sightless, her mouth frozen in an expression of shock. Priscilla placed a hand over her father's nose, hoping against hope that she would feel him breathing. She did not.

"They're dead." There was no remorse in Zeke's voice as he grabbed Priscilla's arm and hauled her to her feet. "Chet never misses. Now it's time for you and me to have a little fun."

The chuckle that accompanied his words left no doubt of his intent. Priscilla's eyes moved wildly, looking for a way to escape. As if he sensed her fear, Zeke tightened his grip and turned toward his brother. "You wanna watch?"

Chet shook his head. "Not this time." A second later, he had mounted his horse and headed after Jake, the coach horses trailing behind him. Priscilla was alone with the bandit named Zeke.

He turned her so she was facing him, then pulled her against his body and ran one hand down her back. Priscilla shuddered with fear and revulsion. She couldn't let him do this. Zeke merely laughed as she struggled against him. Pushing aside his bandana, he grabbed her chin with his other hand, his mouth twisting into a leer. "I wanna see if you taste as sweet as you look."

"No!" As the memory of her parents' lifeless bodies flashed before her, Priscilla gathered every ounce of strength she possessed. Twisting abruptly, she broke Zeke's grip and began to run. *Help me, Lord*, she prayed. *Help me!* The grass was thick beneath her feet, the air filled with the scents of horses and recent rain. She could do it. She could escape. She could almost taste freedom. A second later, she lay face first in the grass, a heavy weight on top of her.

"I always did like feisty ones," Zeke said as he wrenched her arms behind her and tied them. "Now, gal, let's see what you taste like."

He rolled her over, grinding his lips against hers as he lifted her skirts.

"No!" Priscilla screamed the word, but no sound emerged. *No!* She twisted. She turned. She tried to kick, but it was to no avail. Zeke was big; he was strong; he was determined.

18

Please, Lord, help me! As the blood pounded in her ears and she cried out in pain, Priscilla heard the sound of hoofbeats and a single shot.

"C'mon, Charcoal." Zachary Webster stroked his stallion's mane as they forded the river. Though Charcoal preferred galloping on dry land to swimming the Medina and invariably protested when they headed for Ladreville, Zach always smiled when he crossed into town. Though less than fifteen years old, Ladreville had an air of permanence that he suspected was the result of its settlers' determination. When Michel Ladre had arrived from Alsace with his band of French- and German-speaking immigrants, he'd insisted there would be no temporary accommodations in the town that bore his name. Everything would be built to last. Everything would be designed with pride. And it was. With its half-timbered buildings, a part of its Alsatian immigrants' legacy, Ladreville was unlike any place Zach had ever seen. It was true that all of God's creation had its own beauty—all except Perote. Nothing could make the Mexican castle that had been turned into a prison beautiful. Though the rest of the world he'd seen was appealing, somehow this small Texas town touched Zach's heart as no other location had. That was one of the reasons he sought excuses to leave the ranch and come to town. Today, however, he needed no excuse. It was payday, and he was on his way to the post office.

"Mornin'." Steven Dunn, Ladreville's postmaster, greeted him with a broad smile. "I figgered you'd be here today. I told my wife you was regular as clockwork."

Zach chuckled at the realization that he'd become so

predictable. He doubted anyone who'd known him as a youngster would have expected that. "The next thing I know, you'll be accusing me of being stuck in a rut."

The postmaster checked the boxes behind him, then shook his head. "No mail for you or Clay. As far as that rut, with all that's going on, I don't reckon there's much time to get stuck in anything at the Bar C."

"Don't forget the Lazy B." No doubt about it, it was a challenge, being the foreman of two large ranches, but Zach had never been one to shy from challenges. He enjoyed his work, and the fact that Clay Canfield, who hadn't known him from Adam six months ago, trusted him enough to give him complete control over not just his own Bar C but also the neighboring Lazy B was cause for another smile. Two prosperous ranches and a town that had caught his fancy. It was more than a man deserved.

"Heard tell you got some visitors comin' from the East."

Zach nodded. There were few secrets in a small town, not that there was any reason to hide the arrival of Clay's wedding guests. "Clay's happy as can be that the Mortons are coming. You've probably heard that Doc Morton hired Clay as his assistant back in Boston, and the next thing anyone knew, Clay was marrying the older Morton girl."

"She was a right pretty gal, Patience was, but a mite standoffish."

It wasn't the first time Zach had heard that complaint. "Maybe it was just that she was from Boston," he suggested. "Folks are more formal back East."

"Mebbe. My wife sure hopes the parents and the other gal are friendlier." The postmaster cleared his throat and held out his hand. "Got your package ready?"

"You bet." Zach gave him the box. He was certain Steven knew the package contained money, but he'd never asked why Zach sent some each month. That was one of the things that pleased Zach about Ladreville. Though the town loved gossip, its postmaster did not indulge in Ladreville's favorite pastime, and that suited Zach just fine. The good citizens of Ladreville had no reason to know that he sent a substantial portion of his pay to Charlotte Tallman, a woman who was not related to him. If they knew, they would only speculate.

"Thanks, Steven." *For so much.*

As Zach turned to leave, the postmaster stopped him. "I reckon the lady's mighty happy to hear from you so regular like."

"I owe her a lot. Her husband saved my life." Zach blinked at the sound of himself pronouncing words he'd never intended to. Only Clay and his father knew what had happened at Perote and how much he owed John Tallman's widow.

Steven shrugged, as if the revelation were insignificant. "Like I said, she's a mighty lucky lady you write so regular like." He emphasized the word *write*. "Mighty lucky. I reckon she thanks the Lord for you."

Steven was wrong. No woman thanked the Lord for him, not Charlotte and especially not Margaret. *"If you leave me, I'll . . ."* Zach pushed the memories from his mind as he strode out of the post office and mounted Charcoal. It had been fifteen years, half his life. By now a reasonable man should have been able to put the past behind him. Zach had tried and failed. He knew God had forgiven him. He'd begged for and received forgiveness long ago, but he still didn't know why Margaret had refused his offer of help unless she had followed through on her threat. Zach fought back the pain

21

that that thought always brought and nudged Charcoal into the water. Perhaps it was time to accept that he would never understand Margaret's motives. One thing was certain. It was time to learn what God had in store for him next.

⁂

"What the . . . ?"

Priscilla cringed at the sight of the blond man sitting on a horse, his pistol pointed at her. Though the man bit off his words, sparing her what was probably a string of profanity, nothing could camouflage his anger.

"What happened?" he demanded.

Fear caused Priscilla's heart to skip a beat, then begin to pound furiously. Though every instinct shrieked that she should flee, she couldn't, for Zeke's body pressed her into the grass. He was big and heavy and immovable. He had been silent and motionless since she'd heard the shot, and the smell of blood told her he'd been wounded. Perhaps more than wounded.

Priscilla's eyes widened as the blond man slid off his horse, covering the few yards between them in three long strides. What was he going to do? Was he like Zeke? Was he going to . . . ? She couldn't complete the thought. What Zeke had done was unthinkable. *Help me, Lord. I can't bear any more.* Priscilla kept her eyes fixed on the stranger, trying to read his thoughts. She saw anger and something else, perhaps pity. A second later he yanked Zeke off her, tossed him aside like a piece of trash, then straightened her skirts.

"Are you all right, ma'am?"

She would never again be all right. She would never again be clean. She would never again be whole. Priscilla shook

22

her head, then nodded as she managed to sit up. She was as close to right as she was going to be. She was alive, and—as far as she could tell—nothing was broken. No bones, at least. She didn't want to think about the injuries Zeke had inflicted, just as she didn't want to think about the big man standing over her. If she stood, he'd be less threatening, but try though she might, with her hands tied behind her, she could not rise to her feet.

"Who are you?" she asked. He didn't look like Zeke or his brothers. Though he'd worn a bandana, this man had tugged it off as he'd slid from the horse, as if—unlike the bandits—he had no fear of people recognizing his face.

"Lawrence Wood, ma'am. I'm a Texas Ranger." This time there was no question. His eyes were filled with pity. "Let me untie you."

Priscilla shuddered at the thought of him, of any man, touching her. "No, please. Don't touch me." The words came out as little more than a squeak.

He nodded slowly, as if he understood. "I won't hurt you, ma'am. I'd swear that on a Bible if I had one handy. Let me help you."

She had no choice. As Priscilla nodded, the Ranger knelt beside her and slit the bandana that had tied her hands. Then he rose quickly, distancing himself from her as she rose to her feet. She ought to thank him. Priscilla knew that. But somehow the words would not come out. She closed her eyes, trying to block the sight of the bodies lying on the grass. Perhaps if she kept them closed, she could pretend it hadn't happened. Perhaps she could pretend that Mama and Papa were still alive, that they were on the stagecoach, making their way to San Antonio, and she had not been . . . Priscilla shuddered again. She wouldn't pronounce the word, not even in her thoughts.

"How many of them were there?"

The Ranger's voice brought her back to reality. No matter how much she wanted to pretend, today had happened. Everything.

"Three."

He turned Zeke's body over and frowned at the sight. "Zeke Dunkler. I knew I'd catch up with him eventually. The others must have been his brothers, Chet and Jake."

Priscilla nodded. Those were the names she'd heard.

"This one won't be hurting you or anyone else ever again." The Ranger looked around, his eyes assessing the scene. "Just like the other times. They took the horses and anything valuable they could find." He walked slowly toward Mama and Papa's bodies. "Did you know the other passengers?"

"They're . . ." A sob caught in her throat. "My parents."

"I'm sorry, ma'am." The Ranger's voice rang with sincerity. "I wish it were different, but there's nothing I can say to make it better." He scowled as he looked at the bandit's body. "Scoundrels like the Dunkler brothers shouldn't be allowed to live. I can't undo what they've done, but I promise you they'll pay for it." The Ranger rummaged through the back of the stagecoach, emerging with a shovel and a soft cloth.

"What are you going to do?"

"Bury your parents and the driver. I ought to let the coyotes and birds take care of Zeke, but I can't do that." He held out the cloth and nodded toward the small stream she'd barely noticed. "You might want to freshen up a bit while I dig the graves." As if he knew that being too close to her frightened her, he laid the cloth on the grass.

As the rhythmic sound of the shovel hitting soft earth continued, Priscilla scrubbed her skin. The cool water washed away the dirt and blood, but nothing could cleanse her memories, nothing could erase what the bandits had done. The sounds, the smells, the sights, and—worst of all—the memory of Zeke's loathsome touch remained. Priscilla knew those moments would haunt her for the rest of her life. She sank onto the ground and buried her face in her hands. *Oh, Lord, why did you let this happen? It would have been better for me to die. Then I would be with Mama and Papa and Patience. Oh, why didn't you let me die? Where were you when I needed you?* There was no answer, nothing save the pounding of her heart.

She raised her head and looked at the man who was digging her parents' graves. Why couldn't he have come ten minutes earlier? If he had, perhaps Mama and Papa would still be alive. Instead, they would soon be buried in this land Mama had found so foreign. It wasn't fair! The tears Priscilla had been holding back began to flow, accompanied by great body-racking sobs.

Now, child, you know tears solve nothing. When you want to cry, find something to do. As the memory of her father's words echoed through Priscilla's mind, she brushed the tears from her cheeks. Papa was right. There were things she needed to do to help prepare her parents' final resting place. As crude as the grave was, it was all they would have. It was up to Priscilla to do her best. Even though there was no minister in sight, her parents could not be buried without a prayer. She rose and entered the stagecoach, emerging a minute later with her mother's Bible and the reticule she'd hidden from the bandits.

"You ready, ma'am?" The Ranger stood at the side of a single wide grave. The fresh mounds of dirt a distance away told her he'd already buried the driver and the bandit. Dimly, Priscilla realized that he'd dug a single grave for her parents. She nodded slowly. It felt right. Mama and Papa might be in a strange land, but they were together.

Priscilla walked to the gravesite, then bent down and laid the reticule near Mama's hand. A lady, Mama had insisted, never went outdoors without her reticule. She straightened Papa's hat, which the Ranger had placed on his chest. There was nothing else she could do.

"I'm ready," she said. With hands that were still shaking, Priscilla opened the Bible and began to read the familiar words. "The Lord is my shepherd; I shall not want." When she finished and said a silent prayer, the Ranger reached for his shovel. Unable to watch, Priscilla turned away, trying to block the sound of earth covering her parents.

"Where were you heading, ma'am?" the Ranger asked as he stowed the shovel in the back of the stagecoach.

He was matter-of-fact. She would be too. Papa was right; naught was gained by crying. "My brother-by-marriage was going to meet us in San Antonio and take us to his ranch." Had it been less than an hour since she'd been eager to reach Ladreville? The thought brought a fresh wave of pain, and Priscilla squeezed her eyes closed to keep the tears from falling.

"Do you recall the name of the ranch?" If the Ranger saw her distress, he ignored it.

She nodded. "The Bar C. It's just outside a town named Ladreville."

"I've heard of the place. The best thing would be for me

to take you all the way there. If we hurry, we can reach the ranch before your brother-in-law leaves for San Antonio." The Ranger gestured toward his horse. "Let me help you up."

Priscilla stared, horrified by his proposition. Didn't he understand that she couldn't do what he'd suggested? Getting on the horse would mean letting the Ranger touch her. Even worse, once she was mounted, she would have to hold onto him. Priscilla clasped her hands as memories assaulted her. The bandit's fetid breath. The roughness of his hands. The . . . She forced herself to take a deep breath as she pushed the thoughts aside. There was only one thing to do, only one way to survive. She would ensure that no man ever again came that close to her. She would not get on that horse.

"Ma'am, we need to leave."

"I can't." The Ranger stared at her as if she had lost her mind. Perhaps she had. All she knew was that some things were impossible. *You're strong, Priscilla. You can do anything you set your mind to.* Unbidden, Papa's words filled her head, reminding her of the day he'd pronounced them, the day she'd been afraid to strap on a pair of ice skates, lest she break her arm again. With Papa's encouragement, she had skated that day and had rediscovered the pleasure gliding across the ice could bring.

"All right." Priscilla stretched out her hand.

"Isn't she beautiful?" Clay Canfield's grin practically split his face.

Zach looked at the man who'd become his closest friend. Though they both stood six feet tall and had blue eyes, the similarities stopped there. Clay's hair was blond, not almost black like Zach's, and anyone who looked at them could tell that Clay was unaccustomed to physical labor, while Zach had been raised outdoors. Clay was highly educated; Zach had far less schooling. Clay was a renowned physician; Zach ran ranches. On the surface, they had little in common, but despite—or perhaps because of—their differences, they had become almost as close as brothers.

"Isn't she beautiful?" Clay repeated the question.

This was clearly a time for discretion. As far as Zach was concerned, it looked like every other carriage he'd seen. Furthermore, he saw no way to determine that the object of Clay's admiration was female. But Zach knew that uttering either one of those thoughts would not be prudent, particularly when the man who'd hear them was his boss as well as his friend, and so he said only, "Have you given her a name?"

Clay nodded. "Sarah wants to call her Bessie."

"And whatever Sarah wants, she gets." Though he had known Clay for only a few months, Zach had been amazed at how loving Sarah had changed Clay. He was a far happier man since Sarah had agreed to be his wife.

Clay's grin broadened. "Don't look so smug. You'll feel the same way when you fall in love."

He meant well. Zach knew that. He also knew this was not the time for explanations, and so he said lightly, "That day, my friend, will never come."

"I've heard that before, and every time the man was wrong. Your time just hasn't come, but who knows? Your bride might be arriving in the next few days."

"What do you mean?" The words came out seemingly of their own volition. Zach certainly hadn't meant to pronounce them.

"Priscilla." Clay acted as if the answer should have been apparent. "Sunny Cilla may be just the woman for you. She's pretty and smart and has a way of making even a rainy day seem bright. That's why her parents called her Sunny Cilla." Clay gave Zach an appraising look. "She'd be perfect for you."

This conversation had lasted long enough. "Is Bessie ready to travel?"

"Indeed she is, and just in time. Tomorrow's the day we go to San Antonio." Clay patted Bessie. "You're ready, aren't you?"

Zach laughed. What else was he to do? The man was as proud as a new parent, all because he had a carriage.

As a slender brunette emerged from the house, Zach tipped his hat. "I hear you're responsible for this carriage's unfortunate name," he said as Sarah Dobbs, soon to be Sarah Canfield, approached. Though she'd always limp, thanks to a childhood riding accident, Zach was glad to see she had abandoned the cane.

"Am I to infer that you see something odd in giving a carriage a name?" Sarah drew herself up to her full five feet four inches and pretended to glare at Zach as if he were one of her schoolchildren.

"Well, ma'am," he drawled, feigning ignorance, "I reckon this is the first time I've heard of such a thing."

"Zach Webster, you ought to be ashamed of yourself, mocking a child's idea."

"You mean this was Thea's suggestion?" Zach shot his friend a glance and was mollified when Clay appeared as surprised as he by the notion that Sarah's young sister had named the carriage. "You let a two-year-old tell you what to do?"

Sarah shrugged. "Why not? She's very persuasive."

There was no denying that. The little minx had charmed everyone at the Bar C from Clay's father to the ranch hands. Zach clapped Clay on the shoulder. "I don't envy you in another fifteen years. You'll have your hands full, dealing with Thea's suitors."

Clay gave his fiancée a fond glance. "I suspect that's why Sarah's marrying me. She wants some help."

As Zach started to laugh, he heard the sound of an approaching horse. Turning, he saw a palomino with two riders. "You expecting company?" he asked Clay. As far as Zach knew, the visitors were strangers to the area. The man sat tall in the saddle, his gaze vigilant, while an obviously weary woman with reddish blond hair clung to him.

"It can't be."

Zach wheeled around at the sound of Clay's distress. Blood had drained from his friend's face, leaving him ashen. "Something's horribly wrong. I don't know who the man is, but that's Priscilla with him."

2

The long, horrible journey was over. This was the place she had longed to see, the place where Patience had spent her final months. Priscilla gazed at the ranch that had figured so heavily in her sister's letters, trying to see it through Patience's eyes. The land was not foreboding, as Patience had claimed. Like the countryside Priscilla had traversed for the past day, it was gently rolling with trees that had yet to shed their leaves. It was true that the trees were not the slender birches and stately spruces that had decorated their home in Boston and that prickly pear cactus had not dotted the Mortons' front yard, but the Bar C had its own kind of beauty. It was less tamed. Some might say it was less civilized, but even as exhausted as she was, Priscilla saw the vitality. This was a new land, a land meant for adventure. Though the horrible emptiness deep inside her told her she had been wrong to have sought this adventure, she would not deny the appeal of Texas and the Bar C.

Priscilla looked at the outbuildings and the paddock

Patience had described. They were the same. The house was not. Her sister would not have recognized it, for after the fire, Clay and Sarah rebuilt with adobe rather than lumber, but there was no mistaking the man who stood near what appeared to be a new carriage.

As the Ranger slowed the horse, Priscilla took a deep breath. It would be so good to get down from here. The trip had been more painful than she would admit. Riding astride, which was the only option since the horse had no sidesaddle, had stretched already tender muscles and exacerbated the bruises the bandit had inflicted. But that was over. She had arrived.

Three people stood next to the carriage: two men and a woman. Priscilla would have recognized Clay anywhere, for the tall, blond man looked the same as he had in Boston, other than his deep Texas tan. The petite brunette at his side must be Sarah, and the other man was . . . *No! It can't be!* Waves of horror washed over Priscilla, and she closed her eyes, trying to blot out the terrible sight. Her eyes must have deceived her. Zeke was dead. The Ranger had buried him. Priscilla opened her eyes, shuddering when a quick glance confirmed what she'd seen before. What was Zeke doing here?

As the Ranger stopped the horse and dismounted, Clay rushed forward, his blue eyes filled with concern. "Priscilla, what happened?" When he raised his arms to help her off the stallion, she began to tremble. It was silly, she told herself. This was Clay, a man she'd known for years. He wouldn't hurt her. All he was doing was being courteous. Her brain enumerated the reasons she should let him help her. Her heart refused to listen. Priscilla swallowed deeply, trying to fight back the bile that rose to her throat when she thought of a man's hands on her. She couldn't do it. She couldn't let Clay touch her. The only way she had survived the ride was by telling herself that Lawrence Wood was not a man. He was a Ranger. They were a different breed. Even thousands of miles away in Boston, she had heard of the legendary Texas Rangers. The band of lawmen were so well known for their marksmanship and horsemanship, not to mention their almost unbelievable record of capturing outlaws, that peace-loving Papa had spent several dinner hours recounting the exploits he'd read about in the newspaper. That was why Priscilla had known she could trust Lawrence Wood. He was a Ranger.

The Ranger nodded slowly. "Let me help her." Though he phrased it as a request, the look he gave Clay brooked no argument. "It's all right, ma'am." His voice was soft and soothing, the same tone he'd used since they'd first mounted his horse. "You're safe here. They're your family."

But the black-haired man wasn't. Once her feet were on the ground, Priscilla darted another look at him. He wasn't Zeke. She saw that now. This man was taller, his shoulders broader, his features firmer. His brows weren't bushy like Zeke's, and his chin had a cleft that Zeke's had not. Though her mind knew this was not the man who'd hurt her, she could not stop her hands from trembling.

"Priscilla, where are your parents?" Concern colored Clay's words.

How could she tell him what had happened? She and the Ranger had spoken of trivialities, what they would eat, when they would rest. Not once had he referred to the horror he'd witnessed. And that was good, for it was unspeakable. Still, Clay had to know. Though Priscilla opened her mouth, no sounds emerged.

"Who are you, and what are you doing here?" Clay turned to the Ranger, his stance as well as the tone of his voice making it clear that he blamed the man for Priscilla's uncharacteristic silence. The Priscilla he'd known was rarely at a loss for words.

"I'm Lawrence Wood, Texas Ranger. Three bandits attacked Miss Morton's stagecoach about fifty miles east of San Antonio. There's no easy way to say this. They killed her parents and . . ." He paused, apparently searching for the correct word. "They . . . er . . . hurt her."

Clay's face paled; the dark-haired man clenched his fists. Sarah stepped forward and put her arm around Priscilla's waist. Though she was four or five inches shorter than Priscilla, it felt as if Sarah were supporting her. "You poor dear. Come with me. I'll have a nice hot bath drawn for you."

A hot bath. Brittle laughter spilled from Priscilla's mouth. "That's what Mama wanted, a hot bath. Now . . ."

Sarah continued walking, propelling Priscilla toward the ranch house. Despite her decided limp, she kept a steady pace and somehow managed to support Priscilla. Sarah might appear delicate, but appearances were deceptive, for she was strong as well as beautiful. "That's what every woman wants after a long journey," Sarah said, her voice low and soothing. "The Ranger must have had you riding night and day to get here so quickly. I'm sure you're exhausted."

As they entered the low adobe building, Sarah paused to let Priscilla's eyes adjust to the relative darkness of what was obviously a kitchen. A range flanked by cupboards dominated one wall, while a second boasted a window and a deep sink. The third wall was bare, save for a door. It took a moment for Priscilla to notice the woman working at the table in the far corner. Short and stocky, she had hair and eyes so dark they were almost black. That and her black clothing made her blend into the background.

"I was afraid to sleep," Priscilla admitted to Sarah. The few times she'd dozed had been unpleasant. "When I do, the dreams come." They were horrible, replaying all that had happened yesterday, filling her with a terror that was somehow worse than the reality had been. Each time she dreamt, foreboding heightened her fear, for she knew what would happen next. That was part of the reason she had not protested when the Ranger wanted to ride through the night. Being on horseback was so uncomfortable that it made it difficult to sleep.

"I felt the same way after my parents died." Sarah inclined her head toward the woman who continued to knead bread and made brief introductions, explaining that the other woman was Martina, the one indispensable member of the household. As Martina began to heat water for Priscilla's bath, Sarah opened the door on the long wall, revealing a room equipped with a large bathtub, a padded bench, and hooks for clothing. "When we rebuilt the house after the fire, I told Clay that even though he and the ranch hands saw no problem in bathing on the porch, Thea and I needed a room inside. A bathroom was one of the few things I missed from our house in Philadelphia."

Priscilla nodded, remembering that, like her, Sarah had come to Texas from the East. The difference was, Sarah had planned to live here permanently as a mail-order bride, while Priscilla was only visiting.

"Mama would have liked this," she said, her voice choking at the thought of her mother. "It's bigger than our bathroom at home." Home. Tears welled in Priscilla's eyes as she thought of the three-story red-brick building she had shared with her parents. What would it be like, living there alone? She wouldn't think of that. Not today.

"Thank you, Martina," Sarah said as the woman handed her a pile of towels and a fresh bar of soap. When the woman returned to the kitchen, Sarah's eyes registered a new concern. "I didn't see any extra saddlebags, so I imagine the Ranger forgot to bring your clothes."

At the time, Priscilla hadn't cared, remembering how the men had rifled through the luggage. The thought of donning anything the bandits had touched was abhorrent, but what she had on was even worse. This was what she'd been wearing when . . . Priscilla looked at her travel- and grass-stained skirts and frowned. "I'm afraid this is all I have. We left everything with the stagecoach. The Ranger warned me it would probably be stolen before he could get back there."

Sarah gave her a reassuring smile. "Don't worry. We'll find something." When Martina returned to dump the first kettle of hot water into the tub, Sarah turned to her. "When you're done with this, would you ask Zach to ride to the Lazy B? There's a trunk of Mary's clothes in the attic. They'll be a little long for Priscilla, but they'll fit better than mine. Tell Zach to bring the whole trunk."

Zeke was here? Priscilla gasped as the memories rushed back, stronger and more painful than ever. Sarah and Clay knew Zeke?

"It's only until we can have some new clothing made. No one will mind if you wear Mary's in the meantime, least of all her. When she and her son left Ladreville a few months

36

ago, they didn't take much with them, and I doubt they'll be back."

Priscilla grabbed the edge of the tub to keep from collapsing. Sarah obviously misunderstood the reason for her alarm. "Zeke?" She managed to squeak the word.

"Zach." Sarah corrected her. "Zach Webster. He's the dark-haired man you saw outside. Zach is our foreman and Clay's closest friend."

Priscilla took a breath, trying to calm her nerves. The stranger was not the same man. She'd already told herself that Zeke Dunkler was dead. Now she reminded herself that Zach Webster would not hurt her. Still, the similarity in appearance and name was troubling.

When Martina emptied the last pot and billows of steam rose from the tub, Priscilla tried to unbutton her dress, but her fingers seemed incapable of following her brain's commands. "I'm not normally like this." She frowned at her fumbling fingers.

"I can't imagine how you feel after all that happened to you." Like Priscilla, Sarah seemed unwilling to pronounce the ugly word. Sarah took a step closer and deftly unfastened Priscilla's bodice. "But I do know nothing is the same when your parents die. I walked around in a haze for days afterwards." Sarah turned her attention to Priscilla's skirt and soon had it pooling on the floor. "If I hadn't had Thea to worry about, I might have done that for months."

As the last of the petticoats joined her skirt, Priscilla removed her chemise and let Sarah help her into the tub. Though she must have seen them, Sarah made no comment on the bruises Zeke had inflicted.

"Tell me about Thea," Priscilla suggested as she sank into

the warm water. It felt good, so very good, to know that every inch of her would be clean. Maybe if she washed away the last traces of the bandit, the memories would disappear along with the dirt.

Sarah began soaping a cloth. "Where do I start? You already know Thea's my little sister, or—as my parents used to call her—their big surprise. Of course, I can't call her 'little' in her hearing. She's almost three, and she never fails to tell me that that makes her a big girl." Furrows appeared between Sarah's brown eyes. "She was so young when our parents died that sometimes she forgets that I'm her sister, not her mother. As for Clay—she's always called him 'Papa Clay.' The poor man!" Sarah's frown deepened. "Listen to me, babbling about things that mean nothing to you. I'm sorry."

Priscilla shook her head. "I don't mind." Sarah's babbling, as she called it, was soothing, as were her ministrations. Though it had been years since anyone had soaped her arms, Priscilla did not protest. She was so weary and sore that she wasn't certain she could have managed it on her own.

"Lean back," Sarah said, "and I'll wash your hair." She filled a small bucket with water and poured it over Priscilla's head, then began to massage soap into her scalp. "Your hair is beautiful," she said as she reached for the rinse water. "It reminds me of the sky at sunset."

"Unfortunately, freckles seem to accompany reddish hair." They certainly were companions to Priscilla's strawberry blonde locks and her mother's auburn tresses. "I used to have them everywhere. You know how children can be. Even the slightest snub seems monumental. I can remember coming home from school crying because the other children teased me about my freckles. I was so upset that Mama took one of the lemons she'd been saving for a special treat of lemonade and let me rub it on my face, saying it would bleach the freckles. I don't think it did, but it did make me feel better. And now most of them have faded." Priscilla touched the bridge of her nose, where three persistent freckles could be found. "These are all that are left." As the words left her mouth, she frowned. What was happening to her? Her life had changed irreparably, and yet she was talking about something as mundane as freckles. This was worse than Sarah's babbling.

Sarah seemed to find nothing amiss. "Don't be surprised if Thea wants to touch them. She's at a curious stage." Sarah squeezed the water from Priscilla's hair before she helped her climb out of the tub. "Why am I talking about stages? I believe Thea was born curious."

"Mama used to say the same thing about me. She and Papa claimed that if Patience and I didn't look so much alike, they wouldn't have believed we were both their daughters." Her legs suddenly weak, Priscilla sank onto the bench, clutching the towel as if it were a lifeline. "Mama, Papa, Patience. They're all gone. Oh, Sarah, I don't know what I'm going to do. I'm all alone."

Sarah wrapped a second towel around Priscilla's legs. "You have Clay and me. More importantly, you have God."

Shaking off Sarah's hand, Priscilla shook her head. "That's where you're wrong. God has deserted me."

❦

She was afraid of him. That beautiful woman with hair like firelight and grass-green eyes was afraid of him. Zach knew he hadn't imagined it. There was no mistaking the terror in her eyes when she'd looked at him. Though he'd never set eyes on her before, the instant her gaze met his, he'd seen the flicker of recognition, followed swiftly by a look of pure horror. Zach couldn't explain how it could have happened, but somehow she knew his past. It was as if his sin had been branded on his forehead, a modern mark of Cain. Even Margaret's hatred and her bitter words the day they'd parted hadn't shaken him the way this woman's fear had. He was still reeling as if he'd been struck.

That was part of the reason Zach had been reluctant to accompany Clay and the Ranger when Clay had suggested they sit on the front porch. The other part was that he didn't think he could bear listening to the Ranger's tale, knowing that he was not the man to avenge the evil that had been done. But Clay had insisted, and so here Zach was, sitting on the front steps, drinking some of Martina's cool tea.

"What can you tell us?" Clay posed the question.

The Ranger took a long swallow before he replied. "It was the Dunkler brothers' work. There were three of them—tall, dark hair, blue eyes." He stared at Zach for a moment. "They look a bit like you."

A wave of relief washed through Zach. Perhaps that was the reason for Priscilla's reaction. She had seen the physical resemblance and been frightened. That was much better than believing she had looked inside him and learned his shameful secret. Zach took another sip of tea, and this time he savored the cool beverage.

"The Dunkler brothers have been holding up stagecoaches around San Antonio for the better part of a year," the Ranger continued. "Usually their intent is robbery. The unfortunate fact is, they've been remarkably successful in taking large payrolls. That's why the Rangers were called out. I don't know what was different this time, why they killed the driver and Miss Morton's parents and attacked her."

Zach's insides twisted at the thought of three innocent people dying and another suffering the worst harm that could befall a woman. *Oh, Lord, where were you? How could you let this happen?* There was no answer, just as there'd been no answer in that abysmal Mexican jail. Zach rose and walked to the edge of the porch, trying to calm his thoughts. Only then would he hear the voice that directed his life, the voice that had led him here. Was this somehow part of God's plan for him?

"Scum like that deserve to die." Zach heard the anger in Clay's voice.

"One of them already has," the Ranger said. "I killed Zeke Dunkler when I found him with Miss Morton. The others were already gone."

Zach turned and rejoined the conversation. "You said there were three."

"Yeah." The Ranger nodded. "Zeke was the youngest and, from all accounts, the wildest. Jake—he's the oldest—is the leader and the brains of the outfit. Chet's the best shot."

"Any idea where they've gone?" Once again it was Clay who spoke. Zach was trying to tamp back the fury that even now raged like a wildfire inside him.

"Probably north. Judging from the coaches they've robbed recently, that seems to be the direction they're headed." The Ranger frowned. "Trouble is, I can't predict what they'll do once they realize Zeke is dead. They may change their pattern. They may seek revenge."

"Against whom? You said Miss Morton was the only survivor." Surely the remaining Dunklers would not kill her.

But they might. That had probably been their plan all along. Once he'd slaked his lust, Zeke Dunkler would have killed her if the Ranger hadn't shot him first.

The Ranger shrugged. "Most murderers don't like to leave witnesses."

A sudden calm fell over Zach. Perhaps this was what God intended for him. He'd known a change was coming. He simply didn't know what it would be. Perhaps he was meant to accompany Lawrence Wood as he tracked the murderers. He wouldn't kill the men, of course. When he'd left Perote, he'd vowed that he would never again kill. But he could help apprehend the bandits and keep Miss Morton safe. "I'll go with you."

The Ranger shook his head. "No offense, but I'm the one who's trained to deal with the likes of the Dunkler brothers. I'm also used to riding alone."

He would be in the way. Zach didn't need to hear the words pronounced to understand the man's concerns. He couldn't dispute their validity. Though he was a good marksman, he doubted his skill could match that of a Texas Ranger. Those men were legendary. But if God didn't want him to capture the murderers, what was his plan? Zach wished he knew.

Priscilla dragged the chair closer to the window of the room Sarah had said would be hers for as long as she stayed. Though smaller than her bed chamber at home, the room was nicely furnished with a bed, a bureau, and a small table with two chairs. It was one of those chairs that she'd moved toward the window. Opening the sash, Priscilla breathed in deeply. No matter what had happened, there was no denying the beauty of the Bar C and the verdant countryside. It was probably Texas's location, so much farther south than Boston, that accounted for the grass still being green. Perhaps it was the recent rains, which had turned the stagecoach roads into muddy morasses for several days. Priscilla didn't care about reasons. It was enough to look outside and know that something—even if it was only grass—was still alive.

A soft knock was followed by the sound of the door opening. Priscilla turned to see Sarah enter the room, carrying a tray with a pitcher and two cups.

"I brought you some cocoa," she said as she placed it on the table. "That used to be my mother's remedy when I was sad. It didn't matter whether it was summer or winter. Mama was convinced that cocoa was a panacea."

Priscilla smiled at the realization that some aspects of motherhood were universal. "Mine gave me chamomile tea."

Though she'd started to pour the beverage, Sarah's hand stilled. "Would you prefer that? I can brew some."

Priscilla shook her head as she moved her chair back to the table and motioned Sarah toward the other. "The chocolate smells delicious." Priscilla took a sip, enjoying the fragrant beverage.

"It's difficult, isn't it?"

She raised her eyes to meet Sarah's. "What do you mean?"

"At times like this, it's hard to see how God can turn suffering into good."

As memories assailed her, Priscilla's hand trembled so much that cocoa sloshed over the edge of the cup. Placing it back on the saucer, she closed her eyes and tried to will the memories away.

Sarah laid a hand on one of Priscilla's. "He can, and he will."

Slowly Priscilla shook her head and opened her eyes. "I wish I could believe that, but I don't. Nothing good could come from what happened to my parents." *And me.* She wouldn't voice those words, for that would be to allow the memories back inside her head.

As a bird's trilling filled the room, Priscilla bit her lips to keep from crying out. How she wished she were a bird! If she were, she could fly away and not have to deal with a woman who preached God's love. She tugged her hand from Sarah's and picked up her cup. Perhaps the cocoa would soothe her; it was certain Sarah's words would not.

"That's what I thought too." Sarah's voice was low and filled with compassion. "I couldn't understand how God could let me break my leg so badly, but the doctors were sure I'd never walk again." Though Priscilla had seen Sarah's limp, she hadn't wanted to ask what had caused it. "My horse fell on me," Sarah explained. "Poor Daisy. Her leg was hurt worse than mine, and she . . . Well, you know what happens to horses with crushed legs."

Though the accident must have occurred years before, Priscilla heard the note of sorrow in Sarah's voice. Feeling an unexpected need to comfort the woman who had been trying to comfort her, Priscilla said, "You're walking now."

Sarah nodded as she placed her cup back on the saucer. "I'll always limp, but that's a small price to pay for what I've gained."

When she'd accompanied her father on his medical rounds, Priscilla had met several patients with withered or amputated legs. "It must have been difficult to be confined to a chair."

44

"It was, for both me and my parents. I'm honestly not sure who suffered more. All I can tell you is that the day I took my first steps was one of the happiest in my life, and yet walking wasn't the most precious gift I was given."

Priscilla knew her face reflected her confusion. What could be better than regaining use of your legs when you'd thought you had been condemned to life in a chair?

As if she heard the unspoken question, Sarah said, "The knowledge that my suffering helped someone else. Clay's father probably wouldn't be walking again if it weren't for what I learned when I was stuck in that chair."

Clay had written about what he considered the Canfield family miracle, the fact that Sarah's determination had helped his father regain use of his legs after everyone, Clay included, had believed he would never walk again. It was a touching story and an encouraging one. If she were Sarah, she might even believe God had a hand in it. The problem was, Priscilla knew there would be no happy endings to her story. Death was final. Nothing could change that or mitigate its pain. "I cannot imagine anything good coming from losing my family."

Sarah was silent for a moment, as if trying to frame her response. "I don't want to sound as if I'm mouthing platitudes, but times like this are when it's most important to trust God."

Priscilla had trusted God, but he had failed her. "Look, Sarah, I know you mean well and you're trying to help me, but you're wrong. When I prayed to God for help, he ignored me."

Anguish filled Sarah's eyes. "Oh, Priscilla, that's not true. Our heavenly Father never ignores us. Sometimes we just don't hear his answer, because it's not the one we expected."

"It *is* true." Sarah might be stubborn, but so was Priscilla. She wasn't going to let this woman, no matter how well-meaning she might be, continue to believe that her God was a loving one. "He left me alone with the bandit. He wouldn't even let me die. I prayed and prayed that I would die, but he wouldn't even grant me that. That's when I knew he had abandoned me."

Before Sarah could reply, the door was flung open and a small child raced inside, her dark brown braids flying behind her, a rag doll clutched to her chest. The little girl's resemblance to her hostess told Priscilla this was Thea, Sarah's young sister.

"Pretty lady." Thea skidded to a stop in front of Priscilla and pointed.

"Her name is Miss Morton." Sarah reached for her sister, but she eluded her. "Say hello to Miss Morton, and then I want you to go back to the kitchen. I'm sure Martina has some cookies for you."

Though the little girl's eyes brightened at the thought of a treat, she ignored Sarah and climbed onto Priscilla's lap. "Pretty lady. Pretty hair." She stroked Priscilla's hair, looking at her hand occasionally, as if she expected it to have been warmed by Priscilla's flame-colored tresses. When that game paled, she turned her attention to Priscilla's face. Touching Priscilla's nose, Thea announced, "Spots."

Priscilla gave Sarah a quick smile as her earlier prediction that Thea would be curious about them came true. "They're called freckles."

"Feckles." Thea rubbed Priscilla's nose, perhaps trying to remove the spots. It wouldn't work. Priscilla had tried the same technique hundreds of times with no result.

"They won't go away," she told the child.

"But Thea will." Sarah rose. "That's enough, Thea. Let's go."

"No!" Thea closed her eyes, as if that would make her invisible, and snuggled closer to Priscilla, wrapping both arms around her. "Me wanna stay with pretty lady."

"Thea!"

The stern command caused the child to slide from Priscilla's lap. Her ramrod posture telegraphing her annoyance with her sister, Thea picked up her doll and glared at Sarah. "Pretty lady sad," she announced. When Sarah pointed at the door, Thea took a few steps toward it, clomping her feet with each stride. Then she turned, a grin on her face, and scampered back to Priscilla. Before Priscilla had the slightest inclination what Thea intended, the child placed her doll in Priscilla's lap. "Dolly make pretty lady happy."

A tiny flicker of warmth settled in Priscilla's heart as she looked at the child's unselfish gift. It was an ordinary rag doll of minimal monetary value, and yet the love that accompanied it made it priceless.

Sarah's smile was rueful. "I'm sorry for the interruption, Priscilla. I'll be back as soon as I get Thea settled."

Priscilla wasn't sorry. For the first time since the stagecoach had been stopped, she felt something other than anger, hatred, and despair. "Thank you for the doll, Thea." She held it out, urging the child to take it. From the way she'd carried it, Priscilla knew this was one of Thea's prized possessions. In all likelihood, she kept it with her night and day.

The child shook her head vigorously. "Me want you keep her." When Sarah grasped her hand and started to lead her from the room, Thea tugged her hand free. A second later, she'd climbed onto Priscilla's lap again and hugged her. "Me love you."

The flicker of warmth turned into a flame, engulfing Priscilla's heart. She had been wrong when she'd told Sarah that everything had been taken from her. Thea's gesture and her simple words had accomplished what nothing else had been able to. They'd shown her she was not alone. Perhaps God had not abandoned her. Perhaps he had sent this child to comfort her.

3

"Ladre! Get over here!"

Jean-Michel scowled. Albert Monroe was the second most disgusting person in the state of Texas, maybe even in the whole United States of America. Just because he was an empresario, just because he had more money than any one man deserved, he thought he could order Jean-Michel around. Why, the man treated him like little more than a slave. It seemed that no matter where Jean-Michel went, Monroe was watching. It was almost as if he knew Jean-Michel was looking for a way to escape, but that couldn't be. Monroe wasn't that smart. No one was as smart as Jean-Michel Ladre.

"Ladre!"

"Yes, sir." Jean-Michel bowed slightly. The man was so stupid, he wouldn't realize he was being mocked.

"Nelson told me you failed to load your share of bales yesterday. Your father will not be happy when he learns that your pay is being docked."

"No, sir, he won't." Papa would fume and Mama would cry

when they learned that their son was not a model worker. So what? It wasn't his idea to be a common laborer. Jean-Michel was as close to royalty as the town of Ladreville had. All his life he'd been reminded that if it weren't for Papa, there would be no Ladreville, Texas, and that he, Jean-Michel, was an important person. So what if he'd stolen a few things? Papa would never have found out. He was as dumb as Albert Monroe. If it hadn't been for Zach Webster, Jean-Michel would still be in Ladreville. Maybe he'd even be married to Isabelle.

"Make sure it doesn't happen again."

Jean-Michel looked at Monroe. "Yes, sir." It wouldn't happen again. Jean-Michel didn't give a hoot about cotton. Why should he care that his wages were docked when he didn't see a single penny? Everything he earned was sent back to Ladreville. Restitution, Papa had called it. Robbery was more like it. Those days would soon end. He'd find a way to escape, and when he did, Zach Webster had better beware.

Papa would never have believed Clay. He hated the man almost as much as Jean-Michel did, but Zach was different. For some reason, Papa had trusted him. He'd believed Zach's lies, and because he had, he'd sent Jean-Michel into exile. That wouldn't happen again. When Jean-Michel was done, no one would listen to Zach Webster. His days were numbered.

༄

Priscilla awoke, disoriented. The sheets that tangled around her limbs were soft, so different from hotel bedclothes, that for an instant she thought she was at home, but the sweet scent in the air was unfamiliar, almost exotic. Priscilla forced her eyes open, searching for a clue to her whereabouts. Though the room was dark, a faint light sneaking under the door revealed the outline of furniture. Nothing looked familiar. A large bureau. A table and chairs. Perhaps she was still dreaming.

The sound of voices drifted into the room. At first they were muted, a man and a woman speaking of something, their words indistinguishable. As the man raised his voice slightly, memories rushed through Priscilla. *No! Please, no!* She squeezed her eyes closed in a futile attempt to keep the images at bay, but they washed over her like waves after a storm. The sight of bandits brandishing pistols, the stench of Zeke's breath, the grip of his hands on her body, the soft thuds as the Ranger filled the graves. The memories were indelibly etched inside her head.

Priscilla sat upright and wrapped her arms around herself, trying to quell the trembling. She was safe now. That was Clay's voice she heard. She was on his ranch. No one would hurt her here. Priscilla whispered the words aloud. Perhaps if she voiced them, if her ears heard them, she would believe them.

When her teeth began to chatter, Priscilla clenched her jaw. This wasn't working. Thrusting her arms into the dressing gown Sarah had given her, she picked her way to the window and drew back the curtains. Her room, she remembered, was situated on the front of the house, its windows opening onto the porch. She looked outside, wondering where Clay and Sarah were that she heard their voices. Perhaps they were walking close by.

Priscilla gasped. Clay was sitting on the porch swing, his arm around Sarah. As memories of Zeke's arms and their punishing strength assailed her, Priscilla gripped the window-sill, forcing herself to breathe deeply. An engaged couple often touched each other, she reminded herself. Their touches were gentle and loving, not harsh and hateful. Clay wasn't hurting

Sarah. He wasn't like Zeke. He wouldn't force himself on a woman. Though Priscilla's mind knew all that, her heart continued to tremble with fear.

"We'll postpone the wedding until she's recovered." Sarah's words rang clearly in the night.

As Clay drew his fiancée closer, Priscilla shuddered again. She should draw the curtain, return to bed, and pretend she had heard none of this. But she stood there, frozen, as Clay said, "As much as I hate the idea of waiting, I know you're right. Those bruises will take a few weeks to heal."

It was worse than she'd thought. Nothing was private. Priscilla cringed at the realization that, though she had said nothing at the time, Sarah had told Clay of the damage the bandit's fists had inflicted.

"Spoken like a doctor." There was a hint of amusement in Sarah's voice. "The bruises aren't what concern me. I'm more worried about the invisible wounds. As horrible as it was for me to find Mama and Papa's bodies, what Priscilla endured was much worse. She saw her parents being killed and then . . ." Sarah's words trailed off.

"I don't want to think about it either," Clay admitted. "There are some things that are unspeakable, and what happened to Priscilla is one of them." He pressed a kiss on Sarah's head, and this time the gesture did not horrify Priscilla, for she had erected a barrier between herself and the rest of the world, just as she had when she'd ridden behind the Ranger. Though her body had been on the palomino he called Snip, her spirit had been miles away in a place where no one could find her.

Priscilla heard Clay chuckle. "My sweet Sarah, once again you're right. We'll postpone our wedding indefinitely."

As his words registered, the barrier Priscilla had constructed shattered. They couldn't do that! Heedless of her dishabille, she raised the window and leaned out. "No, you mustn't wait."

Both Sarah and Clay turned abruptly, the moonlight revealing Sarah's shock. "Oh, Priscilla," she said as she rose from the swing and walked toward the window, "I'm sorry we woke you. I hadn't realized we were so loud."

Clay followed a pace behind her, his expression filled with concern. Priscilla tightened her grip on the window as she realized that, far from alleviating her friends' worries, she had augmented them.

"You slept through supper," Sarah said when she reached the window. "Would you like me to bring you some food?"

"No." Hunger was the last thing on Priscilla's mind. "I'm sorry to have eavesdropped, but you mustn't delay your wedding."

Sarah gave Clay a quick look before she said firmly, "We've already decided."

"Then undecide. I don't want you to disrupt your lives because of me."

The corners of Clay's mouth turned up, and Priscilla thought she saw grudging respect in his eyes. That was better—infinitely better—than pity. "You sound like Sarah when she first arrived," he told Priscilla. "She kept saying she didn't want to be a burden."

"He wouldn't listen to me," Sarah warned, "so I doubt you'll be any more successful. When Clay makes up his mind, he rarely changes it."

This time would be different. Priscilla leaned her arms on the windowsill, hoping the position and the relative darkness would camouflage the way she was trembling. "You must listen to me. Don't you see? If you change your plans, the bandits will have won again. They've already done too much damage. We can't give them any more power over us." Wasn't it bad enough, knowing that if she hadn't been so insistent on attending Clay's wedding, her parents would still be alive? Priscilla could not undo that, but she could keep Sarah and Clay from suffering because of her.

Clay shook his head. "It's too soon. I owe your parents a formal mourning period."

Priscilla shuddered at the thought of black clothing and all the other trappings of mourning. "They wouldn't have wanted it. You know that, Clay." Though Mama was traditional about most things, she had frequently deplored the refusal to lead a normal life after a loved one's death. "They wanted you to be happy."

"Still . . ."

Priscilla turned toward his fiancée. "Convince him, Sarah. If you can't, send in Thea. She seems to be a master at getting her way."

"Don't remind me." A groan accompanied Clay's words. Priscilla chose to interpret it as acquiescence.

"Then it's settled. You'll be married on December 28, just the way you planned."

Sarah whispered something to Clay. When he nodded, she said, "All right. We won't change the date, but we'll wait a while before we take our wedding trip."

"That's not necessary."

Sarah smiled. "Don't forget that if we go away, you'll be responsible for Thea." Mama had been ecstatic at the idea of caring for a small child while Sarah and Clay honeymooned and had had no reservations when Clay had asked if she and

Papa and Priscilla could extend their visit long enough to help him and Sarah.

Sarah's lips quirked up again. "Be careful, Priscilla. As you reminded us, Thea is quite a handful. You may not want us to leave you alone with her, at least not for a while."

Priscilla nodded. "You win."

"She always does." Clay gave his bride-to-be a fond look.

❧

The next time Priscilla wakened, the sun was high and her stomach was rumbling. She dressed hurriedly, then walked to the kitchen where Martina greeted her with a warm smile.

"I reckon you're hungry," the older woman said when she'd asked how Priscilla liked her eggs cooked. "You slept like . . ." She bit off her words, as if she realized that Priscilla might not appreciate the traditional ending to that phrase. *The dead.* Martina had no way of knowing that words did not hurt. It was only memories that were painful, memories and this horrible feeling of emptiness, knowing she would never see Mama and Papa again.

She would not dwell on those thoughts, Priscilla had resolved when she woke. When she was a child, her parents had nicknamed her Sunny Cilla. Though she didn't feel particularly sunny today, Priscilla would do her best to live up to their expectations.

She took a seat at the small table while Martina cracked eggs into a bowl. "I can't recall ever sleeping so much." Mercifully, she had had only one nightmare.

"Most likely you never rode for so many hours. I heard the Ranger set a fierce pace."

55

"He did." But Priscilla had not complained. Each hour in the saddle meant more miles between her and the Dunkler brothers. "Where is the Ranger? I want to thank him for all that he did."

When she'd poured the eggs into a large skillet, Martina plunked a cup of coffee in front of Priscilla. "He's long gone. I heard him tell Clay he needed to find them others before the trail got cold."

"What about Sarah?" Priscilla had heard no sounds this morning other than those emerging from the kitchen.

"She's off to school. I reckon you know she's the school-marm." Martina chuckled as she scrambled the eggs. "Little Miss Thea didn't want to go with her, not one bit. She near to threw a tantrum."

"I can imagine." Though adorable, the girl appeared head-strong. That wasn't altogether bad. Priscilla thought that if she had a daughter, she'd like her to have Thea's kindness and her independence. But that, she reminded herself as she took a sip of coffee, would never happen. The bandits had killed her dream of marriage and children as surely as they had shot Mama and Papa. Even if the horror faded and one day she could bear the thought of a man's touch, marriage was unlikely. No man would want Priscilla now that she was used goods.

Martina pulled a platter of bacon from the oven and placed several strips on the plate next to the eggs and toast. "Eat up," she urged Priscilla. "I'll fetch more coffee for you."

Priscilla was chewing a bite of eggs that looked delicious but oddly had no taste when she heard the clank of metal and Martina's cry of pain. Somehow the older woman had dropped the coffee pot, spilling hot liquid over her hand.

"Butter. Get the butter," Martina cried as Priscilla rushed to her side.

Priscilla shook her head. "There's something better." She dipped her fingers into the pail of water someone had placed near the sink, nodding when it felt cool to the touch. This was what Martina needed. "Try this." She plunged the woman's hand into the pail. "Do you have any ice?"

Martina shook her head. "Not this late in the season."

Though it wasn't as cold as Priscilla would have liked, the cool water would have to do. "How does that feel?"

"Better."

Priscilla nodded. "The cold helps to numb the pain. You'll also have less scarring this way."

"But I always put butter on a burn." Martina appeared confused by the unorthodox treatment.

"I know. My parents did too, until last winter when Papa was visiting a very poor patient." As Martina's eyes clouded with confusion again, Priscilla explained that her father had been a physician. "The boy's arm was badly burned, but his mother had no butter, not even lard, to spare. In desperation, Papa looked for a way to ease the child's pain. He reasoned that the opposite of hot was cold, so he brought in a pail of snow and instructed the mother to use it on her son's arm. When he came back to check on the boy a week later, Papa was surprised to see that the burn had healed far better than normal. Ever since, he's used ice and cold water to treat burns."

Though Martina appeared skeptical, she did not reach for the butter. Instead, she urged Priscilla to finish her breakfast.

"Good morning, Martina, Miss Morton."

Priscilla was sipping coffee when Zach Webster entered the room. She gasped. A tall man, dark hair, blue eyes. Pain. Unspeakable pain. As the memories swept through her, Priscilla shrank back in the chair, unable to form a word, unwilling to look at the man whose appearance had triggered them.

"Mornin', Zach." Martina appeared not to notice Priscilla's distress. "Have you met Miss Priscilla? She's a mighty fine doctor."

Priscilla clenched her hands, trying to break the memories' grip. Had it been less than an hour since she'd resolved to be Sunny Cilla? That had seemed like such a good plan. She was strong. Papa used to tell her that. But not, it appeared, strong enough, if the sight of Zach Webster sent her into a panic.

"Perhaps another time." His words were clipped, as if he were angry. Before Priscilla could react, he strode out of the kitchen.

"That's odd." Furrows appeared between Martina's eyes. "He's not usually so short with folks."

"It was my fault. I was rude." Zach had done nothing that should have caused her to freeze. "I need to apologize."

Priscilla carried her dishes to the sink, then examined Martina's hand. Though the back was still enflamed, the blisters Priscilla had feared had not appeared. At least one thing had gone well this morning. "Where can I find Mr. Webster?"

"He'll be in with Mr. Canfield." Martina gestured toward the main part of the house. "He's a good man, Zach Webster is."

Priscilla did not doubt that he was good. The problem was, he was a man.

๛

58

"Good work, Robert." Zach smiled at the gray-haired man who'd risen when he entered the room. Though Clay's father moved slowly and awkwardly and needed two canes to take even a few steps, the fact that he was no longer confined to a chair filled Zach with joy. "Before you know it, you'll be riding again." Zach knew that was unlikely, and he suspected Robert did too, but he also knew how important encouragement was. When they'd been imprisoned in Perote, it had been Robert who'd provided the encouragement. Now it was Zach's turn.

"Walking is enough." The words were garbled. Ever since he'd suffered from apoplexy, Robert Canfield's speech had been almost unintelligible. Though Martina and Sarah understood a few words, it was Clay and Zach whose comprehension was the best, and even then there were times when Zach had to ask Robert to repeat his words. How he hated doing that! Each time Zach failed to understand, Robert's eyes dimmed and his shoulders slumped, as if the burden of the failure affected every part of his body.

Zach watched the man who'd befriended him in prison struggle to walk the few feet to the window. It was painful. Zach knew that. And yet Robert pushed himself to go farther each day, determined that he would master the act of walking.

"Every day. I miss her every day." Robert stood by the window, gazing at the small plot where his wife, younger son, and Clay's first wife were buried. Though he'd never voiced the words, Zach suspected Robert's goal was to one day walk to their graves.

"You were blessed with a wife and sons."

Robert turned to face Zach. "Your turn is coming."

This was one time when Zach wished he had not understood Robert. It would be easier to simply ignore the older man's words, and yet he could not. Robert deserved a response, though it wouldn't be the one he expected. "I'm afraid not." Zach had had his chance and lost it. Worse, he had destroyed it.

"Mr. Webster?"

Zach wheeled around, startled by the woman's voice. He hadn't heard her approach, and that was odd. The time in Perote had honed his hearing, just as it had taught him the value of moving silently. But somehow Priscilla had made her way into Robert's room without alerting Zach.

"Miss Morton." He bowed slightly, acknowledging her presence, wondering why she was here. It was clear that she would have preferred to be almost anyplace else. If the nervous darting of her eyes weren't enough, the way she kept her fingers clasped so tightly that the knuckles turned white told him she was uncomfortable in his presence. There was no doubt that he'd caused that nervousness simply because of the way he looked. If Zach could change his appearance, he would, but that was impossible.

As he took a step toward her and saw her recoil, Zach's thoughts whirled. Perhaps it wasn't only his unfortunate resemblance to the bandits that spooked Miss Morton. Perhaps it was the fact that he was male. After what had happened, Zach imagined she would shy from anyone of the opposite gender, at least any who might pose a threat. For years after he was released from Perote, he'd avoided Mexicans, simply because they brought back memories of a horrible time. Though terrible, what he had endured in prison paled compared to Priscilla Morton's ordeal. It

60

was no wonder this lovely young woman's green eyes were filled with fear.

"Have you met Clay's father?" Perhaps if Zach pretended nothing was amiss, she would relax.

She did not. When he had completed the introductions, Priscilla took another step toward him, her hands now fidgeting with her skirts. "I want to apologize." Her words surprised Zach and made him wonder whether her nervousness was at least partially caused by the need to make amends.

"I was rude before, and I'm sorry." She must be referring to the fact that she hadn't spoken to him in the kitchen. Though she might not believe it, he hadn't been offended. When he'd seen her eyes widen and the blood drain from her face, leaving those three freckles on her nose in sharp relief, he'd realized what had happened. "It's simply that you reminded me of someone," she said, her voice a bit stronger now.

Zach nodded slowly, trying to reassure her. "I understand." He wouldn't tell her that the Ranger had commented on his resemblance to the Dunkler brothers. Knowing that she and the attack had been the subject of discussion would merely deepen this woman's distress. "No apologies are necessary."

"Thank you."

Priscilla bolted from the room so quickly that for a second Zach wondered if he'd imagined her visit. Only the faint scent of finely milled soap told him she had not been a figment, that and Robert's attempt to smile as he said, "Beautiful woman." She was indeed. A bit more than average in height, with that glorious hair and green eyes, she was the most beautiful woman Zach had ever seen. She was the kind of woman who could set a man dreaming, if the man were inclined to dream, that is. Zach could not afford to indulge in dreams of that sort.

For the next half hour, he worked with Robert, helping him exercise his legs. It was the same routine they followed each day. Though the bending and stretching challenged Robert, the regimen gave Zach far too much time to think, and today those thoughts focused on Priscilla Morton. The poor woman had suffered so much in such a short time. While it was true that Zach had not inflicted that suffering, his very presence seemed to exacerbate it.

Dear Lord, what should I do? There was no answer to his silent prayer, nothing but the knowledge that he must do nothing to deepen Priscilla's pain.

⁂

Sarah could not recall the last time she had been as anxious as her pupils for the day to end, but today she counted the remaining minutes as often as they did. The children longed for a few minutes of play in the waning sunlight. She wanted to return to the Bar C and the person Thea called "the pretty lady." While she'd taught geography, showing her students a map of the United States and pointing out the location of Texas, Sarah's mind had traced the journey Priscilla had taken, a journey similar to her own and yet vastly different. Sarah and Thea had encountered nothing more dangerous than rutted roads; Priscilla had endured far worse.

While she'd listened to her pupils recite the alphabet, Sarah had pictured Priscilla's face. Though her skin had been burned from too many hours in the Texas sun, there had been an underlying pallor, the result of long hours in the saddle and all that had preceded the ride. Unlike the children with their easy smiles, Priscilla had not smiled. Instead, her expression had remained somber, and her eyes . . . Sarah struggled to keep her own expression calm as she remembered the pain she'd seen reflected in Priscilla's gaze.

She looked at the clock again. Two more minutes. Then she'd release her students and head home. Though she could not undo what had happened, she was determined to do everything she could to help Priscilla recover. But first, Sarah had to tend to practical matters.

As she and Thea approached Ladreville's mercantile, an establishment run by the Rousseau family, Sarah smiled at her sister. "You need to play quietly today," she admonished her.

"Me good." Thea grinned. "Me play with pools."

"Spools." Isabelle Rousseau frequently gave Thea empty thread spools as toys. Perhaps she'd have some today.

The doorbell tinkled as they entered the store, and Isabelle looked up from her position behind the counter. An attractive brunette who was a few inches shorter than Sarah's five feet four, Isabelle was Sarah's dearest friend. Right now that friend was frowning.

"I hope your frown doesn't mean you don't have what I need." Sarah had sent a note to the mercantile, listing the items she hoped to buy. Isabelle rose and smiled, a smile so forced that it bothered Sarah as much as the frown had. Though Isabelle was as perfectly groomed and coiffed as ever, her beauty seemed to have dimmed, reminding Sarah of a lamp with its wick turned down. Something was clearly wrong.

"I was just thinking." Isabelle opened a small cloth bag and gave Thea a handful of spools.

"Of something unpleasant, it seems." Sarah touched her friend's shoulder. "Do you want to talk? You know I'm a good listener." When she'd first come to Ladreville, Sarah had worked in the mercantile with Isabelle. The time together had forged their friendship, a friendship based on shared confidences and ultimately a shared faith.

Isabelle shook her head. "It's nothing." Briskly she turned and pulled two bolts of fabric from the shelf behind her. "What do you think of these? You said Priscilla had strawberry blond hair, so I thought these would suit her."

Though some of the townspeople might look askance at the departure from tradition, Sarah had asked Isabelle to select material in any shade other than black. Priscilla would mourn her loss for far more than a year, regardless of the color of her clothing. Sarah nodded her approval. The bolts Isabelle had chosen were green and rust, shades that would flatter Priscilla's coloring.

"They're beautiful." Sarah looked down, assuring herself that Thea was still engrossed in rolling spools along the floor. Thank goodness the child was easily entertained. It made shopping more pleasant when she didn't have to worry about her sister. Sarah thought about the other items she'd put on her list this morning. "Do you have any fabric for petticoats and chemises?"

This time Isabelle's smile was genuine as she pulled out a froth of white fabric and lace. "I have something better than fabric." She held up a beautifully trimmed petticoat and matching chemise. "You know we don't usually carry ready-made garments, but these were in a shipment that arrived yesterday. We called it our mystery shipment, because no one could remember ordering them." Isabelle smiled again.

"Maman was a bit annoyed, wondering if we'd be able to sell them, but when I read your note this morning, I knew they'd come for a reason." Isabelle handed the garments to Sarah. "Do you think they'll fit?"

Sarah held the petticoat against herself and nodded when she saw it was four or five inches too long. "They'll be perfect." She looked back at Isabelle, noting she was once again wearing a frown. "What I need next are handkerchiefs and some answers."

"Linen or cotton?"

"The truth." As Isabelle raised an eyebrow in surprise, Sarah continued. "What's wrong? And don't say nothing, because I won't believe you. Have there been more problems with Léon?" A few months earlier, the townspeople had turned against Isabelle and her family, blaming her brother Léon for a series of thefts.

Isabelle shook her head. "Léon's fine. We're all fine. Business is good, and everyone's been friendly since you and Clay discovered who was responsible."

Though her words were positive, Sarah sensed that Isabelle was reciting them rather than revealing her true feelings. "What's bothering you?"

"You won't give up, will you?"

Sarah shook her head. "Why would I? That's what friends are for, to help when there are problems." And, though she might deny it, Isabelle had a problem.

Isabelle gazed into the distance for a moment, as if composing her thoughts. "Have you heard that no one's seen Madame Ladre in weeks? She doesn't even attend church any longer."

Sarah wasn't certain what surprised her more, the fact that

the normally active rumor mill had not reported Madame Ladre's absence or that this was what bothered Isabelle. It wasn't as if the mayor's wife was one of Isabelle's friends. Madame Ladre was hardly a frequent visitor to the mercantile, even though her home was only a block away.

"I hadn't heard that."

"The rumor is her nerves have suffered ever since Jean-Michel left." When the mayor had discovered his son was responsible for the town's thefts, he'd banished him to Houston to work for an empresario until he could repay the people he'd wronged. "Some say the shame was too much for Madame Ladre," Isabelle added.

Sarah sighed, remembering her own experiences. "We both know how cruel some people can be and how they blame the whole family for one person's sins."

Before Isabelle could respond, the doorbell tinkled again and a large blond man entered the store. Sarah smiled as she recognized Gunther Lehman, the father of her favorite student and a man who'd been one of her former suitors. With his blunt features, Gunther was far from handsome, but his friendly smile and sparkling blue eyes made a person forget his decidedly average looks.

"Hello, Gunther." Though he nodded briefly in response to Sarah's greeting, his attention was clearly focused on Isabelle. Sarah watched, amazed when Isabelle blushed and looked down at the floor. It wasn't like her friend to be bashful.

"What can I do for you, Mr. Lehman?" Though Isabelle's voice was even, her cheeks still bore a rosy tint.

The German man's lips twisted in annoyance. "I thought you agreed to call me Gunther." When Isabelle blushed again but made no reply, he said, "I would like to see some hand-kerchiefs, Miss Rousseau."

He pronounced her name with mocking formality and clicked his heels, as if saluting her. Isabelle giggled; Gunther smiled; their eyes met, and both of them flushed. It was obvious that neither one remembered Sarah's presence. They stared at each other, their color heightened, until Thea tugged on Sarah's skirt and asked when they were leaving.

"Handkerchiefs." Isabelle murmured the word as she walked to the opposite end of the store.

Gunther's gaze followed her, his expression reminding Sarah of a starving man faced with a banquet he cannot reach. When Isabelle returned with a pile of handkerchiefs, he frowned. "Not those. For a lady."

A moment before her cheeks had been rosy. Now blood drained from Isabelle's face. She bowed her head for a second, then pointed to the selection of women's handkerchiefs that she'd brought out for Sarah's approval. "These are our nicest ones," she said, pulling out one with a delicate lace edging. "Any lady would like these."

Gunther nodded. "Do you like them?"

The simple question appeared to fluster Isabelle. She stared at him for a moment before she said, "Why, yes, I do."

"Then I'll take one."

Nodding shortly, Isabelle reached for a piece of paper to wrap the piece of linen. "Olga will like it."

"Olga?" Gunther sounded as if this were the first time he'd heard the name. How absurd. Everyone in Ladreville knew he was courting Olga Kaltheimer.

Sarah stared at Gunther, wondering what was wrong. In the months he'd wooed her, she had never seen him so addlepated.

"Olga Kaltheimer," she said softly. If he was purchasing a handkerchief for a lady, the recipient had to be Olga.

"Ah yes, Olga. Of course."

As she loaded her packages into the back of the carriage and prepared for the drive back to the Bar C, Sarah's thoughts whirled. The whole encounter between Isabelle and Gunther had been strange. Though the words they'd exchanged had been ordinary, the looks they'd given each other had been anything but. Gunther had regarded Isabelle with the same tender expression Sarah saw so often in Clay's eyes. When she thought no one was looking, Isabelle had darted quick glances at Gunther, each one causing her color to rise.

Sarah's thoughts ceased their whirling and marched toward one conclusion. Could it be? Could the cause of Isabelle's earlier malaise be disappointment that Gunther was courting Olga and not her? Could Gunther's awkwardness have resulted from his attraction to Isabelle? Did Isabelle and Gunther harbor romantic feelings toward each other? The evidence was there, but it raised another, more disturbing question. If Isabelle and Gunther were involved romantically, how would the town react?

Though Sarah loved her new home and the vibrancy the settlers brought with them, there was no denying that the immigrants' legacy was more than storybook beautiful architecture and hard work. The divisions between the French and German settlers were centuries old, remnants of their past in Alsace, where the two countries had been at war more often than not and where trust was rarely given to someone who spoke with a different accent. Unfortunately, though they now lived in a new country, the rifts remained as deep as the ocean they'd crossed.

4

There was no sign of them. Lawrence Wood tightened the reins and urged Snip into a trot. There was no point in remaining here. He'd retraced his way to the place where the Dunkler brothers had attacked Miss Morton, hoping to find a clue, knowing he might be disappointed. He was. Rain had obliterated any clues the men had left. Now only the fresh graves remained as evidence of the violence that had occurred here. Even the stagecoach was gone, probably rescued by an enterprising farmer who sought the reward the company offered for return of its vehicles. It had been a long shot, thinking he would find something here, but he had to try. He owed it to himself, to the Rangers, and especially to Miss Morton.

Lawrence frowned as memories of the beautiful redhead came rushing back, accompanied, as they always were, by worry. Though he told himself there was no reason to worry, that he had seen no sign of the Dunkler brothers heading toward Ladreville, Lawrence was unable to dismiss his concerns.

By all accounts, Jake and Chet Dunkler were among the orneriest creatures in the state of Texas. Heaven help Miss Morton if they decided to avenge their brother's death. That was why he had to find them.

If only they'd left a clue.

⁓ঌ

Priscilla took one last stitch before she knotted the thread. Though she still had another sleeve to set in the dress she would wear to Sarah and Clay's wedding, daylight had long since faded, along with Priscilla's willingness to remain indoors. It made no sense. She was safe inside the ranch house. The bandits would never find her here, and even if they tracked her to the Bar C, Zach Webster had arranged the ranch hands' schedule so there was always someone close. He and the others would not let anyone harm her. The safest place for her was within these walls. Priscilla knew that, and yet by the time night fell, the walls that had been her sanctuary during the day turned into a prison.

Perhaps it was because both Sarah and Clay were home then, and when they were home, they watched her. Their intentions were noble. Priscilla knew they were concerned about her, for she'd heard them speaking of her, worrying about her failure to cry. Didn't they know that crying solved nothing? The damage had been done; crying wouldn't change that.

Priscilla had heard Sarah tell Clay how she requested a bath twice each day, and they'd both wondered how long that would continue. It wasn't that they begrudged her the soap and water or the effort Martina expended. It was simply that such frequent baths were not normal. Perhaps she should stop. The truth was, no matter how often she bathed, Priscilla did not feel clean. Perhaps she should accept the reality that she never would.

It wasn't only her bathing habits that worried Sarah and Clay. Priscilla had heard them discuss her refusal to leave the ranch. Sarah claimed it was normal and that the fear would subside. Clay was not so certain. Nor was Priscilla, for it wasn't only fear of the bandits that kept her here. She also dreaded the speculation that would accompany her if she ventured into town.

Patience had written about how the townspeople had stared at her as if she were an exotic animal that had been brought to Ladreville. How much more would they stare at a woman whose stagecoach had been attacked, a woman who had been violated? They'd know Priscilla was unclean, and they'd either snicker, believing it was somehow her fault, or else they'd view her with pity. Priscilla wasn't certain which would be worse. All she knew was that she would not subject herself to either.

"I think I'll walk outside," she told Sarah as she rose, gathering the unfinished gown into her arms. Though Sarah had offered to accompany her on previous evenings, tonight she simply nodded. A few minutes later, her wool shawl wrapped around her, Priscilla slipped out the front door. She wouldn't go far; she never did; but perhaps the cool night air would clear her mind. Perhaps the exercise would tire her enough that the nightmares would not come. Most importantly, perhaps tonight would be the night God showed her his plan. Though she no longer believed he had abandoned her, she had not heard his voice telling her why he'd brought her to Ladreville.

71

Priscilla shivered, finding the evening colder than she'd expected. Tonight the sky was clear with no clouds to blanket the Earth, holding in the day's warmth. Instead, a tapestry of stars tried to compete with the light of the full moon. Priscilla walked quickly, trying to warm herself, and in the process she ventured farther from the house than she'd done before. When she realized that she had reached the small grove of oak trees, she stopped abruptly. This was not where she wanted to be. There were no answers to be found here where trees sheltered the Canfield burial plot. Priscilla shuddered at the sight of the three headstones, one of which was her sister's. The others belonged to Clay's mother and his brother.

She was here. She might as well stay. Though her feet moved reluctantly, Priscilla made her way to the gravestones and sank down next to Patience's. Her fingers traced the simple words Clay had had chiseled into the marble along with the dates of her sister's life. *Beloved wife, daughter, and sister.* Patience had been all that and more. If she had lived, she would have been a mother herself. Though she had considered Texas a hostile land, Patience had found happiness here as she'd waited for the birth of her first child. Mama and Papa had not found even those fleeting moments of joy. Texas had brought them nothing but a shared grave.

Oh, Mama, I loved you, Priscilla cried silently as she wrapped her arms around Patience's stone. There would be no headstones for her parents. *I didn't mean to bring you and Papa into danger.* But she had. Pain sliced through Priscilla's heart, overwhelming her with its intensity. Not even on the day of her parents' death had she felt a grief like this. She had been numb then, trying desperately to block out the memory of what had happened to them and to her.

72

But now the numbness had worn off, leaving her no shield against the pain. It hurt. Oh, how it hurt to know they were gone. *Forgive me, Lord, if I hurt them.*

Priscilla closed her eyes to murmur a silent prayer for her parents, and as she did, a memory stole into her mind. It had been a late summer evening a month before her seventh birthday and perhaps a week after Grandmama, Mama's mother, had died. Though Mama and Papa had told their daughters that Grandmama had gone to heaven, Priscilla knew they were lying. Grandmama was buried deep in the ground. That was why Mama went to the cemetery each night.

Papa had been gone that particular evening, probably calling on one of his patients, and Patience had been ill, so only Priscilla and Mama made the pilgrimage to Grandmama's grave. As she did each evening, Mama cut a flower from her garden to place on the grave. The flowers, she explained to Priscilla and her sister, were a sign of her love for Grandmama. Always in the past, Mama had carried the flower, but that night she entrusted a rose to Priscilla, warning her to hold it carefully, lest the thorns prick her fingers.

Inordinately proud of the responsibility she'd been given, Priscilla fairly pranced to the cemetery. Afterwards, she could not recall exactly what had happened, why she had tripped and why she had gripped the blossom. All she knew was that she'd destroyed the rose, for the petals had tumbled off the stem, scattering on the ground.

"Oh, Mama, I'm sorry." As tears streamed down her cheeks, Priscilla knelt on the ground, gathering the petals, hoping against hope that she could put them back on the stem. "I didn't mean to hurt Grandmama's flower," she cried.

Gently Mama led Priscilla to a bench and drew her onto

her lap. "It's all right, sweetheart," she said softly. "Everything has its time to die, even flowers. We'll lay a few petals on Grandmama's grave, but I want you to carry the rest of them home."

"Why, Mama?"

"You'll see." When they returned home, Mama pulled a glass bowl out of the china cabinet. Opening Priscilla's hand, she brushed the petals into the bowl, then handed it to Priscilla. "You can keep this in your room. Don't worry when the petals change color. That's what happens when flowers dry. But even though they won't always look the way they do today, they'll still have a nice scent."

Mama wrapped her arms around Priscilla as she said, "I know you miss Grandmama. We all do, but it was her time to leave us, just as it was this flower's time to lose its petals." When thoughts of Grandmama's death brought a fresh spate of tears, Mama turned Priscilla so they were facing each other. Cupping Priscilla's chin in her hand, she waited until Priscilla met her gaze before she said, "Grandmama wouldn't want you to cry. She would want you to remember how much she loved you." Mama touched the bowl of petals. "These are your reminder. Whenever you smell them, I want you to remember how beautiful the flower once was and to know that nothing is completely gone so long as we have memories."

Even after the roses had lost their scent completely and had been replaced with other flowers, Priscilla had kept a bowl of potpourri in her room. Occasionally she would stir it with her finger to release the fragrance, and each time, she'd think of her grandmother, remembering the stories she'd told Patience and Priscilla and how Grandmama had never been too tired to play games with them. As Mama had predicted, the memories had brought comfort.

The wind stirred the oak leaves, breaking Priscilla's reverie. She shivered, but this time the shiver was accompanied by a small smile. It had not been by chance that she'd walked this way. She had been led. Priscilla raised her face to the stars and smiled again. *Thank you, Lord, for showing me that I have not lost everything. I still have memories.*

Feeling more invigorated than she had since she'd arrived at the Bar C, Priscilla walked briskly toward the house, then, changing her mind, she turned toward the paddock. Though the horses might be inside the barn, there was a chance that some remained outdoors. If they did, perhaps one or two would be curious enough to approach her. While her sister had taken great pleasure from gardening, Priscilla had preferred riding and had sought any excuse to accompany her father on those days when he rode rather than took the carriage on his medical rounds.

She had almost reached the paddock when a man emerged from the barn. He strode quickly in her direction, then turned abruptly when he spotted Priscilla. Regret stabbed her as she realized that Zach Webster had recognized her uneasiness around him and was going out of his way—literally— to ensure that he didn't bother her. Since the day he'd interrupted her breakfast, Priscilla had seen him only from a distance. According to Martina, Zach was spending far less time than usual in the house. That wasn't a coincidence, Priscilla knew.

She raised her voice slightly. "There's no need to leave, Mr. Webster. You belong here more than I do."

He turned again and approached her. Instead of his normal

brisk gait, he walked slowly, his hands at his sides, fingers spread wide so there was not the slightest hint of aggression. Priscilla's mouth turned up when she realized this was probably the stance he used when he tried to gain the confidence of a wild animal. Had she seemed wild those first days? Perhaps. She had certainly been frightened.

"You're wrong about me belonging here, Miss Morton," he said when they were a yard apart. "You're family. I'm only a hired hand."

"Mr. Webster, what you are is too modest. Anyone can see that Clay regards you as a brother." Moonlight shone on his face, outlining the firm features. To Priscilla's surprise, it also revealed discomfort. She thought quickly, trying to understand which of her words might have made him uncomfortable, but she could find none.

"Be that as it may, I'll be leaving soon."

His words surprised her, as did the fact that his hands were now clenched. Though he'd volunteered the statement, it obviously caused distress. "May I ask why?" Surely it was not because she was here. "According to both Sarah and Clay, you've been a vital part of the Bar C since the day you arrived. What you do must be even more important now that you and Clay have taken over the neighboring ranch."

Zach shrugged. "It's time." Though his words were matter of fact, he was close enough that she could see the sadness in his eyes. Zach Webster might deny it, but he did not want to leave the Bar C. Priscilla was as certain of that as she was of her own name.

"I'm not meant to stay anywhere for a long time," he said quietly.

Her heart ached at the pain she heard in his voice, and

she sought a way to comfort him. "I'm sorry," Priscilla said, knowing the words were inadequate but unable to find others. "I can't claim to understand how you feel. I spent my whole life in the same house. It was comfortable there, but from the time I was a child, I longed for adventure. I wanted to do things besides paint watercolors and embroider hankies, and I wanted to visit places beyond Massachusetts. That's one of the reasons I was anxious to attend Clay's wedding. I thought it would be an adventure, coming to Texas, seeing more of the country." Priscilla looked directly at Zach as she said, "Now I'd give anything not to have left Boston."

He nodded slowly, his eyes filled with compassion and understanding. "One thing I've learned is that we cannot change the past. We have to make our peace with it and learn to live with our mistakes." He closed his eyes briefly, and Priscilla sensed that he was praying for forgiveness for his mistakes, whatever they might have been. When he opened his eyes again, he said, "I do not believe your journey was a mistake. Clay needed to have Patience's family here."

"Thank you for saying that, Mr. Webster. I wish I could believe I wasn't wrong in insisting we come, but . . ."

"Believe it." He interrupted Priscilla with a command that surprised her by its intensity. "Believe it. One more thing, if it's not too much of an imposition." A wry smile twisted his lips. "Would you call me Zach? No one's ever called me Mr. Webster. When you do, I keep wondering who you're addressing."

"I'm sorry, Mr. . . . . Zach. I should have remembered that Texas is not as formal as Boston. Please call me Priscilla."

His smile broadened. "Good night, Priscilla. Sleep well."

She did. For the first time, there were no nightmares.

"I saw Martina's hand." It was late the next morning, and the family had returned from church. While Sarah and Thea played with her doll in one corner of the room, Clay took a seat across the table from Priscilla as they all waited for Martina to prepare dinner. "I've never seen a burn heal so well."

Priscilla nodded. "Papa was excited when he discovered the value of using cold water instead of butter or lard. That was one of the things he wanted to discuss with you while he was here." As she pronounced the words, Priscilla realized that the pain that accompanied every mention of her parents had lost its sharp edge. For the first time, she'd spoken of her father without triggering the anguish of knowing she'd contributed to his death and the horrible, aching sense of emptiness that his and Mama's absence brought. She took a deep breath, trying to understand what had happened. A second later Priscilla shook herself mentally. Whether it was caused by the realization that she retained sweet memories or by the comfort Zach had tried to provide didn't matter. What was important was that the healing had begun.

Oblivious to her thoughts, Clay winked. "Next thing I know, you'll be taking over my practice."

Priscilla shook her head. Though becoming a physician had once been her dream, she no longer dared to dream so boldly. "I don't think so."

Clay nodded. "I could use an assistant, but the truth is, I doubt Ladreville is ready for a lady doctor. The townspeople are still trying to overcome centuries of mistrust between the

French and the Germans. I don't know what they'd do if I brought you with me."

That was the argument her father had used when she'd spoken of her aspirations. Priscilla managed a smile. "They'd probably run in the other direction."

Clay nodded. "They might." As the aroma of roast chicken wafted in from the kitchen, announcing that dinner would soon be ready, he reached into his pocket. "The reason I asked to talk to you wasn't just to discuss Martina's burn. I want you to have this."

When he opened his hand, tears welled in Priscilla's eyes. Clay was offering her the filigree locket that had once been her sister's. "Are you certain?"

Clay nodded. Rather than hand it to her, he placed the locket on the table and let Priscilla pick it up. She blinked back tears at the realization that he was ensuring he did not touch her.

"It's yours, Priscilla," Clay said. "I had planned to return it when I sent back Patience's fancy dresses, but it was missing for a while."

The tone of his voice told Priscilla there was a story about the misplaced locket, but the expression in his eyes warned her not to ask. "I don't know how to thank you." She cupped her hand, enjoying the sensation of the metal warming in it. "This is more than a pretty piece of jewelry to me. I feel as if you've given me part of my family." Priscilla looked up at Clay. "Patience probably told you that our parents gave us each a locket on our eighteenth birthday. Hers was oval, mine heart-shaped. What made them special was that Mama and Papa put their pictures on one side, ours on the other." Priscilla fingered the delicate filigree, remembering how Patience had claimed that her locket was more beautiful than Priscilla's. It had been Mama who had soothed Priscilla by declaring she had always wanted a heart-shaped pendant. "You know the bandits took all of our jewelry. It may sound strange to you, Clay, but I regret the loss of the miniatures more than the locket itself. And now you've given them back to me." Her hands trembling slightly, Priscilla opened the locket. "They're gone."

"I'm sorry, but I didn't look inside." Clay shook his head, as if regretting his omission. "I don't know where the pictures are. If I had to guess, I would say they were destroyed. Again, I'm sorry."

"It's not your fault." Though he had given her none of the details about the time the locket had been missing, Priscilla knew that Clay was not responsible for the loss of the miniatures. "I'm happy just to have this," she said, sliding her sister's remaining piece of jewelry into her pocket. As beautiful as it was, Priscilla would never wear it. Like the potpourri that had provided so much comfort as a child, it would be enough to touch it occasionally.

Clay rose and walked to the window, then returned to his chair. If she hadn't known that he was not a man given to nerves, Priscilla would have thought he was nervous. He cleared his throat, another uncharacteristic action, before he said, "I don't want you to think I'm rushing you, but I want you to know that whenever you decide you're ready to return to Boston, I'll accompany you. You don't need to fear traveling alone."

For a moment Priscilla was so startled by the notion of traveling East that she could only stare at her former brother-in-law. "That's a very generous offer, Clay," she said when she could once again form words. And it was, for the trip would take him away from Ladreville and his patients for far too long. "Thank you, but I won't be returning to Boston." As odd as it would probably seem to Clay, until he had raised the subject, Priscilla had not thought of going back to Massachusetts. She had been living her life one hour at a time, not thinking beyond the next. But the decision, though it might appear hasty, felt right to her.

Clay's eyes widened with surprise. "What will you do?"

"Ask my father's attorney to sell the house and do whatever is necessary to turn the practice over to Papa's assistant." The words came out with confidence, as if she'd always known them.

"Will you stay in Ladreville?"

For the first time since Clay had initiated the conversation, Priscilla faltered. "I'm not sure." It would be difficult, living here where everyone knew what had happened to her. Perhaps she should make a clean break and move somewhere else. The question was, where. "I don't know. All I know is there's nothing for me in Boston."

Clay nodded slowly. "Sarah felt the same way when she came here." But, unlike Sarah, who had been destitute when she arrived, Priscilla would have no financial worries. The sale of her parents' home and possessions would provide enough money for her to live comfortably for the rest of her life.

"This is your home for as long as you want to stay." Clay gestured around the spacious house. "You know we have plenty of room for you here, but if you'd prefer a house of your own, we can build one." He rose and looked out the window again, as if considering a site. "There used to be a cabin out there. We could rebuild it."

Once again, he was overwhelming her with his generosity. Though Zach had claimed that she was family, the ties no longer existed now that Patience was gone. Yet Clay was treating her like a true sister, not merely a former sister-by-marriage. "That's very kind of you. I would like to stay here a while longer." Once again the decision felt right. "Some days my thoughts whirl faster than a cyclone, and I can't make sense of any of them." It was not a comfortable feeling. "I'd like to stay until I feel more like myself."

Clay settled back into the chair opposite her. "That's a common reaction. I'm telling you that as a physician, not just a friend," he said with a small smile. "Even though you're not a patient, I'll give you the same advice I give them. Don't try to force yourself to make a decision. Give yourself time."

❧

"What do you want?"

Gunther Lehman practically snarled the words. The tall, blond man was in a foul mood. Zach had known it from the minute he set foot inside the mill and saw the miller stomping the floor as if his feet were meant to crush the grain.

"I have some rye to be ground, but I'll come back later." Much later, when he'd given Gunther's mood a chance to improve. Normally the miller was even-tempered, more given to joking than grousing, but today, it appeared, was not a normal day.

"Hand it over. You're here, aren't you? You might as well stay."

Though Zach could think of far more pleasant things to do, he surrendered the sack of rye, watching while Gunther poured it into the hopper, his movements uncharacteristically jerky. "You might as well spit it out," Zach told the man who'd become his friend.

"What are you talking about?" When that friend wheeled around, he looked decidedly unfriendly with his face flushed, his fists clenched as if he intended to punch someone.

Zach hoped he wasn't that someone. "Whatever's sticking in your craw," he said in his most conciliatory tone. "Something's got you madder than a scalded boar."

Gunther ran a hand through his hair. Judging from the spikes, Zach guessed this was not the first time he'd done that. "A man's got a job to do. You'd think the others would help."

"You're looking for a helper?" Gunther hadn't mentioned being overworked, and the mill didn't appear busy.

"*Nein*. The mill is easy. Everything's easy compared to raising a child."

So that was the problem: Gunther's daughter. The miller had been raising Eva alone since his wife had died in childbirth a few years earlier. Unwilling to offer advice when he had no experience with children, Zach kept his mouth shut. Eventually when the silence grew uncomfortable, he asked, "Is something wrong with Eva?"

"Herr Kaltheimer sent Olga to Fredericksburg to live with his brother," Gunther said as if that explained his dilemma. "He claims they need her to help with the new baby. Bah! The truth is, he doesn't want her to marry me."

Gunther's words were starting to make sense. Like everyone else in Ladreville, Zach knew the widower was looking for a new mother for his daughter and that Olga was the latest candidate for that position. If Olga had been sent away, Gunther's plan would have hit a snag or perhaps an impenetrable barrier.

83

The question was, why? Zach had heard of no problem. Instead, the rumor mill had been speculating on the date of Gunther and Olga's nuptials.

"Did you talk to Herr Kaltheimer before you started courting his daughter?" Though Gunther was not an impetuous man, he had started courting Olga soon after Sarah had refused him. Perhaps he'd been so eager that he'd neglected important formalities.

"*Ja*. I'm not a *Dummkopf*. He agreed then, but now he says I have to wait, that Olga's too young to marry." Gunther raked his fingers through his hair again. "I don't understand. I know Herr Kaltheimer wouldn't want his daughter to marry a Frenchman, but I'm German. What could the problem be? Eva's a good girl, and I'm a good provider. It's true I work long hours, but Olga would have a fine house. She could order anything she wanted from the mercantile."

As he pronounced the last word, Gunther flushed and turned his back, as if he didn't want anyone to read his expression. How strange. But then, this whole conversation was strange. Though Zach was hardly an expert on matrimony, he couldn't help noting that Gunther made marriage sound like a business arrangement. Unlike Clay and Sarah, who were visibly in love with each other, not once had Gunther mentioned his feelings toward Olga Kaltheimer or hers toward him. It appeared that he wanted to continue the Old Country tradition of marrying for economic or other practical reasons rather than love.

"I don't see that you have any choice," Zach said at last. "You'll have to wait until Herr Kaltheimer gives his approval."

"That's the problem. I can't afford to wait. Eva needs a

mother now." Gunther scooped the rye flour into a sack and handed it to Zach. "It's not right for a child to be raised by only one parent."

Zach frowned as he counted out the coins for the miller. Thanks to him, it was possible that two children had no father and that two women were raising their children alone. He couldn't dwell on that, for the past could not be changed. What mattered now was the future. It might not be much, but Zach had resolved he would do what he could to ensure that he caused no more pain. If that meant leaving Ladreville and a life he enjoyed so that Miss Morton could live in peace, so be it.

Forcing his lips into a smile, Zach mounted Charcoal and rode into town, intending to stop at the post office. With the wedding less than a month away, Sarah and Clay received parcels almost every day, some of them too large for Sarah to carry. That was why Zach checked the post office frequently. That and the fact that it gave him an excuse to wander through the town that had come to feel like home.

He was looping the reins around a post when Michel Ladre emerged from his house. Though the mayor took pride in the fact that he owned the largest and most elaborate house in town, centrally located between the town's attorney and the post office and across the street from Ladreville's two churches, today his jaunty, almost arrogant step was missing. Judging from Michel's slumped shoulders, his day was not going any better than Gunther's.

"Good morning, Mayor." Zach knew that the man who'd founded the town responded well when addressed formally. Perhaps a reminder of his position would improve his mood. Michel hadn't seemed this despondent the night Zach had brought his son home with proof of his crimes. Though Jean-Michel had screamed obscenities and vowed revenge, Michel had been oddly silent that night, almost as if he had expected the revelation of his son's perfidy. Today was different. Today the mayor appeared to be carrying a heavy burden. His dark hair seemed to have sprouted more gray strands almost overnight, and his brown eyes were dull with pain.

"Name one thing that's good about it." Michel's scowl told Zach it would take more than a friendly greeting to please him.

"The country's elected a new president, and I got my rye ground." Zach accompanied his words with a playful grin. He knew Michel had backed James Buchanan in his campaign against Californian John Frémont and former President Millard Fillmore and had expected him to be pleased with the results of the voting.

The mayor was not impressed. "You're a lucky man if that makes you happy. I need more than that." He glared at Zach, as if whatever was wrong was his fault. "Women! If you ask me, the world would be an easier place if God hadn't made Eve."

Though there were times when Zach might have agreed, telling Michel that would accomplish nothing. Instead he kept his tone light. "It sure would be lonelier."

"Perhaps, but today I'd take loneliness over problems." Michel thrust his hands into his pockets as he said, "I should never have agreed to build that school."

Zach frowned at the apparent non sequitur as he tried to find a connection between women, Michel, and the school. "What's the problem? Everyone thinks the school is good for the community." Though the French and German immigrants

86

agreed on very few things, it appeared that the school pleased both groups.

"The school needs a teacher." Michel gave Zach a look that seemed to say only an idiot would not realize that. "Once Sarah marries, she can no longer teach."

Zach was starting to understand the problem. The mayor had supported the idea of a school. In fact, he had claimed it as his own inspiration. If the school closed for lack of a teacher, he would lose face. "I thought Olga Kaltheimer wanted to replace Sarah."

"So did I. But then Gunther got it into his head to marry her." Michel looked both ways, as if ensuring that no one was close enough to overhear his next words. "What's a man to do? I couldn't let that happen, because then I'd be in the same pickle I am now, so I talked to Olga's father." Zach understood the mayor's desire for secrecy. If Gunther learned this part of the story, fists might fly.

"Herr Kaltheimer said he'd take care of the problem," Michel continued, "but what does he do? Does he simply forbid her to marry Gunther? No. He sends her away. I ask you, Zach, how does that solve my problem? At the end of this month, Ladreville will no longer have a teacher. What do I tell the townspeople? They expect me to find answers."

There was one solution, but Zach suspected Michel wouldn't like it. "You could let Sarah continue teaching."

"Nonsense!" The mayor's reaction was the one Zach had expected. "Everyone knows a married woman's place is at home. Even my wife knows that," he muttered. "Her problem is she thinks our home ought to be somewhere other than Ladreville."

Zach whistled softly, suspecting that marital discord, not

the school dilemma, was the root cause of Michel's ill humor this morning. "This is your town. You founded it. You're the mayor, the sheriff, and the arbiter of most disputes. I'm not saying this to flatter you, Michel, but you're the one indispensable person in Ladreville." Although Zach knew the man craved flattery the way Charcoal did sugar lumps, that was the simple truth.

Michel's scowl faded for an instant, then reappeared. "Jeannette says it's time for us to leave. She claims I spend too much time on the town's business and not enough with her."

Judging from everything he'd heard, Zach couldn't contradict that opinion. There was, however, no point in further riling the mayor. "As a bachelor, I can't claim to know anything about wives, but I might be able to help with the school."

"Are you proposing to teach?"

Zach grinned. The idea was preposterous, and he suspected Michel knew it. "Afraid not. About all I know is horses and ranching. But I also know that Ladreville is a progressive town." As Zach had hoped, Michel's eyes lit with interest, and he straightened his shoulders. "We've got French and Germans living and working together. If that's not progressive, I don't know what is." Michel nodded, a monarch accepting his tribute. "Why couldn't the town's mayor step outside tradition to make his home a better place? It would take a courageous man, but you've already proven you're exactly that." Judicious flattery, Zach told himself, had a place.

"What are you proposing?"

Zach raised his hat to greet two women as they emerged from the post office. He wouldn't venture his proposal until they were out of earshot. When the women were safely inside the mercantile, he turned back to Michel. "I think you should let Sarah continue to teach until summer. That way the children won't suffer, and you would have time to advertise for a new schoolmarm." He gave Michel an appraising look. "I know it's unconventional, but it would be a bold step, one that the rest of Texas would notice."

Perhaps it was only Zach's imagination that the mayor appeared to preen as he considered the suggestion. "It might work," he admitted.

Zach steeled his face to remain impassive, though inwardly he was exulting over the success of his ploy. "I'm confident the townspeople would agree if you presented the idea."

Michel nodded. "You're right. I will do that." The mayor started to return to his home, then turned, as if a thought had suddenly occurred to him. "Oh, Zach, it would be best if no one knew we had this conversation."

"Of course." Zach was smiling as he entered the post office. Flattery had done the trick.

5

"Are you certain you don't mind being saddled with a sick child?"

Priscilla smiled as she attempted to reassure the usually calm woman whose face was now lined with strain. It was a measure of Sarah's distress that she'd entered Priscilla's room while she was dressing. Though she visited occasionally, it was never in the morning. "I don't mind at all." Priscilla smiled again as she fastened the last button on her bodice. Once she'd brushed her hair, she'd be ready. "You needn't worry about Thea. I had plenty of experience helping care for my father's patients."

Sarah's obvious surprise that she knew how to treat sick children caused Priscilla to continue her explanation. "It's true that his wealthy patients might not have appreciated having a child accompany their doctor, but Papa spent one day a week seeing people on the other side of town, the ones who couldn't afford to pay for a doctor. He often took me with him." Priscilla's smile broadened at the memories. "I'm not sure which I enjoyed more—being with Papa or helping the patients feel better. But, thanks to him, I know how to deal with the grippe. I'll be glad to watch over Thea today."

The furrows between Sarah's eyes disappeared. "Thank you. Normally, I'd stay home with her, but I hate to close school, even for a day. The children are so anxious to learn that I feel almost guilty about marrying Clay, knowing the school will close."

Priscilla coiled her hair into a chignon, securing it with the long pins Sarah had purchased at the mercantile, then turned toward her friend. "Aren't you the one who urged me to trust God? Trust him on this. Anyone can see that he meant you to marry Clay, and I'm sure he meant Ladreville to have a school. He'll show us the way." When Sarah nodded slowly, Priscilla headed toward the door. "Let's tell Thea I'll be caring for her today."

Though the child was paler than normal, she grinned when Sarah explained the plan. "Cilla, me want drink," she announced.

"And you'll have one." Priscilla held the cup to her mouth, watching while Thea took several swallows of cool water. "If you're feeling better later, I'll make one of my mother's favorite beverages for you. Right now, though, you and Dolly should sleep."

As Thea settled back on her pillow, the rag doll cradled in one arm, Sarah turned to Priscilla. "What are you going to make for her to drink? Chamomile tea?"

Priscilla shook her head. "That was Mama's sleep potion. I'm going to give Thea mint. When you told me about her grippe, I remembered that Mama claimed mint tea would soothe an upset stomach. I'm sure it's not coincidence that

I saw some growing wild at the edge of the kitchen garden when I was walking yesterday."

Each day, Priscilla managed to venture a bit farther from the house. Though she still looked over her shoulder, ensuring that no one was following her, the fact that it had been two weeks and no strangers had approached the ranch gave her the confidence to explore new areas, that and the knowledge that Zach or one of the ranch hands was close by. Though they had not spoken since the night they'd met by the corral, Priscilla had seen Zach almost every day. He kept his distance, but she knew he was there, ensuring her safety. It was a good feeling.

The day passed more slowly than Priscilla had expected, for she was unwilling to leave Thea's bedside, and there was little to do there other than watch and wait. Despite the cool compresses she applied and the frequent sips of water she encouraged Thea to take, the little girl's fever rose, and she failed to keep even liquids in her stomach. This was, Priscilla knew, the normal progression of the grippe. She was doing everything she could to soothe Thea, but the illness needed to run its course. Only then, when the poisons were out of Thea's body, would the fever break and she be able to sleep normally.

It was mid-afternoon before the change came and Thea slept. Knowing there was nothing more she could do and that her presence now might disturb the child's sleep, Priscilla left the house and headed toward the paddock. The sky was a faultless blue, the air a refreshing change from Thea's sickroom. Priscilla took a deep breath, savoring both the beauty of the Bar C and the knowledge that Thea was mending.

"You're such beautiful horses," she murmured when she

reached the railing. Clay must have taken the buggy into town today, for his stallion was grazing along with the sorrel mare that spent most afternoons in the paddock.

"That they are."

Priscilla wheeled around, startled by the man's voice. "I didn't hear you coming," she told Zach. Her heart began to pound with alarm, and her palms grew moist. It was foolish to react this way. Zach would not hurt her. But her heart returned to normal only when he stopped, leaving a wide space between them.

As he smiled, another thought assailed Priscilla. He already knew she was skittish. What must he think of a woman who talked to herself? "I didn't realize I was speaking aloud. I spent the morning talking to Thea so she'd know she wasn't alone. I guess I forgot where I was."

Though it could have been otherwise, Zach's smile was warm and friendly, not mocking. "How is the little one?"

"Better. She's sleeping now, so I slipped out for a bit of fresh air." This was silly. Priscilla shook herself mentally. She didn't need to explain anything to Zach Webster. Only Sarah and Clay needed to know how she'd cared for Thea. But here she was, acting as if it was important that Zach understood and approved her actions. Silly!

"If you really want fresh air, in my opinion there's no better way to get it than to ride." Zach gestured toward the sorrel mare that was approaching them, apparently curious about the humans. "You could ride her. Nora's a gentle mount."

Priscilla could see that, although Nora was an older horse, she was not yet ready to be turned out to pasture. "I've always loved to ride," she admitted. Riding had been one of her pleasures in Boston, but—with the exception of the time she had spent on the Ranger's horse, which had been anything but pleasurable—she had not been on a horse since she'd left home.

"Then you should. I know Clay would be grateful to have you give Nora some exercise. She was his mother's favorite horse."

Nora's ears pricked up, and she thrust her nose toward Priscilla, as if encouraging her. Sorely tempted, Priscilla stroked the horse's muzzle. The day was perfect for a ride, and Nora would be an ideal mount. Priscilla knew that from the way the mare responded to her touch. "Perhaps tomorrow." She had come out for a breath of air, not a prolonged excursion.

Zach quirked one eyebrow. "Why not now? Thea's asleep, and Martina's inside with her. She'll come for you if you're needed." He propped one boot on the lowest fence rail, the picture of a man at ease. If only she could be so relaxed. Though he stood at least a yard away, Priscilla was deeply aware of Zach's scent and the power of those long arms and legs.

As Clay's stallion came to investigate the humans' activity, Zach rubbed the horse's muzzle. Though he kept his gaze on the horse, he addressed Priscilla. "There's a sidesaddle in the barn. I could have her ready for you in a couple minutes." He turned and gave her an encouraging smile. "C'mon, Priscilla. You'd be doing both Nora and Clay a favor if you took a few laps around the paddock."

"I don't know." Even to her ears, the argument sounded weak.

Zach must have taken her mild protest for agreement, for he nodded. "I'll fetch the saddle. Why don't you and Nora keep getting acquainted?"

Priscilla entered the paddock and approached the mare. "You're a pretty horse, aren't you?" She let Nora sniff her hand, then reached up to stroke her mane. As she did, Priscilla frowned, and her legs threatened to buckle. Though Nora was smaller than the Ranger's stallion, she was still too tall to mount without assistance. That meant . . . Priscilla shuddered as her brain completed the sentence. Riding was a bad idea, a very bad idea.

"Here we are." Zach slung the saddle over the fence, then whistled for Nora.

Priscilla held up a hand to stop him. There was no point in saddling the mare when she wouldn't be ridden. "I'm sorry, Zach, but I can't do this." To her relief, though her limbs continued to quake, her voice sounded normal. Zach was far enough away that he wouldn't witness her fear, since her words had not betrayed her.

Surprise filled those dark blue eyes that reminded Priscilla of the Texas sky. "Why not?"

"It's just . . . er . . ." Oh, it was embarrassing, having to admit her fears. He must know how frightened she was of a man's touch, for he kept his distance. Surely there was no need to put words to her craven thoughts. But Zach, it appeared, did not understand. Priscilla swallowed, mustering her courage. "How would I mount?" she asked.

"I'll lift you." As an involuntary shudder rippled through her, Zach's eyes darkened with understanding. "I see." There was no pity, no condemnation in those two words, only an acknowledgement of a problem. "We'll find another way. You wouldn't want to disappoint Nora, would you?" Nora, who'd been sniffing the saddle, looked at Priscilla, as if she understood her dilemma. "There's a bale of hay inside the barn," Zach continued. "You could climb on that and then into the saddle." Unspoken was the promise that he'd be a safe distance away.

"All right." It was as simple as Zach had made it sound. Within minutes, Priscilla was on Nora's back, watching the mare toss her head, clearly eager to run. "Sorry, girl. I know you want to gallop, but not today." They both needed time to become accustomed to each other. But a few minutes on Nora's back convinced Priscilla they could trot, and so she let the horse increase its pace. It felt so good, so very good, to be riding again, and for a moment nothing mattered but the sensation of being one with this beautiful creature, enjoying the sun, the wind, and the clean air.

"The paddock's a bit confining," Zach said when Priscilla had dismounted, once again relying on the hay bale. "If you'd like, I can show you around the ranch tomorrow."

There was no doubt about it; the opportunity tempted her. When she'd been on Nora's back, Priscilla had been free of fears, released from the prison of terrifying memories. For the length of a ride, she had lived in the present, and it had been a present filled with pleasure, not foreboding. How could she not want to repeat that? When she'd started walking around the ranch, Clay had urged Priscilla to ride, arguing that riding would be an extension of her walks, a way to explore more of the place that was her home, at least temporarily. Each time he'd suggested it, she had refused. Though he had told her that women rode alone here, Priscilla wasn't comfortable with the idea. Zach had solved that problem. With him at her side, she'd be safe. The question was whether she could impose on him. "I don't want to take you away from your responsibilities."

"Who said anything about shirking responsibilities? You can help me check the fences. I need to do that occasionally."

Her last concern assuaged, Priscilla smiled. "I'd like that." When Zach looked at the sky, as if assessing the sun's position, Priscilla glanced at her watch and blinked at the realization that she'd been outside for more than an hour. The time had been so pleasant that she hadn't been aware of its passage. "I'd better check on Thea."

The little girl was awake and restless, both good signs. "Tell me a story," she demanded when Priscilla had coaxed her to drink a few sips of mint tea.

"What kind of story would you like?"

"The one with the coach."

The coach. Priscilla's smile faded and her limbs began to tremble as images of the bandits attacking her stagecoach filled her mind. How did Thea know about that, and why—oh, why—did she want to hear that story?

"No, sweetie." That was one story she would not recount, not to anyone, especially not to an innocent child.

"Please, Cilla." Thea's voice was filled with entreaty. "Pumpkin coach."

Pumpkin. Of course. Relief washed over Priscilla at the realization that Thea wanted to hear the tale of Cinderella. It was only Priscilla's traitorous mind that had turned a simple request into a terrifying memory.

"Once upon a time . . ."

It was easier than he'd expected. Jean-Michel slipped the key into the lock and turned it. Perfect! The gal who cleaned

Monroe's office was even dumber than the great man himself. A few kisses, some sweet words and she'd told Jean-Michel everything he needed to know. Thanks to her, he hadn't had to break down the door, possibly alerting the guards Monroe stationed near his office. Thanks to her, he knew about the safe and the strange set of numbers she'd found glued to the bottom of a paperweight, numbers Jean-Michel was betting were the combination. Thanks to her, Jean-Michel Ladre would soon be a wealthy man . . . and a free one.

He closed the door behind him, grateful that the bars Monroe had installed on the windows did not block the moonlight. It might not be easy, opening the safe in near darkness, but Jean-Michel couldn't take the chance of carrying a lantern. That would be dumb, and he was not dumb. No, sirree. He'd always known he was the smartest man in Ladreville. As the safe swung open, revealing pouches filled with coins, Jean-Michel chuckled. He wasn't just the smartest man in Ladreville; he was the smartest man in the whole state of Texas.

With all this money, he'd have no trouble getting home, and when he did, everyone would see what an important, powerful man he was. Isabelle would beg him to marry her. Zach Webster would do his share of begging too, only his would be done at the point of a rifle.

Jean-Michel was still laughing as he loaded the gold into saddlebags and mounted the horse he'd taken from the livery. He was on his way to Ladreville, where the two sweetest things in life awaited him: marriage and revenge.

The trail was cold. Lawrence Wood paused at the top of the hill and looked at the countryside. This was what he had feared. Though he'd followed the route he thought the Dunkler brothers were taking, he'd been unable to find them. Perhaps they'd changed their minds; perhaps they were holed up somewhere, trying to decide what to do without Zeke. Lawrence didn't pretend to understand a bandit's mind. All he knew was that he hadn't found them.

He should have chased them immediately. They would have had no chance of escape if he'd gone after them as soon as he'd sent Zeke to meet his Maker. That would have been the prudent course of action if he hadn't been worried about Priscilla—Miss Morton, he corrected himself. No matter how much he wanted to capture Chet and Jake Dunkler, he couldn't simply abandon her. A man had responsibilities, and caring for an injured woman was more important than apprehending criminals.

Lawrence studied the valley one more time, assuring himself there were no signs of the bandits. This valley was like the last three he'd checked—filled with pastoral beauty but no trace of riders. They couldn't have vanished. No matter how seemingly insignificant, they had left clues, and it was up to him to find them. More than his reputation as a Ranger was at stake. That was important, for he'd made a vow he intended to honor when he'd joined the Rangers, but there was also the matter of his promise. He kept his promises, including the one he'd made at the Bar C. How could he tell Priscilla—Miss Morton—that he'd failed to catch the Dunkler brothers? He couldn't.

Lawrence let out a short laugh as he urged Snip to gallop. Wouldn't his sister gloat if she could see him now, his head filled with thoughts of a beautiful woman with strawberry blonde hair and green eyes? He couldn't explain it. This wasn't the first time he'd rescued a damsel in distress. Lawrence smiled at the term his sister had used. When he'd told her he was joining the Rangers, she'd declared it was because he had an inner need to be a savior of women. He'd scoffed at the time. He wasn't scoffing now. Though he couldn't claim that he'd saved many, Lawrence had seen women after brutal Indian attacks, others who were injured in saloon brawls, still others left half-dead by robbers. They had all been damsels in distress, but none of them had lingered in his memory the way Priscilla did.

Perhaps it was because he'd spent more time with her than he had with the others. This was the first time he'd done more than deal with the crime itself. In taking Priscilla to the Bar C, Lawrence had gotten to know her, and what he'd learned had surprised him. She'd been plucky on the trail, never complaining, even though her injuries must have made riding painful. Other women would have wailed and wrung their hands when he suggested riding through the night. Not Priscilla. She had borne the hardships of their journey staunchly. There'd been no tears except for that first spate that had ended so abruptly.

No doubt about it, Priscilla Morton was unlike the other women he'd met. That must be the reason why he couldn't get her out of his mind, why he felt such a longing to return to the Bar C and announce that he had captured the Dunkler brothers. He would do it. Somehow.

❦

"I need your help."

Though Clay did not normally join Zach when he rode the range, this afternoon he'd volunteered to accompany him. The reason was now apparent. Clay wanted advice of some sort, and judging from the fact that Clay had waited until they were out of earshot of the ranch, that advice probably concerned his bride-to-be. Zach cringed at the thought of being drawn into another discussion of women. Gunther, Michel, now Clay. Why did they think he had any knowledge of the female of the species? They'd all been married; he had not.

Clay stared into the distance, as if the cumulus cloud that threatened to block the sun would provide inspiration. When he spoke, his words confirmed Zach's fears. "Since we're postponing our wedding trip, I need to think of something special to do for Sarah after we're married."

Perhaps humor would diffuse his friend's seriousness. "You're asking me?" Zach didn't have to feign incredulity. "C'mon, Clay. This is your second marriage. You're the expert, not me."

"But you're the one who helped me plan Sarah's birthday party. That turned out well, even if you did tell me I ought to invite Gunther."

Zach chuckled, recalling his friend's discomfort at the thought of inviting one of Sarah's suitors into his home. Clay had been so annoyed, he'd almost started a fist fight. "Gunther never had a chance of winning her hand. Even I could see that." Gunther. Zach's mood brightened at the realization that he could change the subject. "I feel sorry for the man. He wants a new mother for Eva, but no one's interested."

Clay's lips twisted into a grin. Though Zach refused to smile, he couldn't help being pleased that Clay had taken the bait. "Sarah's got it into her head that Gunther and Isabelle belong together."

"Isabelle Rousseau?" The idea was so unexpected that Zach thought he must have misunderstood. Why would Sarah even suggest that Gunther, a German, should marry Isabelle, a Frenchwoman?

"As far as I know, there's only one Isabelle in Ladreville."

"They're both nice enough people," Zach conceded, "but I can't picture them marrying. The way I see it, it'll take at least another generation before the town's ready for that." Though they worked together, for the most part peaceably, there was no ignoring the divisions between the German and the French settlers. Each group had its own church, and for a long time, the children had not been permitted to attend school together. While some of the barriers had been breached, there had been no intermarriage.

"That was my reaction too," Clay admitted. "Sarah thinks otherwise. Let me give you some advice, Zach. Beware of women when they have matchmaking on their minds. I've never seen Sarah so determined."

They rode for a few seconds in companionable silence before Clay said, "Come to think of it, you should be grateful Sarah has Gunther and Isabelle to worry about. Otherwise, she might turn her attention to you."

Zach flinched. Maybe it hadn't been such a good idea to change the subject. "I'm not interested. Some men are meant to be bachelors, and I'm one."

"You've said that before." Clay's expression reflected his skepticism. "My answer is the same as it was then: your time is coming, one way or the other. If you're wise, you'll take my advice and find yourself a bride before Sarah decides to pick one for you."

"I'm not interested." As Zach repeated his words, an image

102

of Priscilla flashed before him. He might not be interested in the state of holy matrimony, but she should have been. The rides they'd taken together and the conversations they'd had during those rides had confirmed his initial impression of a kind, loving woman. If ever a woman was meant to marry, it was Priscilla, but now—thanks to the Dunkler brothers— she was afraid of men. For the life of him, Zach could not understand why God had let that happen.

Priscilla clutched her stomach as she tried not to gag. This wasn't like her. Unlike her sister, who'd suffered from frequent mild ailments, Priscilla had always been healthy. In fact, Patience had pronounced her disgustingly healthy. She wasn't healthy now.

Priscilla gagged again, then swung her legs out of bed. There was no reason for her to feel so queasy. She hadn't eaten anything unusual yesterday, and she had no other symptoms of illness. Unfortunately, rationalizing was accomplishing nothing. As much as she wanted to deny it, there was no doubt about it. Last night's supper was not staying in her stomach. She must have caught the grippe from Thea.

Priscilla grabbed the chamber pot and retched.

6

Thank goodness her stomach had settled. Priscilla laid the green poplin dress on the bed and smoothed the lace trim that she and Sarah had spent hours applying. The dress was lovely and would not look out of place at this afternoon's wedding, so long as the wearer's face wasn't green. Though the mirror told her otherwise, that was how Priscilla felt each morning when her stomach rebelled against even the thought of food.

The reason for her queasiness wasn't hard to find. After the first two days when she'd had none of the other symptoms, she'd realized she wasn't suffering from the grippe. Her problem was anxiety. Papa had taught her that the mind could cause illness just as surely as a festering cut. That was most assuredly Priscilla's case. First she had dreaded Christmas, and now there was Clay and Sarah's wedding. Under other circumstances, both would have been joyous occasions, but these weren't other circumstances.

As it had turned out, Christmas had been less painful than

Priscilla had expected. Though the joy she normally found in the celebration of her Savior's birth was tempered by the absence of her parents, the fact that she was in a place that held no memories of them seemed to assuage the worst of her sorrow. Those first few days of almost unbearable pain, remembering the bandits' attack and the shock on her parents' faces when they'd realized what was happening, had faded into a dull ache.

Though Sarah had extended the invitation, she had not pressured Priscilla to attend Christmas Eve services. Clay, ever the pragmatic physician, had urged her to leave the ranch, claiming that Christmas was the perfect time to meet the citizens of Ladreville. One look at Priscilla's face had been all Sarah needed. She'd shooed Clay away and assured Pricilla there was no reason to go into town until she was comfortable. Instead, while the family had been at church, Priscilla had opened her Bible to the second chapter of Luke. She'd memorized the words long ago, but there was an undeniable comfort in holding the leather-bound book her grandmother had given her. "And she brought forth her firstborn son, and wrapped him in swaddling clothes, and laid him in a manger, because there was no room for them in the inn." As she spoke the words aloud, a shiver of wonder rippled through Priscilla. Papa had always said that birth was a miracle, and the birth in the stable so many years ago was the greatest miracle of all.

Christmas Day itself had been pleasant. Thea had wakened everyone in the household with cries of delight when she snuck out of her room and saw the tree with its decorations and packages underneath it. Unable to resist her sister's pleas to open gifts, Sarah had postponed breakfast and had asked Martina and Miguel as well as Zach to join the rest of the family.

Oddly, the most memorable moment was not Thea's excitement when she found a miniature wagon for her doll. It occurred later in the morning when Zach walked around the Christmas tree to admire the décor. "What's this?" he demanded, pointing at what appeared to be a pickle hanging from one of the branches.

Sarah's eyes widened in faux surprise. "It's a pickle, Zach. Can't you see that?" she asked, her tone one she might have used with a difficult pupil.

Zach responded with a frown. "Of course I can see that it's a pickle. What I don't understand is why you have one on the tree. I understand berries and popcorn, but a pickle?"

Priscilla watched the exchange, puzzled. It wasn't like Sarah to tease, and yet Priscilla sensed that was exactly what she was doing, for her eyes sparkled with mirth, though her voice was solemn. "It's an old German tradition," Sarah explained. "The woman of the household always hides a pickle on the tree, and whoever finds it is destined to be the next to marry."

When the blood drained from Zach's face, Clay clapped his friend on the shoulder and muttered, "Matchmaking. I warned you."

Later Sarah had admitted that she'd stretched the legend a bit. Normally children searched for the pickle, and whoever found it received an extra surprise. She had reserved a piece of candy, expecting Thea to spot the unusual ornament, but when Zach discovered it, she couldn't resist teasing him. "He's too serious," she told Priscilla. "Besides, a bride would be a surprise for him, wouldn't it?"

Priscilla raised her arms to slide the last petticoat over her head as she thought about Zach's reaction. Without a doubt, a bride would be a surprise, an unwelcome one. That puzzled Priscilla. Although most men weren't as overtly eager for marriage as many women, Zach's expression had verged on horror. Surely that was an extreme reaction. Perhaps it had only been shock. That made more sense, for Priscilla thought the revulsion had been mingled with regret. Whatever the cause, she'd felt a kinship with him, for she knew all too well the feeling of discomfort.

Priscilla tried not to frown as she reached for the green poplin dress. No matter how she tried to quell her fears, they returned, turning her legs to jelly and dampening her palms. It was no wonder her stomach had been upset each morning. Today wasn't simply her first time leaving the safety of the Bar C. It was also her first foray into Ladreville's society. They'd stare at her. She knew that. What roiled her stomach was not knowing whether the townspeople would regard her with pity or scorn. Priscilla wasn't certain which would be worse.

She fastened the last of the buttons, then headed toward Sarah's room. The house was quieter than normal this morning, for, mindful of the ancient tradition that a groom should not see his bride's face before the ceremony, Clay had spent the night at the neighboring ranch, an event which had displeased Thea enough that she'd thrown a tantrum. Priscilla preferred not to consider how Thea would react tonight with both Sarah and Clay gone. When Granny Menger had offered the newlyweds her house for their wedding night, Priscilla had agreed she'd watch over Thea. It was, she had reasoned, the least she could do for the people who'd been so kind to her. But that was before she'd experienced one of Thea's tantrums.

"I'm glad you're here," Sarah said as Priscilla entered her room. "My hands are shaking so much I can't fasten a single button."

Priscilla smiled. "That's bridal jitters. Patience was the same way. She couldn't get dressed by herself, and I had to fix her hair." Giving Sarah's coiffure a quick look, Priscilla gestured toward the dressing stool. "Sit down. I'll do yours too." She took the curling iron to the kitchen to heat, then began to brush Sarah's hair.

"I don't know quite how to ask this," Sarah said a moment later. "It's almost too late, but . . ." She hesitated, as if uncomfortable with the subject. At last she blurted out, "Are you sure you don't mind that Clay's marrying again? I'm not trying to take your sister's place."

Though she'd been standing behind her, Priscilla moved so Sarah could see her face. Today of all days it was vital that Sarah believed what she was about to say. Priscilla had already told Clay how she felt. Sarah needed to know, as well. "I'm happy for both you and Clay, and I know Patience would be too." Her sister had never been a selfish woman. "She loved Clay dearly. I'm certain Patience would be glad he's found happiness a second time." As Sarah nodded, apparently convinced of Priscilla's sincerity, Priscilla reached for the curling iron. "Perhaps you'll be able to give Clay the children he longs for."

Sarah colored slightly as she nodded. "We're praying that God will bless us with many babies."

Half an hour later, Sarah was dressed, her dark hair arranged in ringlets framing her face. Though she was beautiful on an ordinary day, today she was radiant.

"Are you two almost ready?" Zach's voice carried through the door. "Clay will never forgive me if you're late."

Priscilla opened the door and ushered the bride into the main room, her gaze stopping abruptly at the sight of Zach. Though this was not the first time she'd seen him in a suit, for he'd worn one on Christmas, today he looked more distinguished, more handsome, than ever before. Perhaps it was because he'd visited the barber, and his hair was freshly cut. Perhaps it was the new cravat, a Christmas gift from Sarah and Clay. Perhaps it was simply the smile that softened his face at the same time that it emphasized the cleft in his chin. Priscilla didn't know. All she knew was that he was an arresting figure, and something—she couldn't imagine what—was making her heart beat faster. She had never before felt like this, all fluttery inside, her legs turning to jelly. It was different from the grippe that plagued her each morning. That was unpleasant. This was . . .

"Me ready!"

Priscilla wrenched her gaze from Zach and turned her attention to Thea, relieved that the odd sensations had vanished as quickly as they'd appeared. Bless Thea for the interruption! The little minx had escaped Martina's grip and was racing toward her sister.

"Me ready!" Thea skidded to a stop and stared at Sarah and Priscilla. "Sarah pretty. Cilla prettier."

It was not the best thing to say to a woman on her wedding day. Far from being insulted, Sarah laughed. "Leave it to my sister to put me in my place." She bent down to give Thea a kiss. When she rose, she turned toward Priscilla. "Are you certain you're ready to care for her?"

"Of course." It was, after all, only for one night. If she was fortunate, Thea would consider it an adventure, not punishment. "We're good friends, aren't we, Thea?"

"Yes! Me love Cilla."

Zach grinned at the exchange. "Now that that's settled, may I escort you three beautiful ladies to the carriage?"

"We need a bridge," Sarah said ten minutes later as the horses descended the shallow bank into the river. She and Priscilla occupied the rear seat, while Thea was happily ensconced in front between Zach and Clay's father, seemingly oblivious to the fact that neither man was responding to her chattering.

Sarah gestured toward the water, which was now only three feet deep. "Isabelle warned me that summer rains bring flash floods, and it's impossible to cross the river for days. Fortunately, that didn't happen this past summer, but I still worry."

The words, though ominous, barely registered, for Priscilla's attention was focused on the town they were approaching. Patience had described it as quaint, but that word hardly did justice to the charm of the half-timbered houses with their steep roofs. Other than the streets, which were laid out on a precise grid rather than twisting and turning, and the distinctly Texan trees, Ladreville looked like a scene from a picture book, the quintessential European town.

"It's beautiful," Priscilla said softly as she admired the small town. Even from this distance, she could see that the streets were spotlessly clean. In summer, she suspected, the window boxes would be filled with flowers, bright splashes of color against the black and white buildings. At any time of the year, the two church steeples would remain the dominant features, standing taller and prouder than the other buildings.

Sarah nodded. "I'd forgotten this was the first time you'd

seen the town. That's the school." Unlike the older buildings, the school was a simple wooden building, utilitarian rather than ornamental. Still, there was no mistaking the pride in Sarah's voice. As the horses emerged from the water, she pointed at the street. "For some reason, the townspeople named the east-west streets after rivers. This one's Rhinestrasse." She gestured toward the right. "The next one's rue de la Seine, and the third is Potomac Street."

Priscilla smiled. "I see all three countries are represented." Though she'd failed to describe the town's appeal, Patience had mentioned the rivalry and occasional hostility between the German and French settlers and their mistrust of the original Anglo settlers. Those problems appeared resolved, at least for the day, for the entire town had been invited to Sarah and Clay's wedding. Lest anyone be insulted, the bride and groom had been careful to include everyone. Though the ceremony was to be held in the German church, both ministers would officiate, and the reception was being hosted by the French church.

When they arrived at the German church, Sarah and Thea were whisked off by her friend Isabelle, leaving Zach to lead Priscilla and Clay's father into the sanctuary. Once they were seated, the church would be opened to the guests. "You'll be in the front row," Zach said as they walked slowly, pacing themselves to Mr. Canfield's halting gait. Even with two canes, he had difficulty moving smoothly, but it was, Sarah had assured Priscilla, a miracle that he could walk at all, a miracle Clay attributed to both Sarah and Zach. Sarah had started the process, but it was Zach's persistence that had resulted in Robert Canfield leaving his wheeled chair.

Priscilla had seen the love Sarah lavished on her soon-to-be father-in-law and was not surprised that, although his infirmity kept him from escorting her down the aisle, Sarah had asked him to join her at the altar and be the one to give her hand in marriage.

Once they were seated, Priscilla spent a few moments studying the church. It was far different from anything she'd seen in Boston, devoid of stained-glass windows and padded pews. The altar was simple, graced with two elaborate silver candelabra that must have been brought from Europe. In sharp contrast was the rough-hewn cross, which Sarah had told her the parishioners had constructed from a local tree during their first Lent in Ladreville. Despite the obvious differences, the peace Priscilla had always found in church began to envelop her, and she closed her eyes in prayer.

"That must be the sister." A piercing whisper disturbed her meditation. This was what she had feared. This was the reason her stomach had been so queasy. It was one thing to know she was the subject of speculation, quite another to face it.

"Her hair's the same color as Patience's." Priscilla realized the woman with the French accent was seated directly behind her. Though she'd been aware of sounds and muted conversation as the church filled, this was the first time she'd distinguished words. These words were innocent. The next ones might not be.

"It's downright sinful what happened to her parents." A second French woman joined the conversation. Priscilla stiffened. Clay's father must have sensed her disturbance, for he murmured something. His words might be unintelligible, but his tone was comforting.

"I heard the Texas Ranger still hasn't caught the bandits," the first woman said.

"He will." The second voice was firm. "That's one thing you can count on. The Rangers always get their man."

As the women continued their conversation, Priscilla began to relax. Though they'd spoken of her parents' death, neither of them had mentioned what had happened to her. Was it possible they didn't know?

"I haven't seen her yet." Judging from the rustling of skirts, the first woman was turning to look behind her.

"It's not time for the bride," her companion reminded her.

"Not the bride. Jeannette Ladre. She hasn't been to services in months, but I thought she'd be here." Relief flowed through Priscilla at the realization that she was not the primary object of speculation in Ladreville.

"Michel's over there. See?" Michel, Priscilla remembered, was the mayor's first name. Jeannette must be his wife. "He's not saving a seat next to him, so I doubt she's planning to come."

"I wonder what's wrong."

The organist paused, then began the processional, effectively ending the women's conversation. As Sarah had planned, Isabelle preceded her down the aisle, followed by Thea. Isabelle's pace was slow and stately, befitting a wedding. Thea, however, scampered, causing laughter to ripple through the congregation. Priscilla suspected Sarah would be pleased, for she'd claimed there was too much solemnity in Ladreville. Life, Sarah said, was meant to be enjoyed.

"Here, Thea," Priscilla said as the child skipped by the pew. Knowing how easily her sister was bored, Sarah had asked that she sit between Priscilla and Mr. Canfield rather than stand at the altar with her and Clay.

"Sarah!" Thea crowed when the bride entered the sanctuary. "Sarah's coming." Perhaps Thea's shout of joy distracted the parishioners. Priscilla didn't care. What mattered was that no one commented on Sarah's pronounced limp. Instead, there were oohs and aahs from the young women and a few muted comments on the beauty of her apricot silk gown.

Clay appeared oblivious to everything except his bride's approach, but the man at his side smiled when he looked at the first pew. Priscilla saw pride in Zach's expression and guessed it was caused by Robert Canfield's slow but steady progress as he moved from the first pew toward the altar. There was no question about the source of Zach's amusement. Thea's exuberant wave turned too-solemn Zach's smile into a full-fledged grin.

The service was longer than normal, for both Pastor Sempert and Père Tellier delivered homilies. To Priscilla's relief, Thea sat quietly while the German minister reminded the parishioners of the sanctity of marriage and the French pastor urged every married couple to renew their vows silently as Sarah and Clay took theirs. When at last the two men spoke in unison, pronouncing Sarah and Clay man and wife, their words were greeted with applause.

Priscilla smiled, thankful that her friends' marriage was so well received, then put a restraining arm around Thea, who was eager to join her sister and the man she called Papa Clay. "No, sweetie. We're going to sit here." Clay had suggested that, in deference to his father's difficulty walking, they wait until the church was almost empty before they proceeded to the receiving line. Though Thea was obviously displeased, she quieted when Priscilla began to tell her a story about a beautiful princess named Sarah and a prince named Clay.

"And they all lived happily ever after." Priscilla was wracking her brain for another story when she heard the sound of footsteps.

"We're ready now." Zach stood at the end of the pew and watched as Mr. Canfield rose. Perhaps it was only Priscilla's imagination, but it seemed as if the older man's balance improved each day. Though he'd never walk without the two canes that now supported him, he wobbled less. Even standing at the altar with Sarah and Clay had not tired him as much as Priscilla had feared. *Papa, you should see this.* As her brain completed the thought, sorrow shot through Priscilla. Never again would she share medical triumphs with her father. She took a deep breath and gripped Thea's hand so tightly that the child winced.

"Ready, ladies?" As Clay's father started toward the back of the church, Zach bent his arm, inviting Priscilla to put her hand in the crook of his elbow. It was pure instinct. She recoiled. A second later, seeing the pained expression on Zach's face, Priscilla regretted her reaction. How foolish she was! Zach was simply being a gentleman, offering her the courtesy of his assistance. Priscilla knew that, and yet she continued to tremble at the thought of being touched by a man. Any man.

"What do you say, Thea?" Though she knew otherwise, Zach spoke as if he had not noticed Priscilla's reaction. "Want to ride on my shoulders so you can see everyone?"

"Yes!" Thea squealed with delight. "Me ride."

It was, Priscilla realized as she walked at Zach's side, an incredibly thoughtful gesture. With Thea on his shoulders, no one would expect him to have Priscilla's hand on his arm. No one would look askance at either of them. How kind of him!

Zach looked around the room where the citizens of Ladreville were gathering and tried not to frown. If Clay hadn't been his closest friend, he would not have come, not to the wedding and especially not to the reception. This was the first marriage he'd witnessed in fifteen years. When he'd been growing up in the small southeastern Texas town of Haven, his mother had dragged him to every wedding, insisting that his presence was vital. Even as a child, bored by the ceremony and convinced that the only reason anyone attended was the presence of cookies, cake, and punch at the reception, he'd doubted that anyone would miss him if he went fishing instead. But as he'd grown older, though he'd never outgrown finding the ceremony boring, the reception had taken on a new appeal.

"There she is," his friend George had announced as they wandered around the field where the reception was being held. "She keeps looking this way."

A few minutes ago, the girl in question had been surrounded by a bevy of friends. Now she stood alone, one hand touching the trunk of an oak tree. Zach felt heat rise to his face and turned abruptly, hoping George hadn't noticed the telltale flush. For Pete's sake, it was almost as embarrassing as the way his voice used to crack. He should be past such childish things. "You sure?"

"A fellow would have to be blind to miss the signals she's sending. That filly wants you by her side. I reckon you better go." When Zach didn't move as quickly as his friend liked, George gave him a shove. "Go on now."

Stuffing his hands in his pockets and walking with what he hoped would appear to be a casual saunter, Zach headed toward Margaret Early, still unable to believe she was interested in him. *Why would she want him?* Margaret was the prettiest girl in the class, tall, with brown hair and eyes and soft curves that a boy couldn't help admiring. She could have her pick of the boys, so *why was she interested in Zach Webster?*

"Nice wedding, wasn't it?" he asked when he was close enough to be heard.

She smiled, and once again Zach felt his face flush. *Stop it!* he admonished himself. *You can't let her see that you care.*

"The flowers were nice," Margaret said with another smile. This one made his knees feel as if they were melting. "When I get married, I want to have flowers like that and a cake like Charlene Morgan's."

Weddings. Is that all girls think about? Zach knew better than to voice those words. "What was special about Charlene's cake?" he asked, feigning interest. *It didn't matter what they talked about. What mattered was the fact that Margaret Early was talking to him.* "They all taste the same to me."

Margaret's smile turned arch. "Of course they do. It's the way they look that matters. Boys never notice things like that." The way she was fluttering her eyelashes made his heart pound.

"I may not notice some things, but I noticed that you look right pretty today." Somehow, he managed to get the words out without stuttering.

Margaret smiled again. "Why, thank you, Zach." The tip of her tongue traced her upper lip. "My throat is awfully parched," she said. "Would you fetch me a glass of punch?"

He had, practically tripping over his feet in his rush to

do her bidding. Zach and Margaret had spent the rest of the afternoon together, and before the day ended, they had shared their first kiss.

Zach frowned again. He didn't want to think about that day or all that had happened since then. Rocking back on his heels, he looked around the crowded hall. It was no surprise that most of Ladreville's residents had come. As the town's doctor and its teacher, Clay and Sarah were prominent figures. It was logical that everyone would wish them well, especially since Michel Ladre had announced that Ladreville—progressive Ladreville, the town that was serving as an example for the rest of the state—would allow Sarah to teach until her replacement could be hired. Zach's frown turned into a wry smile as he considered the origin of that declaration.

The mayor was holding court in one corner, probably explaining why he'd decided to defy tradition. Zach looked around again. While the majority of the people were clustered around Sarah and Clay, a smaller group surrounded Priscilla. His gaze moved on, then returned to her. Perhaps it was only his imagination, but she appeared uncomfortable, almost as uncomfortable as she had when he'd stupidly offered her his arm. How dumb could a man be? He should have realized that the wounds Zeke Dunkler had inflicted would not heal easily. That explained Priscilla's reaction in the church. Zach wondered what was causing her discomfort now. There were no men anywhere near her, only women who seemed friendly. Still, there was no denying the fact that Priscilla was pale.

Someone ought to do something. Zach could have kicked himself for that thought when he realized there was no one else. On another day, Priscilla might have welcomed him, but after the faux pas with the arm, he wasn't certain she would want to be near him. The only alternative was to ignore her distress, and Zach could not do that.

"Excuse me, ladies," he said as he inserted himself into the group around Priscilla. "I promised the bride and groom I'd make sure Priscilla tasted the punch and cookies before they're all gone." As he'd hoped, the women parted.

"Thanks, but I'm not thirsty." Priscilla spoke softly so that her words would not be overheard.

Though he wasn't certain whether that was the truth or whether she judged his company even less appealing than the women's, Zach kept the smile fixed on his face and gestured toward the refreshment table. "Take a glass, anyway. We're being watched."

"I know." Priscilla's eyes widened in what appeared to be panic. "I didn't expect . . ."

The poor woman. She was regarding the hall as if it were a prison. Relief rushed through him at the realization that he was not the cause of her discomfort. "Let's find your cloak and go for a walk."

Once they were outdoors, Zach stopped and looked at Priscilla. She was still far too pale, the whiteness of her skin making her freckles appear like beacons on her nose. "Take a deep breath." When she complied, he encouraged her to take two more. "Now, let's walk." Mindful of her reaction when he'd offered his arm in the church, he made no attempt to guide her. Instead, he darted glances at her as they strolled silently down rue de la Seine toward the river. When they'd reached its banks, he stopped and looked at her. As her color returned, the freckles on her nose were less prominent. "Feel better now?"

"Yes." Priscilla's expression was pensive as she nodded. "I don't know what was wrong. I was afraid I might faint."

119

"I don't claim to be a doctor, but you looked pale and shaky."

Though there was nothing amusing about his statement, Priscilla laughed. "If I might make a suggestion, Zach, it's never a good idea to tell a woman she looks awful."

"I didn't say that!"

"Close enough." She punctuated her words with a chuckle. It was one of the most reassuring sounds Zach had heard.

"Now you sound like Sunny Cilla."

Priscilla raised an eyebrow. "Where did you hear that name?" Curiosity colored her voice. "No one's called me that in years."

Zach turned at the sound of horses. It appeared the first guests were leaving the wedding reception. Fortunately, he and Priscilla were standing under a large oak tree. Unless someone headed toward the river, they would not be seen, and Priscilla— Sunny Cilla—would not be subjected to more gossip.

"Patience told Clay that your parents used to call you that," Zach explained, "and Clay mentioned it to Sarah and me."

Priscilla shook her head in mock disgust. "I can see there are no secrets here."

"Everyone has secrets," he countered. "It's what makes us unique." In Zach's case, the secrets were unpleasant ones, but that wasn't true for everyone. "Do you want to talk about what happened back there and why you were so . . ." He paused, searching for an appropriate word. "So fetchingly pale?"

Priscilla laughed again. "You're a good learner. 'Fetchingly pale.' I'll have to remember that." Her expression sobered. "It seems silly now, especially since everyone was so nice to me. The fact is, I didn't expect such kindness. All the while the women were talking to me, I kept expecting them to turn away when they realized what had happened to me."

Her shudder told Zach she was referring to Zeke Dunkler. But why? If she'd said she expected the Man in the Moon to appear at the reception, he wouldn't have been more surprised. "Why would anyone shun you? You didn't do anything wrong." Unlike him.

Priscilla shook her head slowly. "It happened, Zach." She wouldn't pronounce the ugly word. "No matter what, the woman is always blamed."

Zach's breath left him in a whoosh, replaced by blinding anger. He clenched his fists, trying to control his fury. Priscilla had already suffered unbearably, but it appeared that her suffering would not end, for the wounds Zeke Dunkler had inflicted were festering. The injuries might have healed, but now Priscilla lived with the fear of shame and ostracism.

"You won't be blamed. Not here." Though she looked as if she needed physical support, all he could offer were words of reassurance. Zach hoped they'd be enough. "No one outside the Bar C knows anything more than that your parents were killed, and they never will."

A glimmer of hope shone in Priscilla's eyes. "I wish I believed that was possible."

"It is." Zach filled his words with certainty. "This is one secret that's safe."

❧

"You're a pretty bride, Miss Dobbs." Though Sarah gave the girl who was holding Thea's hand a warm smile, six-year-old Eva Lehman flushed with embarrassment. "I'm sorry. My father told me you're Mrs. Canfield now."

"Don't tell anyone," Sarah said in a conspiratorial tone, "but I forget my new name too." After all, she'd been Clay's wife for less than two hours. As the little girl giggled, Sarah continued. "You look very pretty today. If I'm not mistaken, that's a new dress."

Eva nodded so vigorously that her blonde braids bounced against her cheeks. "Miss Rousseau chose the material. She said it would make me look grown up."

"It does. Why, I could think you were at least seven." As Eva grinned, Sarah laid a hand on her head. "You don't need to be in a hurry to grow up."

"But I do, Miss . . . Mrs. Canfield. I need to grow up. Maybe if I do, *Vati* won't be so sad." Though Eva had taken Sarah's admonitions to heart and rarely laced her sentences with German words, she had not abandoned the affectionate term for her father.

"It's normal for him to be sad sometimes. I know he misses your mother."

Eva nodded. "*Vati* thinks I need a new mother, but I don't. He won't listen when I tell him that. I'm right, though. I don't need a mother, but *Vati* needs a grown-up friend. That's why I have to grow up, so I can take *Mutti's* place and he won't be sad anymore." A frown crossed Eva's face. "I've been trying. I cooked supper, but it burned."

Sarah kept her face impassive, though inwardly she shuddered at the thought of such a young child attempting to cook. No wonder Gunther was so anxious to remarry. He probably feared that Eva would set the house on fire and kill herself.

Where was he? While Sarah and Clay had defied tradition and had separated for a few minutes, Gunther normally kept Eva close to him at social occasions like this. Though the room was crowded, Gunther stood a couple inches taller than most of the townspeople. It was not difficult to spot his blond head or to see that he was laughing. What Sarah couldn't tell was the reason for his laughter.

"Your father looks happy now," she told Eva.

The child nodded. "That's cuz he's with Miss Rousseau. He likes her."

And Isabelle appeared to like him. Sarah smiled. She hadn't been wrong. There was more than simple friendship between her best friend and her former suitor.

It appeared there was no limit to Zach's kindness, Priscilla thought as she approached the punch bowl for the second time that afternoon. First he'd hoisted Thea to his shoulders to keep Priscilla from having to touch him. Then somehow he'd sensed her discomfort when she'd been surrounded by that group of women and had rescued her. The walk they'd taken to the river had soothed her spirits, but what had helped the most was his revelation that her shame was not common knowledge. With those few words, Zach had lifted a heavy weight from her, leaving her feeling as if she could float on air. Now he stood at her side, far enough away that she did not feel threatened but close enough that she knew he was there.

Priscilla accepted a cup of punch, then turned, almost bumping into a short, heavy-set older woman.

"You must be Priscilla." The woman's light accent revealed that she was one of the German immigrants. "You resemble your sister."

Though she knew that to be stretching the truth, for no

one could be as beautiful as Patience, Priscilla said simply, "Thank you."

"Priscilla, this is Granny Menger." Zach began the introductions. "Besides being one of the wisest women in Ladreville, Granny's also the town's midwife."

Priscilla looked at the woman with interest. If her mother hadn't declared it unseemly, she might have pursued midwifery when her parents had forbidden her to study medicine. But Mama had claimed that ladies would not trust their babies to an unmarried woman and that their husbands would be equally unwilling to entrust their wives' lives to someone who'd never experienced childbirth. "You should be thankful you have no need to work," Mama had said. "What you need is to find a good husband." But Priscilla had not.

Banishing those thoughts, she studied Ladreville's midwife. Only a few inches above five feet, Granny Menger seemed almost as wide as she was tall. She wore her brown hair, now liberally laced with gray, braided and wound around her head in a coronet, giving her an almost regal appearance. From a distance, Priscilla would have believed Granny to be just another aging matron, but that impression disappeared the moment she looked at her eyes. A warm brown, they radiated both intelligence and compassion. It was no wonder Zach called her wise and why she was a successful midwife. This was a woman other women would trust.

"Run along, Zach." The older woman's fond smile made it clear the command was given playfully. "We ladies can talk more freely if you're not here." When Zach left, Granny nodded toward Priscilla. "Now, child, let's find some chairs. These bones tire more easily than they used to. I reckon it's God's way of telling me it's time to slow down."

"My father used to say the same thing," Priscilla admitted as she and Granny made their way through the crowd. "That's why he hired an assistant. He claimed Clay was the answer to his prayers."

Granny sank onto one of the chairs that had been arranged along the wall. "God has plans for everyone, if we just listen to him. Look at how he brought Sarah and Clay together." The older woman smiled as she regarded the bridal couple. "Did you ever see two such happy people?"

"No." It was the truth. "Clay didn't look this happy even when he married my sister."

Granny's gaze met Priscilla's, and she nodded sagely. "That's because he's older now. He knows how precious love and life are, and he appreciates them more than he did in Boston. It's all part of God's plan."

Priscilla didn't doubt that, for Sarah had told her much of what had transpired since she'd come to Ladreville and how it had been the Lord's plan. "I wish I knew his plan for me. Some days I feel like a boat going in circles because it has no rudder."

"We all feel that way sometimes." Granny placed her hand on top of Priscilla's. "It happens when we don't let God be our rudder. Trust him, and he'll show you the way."

Soon, dear Lord. Make it soon, Priscilla prayed.

7

It was harder than he'd expected. Jean-Michel tugged on the reins. Who would have thought that the horse he'd taken from Albert Monroe's stable would go lame? That was bad enough, but when he'd stopped at the farrier's shop to have it shod, the man had started asking questions. Jean-Michel's horse, he claimed, looked a lot like the one that was reported stolen, and Jean-Michel himself bore a remarkable resemblance to the man who was thought to have taken Albert Monroe's favorite gelding.

An amazing coincidence, Jean-Michel had explained, but he knew no one named Albert Monroe. As for stealing horses, did he look like a man who needed to steal? When the farrier, obviously impressed by his new clothing, shook his head, Jean-Michel gave him an extra silver coin.

"There's no need to tell anyone you've seen me," he cautioned. "The truth is, I'm on a secret mission for Sam Houston. He wouldn't be pleased if anyone learned I'd been in this part of the state."

126

The farrier had nodded again, proving what Jean-Michel had always known: the rest of the world was dumb, as dumb as a horseshoe. He wasn't taking any more chances, though. That was why he'd avoided towns and had spent his nights in abandoned barns or, when none of those presented themselves, outdoors. It was not the way a man of his stature should live, but until he was certain he was far enough from Houston that no one would connect him with Albert Monroe, he could do no less.

Jean-Michel's stomach rumbled. Though he'd been fortunate the last two days, finding lonely women who had believed his tale of rushing home to his father's deathbed and who'd been more than happy to provide him with a hot midday meal and provisions for his supper, there were no farm houses in sight today. Unless something appeared in the next few minutes, he'd be forced to eat some of the jerked meat he'd taken from the last widow and another of those biscuits that were harder than rocks. Zach Webster was going to pay for this. Indeed, he was.

Jean-Michel spurred the horse, anxious to crest the hill. If luck was with him, he'd spot a house. When he reached the top, he reined in the horse and looked around. No house. But—wait—there was something in the road. A wagon. Not an ordinary wagon. Jean-Michel smiled. This one had closed sides, and if he wasn't mistaken, it was one of those peddlers' wagons. Peddlers, Jean-Michel had heard, carried food— good food—as well as trinkets. Luck was with him.

❧

"Cilla sick."

Sarah and Clay stopped in midstep. It was early afternoon,

127

and they had entered the ranch house for the first time since their wedding, their faces glowing with happiness. At Thea's announcement, their smiles faded.

"What is it?" Clay asked. His eyes searched Priscilla's face, looking for symptoms. He would find none, for they had ceased as they did by this time each day.

"It's nothing." Priscilla had tried to tell Thea that this morning, but the child, who had insisted on spending the night in her room and had heard her retching, was not convinced. Though Priscilla had hoped she would forget by the time Sarah and Clay returned, she had not been so fortunate.

Sarah's eyes narrowed as she looked at Priscilla. Though Priscilla thought she had schooled her features to reveal nothing, she must have failed, for Sarah gave Clay a quick look before she said, "Thea, we have lots of bags. Could you help Clay bring them in?" As the little girl, flattered to be asked to help an adult, tugged Clay's hand and scampered away, Sarah turned to Priscilla. "I figure we have four or five minutes before Thea reappears, so tell me what's wrong. I won't believe it's something inconsequential."

It wasn't. Priscilla sank into one of the deep settees and waited until Sarah took a seat next to her before she spoke. "I tried to pretend it was simply something I ate, but it's been two weeks now. I'm sick every morning. That's what Thea saw." Though she wanted nothing more than to hide her face, Priscilla forced herself to look directly at Sarah as she said, "I'm afraid I'm pregnant."

Sarah gasped, though Priscilla wasn't certain whether it was at the idea itself or the fact that she had used such a blunt term. While Papa believed in speaking clearly, Mama would

128

have shuddered and reprimanded Priscilla for not cloaking her condition in euphemisms.

"Have you missed . . ." Sarah let her words trail off.

"Yes." Priscilla tried to blink back the tears that welled in her eyes. Crying solved nothing. "Oh, Sarah, what am I going to do? I can't have this baby. I can't!" Though she had tried to ignore the symptoms, she could no longer delude herself. Priscilla had spent too much time reading her father's medical books to pretend she didn't know what had caused her sickness. Though most of Papa's patients had been pleased by the prospect of a new life, she was not. She brushed away the tear that had made its way down her cheek.

"You know I love you, and I want to help you." Sarah wrapped her arms around Priscilla and drew her close as she said, "I don't know what to do. I wish I could say that I understood, but, the truth is, I can't imagine how you feel. I've always believed babies were a blessing, a gift from God."

"This one is not." Far from being a blessing, Priscilla's child would be a curse, a constant reminder of the most horrible day of her life.

For a while Sarah said nothing, merely stroked Priscilla's back. It was, Priscilla guessed, the way she would comfort Thea. When she spoke, Sarah kept her voice low. "I know it's hard to believe right now, but God will turn this into good for you."

He wouldn't. Nothing could make this good. Priscilla wrenched herself out of Sarah's arms and glared at the woman who was mouthing platitudes. "I don't believe that anymore. Don't you see, Sarah? I've spent my whole life trying to discover God's plan for me. I thought that coming to Texas

129

was part of it, but look how that turned out. My parents were killed, and I'm carrying a bandit's baby." Though she saw the pain her words were causing Sarah, Priscilla couldn't stop. Not now. Sarah had to hear the rest. "Just last night I prayed that he would show me his plan. This morning I awoke knowing I was pregnant. If this is God's plan for me, if he wants me to be an unwed mother and face scorn every time I show my face in public, then I reject it and I reject him. He's not a loving God."

Tears filled Sarah's eyes. "Oh, Priscilla, I know you're hurt, but you're wrong. God loves you. I'll pray that you realize how deep his love is."

Prayers. Priscilla clenched her fists. What was the point in praying, when he didn't listen? "Don't waste your breath. You can see what my prayers brought."

Something was wrong. A man didn't need to be a genius to see that. As if the slumped shoulders and the bowed head weren't enough proof, there was the fact that he was heading toward the family burial plot, a place he rarely frequented and one of the last places he should have been going less than twenty-four hours after his wedding.

Zach had been in the stable, putting the buggy away, when he'd heard it. The voice deep inside him that had urged him to come to the Bar C last summer was telling him to leave the barn. As he had before, Zach obeyed immediately, though he had no idea where he was meant to go. Once outdoors, his feet moved unerringly toward the small cemetery. When he saw Clay's posture, he knew this was the reason God had sent him and quickened his pace.

"What's wrong?" Zach caught up with his friend before he reached the small grove of oak trees.

Clay swiveled. If Zach needed further proof that something was amiss, the lines stamped on his unnaturally pale face provided it. "Nothing."

"I'm disappointed in you, Clay. I didn't think you were a liar, but that was nothing short of a bald-faced lie." Clay thrust his hands into his pockets, but not before Zach saw him clench them. Though the fists suggested anger, the expression in Clay's eyes was sorrowful.

It was clear Clay intended to say nothing, so Zach continued, hoping that something he said would trigger a response. "When you and Sarah returned to the Bar C this afternoon, you looked the way I expected—like the happiest man on Earth." That had been less than an hour ago. "Now, if I didn't know better, I'd say you were on your way to a loved one's funeral." A newly wedded man did not visit his first wife's grave unless something was drastically wrong. Though Zach was concerned by the fact that Clay and Sarah were parted, he did not believe Sarah was the reason for his friend's distress.

Clay looked down at the ground and gave an acorn an impatient kick. Like the fisted hands and the long silence, this was not normal behavior for Clay. When he finally spoke, his voice was heavy with sorrow. "I might as well tell you. As much as I wish it were otherwise, we won't be able to hide the truth for too long." Clay clenched his fists again, releasing them slowly before he met Zach's gaze. "You know what happened to Priscilla. Without being too clinical, let me say there were consequences."

The tone of his voice told Zach what those consequences

were. "You mean she's in what my mother would call 'a family way.'"

"Exactly. Only, as you may have noticed, there's no family. When Sarah told me, all I could think of was how different it had been for Patience." Clay looked at his first wife's grave. "We were both so excited and happy at the thought of being parents. Even though the baby died with Patience, we had months of happy anticipation. It's not like that for Priscilla."

A wave of anger swept through Zach at the thought of the pain the bandit had wrought. Two days ago Zach would not have realized the full implications of Priscilla's situation, but her words yesterday had shown him the devastating consequences of the bandit's attack. This was worse, much worse than what she had feared then. Thanks to Zeke Dunkler, Priscilla was alone and in the worst predicament a woman could face.

It was difficult enough raising a child alone. Zach's mother had told him that numerous times. But Mama had been a widow. That had made her respectable in the eyes of the town. Priscilla was not a widow, and so she would bear the shame. People would snicker. They might shun her, and, through it all, she would be powerless, for the woman was always blamed. That's what she had told him.

Zach took a deep breath and tried to catch his anger. *Help me, Lord,* he prayed. *I'm here, my son.* But instead of the peace he'd prayed for, Zach was barraged with memories. He saw Margaret's tear-stained face, her father's fierce scowl, his own mother's look of disappointment. Anger turned to sorrow as he thought of what he'd done. Had Margaret faced scorn and shunning? Was that why she had threatened to kill their baby? He hadn't considered that. The truth was, he hadn't considered anything but himself the day Margaret's father had demanded Zach marry her. He'd been little better than the bandit, for he'd left Haven without giving a thought to Margaret or their child. While it was true that he'd tried to make amends later and had been rebuffed, he hadn't been there to protect her. Zach closed his eyes as pain washed through him. He couldn't undo what had happened fifteen years ago. He couldn't change Margaret's life, but he could ensure that Priscilla did not suffer, and perhaps in doing so he could atone for his sin.

Oh, Lord, is this what you planned for me? Is this the reason I've believed a change was coming? The warmth that filled him gave Zach his answer. He took a step toward Clay, and his voice was firm as he said, "Priscilla needs to marry. If she does, even though the baby's born early, talk will die down." Neither she nor the child would face a lifetime of disgrace.

"You're right, of course, but who?"

"I'll marry her, if she agrees."

Clay didn't bother to hide either his surprise or his relief. "Are you certain?"

"Yes." More certain than he'd been of anything since the day he'd known God wanted him to find Robert Canfield.

"Thank you, Zach. I'll tell Sarah." Clay turned toward the house.

Though Zach appreciated his friend's offer, that was not the way it would be done. "No. This is between Priscilla and me. I will ask her. If she agrees, we'll tell you and Sarah, so you can make plans."

Clay clapped Zach on the shoulder. "You're right. It would

be better that way. I don't know how to thank you, Zach, other than to say that it's a very Christian thing to do."

"I believe it's what God wants." Although not for the reason Clay imagined.

☙

"Howdy." Jean-Michel detested the greeting. No self-respecting Alsatian would have used such a crude salutation, unaccompanied as it was by a personal address. In Alsace, he would have greeted a stranger with the more courteous "*Bonjour, monsieur*," but things were different here. Jean-Michel didn't want to draw undue attention to himself, and so he called out the way an Anglo like that despicable Zach Webster might have.

The peddler looked up from the pot he'd been stirring. It hadn't been Jean-Michel's imagination. Those were pork and beans he'd smelled as he'd approached.

"Somethin' I can do for you?" The man's face was brown and wrinkled, the result of years in the sun, his hair liberally threaded with gray, his smile welcoming. He looked like every other old man Jean-Michel had seen, except for his eyes. Cold and blue, those eyes appeared to be looking right through him, as if they could read his thoughts. Absurd! Still, Jean-Michel resolved to think only good thoughts while he was with the peddler. A man couldn't be too careful.

Mindful that he had not answered the old man's question, Jean-Michel looked down at the bubbling beans. "Those smell mighty good," he said with what he hoped sounded like a Texas accent. "I wonder if I could trouble you for a bowl. I can pay for it."

The peddler's eyes moved from Jean-Michel's expensive

134

hat to his highly polished boots. "I can see that. Sit down." He gestured toward the ground. "I reckon I've got enough to share with a hungry traveler." The man stuck out his hand. "Tom Fayette."

Jean-Michel shook the proffered hand. "Jean-Michel Ladre." As soon as the words were pronounced, he regretted them. He should have invented a name, something that sounded more Texan.

"Glad to meet you, Jean-Michel." Apparently unconcerned by the name or, more likely, too dumb to realize that it was a foreign name, the peddler rose to retrieve an extra plate and spoon from the back of his wagon. "What brings you to this part of Texas?"

"I work in Houston." That wasn't a lie. "When I heard my mother was doing poorly, I realized it was time to go home." That wasn't a lie, either. Not exactly. With him gone, Mama would be feeling poorly. She had cried buckets when she learned that Papa planned to send him to Houston, but all her tears and entreaties had accomplished nothing. Michel Ladre, the great and powerful Michel Ladre, would not be dissuaded.

"I like a man who cares for his mother."

Jean-Michel nodded as he took another spoonful of beans. They weren't fancy food like his mother made, but they were a sight better than rock-hard biscuits and jerked beef. "Where are you headed next?" While he'd chewed the morsels of pork, Jean-Michel had looked at the peddler's wagon. Unless he was mistaken, a peddler—or at least this one—earned a good living.

Luck was definitely with him.

ॐ

Zach waited an hour before he approached Priscilla. He wasn't certain whether she'd seen him and Clay talking, and he didn't want her to think he'd been coerced, or even persuaded, to make his offer. Besides, he'd needed time to outline his strategy. "There's still some sunlight left," he said when he found her sitting with Clay's father in the main room. Robert had dozed and Priscilla held a book, though the fact that she had turned no pages in the minutes he'd watched her told Zach she wasn't reading. She was so beautiful, so innocent, and so very sad. Marriage might not have been his plan, but Zach did not regret the decision he'd made, for it was the only way he knew to help Priscilla.

"Would you like to go for a ride?" Riding was one of the things she enjoyed. It was also something that relaxed her, and today of all days, Priscilla needed to relax.

"I'm not feeling too well."

Though she was unnaturally pale, he wouldn't make the mistake of telling her that. "All the more reason to go. Dr. Zach is convinced of the therapeutic effect of contact with members of the equine family, preferably contact achieved by mounting one."

As he'd hoped, his deliberately pompous tone made Priscilla smile. "Far be it from me to dispute Dr. Zach's wisdom."

A quarter of an hour later, they were headed away from the house with Zach leading the way toward their destination: a small grove of trees near an equally small pond. He slowed his horse and gestured toward the pond. "Would you like to walk a bit?" Before she could demur, he added, "That rock is big enough that you could use it for mounting." He'd seen the way she shied from contact with men and knew she would refuse to leave the horse unless she could remount without assistance. The rock was one of the reasons he'd chosen this particular spot.

"All right." When they reached the pond, Priscilla dipped her hand into the water, then pulled it out and shook it vigorously. "It's cold."

"That's what you get when you're two days away from January. That's our coldest month." Zach took a deep breath, exhaling slowly as he mustered his courage. It was time to begin. "I didn't bring you here to talk about the weather." Priscilla raised an eyebrow. "I heard about your situation." He would not refer to it as a problem, for that would only distress her. It was bad enough that what he'd said so far had caused her to blanch. "I'd like to help you, Priscilla. I don't imagine this is the way you thought it would be, but if you're willing, I would be honored to have you as my wife."

Zach hadn't thought her pallor could increase, but it did. "You want to marry me?" She took a step backward, as if she felt the need to distance herself from him.

"I want to protect you and your baby." He wouldn't claim that this was an ordinary proposal of marriage, for it was not. "As I see it, the best way—perhaps the only way—to do that is for me to marry you and be a father to your child." Priscilla backed up until she was touching one of the trees. This was not going the way he'd expected. He had thought she would either agree or refuse. He hadn't expected the palpable fear now etched on her face. Zach wished he knew whether the fear was caused by the thought of marriage or of marriage to him.

"I know you must have had scores of beaux in Boston, people of your social standing. I'm sure that when you imagined marrying, it was to one of them, not an uneducated ranch foreman." Zach wasn't going to pretend that he was the ideal husband. Though he wanted to believe he'd matured since he left Haven, the simple fact was, he knew nothing about being married. What he did know was that Priscilla needed the protection a wedding ring would provide. "I'm sure you have other suitors. The problem is, all those men are in Boston. They can't help you. I'm here, and I can. So, yes, I want to marry you."

Priscilla took another step backward, stopping only when she bumped into a tree. "I don't know what to say."

"Say yes."

Her eyes darkened, and she gripped the tree trunk as if for support. "I can't. I can't marry you or anyone."

Though the fear he'd seen on her face had turned to terror, Zach felt relief flow through him. It was marriage she feared, not him. That made sense. If she feared the simple touch of a man's hand, how terrifying must the thought of marriage and all it entailed be? "You don't need to worry." He kept his voice low and soft, the same tone he used when taming a wild horse. "The marriage is to protect you. It will be a marriage in name only."

For the first time he saw a glimmer of hope in Priscilla's eyes. "You mean . . . ? You wouldn't . . . ?"

Zach wasn't sure whether to nod or shake his head. Instead, he kept it steady as he said, "It's true we'll share a house, but you'll have your own room. I promise I will not insist on my marital rights."

"House?" She grasped at what Zach believed to be the least important part of his declaration. "Where would we live?"

That was one of the things he had considered during the

hour he'd spent planning this moment. "For the time being, at the Lazy B." In case she didn't recognize the name, Zach explained that that was the neighboring ranch Clay had taken over when its owners left Ladreville. "Clay keeps saying it's a shame that the house is empty, so I know he'd agree that we could live there. You'd have your own house and privacy."

He could see that Priscilla was considering the idea. When she spoke, he heard wonder in her voice. "It's a generous offer, Zach. I don't know how to thank you for making it." She managed a small smile. "I understand what I'd gain, but what about you? You said you were planning to leave Ladreville, that you never stayed anywhere for too long. Why would you want to saddle yourself with another man's child and a wife who isn't a true wife? What would you be getting?"

Though he hadn't expected the question, Zach had no trouble answering. "A home of my own. I've never had one. Since I was fifteen, I've been on the move, first with the army, then living on other people's ranches. There comes a time in a man's life when he wants to settle down. I've reached that time. I like Ladreville and want to remain here." Permanently. "It's true I thought I would leave, but only because it was obvious that having me around distressed you. Everything's different now. If you marry me, I'll try to buy the Lazy B." Zach felt his lips curve in a smile at the thought of the white frame house. "I can't imagine that Clay will object. The current owner asked him to sell it, and Clay doesn't want it. If this works out, for the first time in my life, I'll have land, a house, and a family to fill that house."

Zach paused for a deep breath. "Will you marry me, Priscilla? Will you help make my dreams come true?"

This time there was no hesitation. The beautiful woman

who had invaded his thoughts since the day she'd arrived at the ranch nodded. "I will."

Zach closed his eyes for a second, letting relief flow through his veins. It had been such a short time since he'd made his decision that he hadn't realized how much he wanted Priscilla to accept his proposal, yet now that she had, it felt good. More than good, it felt right.

"Thank you." It was time to think about practicalities. "Would you prefer to be married in the French or the German church?"

"Neither. The judge can marry us."

Though the vehemence of Priscilla's response surprised Zach, it was the content that shocked him. He stared at the woman who would soon become his wife and tried to understand her reaction. "There is no judge in Ladreville," he said as gently as he could, "but even if there were, I wouldn't agree. Marriage is a sacrament, a contract between a man, a woman, and God." When Priscilla started to shake her head, Zach held up his hand. He wasn't finished. Realizing that she might fear being married in a public place, he was willing to concede one point. "If you insist, I will agree that we don't have to be married in one of the churches, but we must have a minister."

Priscilla's eyes widened, and he could see the confusion in them. "Why? The results are the same, regardless of who performs the ceremony."

"Not to me, they're not." The day he'd given his life to the Lord, he'd vowed that he would live according to his commandments. As much as he wanted to help Priscilla, Zach knew he would be breaking his promise if their marriage were not a religious ceremony. He couldn't—he wouldn't—do that. "You need to make a decision, Priscilla. I want to marry you, but the only way I'll do that is if we say our vows before God."

She was silent for a moment, her eyes focused on the distance, and Zach sensed that the decision was a difficult one for her. He forced himself to breathe steadily while he waited for her to speak. It was probably only a minute, but Zach felt as if a lifetime had passed before she turned back to him and nodded. "All right. We'll do it your way."

There was no moon tonight. Jean-Michel smiled with pleasure. What he had in mind was best done under the cover of darkness. That was why he'd waited the extra three days. When he'd left the peddler, Jean-Michel's stomach had been filled with tasty food, his mind with possibilities. The old man had money. Though he thought Jean-Michel had not noticed how his eyes had flickered toward the wooden chest in the far corner of the wagon, Jean-Michel was too smart to be fooled. He'd seen the peddler's worried glance and had known what it meant. Money. Lots of it. Soon that money would be Jean-Michel's.

When he had finished his meal, Jean-Michel had taken his leave, purportedly to rush to his dear mother's side. Instead he had ridden only a few miles, then concealed himself and the horse in a stand of trees. From there he'd been able to observe the peddler's approach and confirm that the old man had gone to the town he'd named. The peddler had stayed there for two days as he'd planned, but tonight he was camped by the river. Perfect. There would be no witnesses.

Jean-Michel waited and watched. When he was certain

the old man was asleep, he snuck out from behind the tree. It was time. Moving carefully, he cracked open the back of the wagon, reaching up to silence the bell the peddler had installed, presumably to alert him if anyone tried to break into the wagon. It might work for others, but Jean-Michel was too smart. He'd seen the bell. He knew what to do.

He climbed inside the wagon and inched forward. There it was! He could feel the leather straps that hinged the top and bottom.

"Lookin' for somethin'?"

Jean-Michel turned and faced the barrel of a shotgun. What was going on? The peddler was supposed to be asleep. "You can put that down." Jean-Michel doubted the old man planned to fire his weapon, but he wasn't taking any chances. "I didn't mean any harm."

"Just as you didn't mean any harm when you stole Albert Monroe's money and his horse?" The man's voice sounded different than it had at dinner that day. Tonight he was angry. "I knew somethin' was wrong the minute I set eyes on you. It didn't take long to find out who you were. That's why I figured you'd be paying me a visit one of these days." He glanced at the chest that Jean-Michel had pulled from the back of the wagon. "I reckon you can't resist my supply of crocheted antimacassars."

"What are you talking about?" The man was bluffing. No one kept silly doodads in a chest. A chest like this was designed for money, nothing else.

"Open it up." The peddler's voice taunted him.

"All right." Jean-Michel unbuckled the straps and lifted the lid. Though there was little light, he could see that the old man hadn't lied. Layer upon layer of fancy white doilies greeted him. Of course! They were a trick, designed to fool men who weren't as smart as he. The silver and gold were on the bottom. "It's got to be here." Jean-Michel dug down, searching for the moneybags he was certain were hidden beneath the crocheted antimacassars. When he reached the bottom and had found nothing but silly doilies, he heard the peddler chuckle.

It was too much. No one laughed at Jean-Michel Ladre. No one. His blood boiling with rage, Jean-Michel picked up the chest, wheeled around, and flung it at the peddler. Though the chest was surprisingly lightweight, the force was enough that it knocked the old man backward. A second later Jean-Michel heard his body hit the ground.

He scrambled out of the wagon and stared at the man who'd fed him dinner, the same man who'd laughed at him. It appeared that the fall had knocked him unconscious, for he did not move, though the rise and fall of his chest said he was still alive. Not for long. Jean-Michel smiled at the sight of the peddler's shotgun lying a few inches from his hand. That was all the invitation he needed. He reached for the gun and pulled the trigger. The peddler would never laugh again.

It was not the way she had pictured her wedding day. There was no church filled with hundreds of guests, flowers, and sacred music. There had been no months of preparation, no parties celebrating the upcoming nuptials. Most of all, there was no sense of anticipation knowing she was about to marry the man God had intended for her. Instead, there would be a small ceremony at the Bar C, with only Sarah, Clay, Thea, and Mr. Canfield present when Pastor Sempert pronounced Priscilla and Zach man and wife.

"You look lovely." Had it been only a week since Priscilla had said the same thing to Sarah? Now she was the one dressing for her wedding. "Are you ready?"

Priscilla looked down at the green dress she'd worn last week. Though Sarah had insisted they had time to make her a new gown, she'd refused. This one was good enough. If the bride was used goods—and she was—why shouldn't her dress be used too? "I'm as ready as I'll ever be," she told Sarah. Her hands were shaking, her palms sweating. Fortunately, since it was afternoon, her stomach was no longer queasy.

"Zach's a good man."

Priscilla pinched her cheeks, trying to give them some color. It wouldn't do to look as if she were on the verge of fainting. Zach might take her arm if she did. Though he knew how much she feared a man's touch, he was too gentlemanly to let her collapse. It was up to Priscilla to avoid the problem by appearing healthy. "I know he's a good man. That's why this is so difficult. Zach could do better than me. He should be marrying a woman he loves." She still could not believe he'd made such a generous offer. Though she'd known dozens of men in Boston and had even considered marrying several, she could not imagine one of them doing anything so selfless.

Sarah pursed her lips, giving Priscilla an intimation of how she dealt with unruly pupils. "Zach is thirty years old. If he loved someone else, don't you think he'd have married her by now?"

"Yes, but . . ."

"No buts. He's a grown man who does what he wants, and what he wants is to marry you. So, put a smile on your face, Priscilla Morton. Your bridegroom is waiting."

He was indeed. When Priscilla entered the main room,

she saw him at the far end, smiling at her as if she were the woman he'd waited for all his life. She took a deep breath and tried to return the smile. Zach was a good man. He did not deserve a bride who looked as if she were facing a firing squad.

Pastor Sempert nodded solemnly as Priscilla and Zach stood before him, then began to speak. "Dearly beloved, forasmuch as marriage is a holy estate . . ." His voice resonated throughout the room as he recited the familiar words.

"Wilt thou, Priscilla Morton . . ." Though Priscilla had heard wedding vows dozens of times, today she could not have recited a single one. Now she understood why it was customary for the minister to read the vows first, asking the bride and groom to repeat them.

"And thereto I plight thee my troth," she recited the final vow.

Pastor Sempert looked at Clay. "The ring please."

A ring! The smile Priscilla had kept on her face faded. Why hadn't she remembered that a wedding involved a ring and that the bridegroom placed that ring on his wife's hand? She flinched.

Unaware of her distress, the minister handed the simple gold band to Zach, then looked at her expectantly. "Give him your left hand, Priscilla."

She couldn't. Though she tried to force them away, memories of Zeke Dunkler grabbing her hands and twisting them behind her flooded through Priscilla's mind, and her hand remained frozen at her side.

"Your hand." Pastor Sempert repeated the command. It was simple enough, unless you were Priscilla Morton. Desperately, she looked at the man who was about to become her husband. Surely Zach would find a way to help her. His eyes were warm and understanding, and he nodded ever so slightly, as if asking her to trust him.

You're strong, Priscilla. You can do this. She heard her father's admonitions echoing in her head and saw Zach's steady smile. He was giving up so much for her. Surely she could do her part. The marriage was designed to protect Priscilla and her unborn child. All she had to do was let him put a ring on her finger. That was nothing, compared to all that had come before. Slowly, Priscilla extended her hand. It was only one finger. That's all he would touch. It would be over in a second. She would survive. But still her hand trembled as Zach slid the circlet of gold onto her finger.

"With this ring, I thee wed." It was done. She was Zach's wife.

8

"You're a sly one." Though Priscilla winced when Gunther slapped Zach on the back, her new husband didn't seem to mind. He simply smiled as the miller said, "You've gone and gotten yourself married, and you didn't even tell your friends."

Gunther gestured toward the dozen guests who'd been invited to the Bar C for supper, not realizing that the supper was to be a wedding reception. While Sarah and Clay circulated among their friends, making everyone feel welcome, Priscilla and Zach remained at the far end of the room, accepting felicitations, including those of Gunther and his daughter.

The guests' reactions had been amusing. While they'd all evidenced varying degrees of surprise when Sarah and Clay had introduced the newly married couple, the Rousseaus had greeted the news with enthusiasm. Frau Friedrich, on the other hand, had nudged her son and muttered something that sounded suspiciously like, "Why are you waiting?

You ought to be married too." And then there was Gunther, feigning horror.

"What kind of friend are you?" he demanded.

"A prudent one." Zach grinned at the miller. "You don't think I'd ruin my chances with a beautiful woman like Priscilla by introducing her to you, do you? No, sirree. I carefully kept her away from all you eager bachelors until she had my ring on her finger." Even though she knew it was for show, Priscilla couldn't find a flaw in Zach's performance. He looked and sounded like a happy bridegroom. She hoped her smile was as convincing. With all that Zach was doing for her, she didn't want to embarrass him in front of his friends.

"You're a lucky man." Gunther gave Zach another slap on the back. "And you, ma'am. As much as it pains me to admit it, you've got yourself a good husband. They don't come much finer than Zach Webster."

The child who'd been standing quietly at his side tugged on his hand. "You're a fine man too, *Vati*."

Gunther looked down at his daughter, as if surprised to see her. "Why, thank you, little one." He gave her head an affectionate pat. "You don't need to stay with your boring old papa. I imagine Thea is looking for you."

Eva shook her head, then fixed her gaze on Priscilla. Priscilla remembered the child having stared at Sarah the same way during her wedding reception. Eva, it appeared, was at the age of being in awe of brides. "Thea had to take a nap," Eva announced. "I don't take naps anymore. I'm a big girl."

"Yes, you are." But she was also the only child in the room. Until Thea wakened, she needed something to do. "I think Martina might need some help with the cookies. Would you like to help her?"

Her eyes lighting with enthusiasm, Eva nodded and followed Priscilla to the kitchen.

"What are you doing here?" Sarah's smile softened her words when she found Priscilla seated at the small table, supervising Eva's placement of small cakes and cookies on a platter. "You're the guest of honor."

Priscilla shrugged. "I've met everyone, and right now, I'm feeling a bit overwhelmed." It wasn't as if this was the wedding of her dreams. It wasn't as if this was a real marriage. Oh, it was legal, but it wasn't the sort of happily-ever-after marriage Sarah and Clay had. And, because it wasn't, Priscilla wanted no fuss made. "So much has happened so quickly." Only six weeks ago, she'd been on her way to a wedding, never dreaming that the journey would end with her own marriage.

"And now you're a bride." Sarah's smile faded, as if she were remembering the circumstances of Priscilla's wedding. "That is overwhelming, isn't it?"

"*Vati* doesn't need a bride." Though Eva had appeared intent on arranging the cookies, she raised her head and looked directly at Sarah. "I'm a big girl now. Miss Morton . . . er . . . Mrs. Webster said so. I can take care of *Vati*."

The expression in Sarah's eyes said she wasn't convinced. An hour later, when they were seated for dinner, Priscilla realized that, not only was Sarah unconvinced that Gunther had no need of a wife, but she was doing her best to encourage him to find a new one. That had to be the reason she'd seated Isabelle next to him rather than placing her beside her parents and brother. It appeared to be an arrangement that pleased both Gunther and Isabelle, for they recounted amusing anecdotes, each completing the other's sentences, laughing when they pronounced a phrase in unison. The fond look on Sarah's face said she was pleased by her matchmaking efforts. The frowns the older Rousseaus exchanged told another story.

The hours passed quickly, and before Priscilla knew it, the guests were preparing to depart. Zach appeared at her side, silently reminding her that tradition dictated he and Priscilla leave first. "It's time to go home."

Though Zach's words were matter-of-fact, they sent shivers down Priscilla's spine. Home, at least for the foreseeable future, was the Lazy B's ranch house, a building she would share with the man who was now her husband. It was true they had ranch hands, and Zach had hired a woman from town to do the laundry, but all those people lived elsewhere. Priscilla and Zach would be alone in the house. It was that prospect and the fact that the man she had promised to love, honor, and obey was practically a stranger that caused her hands to shake.

After waving gaily as their guests bade them farewell, Priscilla kept her eyes focused on the road. Surely that was preferable to looking at the man who sat only a foot away. Zach was a kind man, she told herself. He had made promises. Though she continued to remind herself of that, she could not dismiss the fear that once they were alone, he might not keep them. There was no guarantee.

The fact that he was as silent as she did nothing to still the trembling of Priscilla's limbs. Perhaps it was simply that he found the situation as awkward as she did. They were married, and yet this would not be a traditional wedding night, any more than the coming months would be a traditional marriage. Did he regret their agreement? Priscilla couldn't ask, for her mouth was so dry that words were impossible.

When they reached the ranch, she climbed out of the wagon as quickly as she could, then started to mount the front porch steps. Sarah had shown her through the house yesterday, and Priscilla had chosen the room that would be hers. If she could reach her bedroom, she would be safe, for she could slide the bolt. Though no one in Ladreville locked their houses, when she'd told Zach that she still feared the Dunkler brothers, he had volunteered to install bolts on the front and kitchen doors as well as the one to her bedchamber.

There is no reason to fear Zach, Priscilla reminded herself, but her feet refused to listen, and she hurried to get inside before him. Unfortunately, Zach was right behind her. As they approached the door, he stretched out his arm. Priscilla cringed and took a step backward. Surely he didn't mean to carry her over the threshold! It had been difficult enough to feel his hand when he slid the ring onto her finger, and that had taken only a second. Being held in his arms would be much, much worse. She couldn't let him do that.

Priscilla took a deep breath as she debated which direction to run. He was beside her now, so close that if she turned, she would touch him. Which way was best? Before she could move, Zach took another step forward and opened the door with a flourish. Color flooded Priscilla's cheeks as she realized how foolish she had been. Zach had no intention of touching her. He was only being a gentleman.

Standing back to allow her to precede him, he said, "Welcome to your new home, Mrs. Webster."

ॐ

Priscilla smiled as she slid the supper plates into the sink. Her first week of marriage had gone well—better than she'd

151

expected, except for the morning sickness. The summer she'd been pregnant, Patience's letters had been filled with excitement over every aspect of her condition. She'd even managed to make what she referred to as her daily encounters with the chamber pot amusing. Priscilla was not amused. Of course, their situations were vastly different. Patience had been married to a man she loved, and their baby had been the answer to prayers. It was true that Priscilla was married to a good man. Zach was kind, but he was not a man who loved her or whom she loved, and her baby was most definitely not the answer to prayers. Still, she could not complain about life at the Lazy B.

From that first night when he'd ushered her into the house, Zach had made it clear that he would make no demands of her. Although they had agreed there was no need to hire a cook and that Priscilla would prepare meals, once he became aware of her morning sickness, Zach announced that he did not expect her to make breakfast for him. Instead, each morning he brought her weak tea and toast before leaving for the range. Priscilla suspected that not even Clay had been so considerate.

Though she had not expected it, supper time was the best part of the day, for that was when she and Zach were together. Far from fearing his return, Priscilla found herself counting the hours until he'd be home. Once he'd cleaned off the range dust, he would join her in the kitchen and would entertain her with tales of his day, somehow making cattle ranching sound amusing. Both Patience and Clay had had a far different view of ranch life. Neither one had found it amusing or even remotely enjoyable. But, then, Zach seemed to find something positive in almost everything that happened. He even joked when Priscilla burned the biscuits, announcing that he'd heard charcoal was good for the digestion.

It was pleasant to share a table with Zach. Priscilla scrubbed the first plate, then rinsed it. As much as she enjoyed suppers and evenings spent with Zach, she wondered if the appeal wasn't simply the contrast to her days. They were undeniably lonely. In Boston, there had always been other people around. Here there was no one. The woman who'd been hired for laundry would not come until next week, and though she was only two miles away, Priscilla did not want to visit Sarah. After all, Sarah was still on her honeymoon. It was bad enough that she was teaching. Sarah didn't need another intrusion on her time with Clay. The problem was, Priscilla hadn't realized how much she would miss human companionship.

She had considered asking Sarah if she could care for Thea during the day, even though Sarah had mentioned how much Thea enjoyed being at school. "It makes her feel like a big girl," Sarah had said with a fond smile. But, even if Sarah would agree, Priscilla couldn't consider having Thea here until her morning sickness ended.

"I don't want you lifting the tub." She turned, startled by Zach's voice. Normally he checked the horses after supper, but tonight he'd come back from the barn earlier than normal. "If you heat the water, I'll pour it."

Priscilla looked down at the pan filled with soapy water and wondered what he meant. She had all the water she needed to finish the dishes. "Water for what?"

"Our baths." Zach gave her a piercing look as he added, "Today's Saturday. I like to get cleaned up before church."

"Oh!" Priscilla felt the color rise to her face. Though he hadn't chided her, she felt silly. "I haven't been keeping track of the days." Just the hours.

"That's because you've been working too hard. The house

looks nice, but are you sure moving all that furniture is wise? You don't want to hurt the baby." To Priscilla's amusement, this time, it was Zach's face that flushed. Men, he'd undoubtedly been counseled, did not mention anything related to upcoming blessed events. Not that this baby's arrival would fit into that category. Still, it was kind of him to be concerned, just as it was kind of him to appreciate the effort she had put into the house. When she'd first seen it, though the furnishings were attractive, she'd found the rooms unwelcoming, but she'd soon realized that there were relatively simple ways to make the house more appealing.

"The baby's all right, isn't it?" Zach sounded worried.

"I don't think anything will hurt this child." She tried to make Zach laugh by feigning indignation. "I'm the one you should feel sorry for, being sick every morning."

Unfortunately, he did not laugh. If anything, the consternation in his blue eyes increased. "That doesn't last the whole time, does it?"

"It's not supposed to. The next thing you know, I'll be fat."

"But beautiful."

It was Priscilla who laughed, remembering the day he'd commented on her pallor. "You learned your lesson well, didn't you?"

"'Pears that way, doesn't it?" To her surprise, Zach reached for a towel and started drying the plates. She'd never heard of a man helping in the kitchen. They were women's domains, and all work associated with them was women's work, or so she'd been taught. But there was Zach, looking as comfortable as could be with a towel in his hand.

"This is my week to attend the French church," he said

casually when he'd returned the plates to their shelf. "I'd be pleased if you'd accompany me." His voice was diffident, probably because of her refusal to be married in a church. That had been only a week ago.

Priscilla started to decline, but as memories of this week's solitude resurfaced, she changed her mind. Though she wasn't certain God wanted her in his house, at least for those hours she'd have company. Besides, if she was going to live in Ladreville—and she was—she needed to meet the townspeople. It would be easier and safer to do that with Zach at her side. "All right."

Though the next morning was sunny, the cool temperatures discouraged parishioners from lingering outside the church before the services, and Priscilla felt herself relax. It would be better to converse with the townspeople afterward. First she needed to make peace with God. She looked up at Zach and nodded when he asked whether she was ready to go inside. Even if the parishioners were as friendly as he claimed and as they'd seemed at Sarah and Clay's wedding, they would not engage in more than brief greetings inside the sanctuary. Or so Priscilla believed.

As she and Zach entered the vestibule, Isabelle Rousseau rushed to their side. "I'm so glad you came!" The petite brunette who was Sarah's best friend and the object of her current matchmaking campaign gave Zach an arch look. "Now, Mr. Webster," Isabelle said with feigned severity, "there's no reason to hide in back. You and Priscilla must sit with my family."

And so, though she had hoped to attract little attention, Priscilla found herself in the second pew. The French church bore little resemblance to the one the Germans had built.

While the other church had no stained glass, this one had two magnificent windows, one depicting the birth of Christ, the other his ascension to heaven. While the German crucifix was rough-hewn wood and had been created by the settlers, the one that hung over the altar here appeared to be carved of centuries-old marble. If the cross was old, though, the minister was not. While Pastor Sempert was in his seventies, Père Tellier could not be more than thirty-five. Pastor Sempert was tall, although a bit stooped with age, and sturdily built. Père Tellier was of short stature and a slight frame.

And yet, for all their differences, both churches exuded the same sense of peace. Simply sitting in the pew made Priscilla realize she had not made a mistake by coming. God had not excluded her because of her anger. Instead, she felt him welcoming her, and she knew that the contentment she'd felt at the Lazy B this week had been his doing. He had brought Zach into her life to make it better. *Thank you, Lord.*

Priscilla glanced at the man who sat next to her, his eyes fixed on the minister, and wished his life could be different. This week had shown her what a generous, thoughtful man Zach Webster was. Surely he deserved better than a loveless marriage.

When the services ended, Priscilla and Zach were surrounded by a group of parishioners, each felicitating them on their marriage, no one commenting on its hastiness. The men clapped Zach on the back or shook his hand; the women smiled brightly at Priscilla; the children appeared bored. And all the while, Zach stood at her side, accepting congratulations, telling everyone how fortunate he was.

"That wasn't so bad, was it?" he asked half an hour later as he guided the wagon into the river.

Priscilla loosened her cloak. With the sun at its zenith, the day had turned warmer than she'd expected. "It wasn't bad at all. I was surprised at how friendly everyone was." Though she'd seen curiosity on many faces, it seemed to be the normal curiosity about a new resident, nothing more, and that was a pleasant surprise. Zach had claimed that no one knew what had happened, but surely they must have suspected something was amiss for her to have married so quickly.

Zach's smile accentuated the cleft in his chin. "I keep telling you that this is a good town. Oh, it has its idiosyncrasies, but overall it's a fine place to put down roots. You and your child will be safe here."

Priscilla knew that. It was Zach whose situation concerned her. "I wish you were getting more from this arrangement."

"Don't worry about me. I'm happy with our agreement."

If only she could believe him.

～

Zach rode slowly, his eyes scanning the horizon for calves separated from the herd. It happened each winter, the weaker animals being left behind to fend for themselves. Each year Zach searched for them. If they were injured, he'd do what he could to tend the wound. If they were hungry, he'd feed them. If they were simply lost, he'd guide them back. Clay claimed that, short of branding, this was the aspect of ranching he detested the most. Zach felt differently. This was the time when he felt useful. Oh, it was true, as Clay claimed, that cattle were not the most intelligent of God's creatures, but that was all the more reason why they needed his care.

He settled back in the saddle and raised his eyes to the sky. *If this is your plan, Lord, and I think it is, I like it.* Not just helping the cattle. His life in general. When he'd come to the Bar C, Zach hadn't known what the Lord had in mind for him. He thought he'd been sent to help Clay and his father. Never once had he considered the possibility that he would wind up married, but here he was, a husband.

Zach whistled softly. Charcoal seemed to like the sound, and it helped Zach relax. Marriage was not what he'd expected. Of course, he hadn't spent much time contemplating married life, so it was hardly surprising that he had few preconceived ideas. He certainly hadn't thought it would feel so right. Part of the reason was having his own house. Zach enjoyed that more than he'd thought possible. He liked the privacy, the quiet, the comfort. But part of the appeal was Priscilla. To say the least, living with her was very different from life in the bunkhouse. He'd traded a dozen rowdy men for one quiet woman. One puzzling woman.

Zach had been taught that women were weak, but she was strong. She possessed not just physical strength, although it certainly took that to accomplish all she'd done around the house. What surprised him was her emotional strength. Though Priscilla had been through harrowing experiences, she never cried, not even when she was in the midst of a nightmare. Zach knew she was plagued with them, for each night he heard her whimper and then light a candle to banish the darkness. But, unlike him who would remain caught in remembered horror for hours, she seemed to recover quickly. Not once did she refer to her troubled dreams. Instead, Priscilla did her best to find something humorous to recount each day. No wonder her family had called her Sunny Cilla.

Zach suspected that wrestling with the horsehair settee in the parlor had been far less amusing than the tale Priscilla had told, but he admired her fortitude and her willingness to laugh at herself. Not many women would do that.

When a spot of black caught his eye, Zach leaned forward. "Let's go, Charcoal." The spot, his trained eye told him, was a calf. Though Charcoal was trotting now, Zach would slow him to a walk as they approached the animal. The last thing he needed was to spook an injured calf.

Or a wife. As strong as she was, where men were concerned, Priscilla was like a wounded animal, fearful of predators. Though she seemed to be a bit more relaxed around him each day, Zach knew it was only because he kept a distance between them. *Heal her, Lord*, he prayed silently. *Show me how to help her.* As the days passed, he had been moving slowly, gradually narrowing the distance between himself and his wife. Drying dishes had been his first test. Though he'd stood closer to her than normal, she had not been spooked. Perhaps it was because his hands had been occupied, and she hadn't feared he would touch her. Zach wasn't certain. All he knew was that he would continue. Building Priscilla's trust would take time, but if he was careful, one day the fear would leave her eyes.

He slowed Charcoal again, watching the calf. There was no doubt about it; it was limping. Slowly and deliberately Zach reached for his rope. The calf did not move. Good. He spun the rope over the calf's head, then, so quickly that the calf had no warning, looped it around the animal's shoulders, and tugged it to the ground. An instant later, Zach had dismounted and was running toward the frightened calf.

"It'll be all right," he said, as much to reassure himself as the animal. "Let's see what's wrong." The calf continued to struggle, attempting to rise. Zach tied the three good legs together so that he could inspect the injured one without worrying about being kicked. No broken bones. The problem was a deep gash that had already begun to form a scab. Excellent! Zach released the calf, knowing it would heal on its own. He prayed that Priscilla would too.

Back on Charcoal, Zach was continuing on the route he'd planned for the day when he suddenly stopped. He couldn't explain it. All he knew was that he needed to return to the house. Immediately. The feeling was so urgent, so insistent that he wheeled around and headed home, despite the fact that other injured cattle could be over the next rise. Half an hour later, when he and Charcoal reached the ranch, Zach had second thoughts. Perhaps it was all his imagination. Perhaps there was no reason for him to be here. He scanned the yard. Nothing looked amiss. He'd go inside, reassure himself, then head out for the range again. But as he entered the house, he heard sobs, and he knew he'd been called here for a reason.

Chills raced down his spine as he ran through the house looking for Priscilla. There she was, doubled over on the settee, crying as if her heart were breaking. Deep and heart-wrenching, the sobs could have been caused by pain or anguish. Zach's heart lurched at the knowledge that something was desperately wrong for the woman who never wept to be sobbing like this.

"What's wrong?" he demanded, his voice harsh with worry. Though he longed to wrap his arms around Priscilla, he dared not, for that would only increase her distress. All he could do was talk. "Are you ill? Did something happen to the baby?"

She looked up, her eyes swollen, her nose red. "The baby's fine. I'm fine."

She was not, for the fear he had seen the day she arrived at the Bar C had returned to her eyes. Sensing that she was frightened by his standing over her, Zach sank into a chair opposite her.

"You're not fine, not if you're crying like that." He wondered whether this was a daily occurrence, and he'd never known. Though she seemed cheerful when he returned each evening, Zach hated the possibility that she spent hours weeping. "Tell me what's wrong." If it was within his power, he would fix it.

Priscilla wiped her tears and blew her nose before she spoke. "It's nothing, Zach. Really nothing. I was just being silly."

He wouldn't believe that. "You're the least silly person I know. Now, tell me what's wrong."

"You'll think I'm crazy." When Zach shook his head, trying to reassure her, she dabbed at her eyes again. "It's my locket." Priscilla's voice broke. "They took my locket. The bandits killed my parents and they hurt me and they took my locket." The words came out like water rushing over a dam. "It was all I had and they took it. They took everything."

Zach tried to make sense of what she was saying. Clay had warned him that women in Priscilla's condition could be emotional. Perhaps that was the reason for her spate of tears, though it seemed unlikely. Why would a normally sensible woman be so upset about a locket? Whether her sorrow was logical or not, Zach needed to help her.

"Tell me about your locket," he urged.

Priscilla looked at him as if surprised by his request, then swallowed deeply in an obvious attempt to calm herself. "It was a birthday gift from my parents. When you opened it, their miniature was on one side, one of Patience and me on the other." The tone of her voice told Zach she had treasured the family portraits even more than the locket itself. He watched as tears welled in Priscilla's eyes. Defiantly, she brushed them aside, her next words confirming his supposition. "The locket had the only pictures I had of my family, and they took it. Now I have nothing."

It was no longer sorrow that colored her words; it was desperation. Zach closed his eyes. *Help me, Lord. Show me the way to comfort her.* When he opened his eyes, he fixed them on Priscilla. Even with her eyes reddened and her face blotchy, his wife was beautiful. More than that, she was lovable. "You're wrong, Priscilla." Zach kept his voice soft but firm. "You have not lost everything. You still have God's love, and he's given you a new life to raise."

Those were not the words she wanted to hear. Priscilla's lip curled in scorn. "A bandit's baby."

"Your baby." Zach paused. "Our baby." Though her eyes widened in surprise, Zach wouldn't rescind the words, not when it felt so right to have pronounced them. "You're safe here. Our child will be safe here."

She nodded slightly, and the fear in her eyes began to fade. *Thank you, Lord.* Encouraged by the progress he was making, Zach continued. "We can have a good life here." Again she nodded. "I will do everything I can for you, but there's something you have to do for yourself. If you want true peace, you need to forgive the bandits."

The hope that had flickered was extinguished. "I can't."

෴

162

Priscilla was in the kitchen cutting vegetables for stew when she heard a carriage approaching. Wiping her hands, she hurried to the front porch, her heart filling with pleasure at the sight of Sarah and Thea. "I'm glad you came." It had been three days since their last visit. After the first week, Sarah and Thea had stopped at the Lazy B every few days, and even if they stayed only half an hour, their arrival was cause for rejoicing.

Priscilla opened the front door. "Come in. I'll make us some coffee." She ushered her guests into the parlor, waiting until Thea appropriated one of the chairs and began an animated discussion with her doll.

"I'm still impressed with the changes you've made," Sarah said. "Everything looks so much brighter and more inviting."

Zach had said the same thing. "All I did was wash curtains and rearrange the furniture." Priscilla had also taken down the somber portraits, feeling that bare walls were better than ones with the former owners' disapproving ancestors staring down at her.

"You've turned a house into a home." Sarah settled onto the settee. "I like it."

When Priscilla returned with a tray of coffee, milk, and cookies, Thea held up her doll. "Cilla wanna play?"

Sarah shook her head and gave her sister a cup of milk. "Not now, sweetie. You and your dolly can play by yourselves for a few minutes." When Thea started to pout, Sarah added, "You may have two cookies if you're quiet while Priscilla and I talk." She waited until Thea had drunk her milk before she turned to Priscilla. "I want your advice on something, but first, it's not just the house that looks different. You look

. . . Oh, how can I describe it? Contented. That's the word. Are you?"

Priscilla thought for a moment. Though that wasn't an adjective she might have used, she couldn't dispute the fact that it applied to her. Other than the nightmares and that horribly embarrassing day when Zach had caught her sobbing over her locket, she had been content. "More than I thought possible," she admitted. "I'm comfortable here and safe, so, yes, you could say I'm content."

Zach probably wouldn't believe that after the crying spell he'd interrupted. The odd thing was, it had helped. Not simply the crying, although that had been beneficial. If he'd been alive, Papa might have told her she had a wound that needed lancing, and the tears had provided that release. But what had made the most difference were Zach's words of comfort. Priscilla had been startled when he'd referred to the life growing inside her as their baby. She hadn't expected that, hadn't even considered the possibility that he would regard the child as his. Oh, she'd known that he would protect the baby and would help her raise it, but she had never dreamt that he might treat it as if it were his child. She had been wrong. Zach had said the word *our* twice, and ever since that day Priscilla had clutched the memory close, smiling whenever she recalled it. That one small word had brought comfort. His other words had not. She would cling to Zach's promises of comfort, not to his insistence that she forgive the bandits. Some things were not forgivable.

Oblivious to Priscilla's internal turmoil, Sarah smiled. "I know I must sound like every new bride, but I think marriage is wonderful. That's why I want Isabelle and Gunther to marry. They deserve the same happiness."

164

It was Priscilla's time to smile. "So you've decided to be a matchmaker. I thought that might be why you seated them next to each other at our wedding supper."

Sarah nodded. "They'd make a wonderful couple. The problem is, they don't seem to realize that. That's why I wanted your advice."

The reluctant bride as matchmaker. Priscilla wanted to laugh at the notion until she realized that she had some experience, albeit secondhand. "My mother used to claim the best way was to find reasons for a couple to be together. She was convinced that Clay was the perfect man for Patience. That's why she insisted he take his meals with us most days. It would give him time with Patience."

Sarah appeared surprised. "Clay never said anything about your mother's matchmaking."

"He probably wasn't even aware of it. Mama was subtle."

Sarah laid down her coffee cup and raised an eyebrow. "Are you saying my seating arrangement wasn't subtle? No, don't answer that. I don't want to know. Your mother was probably right about proximity." Sarah grinned. "It certainly worked for Clay and me. The problem is, Gunther has no reason to visit the mercantile more than once every month or so, and Isabelle never goes to the mill. How do I get them together?"

That was a problem, but there was a greater one. "We can't forget Eva. My impression is that Gunther won't marry anyone unless he's convinced she'd be a good stepmother, and Eva seems protective of her father. You heard her. She doesn't think he needs a wife."

"You're right." Sarah nodded and took another sip of

coffee. "At one time, I was the logical choice, because Gunther saw me with Eva every day and knew how much I loved her. It was the same with Olga Kaltheimer. She and Eva were together at the school, and Eva considered her a friend."

"So we need a reason for Eva to spend time with Isabelle."

"Are you and Cilla done talking?" Thea climbed onto Sarah's lap and hugged her.

"Just a little while longer." Sarah pretended to offer Thea's doll a sip of coffee.

"Another cookie?"

"No. You may sit here, but you may not have another cookie."

While Thea pouted, Priscilla considered the problem of Isabelle and Gunther. "He seems to think that teachers would make good mothers."

"True, but Isabelle's not a teacher." Sarah's face brightened. "She's an excellent seamstress. Perhaps she could teach Eva to sew."

"I imagine there are several unmarried German women who could do that." Though neither she nor Sarah had broached the subject, Priscilla was certain that Isabelle and Gunther's different heritages were a barrier to their romance. "What if Isabelle were to teach Eva to speak French?"

Sarah nodded slowly. "It would be a good idea, if Gunther believed that his daughter needed fluent French. The problem is, we're trying to convince everyone in Ladreville that English is our common language."

"You and I learned French, even though we speak English every day. I don't know about you, but my mother claimed that all well-bred girls spoke French."

166

Sarah cuddled her sister, who had started to fuss over the enforced inactivity. "My parents planned to take us to Europe. Mama said that was why I needed to learn it."

"You could use that argument with Gunther. Tell him that Eva might want to travel to Europe some day, and she should speak both French and German when she goes."

"That might work," Sarah conceded. She narrowed her eyes. "There's one more problem. We need someone to persuade him. I could try, but I'm not sure how effective I'll be. Things have been a little strained since I refused Gunther's offer of marriage. Besides, the idea would probably be best coming from a man."

When Sarah refused to meet Priscilla's gaze, she knew why the other woman had come to the Lazy B today. This was more than a neighborly visit, and Sarah wanted more than advice. She wanted Priscilla's husband to help her. "All right. I'll ask Zach."

"You want me to be a matchmaker?"

Priscilla had waited until after supper before she broached the subject. One of Mama's precepts had been that men were more amenable to suggestions when they were well fed. This was the first time she'd had to test the theory, and she hoped the stew and fluffy biscuits had done their job. "Not exactly," Priscilla hedged. "Oh, all right—yes, I want you to help Sarah." When Zach continued to look dubious, she added, "It's not as if you'd be pushing Gunther and Isabelle together."

"Just nudging my friend in that direction." Though Zach had been sitting on the opposite side of the table, he rose

167

and strode toward the door. When he reached it, he wheeled around. "Tell me, Priscilla, why do women feel this need to see their friends married? Can't they understand that some men are meant to be bachelors?"

His words were spoken so vehemently that she knew he felt strongly, but he was right: she didn't understand. "Who's meant to be a bachelor? Gunther's already been wed, so you can't be speaking of him."

"I . . ." Zach fell silent. "You're right," he said at last. "Gunther wants to marry again, and your plan might help him. I'll do it."

Late that night, Priscilla remained awake, remembering the conversation. Though he'd agreed, the troubled expression on Zach's face told her he had misgivings. Those misgivings, she sensed, were not related to Gunther but to the fact that he believed some men were born bachelors. Who? He'd started a sentence with "I" but had said nothing more. Was he speaking of himself? Did he believe he was one of those men meant to remain unmarried? Priscilla cringed at the thought. If that was the case, he'd sacrificed even more than she'd known when he asked her to be his wife. Poor Zach!

Priscilla gripped the windowsill and stared into the distance. The bandits' evil was like a stone tossed into a pond, sending out wider and wider ripples until it disturbed the entire pond. They'd hurt her, and through her, they'd hurt Zach. *Oh, Lord*, she prayed, *why did you let this happen? Zach deserves better.*

9

"Did you ever think about children? Before Eva was born, that is." Zach leaned against the doorframe, feigning nonchalance. The truth was, he couldn't recall when he'd dreaded an encounter more. It was one thing for Priscilla and Sarah to claim that Gunther wanted a new wife and that Isabelle was the perfect candidate. It was quite another to involve Zach in their schemes. But here he was at the gristmill, pretending this was a casual visit.

Perhaps he'd been a fool to agree. After all, he knew nothing of matchmaking and had even less desire to learn. If Sarah had asked, he would have refused, but it was far more difficult to deny Priscilla anything. The day he'd found her crying over her missing locket had shown him that her seemingly calm exterior was only a fragile shell. Inside she was vulnerable, and that made Zach determined to do anything he could to help her, which was why he was having a sack of corn ground when no one needed cornmeal. That was the only excuse he had found to visit Gunther and ask inane questions.

Fortunately, Gunther seemed to find nothing odd in Zach's question. "There wasn't a lot of time to think," he said with a grin. "Eva got started right away. It happened so quickly that Frieda was afraid if the baby came early, folks would think we jumped the gun, so to speak." Gunther raised an eyebrow. "Why are you asking? You and Priscilla got babies on the mind?"

"Don't all newly wedded folks?" Zach and Priscilla did, but not for the reason Gunther probably imagined. In another few months, it would be obvious that Priscilla was with child and that Zach was not the child's father. He could only pray that the townspeople would not distress her with their speculation. He would not speak of that today. Instead, he said, "I've been thinking about all the responsibility—feeding them, clothing them, taking care of them when they're sick." That was nothing less than the truth. Though he'd never admit it to Gunther, the prospect scared Zach. How was he going to care for a tiny, helpless infant? He knew nothing about babies. But that wasn't the reason he was here. He had to persuade Gunther that Eva needed Isabelle.

"It gets easier once they can talk. Then they tell you what they need."

Thank you, Gunther. He'd provided the opening Zach sought. "I suppose that does make it easier, and the school helps, but don't you still worry about whether they're learning everything they should? Last night at supper Priscilla was talking about the school she attended. They learned to do needlework, play the pianoforte, and speak both German and French."

Gunther frowned. "Why do young'uns need all that?"

Zach had asked the same question, pointing out that life

170

in Texas was different from Boston and Philadelphia. His wife's answer had prepared him. "According to Priscilla, that's what's expected of ladies in America."

The miller's frown deepened. "I didn't know that. Looks like I need to talk to the mayor. When he hires the next school-marm, he'd better make sure she can teach the piano and stitching."

"Don't forget French and German."

Though he was normally affable, it was clear Gunther did not like the idea. His frown became a full-fledged scowl. "Eva already speaks German." It was a measure of Gunther's anger that his normally light accent grew more pronounced. "There's no need for her to learn French. We're Americans now."

"True." Zach had expected this argument. He had made it himself. "If Eva never leaves Ladreville, she'll be fine, but what if she wanted to visit a big city? Priscilla said cultured ladies do that. They go to museums and opera houses and eat in fancy restaurants." When Priscilla had ventured the explanation, Zach had cringed. Cities and crowds held no attraction for him. "I heard fancy restaurants serve French dishes. You wouldn't want your daughter to seem ignorant in front of some waiter, would you?"

Gunther clenched his fists, clearly appalled at the thought that Eva might not be prepared for every social eventuality. "Of course not! Maybe Sarah can start those lessons right away. She speaks French."

Zach repressed a smile. The morning was going better than he'd expected. Gunther had taken the bait. All he had to do was reel him in. "True, but she's mighty busy, what with being a bride and caring for her sister. I reckon it would be

171

a real imposition. Still, you're right. The sooner Eva starts learning, the better." Zach paused, as if searching for an alternative. A few seconds later, he clicked his fingers. "There might be a way."

"What do you mean?"

The fish was in the air, headed for the creel. Zach kept his voice even, though inwardly he was chuckling. "I heard Miss Rousseau is good at fancy stitching, and she speaks French. I wonder if she might agree to tutor Eva. That would give your daughter a leg up when classes do begin."

"*Sehr gut*. It's a good idea," Gunther said with a grin. As he handed Zach the sack of freshly ground corn, he narrowed his eyes. "If you want my advice, Zach, you and Priscilla shouldn't wait too long before you start your family. Children are God's greatest blessing."

The pleasure Zach had felt in accomplishing his mission for Priscilla evaporated. Though he nodded in apparent agreement with Gunther's statement, he doubted either Priscilla or Margaret considered their children blessings.

≈

Married! She was married! Lawrence Wood schooled his face to reveal nothing, even though he felt as if someone had rammed a rifle butt into his stomach. He'd been whistling with anticipation when he'd ridden onto the Bar C. He wasn't whistling now that the Canfields' housekeeper had delivered unwelcome news. Though he hadn't been sure what to expect and had even considered the possibility that she might have gone back East, one thing was certain: he hadn't expected Priscilla to be married.

Why not, Lawrence? he asked himself as he strode away

from the ranch house. *She's a beautiful woman. If you can't stop thinking of her—and admit it, man, you can't—what makes you think another man wouldn't react the same way?* Women were scarce out here. As for beautiful, courageous women like Priscilla Morton—well, they were one in a million. It was no wonder Zach Webster had seized the opportunity. Chances like that didn't come more than once in a lifetime.

Lawrence kicked a rock, deriving scant satisfaction when it skittered away. He'd been a fool. An utter fool. Only a fool acted like a schoolboy, dreaming dreams that would never come true. Only a fool took on a new assignment when the first one wasn't finished, simply because it would bring him close to her. And, worst of all, only a fool believed a woman like Priscilla would care about him.

His heart heavy with the weight of shattered dreams, Lawrence mounted his horse. He ought to leave right now. He knew that, just as he knew he wouldn't. It might be foolish, but he had to see her one last time.

Jean-Michel pulled the six-shooter from its holster and aimed it. Bull's-eye! The prickly pear pad had a hole precisely in its center. He laughed out loud, pleased by this latest proof of his prowess. He had always known he was smarter than ordinary men, but until recently he hadn't realized he was so much more powerful. That had changed the night he'd killed the peddler.

Why hadn't anyone told him how wonderful it felt, knowing you had the power of life and death? And wielding that power—was there anything so magnificent? He'd felt a rush of pleasure greater than anything he'd ever experienced when he saw the peddler lying there, his eyes open and sightless. That was what being a man felt like.

He, Jean-Michel Ladre, knew what it was to be a man. The others were too stupid to recognize how much power they held in their hands. They never dared to kill. Then there was Zach Webster. Everyone in Ladreville knew he'd vowed never to kill again. How could he give up such pleasure? The man was weak; he was stupid; he was a fool. Soon he'd be a dead fool.

⋦⋗

It was early afternoon when Priscilla heard the sound of hoofbeats. Setting aside the embroidery that had failed to hold her interest, she hurried to the window, her heart beating faster at the thought that Zach might have come home early. Anticipation turned to fear when she saw that the horse was a palomino, not Zach's charcoal black stallion, and the rider a stranger. A strange man. Her heart thudding with dread, Priscilla looked around, searching for something to use as a weapon. She couldn't let the man come near. She couldn't let him hurt her. No matter what she had to do, no man would ever again touch her.

He was closer now. Priscilla shuddered. Why, oh why, hadn't she listened when Zach had told her she needed to learn to fire a shotgun? It was too late now. All she could do was try to defend herself. Quickly she latched the front door. She would barricade herself in her room and hope that one of the ranch hands was close enough to hear her scream.

As she hurried toward her room, she glanced out the window at the rider who was now dismounting. *Silly Priscilla.*

There's no cause for alarm. This was not a stranger. It was the Ranger, Lawrence Wood. Mentally castigating herself, Priscilla realized she should have recognized him or at least the palomino she'd ridden for two days. Instead, fear had blinded her, causing her heart to beat faster than a runaway horse's hooves. Would it always be this way? Would nothing more than the sight of a man cause her to panic? Though she hoped not, Clay had not been able to answer the question, and Papa's medical books had not discussed the aftermath of a bandit attack.

Taking a deep breath and willing her heart to return to normal, Priscilla opened the door and walked onto the porch to greet the Ranger. He'd promised he would tell her when he'd caught the bandits. That must be why he was here.

"Good afternoon, Ranger Wood." She beckoned him onto the porch. Thank goodness her voice no longer betrayed her fear.

"Good afternoon, Miss Morton. The folks at the Bar C told me I could find you here." The Ranger doffed his hat as he climbed the steps, then corrected himself. "Sorry. I heard you're Mrs. Webster now. May I offer my best wishes?"

Though the Ranger looked the way she remembered—tall, blond, *big*, with eyes almost as deep a blue as Clay's—something was different. Priscilla didn't recall any signs of discomfort when they'd traveled together, but today he seemed unwilling to meet her gaze. Surely it was her imagination that his voice sounded strained. It must be her imagination, for the words were ordinary, and there was no reason to think he was somehow distressed by her marriage.

Recalling her mother's lessons in deportment, Priscilla gave her visitor a warm smile. "You look as if you've traveled quite a distance. May I offer you some refreshment? It won't take long to make a pot of coffee." Fortunately, the day was warm enough that she could serve it on the porch. Though she knew there was no cause for fear, for this was the man who'd rescued her, Priscilla did not want a man—any man other than Zach, that is—inside the house.

The Ranger appeared to hesitate. "I can't stay long, but I wanted to see you. That is, I wanted to see how you were faring." This time there was no doubt about it. Priscilla heard discomfort in his voice.

"At least sit down." She gestured toward the swing as she settled herself in one of the chairs. When she'd rearranged the furniture, she had placed a small table between the two chairs, ensuring that if Zach sat in the other one rather than taking a seat on the swing, he would be far enough away that their arms would not inadvertently touch.

The swing creaked under the Ranger's weight. "I'm mighty glad to see you looking so well."

Though he seemed reluctant to meet her gaze, he had obviously glanced at her. Priscilla was thankful he hadn't come in the early morning, for she hadn't looked well then. "I feel much better than the last time you saw me." She had been battered and bruised then, and the intense fear that had shocked her by its reappearance today had been her constant companion on the trip to the Bar C.

A flush stained the Ranger's face. "Well . . . um . . . about that . . ." He rolled his hat brim as he spoke. "I'm sorry to say I haven't caught Jake and Chet yet."

He hadn't? Then why was he here? As an involuntary gasp escaped her lips, the Ranger's flush deepened. "I assure you I will catch them. Those two will pay for their crimes."

Fear snaked up Priscilla's spine. Though she knew she wasn't meant to overhear it, she'd heard Zach and Clay discussing the Ranger's worry that the Dunkler brothers might seek to avenge Zeke's death by killing her. "Do you think they've come this way?" That must be why the Ranger was in Ladreville.

He shook his head. "No. All indications are they holed up for a few days, then headed north."

"But Ladreville isn't north."

"And you're wondering why I'm here." He stopped fussing with his hat and looked directly at her, his expression solemn. "It's true I wanted to assure myself you were all right, but I have another reason. It appears a young man named Jean-Michel Ladre stole a good sum of money from the empresario he was working for and ran away. Since he used to live in Ladreville, I thought he might have headed back here."

Though Priscilla had been told the story of Jean-Michel's earlier misdeeds and his banishment, she thought he was still in Houston. "I don't go into town very often, so I can't say whether he's returned. You'll have to ask Zach. My husband." Priscilla added the explanation.

The Ranger stared into the distance, as if he were once again unwilling to meet her gaze. Perhaps it had not been her imagination that something about her marriage had disturbed him. "If you don't mind my saying, ma'am, I was surprised to hear you married so quickly."

Priscilla bit her lip, debating what to tell him. Though certain things were not mentioned in polite company, the Ranger knew what had happened to her. Why not admit the truth? "It was because of the baby."

The flush which had faded returned to his face. "Oh."

"I heard you had a visitor today." To Zach's relief, his voice did not reflect the jolt of something—surely it could not be jealousy—he'd felt when Miguel had told him Lawrence Wood had returned to Ladreville.

"The Ranger came." Though he watched carefully, Zach saw no sign of discomfort on his wife's face. Priscilla pulled the pan of biscuits out of the oven, carefully placing them on a plate. Only when she'd covered the plate with a towel did she add, "He wanted to tell me he still hasn't caught the bandits." She might have been discussing the weather for all the emotion she displayed. Evidently Lawrence Wood's visit had not been an important part of her day. That was good news.

"I see." A progress report. That was the first time Zach had heard of a Ranger reporting to anyone other than his captain. Normally, folks simply assumed the lawmen would do their job, and eventually the stories of how justice was meted out filtered back to them. Lawrence Wood, it appeared, had a different approach. A more personal approach. It certainly wasn't jealousy, but Zach couldn't say that he approved, particularly since coming here took time away from what the Ranger was supposed to be doing: hunting the Dunkler brothers.

As Priscilla placed the last bowl on the table, Zach pulled out her chair, taking care not to touch her. Someday, he hoped, she would not shy from a casual touch, but that day had not arrived.

When they'd given thanks for their food and started to eat, Priscilla looked up, a question in her eyes. "Did you know that

Jean-Michel Ladre has run away from Houston or Galveston or wherever it is he's supposed to be?"

The question took him aback, for Zach couldn't imagine why she was asking about a man she'd never met. Before he could say anything, she continued, "That's why the Ranger was in Ladreville. He said Jean-Michel had stolen some money and ran away. He thought he might have come here."

Relief washed over Zach. He'd been mistaken, thinking Lawrence Wood had come to Ladreville specifically to see Priscilla. Apparently she was nothing more than an afterthought. Good. Excellent. As he looked at Priscilla, admiring the way her hair seemed to bring light to the whole room, Zach said, "I hadn't heard of Jean-Michel's escape, but I wondered why I hadn't seen Michel around town recently." At the time, Zach had thought the mayor was spending more time with his wife in an attempt to prove that she was as important to him as the town. It appeared that Zach was wrong. "If he got word of his son's latest crimes, Michel is probably ashamed to be seen in public."

Priscilla took a biscuit, then passed the plate to Zach. Tonight's supper was some kind of thick soup—barley, he guessed—with biscuits. Other than the one time when they'd been almost as black as his horse, her biscuits had been delicious, proving what Zach had suspected: his wife learned very quickly.

Right now that wife was frowning. "But the Ladres didn't do anything wrong."

Zach buttered another biscuit as he searched for the right words. If only he hadn't opened the Pandora's Box of rumors and condemnation, but he had. "Folks might claim they didn't raise Jean-Michel properly. My ma used to tell me that the reason I had to behave was so the neighbors wouldn't think she was a poor mother." Though Zach tried to make light of it, he could see that Priscilla was concerned.

"That might be true of small children, but once a person's an adult, he's responsible for his own behavior." The way Priscilla toyed with her spoon told Zach she was more concerned with the townspeople's possible shunning of the mayor than with eating. Did she fear that she would be subjected to the same shunning when her baby was born less than nine months after their wedding?

Priscilla took a sip of coffee, then looked directly at Zach, her green eyes filled with pain. When she spoke, her words surprised him. "Do you suppose some people are born evil?"

She wasn't speaking of Jean-Michel. Zach was certain of that, for when she'd asked the question, Priscilla had placed her hand on her abdomen. Her worry was for her unborn child. This was, Zach guessed, a new fear and, in all likelihood, one that troubled her far more than the prospect of being shunned. "No, I don't." Zach spoke forcefully, willing her to believe him. "I believe everyone has the potential to be either good or evil. We all make choices, and some of us make the wrong ones."

"Like the bandits."

"And Jean-Michel."

To Zach's surprise, his words appeared to have restored Priscilla's appetite, for she took a spoonful of soup and followed it with a bite of biscuit. When she looked up, some of the pain in her eyes seemed to have receded. "Do you ever wish you'd made different choices?"

Zach had no intention of admitting how one bad decision had affected his life. Instead he said simply, "Yes."

To his relief, Priscilla did not ask him to elaborate. She nodded slowly as she said, "So do I."

"What would you change?" Several times she'd mentioned wishing she hadn't come to Texas, for she believed that if she hadn't insisted on attending Clay's wedding, her parents would still be alive and she would not be carrying a bandit's child.

A small smile curved the corners of Priscilla's mouth, as if she knew what Zach expected but had no intention of repeating the same story. He didn't care what she said. What mattered was that she seemed to have recovered from her earlier distress.

"I wish I hadn't listened to my parents." Zach tried but failed to mask his surprise. Priscilla struck him as a dutiful daughter, and from what she and Clay had said, it was difficult to picture her parents making unreasonable demands. Rather than speak, he raised an eyebrow and waited for her to explain. "I wanted to be a doctor, and they discouraged me."

"You wanted to be a doctor?" His voice rose in disbelief. It was the wrong reaction, for Priscilla's smile disappeared.

"You sound like my parents—shocked by the very idea. Why can't a woman be a doctor?"

Zach could think of a dozen reasons, starting with the fact that patients would not accept a woman in that role any more than they'd accept a woman standing at the pulpit on Sunday morning. But he knew Priscilla didn't want to hear that, and so he said, "It's not impossible, but it's always difficult to be the first to do anything. Trailblazers have a hard time."

"I wouldn't have been the first. A woman named Elizabeth Blackwell is a doctor, and I heard that her sister is too. Papa

181

considered it a bit of a scandal, but they're planning to open an infirmary for women and children in New York City."

Zach didn't care about Dr. Blackwell; he cared about the woman who was now his wife. Though the decision had been made some time in the past, her dream and the fact that it was unrealized had helped shape the woman Priscilla was today. "What made you want to travel such a difficult road?"

When she met his gaze, Zach saw a sparkle of enthusiasm in her eyes. "I loved helping my father with his patients. I saw how he made a difference in their lives, and I wanted to do the same."

It was an admirable goal and one Zach shared. He liked thinking that he was helping Clay and his father. That was why he spent time each day teaching Robert to walk again. But surely Priscilla realized that practicing medicine was not the only way to help others. "Women make differences too." He nodded when she held up the coffeepot and waited until she'd refilled his cup before he continued. "Women do things that only they can do. They create a home and raise children."

Priscilla took another sip of coffee. "I worried I'd never marry."

Though he'd been startled by the idea that Priscilla longed to be a physician, that shock paled compared to the one he'd just received. "Why on earth not? You must have had suitors by the score."

She shrugged. "There were none I wanted to marry. I knew not one of them was the man God had chosen for me."

Zach swallowed deeply at the realization that he wasn't either, and yet she'd married him. Zeke Dunkler's attack and its aftermath had left her no choice. Zach couldn't change that, but perhaps there was a way to help Priscilla achieve her dream. "Have you talked to Clay? Now that Dr. Adler can't practice, he's complained about being too busy." When the town's sole doctor began to lose his sight, Clay had taken over his responsibilities. That was one of the reasons he'd hired Zach to manage the Bar C.

Priscilla shook her head. "Even if he might have considered it before—and I doubt that—there's no chance now that there's a baby on the way. Clay was very protective of Patience when she was in my condition. He told her women needed to care for their babies, both before and after they were born."

Zach couldn't disagree. He knew how unpredictable a doctor's schedule was and could not imagine how a woman with children could handle it. The bandits, it seemed, had destroyed more than one of Priscilla's dreams.

"I don't mean to complain," she said as she placed a piece of apple pie before him, "but the days go slowly."

"It'll be different after the baby comes."

Though Priscilla nodded, her eyes darkened with regret. "That's still a long time away."

Zach had no answer for her.

The next morning Priscilla was still thinking about her conversation with Zach. She wasn't surprised that he'd been surprised, even shocked, by the fact that she'd once dreamt of becoming a doctor. Her parents had had even stronger reactions. Papa had told her it was impossible, that no school would accept her and that, even if one did, she would never be able to attract patients. "Ladies aren't doctors," he'd told her firmly. "I was wrong to take you with me." And from that day forward, he'd refused to let her accompany him on his rounds.

Mama had simply cried, demanding to know how she'd failed in her duty as a parent, for she must have failed if Priscilla, who could have her choice of eligible husbands, would even consider such an unwomanly occupation. Only Patience had offered sympathy, but she, too, had discouraged her sister from pursuing the idea, admitting that she wouldn't allow a woman physician to treat her, even if that woman was her sister.

There was no point in thinking of a career in medicine. Though it was true that her parents were not here to disapprove, Priscilla knew that becoming a doctor was no longer a possibility. She had new responsibilities to Zach and her unborn child. But that didn't mean she couldn't improve her days. When she'd wakened this morning, she had been filled with the conviction that she had to do something. The time she spent with Zach was surprisingly pleasant, but it wasn't enough.

What she craved was the company of others. As Priscilla had feared, when she discussed having Thea spend days with her, Sarah had confirmed that Thea would throw a tantrum if she didn't go to school like all the other big girls. The Ranger's visit, even though it had frightened Priscilla initially, had been a welcome change from the boredom that characterized her life now that she'd finished rearranging the house. He wouldn't be back, and there were no other women on the ranch, but there was a solution to her ennui. She didn't have to stay home. All she had to do was muster the courage to go into town.

Two hours later, Priscilla hitched the horses in front of

the mercantile. Though her palms were sweating inside her gloves, she tried to reassure herself. While it was true that this was the first time she'd visited Ladreville without Zach, there was nothing to fear. She was going into a store, not paying a personal visit. Besides, each time Priscilla encountered Isabelle, the lovely brunette urged her to come for a visit. It was time for that visit. Not only was Priscilla assured of a warm welcome at the Rousseaus' store, but she would have the opportunity to learn whether Gunther had spoken to Isabelle.

Closing the door behind her, Priscilla looked around. As she'd expected, the mercantile was smaller than the stores she had frequented in Boston, and some of the merchandise, including a stock of braided lariats, was different from anything she had seen back East. Despite the differences, it had the same mixture of aromas, a blend of spices mingled with leather and grains. It also had the person she sought. Isabelle sat behind the counter, perched on a high stool, chatting with another customer. Though the woman's back looked familiar, Priscilla could not place her.

"I can wait," she said in response to Isabelle's greeting. Priscilla was in no hurry, and the other customer had been here first. Though she headed toward the yard goods display, Isabelle had other ideas.

"Come over here." Isabelle crooked her finger to emphasize the invitation, although her tone of voice was little less than a command. Isabelle, Priscilla had learned from their encounters at church, was a determined woman. "There's someone I want you to meet." Isabelle waited until Priscilla was near the counter before she said, "I'd like to introduce you to Yvonne Beauvais."

When the other woman turned, Priscilla realized why she

seemed familiar. Yvonne had been seated a few pews in front of her and Zach last Sunday. A couple inches shorter than herself, Yvonne had hair so dark a brown that it appeared almost black and sparkling brown eyes. Though her face would never be called beautiful and her figure was plumper than current fashion dictated, Yvonne's sweet smile made an onlooker forget her physical shortcomings.

"Your arrival is providential." Isabelle continued the introductions. "Yvonne has been married a little longer than you, and she was just now telling me how she longed for the company of another young married woman."

Priscilla's smile broadened. She'd come in search of one companion, but it appeared she might have found two.

"When I saw you and your husband in church last week," Yvonne said in heavily accented English, "I told Neville we should invite you to join us for Sunday dinner. I'd like a new friend."

"So would I." Friendship was what she sought, not a spool of thread.

The three women chatted for the better part of a quarter hour, talking about everything and nothing, and for that space of time Priscilla was content. This was what she needed. If only it could happen more often. She thought of Yvonne's invitation to Sunday dinner. Though an excursion with Zach would be pleasant, it would do nothing to relieve Priscilla's boredom during the week. "Perhaps you'd also like to visit me. I don't know what your house is like, but when Zach is gone, the ranch seems lonely."

"*Exactement!*" Yvonne nodded then repeated in English, "Exactly. Isabelle is too polite to complain, but I suspect she wishes I were a less frequent visitor here."

Isabelle pursed her lips and feigned dismay. "I would never chase away a customer."

"True. Unfortunately, I do not always make a purchase." Yvonne's eyes sparkled. "So, yes, Priscilla, I accept with pleasure. You and I have many things to discuss."

Her spirits lighter than they'd been in days, Priscilla turned to Isabelle. "I know you have to work here, but you close the store at midday. Would you be able to join us for dinner? Perhaps you and Yvonne could ride together."

"*Magnifique!*" Isabelle clapped her hands, her enthusiasm telling Priscilla that, though she spent hours with customers, she still longed for quiet conversation with other women. It appeared it wasn't only Priscilla who felt that need. Perhaps this was the reason Mama had belonged to so many organizations. A quilting club, another devoted to tatting, still another that knitted layettes for the poor—every day of Mama's life had been filled with meetings. At the time Priscilla had not understood. She had enjoyed quiet times, reading, walking in the park, visiting Grandmama's grave. But now, faced with days of silence, she thought she understood her mother's craving for adult companionship.

"We wouldn't have to rush our visit," Isabelle continued. "Maman can mind the store on her own for an hour or so. That would give us time to talk." Isabelle's enthusiasm faded. One second she was smiling at both Priscilla and Yvonne. Then it was as if a cloud obscured the sun, sobering her expression. "Are you sure you want me to come? After all, you're both newly wedded, and I'm . . ."

"Our friend." Priscilla would not let Isabelle complete her sentence. She saw the loneliness in her eyes, the fear that she would forever be an outsider when young married women met. In that moment, Priscilla understood why Sarah was so adamant about matchmaking for Isabelle. She also knew that Gunther had not spoken to her. "Of course we want you to come," Priscilla said with a bright smile. "Who else will keep us informed of all the latest news?"

Isabelle read the newspapers as soon as they arrived and could be counted on to recount the most important items. Just last week she had told Priscilla there was speculation that the delegation from Buffalo, New York, would not attend President Buchanan's inauguration. According to the paper, they were disappointed that fellow Buffalonian Millard Fillmore had not been elected. Priscilla had scoffed when she'd heard the former president had run as part of the Know-Nothing party and had asked her friend how anyone could vote for a group with such an inauspicious name. Isabelle had simply shrugged her shoulders.

"Who cares about the news?" Yvonne looked at the stack of bolts behind Isabelle. "Who else can offer good fashion advice, like which flannel I should buy?"

"For a petticoat?"

"No." Yvonne shook her head as color rose to her cheeks. "A layette."

"You're expecting!" Isabelle clapped her hands again.

Yvonne smiled again. "All the signs are there. I haven't spoken to Granny Menger yet, and Mama said I shouldn't tell anyone other than Neville, but I couldn't wait to start sewing, and I didn't want to lie about the reason for the flannel." Yvonne paused long enough to chuckle. "Red flannel might make a fine petticoat, but I don't want to swaddle my baby in it. Oh, I'm so excited."

188

Isabelle hurried from behind the counter to hug her friend. "So am I. That's wonderful news."

"Indeed it is." *For you*, Priscilla added silently.

༖

"I feel awful." Priscilla picked at the food on her plate. Since she'd caught cold yesterday, she'd had no appetite. Now all she wanted was to finish the meal so she could climb back into bed.

Reaching for his coffee cup, Zach smiled. "You're the only woman I know who can look beautiful with a red nose."

Priscilla couldn't help it. She laughed. "And you're the only man I know who'd lie about something like that." She cringed each time she looked in the mirror. It wasn't only her nose that was red. Her eyes were bloodshot and red-rimmed too. She felt miserable, and she looked worse.

Zach shrugged, sloughing off her accusation of prevarication. "That lie, as you refer to it, got you to laugh, didn't it? Besides, you'll be over this in a few days."

"I know." Priscilla had spent enough time with Papa's patients to know that this particular malady was not serious and that it would run its course in less than a week. "It's not the stuffy head that's making me feel awful. It's having to cancel Isabelle and Yvonne's visit." She had spent days planning the menu, trying to make their first trip to the Lazy B a memorable one. "I can't entertain guests when I feel like this."

"There's always next week."

"You're right." A sneeze punctuated her words. "It is silly to be so disappointed. It's just that I was looking forward to having company during the day."

Zach looked up from his plate. Unlike hers, his appetite

had not diminished. "If it's company you crave, I can always stay home."

Priscilla shook her head. Though the offer was generous, she could not accept it. "You'd never catch up if you did that." In Priscilla's estimation, running a ranch involved an incredible amount of work, and Zach was responsible for two. He'd regret even a day of idleness. "You've got fences to check and cattle to feed, but thanks for the offer. It was very kind of you."

"My mama taught me to be kind to ladies." Though his lips were still curved in a smile, Zach's eyes were serious.

"This lady appreciates it." Priscilla could not recall her father ever staying home to be with Mama when she suffered from the vapors or one of her other ailments. Perhaps that was because he knew Mama was surrounded by servants and that friends were as close as next door. Priscilla had no servants, only the woman who came two days a week to do the laundry, and her closest neighbors were two miles away.

"You never talk about your parents," she said, abandoning the pretense of eating. Her head hurt so much that chewing was painful, and her stuffy nose robbed the food of its flavor. "Are they still alive?"

Zach eyed her plate, then taking care not to touch her, he reached for it and emptied the contents on his. "No point in wasting good food," he said as he forked a potato. "Pa died when I was eleven, Ma about ten years ago."

So Zach had lost both parents too. "I'm sorry. I would have liked to have met them."

"They'd have liked you—especially Ma." Zach cleaned his plate, then rose and gestured toward the notes Priscilla had written to Isabelle and Yvonne, advising them of her illness.

He had agreed to deliver them as soon as supper was over. "I'd better head into town now. I don't want to disturb the ladies too late."

With the unfailing courtesy that seemed to be his hallmark, Zach pulled out Priscilla's chair. She had taken only a few steps toward the sink when the world turned black and her legs began to crumple.

"Priscilla!" The next thing she knew, Zach had his arms around her.

10

It was only a matter of seconds before she was once more seated, but for the space of those seconds, she felt warm and comforted. Priscilla took a sip from the glass of water that he pushed toward her. "Thank you, Zach. I don't know what happened."

"I do." Zach's voice was as strong as his arms had been. He stood next to her, not touching but close enough that he could catch her if she tumbled off the chair. When she looked up at him, she saw concern reflected in his eyes. "You're sicker than you realize. I'm going to get Clay."

Priscilla took another sip of water. Though her head was still dizzy, she no longer felt as if she would collapse. "No. Honestly, Zach, it's nothing serious. I just stood up too quickly. I'm fine now." That was an exaggeration, but she needed to chase the worry from his eyes.

"I know I promised to deliver those notes, but I don't want to leave you alone."

His solicitude did more to clear her head than the cool

water he'd insisted she drink. "I'll be all right. I'll rest until you're back." Priscilla rose, slowly and deliberately, waiting until her head stopped spinning before she took a step. Though her bedroom was only a short distance away and blessedly not up any stairs, she did not want to stagger while she walked. That would only increase Zach's concern.

He stayed at her side, and though he was close enough that she could feel his warmth, he was once again careful not to touch her. When they reached her room, he remained in the doorway, watching while Priscilla removed her shoes and lay on the bed, pulling a quilt over herself.

"Promise you won't move until I return." Zach's voice was husky with worry.

"I promise." As his footsteps faded, Priscilla closed her eyes. Though her head still hurt, her heart was filled with an unfamiliar warmth as she realized what had happened. Zach had touched her, and it had not hurt. This was not like their wedding day. Tonight he'd done far more than slide a ring onto her finger. Tonight he'd wrapped his arms around her and practically carried her back to the chair. By all rights, she should have been terrified. She should have trembled the way she did when the nightmares overtook her. But she hadn't. Instead, she had known that he meant her no harm, and she had felt safe and cared for. *Thank you, Lord.*

❦

The man looked as out of place as a silver bowl in a pile of muck. Isabelle tried not to smile as she watched Gunther stroll around the store as if he were searching for something. He wasn't, of course. She could tell that by the way he never paused to touch anything. Besides, with the exception of

Christmas shopping, he brought Eva with him. Today he was simply passing time until Frau Bauer left.

While she waited for her customer to choose between the red and the blue gingham, Isabelle considered the reasons Gunther Lehman was now pacing the floor. The last times he'd done this had been when he'd sought her advice on courting. First he'd come with questions about Sarah, then Olga. Who was next? And why did he think she was the town's expert on wooing? Just because Pierre Erté and Jacques Gris had asked her father for permission to court her didn't mean she knew more than any other woman in town. After all, her father had refused both men's suits, claiming neither man was worthy of his daughter. That was just as well, for Isabelle could not imagine herself wed to either one. When she married, she wanted it to be to a man who was her friend as well as her husband, a man like . . . Isabelle flushed when she realized that the man who was wandering aimlessly through the mercantile fit the description. It was foolish to harbor such thoughts. Papa would never agree to her marrying a German. Besides, Gunther did not regard her that way.

"Can I help you find something?" Isabelle asked him when Frau Bauer had finally selected and paid for the blue gingham and they were alone in the store.

"*Nein. Ja.*" Gunther shook his head, as if he weren't sure which response was correct.

Isabelle repressed another smile. A friend didn't laugh at her friend's discomfort. Still, the fact that Gunther had reverted to German told her he was more flustered than usual. Whoever this woman was, he was worried about wooing her. As his friend, Isabelle was responsible for helping him. "We have some nice candies," she offered. "I can make a pretty arrangement in one of these tins." She held up a potential container.

"But I don't need candy. I need . . ." He stopped abruptly, his face flushing.

"What is it you need?" Isabelle softened her voice.

"I need you." Though she'd thought his face could not redden any more, she was wrong. He flushed, and—to her further embarrassment—so did she. "That is," Gunther corrected himself quickly, "I need your help. I don't know how to ask."

Her help. Of course that was what he needed. It was quite silly—ridiculous, really—to have imagined he meant anything else. Isabelle came out from behind the counter so she could stand next to Gunther. Perhaps that would ease his discomfort. He often laughed at the fact that he was a full foot taller than she. Perhaps being so close would amuse him.

"We're friends, Gunther. You can simply ask me. I'm curious, though. Who is she?" For once, there had been no rumors. Normally the gossipmongers hurried into the mercantile to discuss possibilities, but they'd been oddly silent since Olga Kaltheimer had left Ladreville.

Furrows appeared between Gunther's eyes as he asked, "Who is who?"

"The lady you're courting, of course. That's why you came here, isn't it? For advice or maybe a gift."

"*Nein!* I'm not courting anyone." Though his color remained high, Gunther shook his head vigorously.

The relief that flooded through her startled Isabelle by its intensity. It was foolish to feel as if a burden had been lifted. Gunther was her friend. He needed a wife. Isabelle knew that, just as she knew she ought to be encouraging him to find the perfect woman. Instead, she was almost grinning with pleasure that he had not chosen the next Frau Lehman.

"I'm not courting, but I still need your help," he said.

"All right." It was more than all right, but she wouldn't say that. "How can I help you?"

"It's Eva."

The pleasure Isabelle had felt evaporated, replaced by alarm at the realization that his daughter was the reason Gunther had been so flustered. The little girl who tried so hard to be an adult was one of Isabelle's favorite customers. "Is something wrong?"

"No, yes." At least he was speaking English. That was a good sign, wasn't it? Gunther took a step closer to Isabelle, his eyes earnest as he began his explanation. "Zach said that Priscilla and Sarah said that every lady should know how to embroider and play the pianoforte and speak French."

Eva did none of those. But, though Gunther appeared to believe that his daughter's life would be ruined by her failure to master lazy-daisy stitches, Isabelle did not share his concern. "What Zach said is probably true in Philadelphia or Boston," she agreed. "Life is different here. You know that, Gunther. Folks don't put as much store in what Easterners call social graces. What's important here is knowing how to survive a blue norther, when to plant the crops, and how to shoot straight. Don't worry that Eva can't play a Chopin prelude."

Though she meant her words to reassure Gunther, they failed. He was clenching his fist and looked as if he wanted to pound the counter. Apparently thinking the better of that, he opened his hand and placed it palm down on the flat surface. "I do worry. I want my daughter to have every advantage."

Isabelle waited until Gunther met her gaze before she

196

spoke. "You're a good father." She accompanied her words with a smile.

"You think so?" Gunther seemed genuinely surprised by the compliment.

"I know so. Eva is fortunate to have you as her father." While it was true that he wasn't adept at braiding hair and needed advice about clothing suitable for a child Eva's age, no one doubted the love Gunther lavished on his daughter.

"She needs more. She needs . . ."

"A mother." Isabelle completed the sentence. "Everyone in Ladreville knows you're looking for a new mother for her."

Gunther shook his head. "Not today. Today I'm worried that my daughter cannot speak French. If she ever goes to Boston or Philadelphia, I want her to fit in."

"Gunther," Isabelle said as gently as she could, "they speak English there, not French."

"I'm not a *Dummkopf*. I know that. But Priscilla told Zach that food has French names. I don't want my Eva to look like a *Dummkopf* if she goes to a fancy restaurant."

Isabelle forbore mentioning that Eva was years away from eating in a restaurant, plain or fancy. To say that would only distress Gunther, and she couldn't do that to her friend.

"How can I help?"

Gunther's eyes brightened, and the look he gave Isabelle was so warm that she knew she'd do anything he asked.

"Teach her how to speak French, not just the names of foods, but all the words. And if you know how to do those other things—fancy stitching and the piano—could you help her with those too? I want my daughter to have every one of those things you call social graces. Don't worry, though, I'll pay you."

It was the longest speech Isabelle had ever heard him make. It was also the most insulting. "Shame on you, Gunther Lehman. Friends don't ask for payment."

The sparkle fled from his eyes. "Then you won't help?"

"I didn't say that. I simply said there will be no further talk of payment." Isabelle waited until he nodded in agreement before she continued. "We don't have a pianoforte, so I cannot teach her that, but I can help with the others. You understand that these will not be formal lessons. We'll be interrupted by customers, but if you agree, we'll start after school tomorrow."

"*Danke schoen.*" Gunther's smile radiated both relief and gratitude.

Feigning indignation, Isabelle wagged a finger at him. "It wouldn't hurt you to learn some French. 'Thank you' is *merci beaucoup.*"

"Mercy bo what?"

"Coo."

"Mercy bo coo." Though his accent was deplorable, Gunther repeated the words.

"That wasn't so difficult, was it?"

"*Nein.*" As the German word came out of his mouth, Gunther laughed. Isabelle joined him, her heart lighter than it had been in weeks. This could be fun.

Priscilla slid down from the horse and tied it to one of the hitching posts. Today, since she intended to buy only a few items, she'd decided to ride rather than bring the wagon into town, and Zach had brought her favorite mare from the Bar C. Though he had warned Priscilla about Charcoal's aversion to water, Nora appeared to enjoy crossing the river, for she whinnied and tossed her head the instant they started descending to the Medina. Nora might be old, but she had not lost her zest for life.

The same could be said about the woman who greeted Priscilla.

"Good afternoon, my child." Even if she hadn't recognized the voice, only one person in Ladreville called Priscilla "child." She turned and smiled at Granny Menger. As the midwife returned the smile, her eyes moved slowly, appraising Priscilla. "It's good to see you out and about."

"It was nothing serious. I just caught cold."

Granny Menger nodded at the bench the Rousseaus had placed in front of their store. "Let me rest my bones a bit," she said as she lowered herself onto the seat Isabelle claimed had been designed for husbands whose wives were inside the store. When Priscilla had taken the place next to her, Granny nodded again. "Your ailment may not have been serious, but that husband of yours was mighty worried."

Though Zach had mentioned that he'd met Granny Menger when he delivered the notes to Isabelle and Yvonne, he had neglected to mention that he'd discussed Priscilla's illness with the midwife. "I told Zach there was no reason to worry."

"But he did. God chose a good man for you."

"I don't think marriage was part of Zach's plan." The instant the words were out of her mouth, Priscilla regretted them. While they were nothing less than the truth, there was no reason for Granny or anyone other than Zach, Sarah, and Clay to know the circumstances of their marriage.

Apparently unfazed, Granny asked simply, "Why not? It

seems to me that you and Zach are good for each other. You can heal each other's wounds."

Was Granny a mind reader? That was the only reason Priscilla could imagine for her to be speaking of wounds. "What do you know of Zach's past?"

As two women left the mercantile, they stopped to greet Granny and Priscilla. It was several minutes later that Granny turned back to Priscilla, her eyes serious. "I know no more than anyone else in Ladreville," she said, dashing Priscilla's hopes. "Zach is mighty closed-mouthed, and he doesn't frequent the saloon, so nobody's heard anything he doesn't intend them to know." Granny paused before she added, "He's a bit like you that way. Still, you only need to look into Zach's eyes to know he's suffered and is still suffering." Granny stared into the distance for a moment. "I reckon if he tells anyone, it'll be you."

"Maybe not. There are some things no one wants to talk about."

"Like what happened to you." It was a statement, not a question.

Priscilla frowned. "How do you know? Zach said no one would learn what happened."

"I guessed." Granny patted Priscilla's hand. "You needn't worry. If anyone suspects the baby isn't Zach's, they won't say anything."

This was worse than she'd expected. "You know about the baby? Did Zach tell you?"

"No. Like I said, he's closed-mouth. I guessed the first time I met you." When Priscilla let out a small sigh, Granny said, "I'm a midwife, child. I know what to look for. If I'd had any doubts, they would have vanished when I saw Zach

200

that night. He was so worried about you. He was acting just like an expectant father."

Zach, it seemed, had accepted the baby more easily than Priscilla. "There's no point in denying what will soon be obvious, is there?"

Granny shook her head. "How are you feeling? Still queasy in the morning?"

"Yes, but by afternoon I feel fine." Which was why she'd waited until then to come into town. "The only other difference I've noticed is that I'm hungrier than before."

"That's natural." Granny gave her hand another pat. "Now, don't you fret. Women have been having babies since Eve. You just call me when your pains start, and I'll be there. Lord willing, you and Zach will have a healthy baby. Now, you go on and do whatever it was that brought you into town."

Though she could not have predicted it, her conversation with Granny Menger, though brief, marked a turning point for Priscilla. As she entered the mercantile, for the first time, she thought of the life that was growing inside her as *her* baby. Always in the past, it had been "the baby" or simply "it." In the middle of the night, when the nightmares wakened her, it was "the bandit's child." Even when Zach called it "our baby," she had never used the words. But today, Priscilla smiled as she touched her abdomen. Granny was right. This would be her child and Zach's.

"I saw Granny Menger when I went into town today," Priscilla told Zach that evening as they ate supper. "She guessed about the baby."

Apparently unperturbed, Zach nodded. "It won't be long before others notice. I figured that we'd wait another month or so before we told anyone. Mentioning it to one or two is all it will take. After that, the Ladreville rumor mill will spread the news." When Priscilla frowned, he shook his head. "That's not bad. After all the troubles we had last year, folks need something happy to talk about."

"I suppose they do." And new life, no matter how it began, was cause for rejoicing.

"Have you thought about what you want to name the child?"

The question, which seemed to be additional proof that Zach regarded the baby as his, surprised Priscilla. She nodded slowly. "Halfway. If it's a girl, I'd like to call her Patience after my sister, but I can't think of any boys' names I favor." Perhaps that was because she continued to pray that the baby would be a girl. A girl, Priscilla reasoned, would be less likely than a boy to remind her of Zeke Dunkler.

"Would you consider John?"

"John Webster." Priscilla liked the way it sounded. "Was that your father's name?"

"Nope. He was Zach like me. Or rather," Zach said with a wry smile, "I was named Zach like him." The younger Zach Webster's expression sobered. "I always thought that if I had a son, I'd like to name him after John Tallman. John's the man who saved my life."

Though he said the words calmly, Zach's eyes filled with remembered pain. Priscilla took a deep breath as she considered that Granny Menger might be right: Zach might be ready to confide in her. "I understand if it's too painful, but will you tell me what happened?"

He nodded slowly. "I've come this far. You might as well know the rest." Zach took a long swallow of coffee before he began. "I was just a kid, barely fifteen, when Sam Houston mustered an army to march to Mexico. This was late in '42."

Priscilla's knowledge of Texas history was sketchy, but she remembered reading that there were numerous skirmishes between Texas and Mexico, even after Texas gained its independence.

"At first, things were going our way. We captured Laredo and thought we were winning the war, but later that month a bunch of us were captured and taken to a place called Perote." Zach's eyes darkened with the memory. "The Mexicans call it a castle. I call it the worst place on Earth. Conditions were unspeakable—not enough food, brutal guards, locked in a dungeon with no sunlight. We were sure it couldn't get worse, but it did the day they decided to punish us with decimation."

"You mean killing one out of every ten?" Priscilla had heard the term but had thought the practice had been discontinued.

"That's right." Zach nodded. "Our jailers had a pot of beans, one black for every nine white. We stood in a line, and one by one, we had to pull a bean out of the pot. Whoever picked a black one would be killed. That's what I got."

Priscilla shuddered as she imagined the terror Zach must have felt. He was, as he admitted, little more than a child. Though he must have known that death was a possibility when he'd joined the army, it was one thing to die on a battlefield, another to face a firing squad. "How did you survive? Did John Tallman help you escape?"

Zach shook his head. "We were too heavily guarded for there to be any possibility of escape." He stared into the distance for a moment, his eyes so filled with anguish that

Priscilla knew he must be reliving that horrible day. "John was as close to a saint as any man I've met." Zach's voice quavered. "When he saw how scared I was, John switched beans with me. He took the black bean and died in my place."

Priscilla's eyes filled with tears. No wonder Zach looked haunted. He was. He was haunted by the memory of a man who'd given him the most precious gift of all: life. "Oh, Zach, what a wonderful gift!"

"It was, but it came with one stipulation. John wanted me to forgive our jailers. He told me that was the only way I'd be truly free."

"Did you?" The Bible told of Jesus asking his Father to forgive the men who crucified him, but he was divine. It was far more difficult to imagine an ordinary man being so forgiving.

"Not at first," Zach admitted. "I was so ashamed of my cowardice that I could hardly bear each day. At one point, I even thought of killing myself."

Priscilla shuddered. "If you'd done that, you would have squandered John Tallman's gift."

"Clay's father said the same thing. He told me only a coward would take that road, that a brave man would live and make each day of his life a testimonial to John's generosity. But first I had to learn to forgive." Zach drained his cup and placed it back on the table. "It was the hardest thing I've ever done, to give up my anger and hatred, but once I did, I found a greater peace than I dreamt possible."

As she looked at the man she'd married, one thing was clear. "That's why you advised me to forgive the bandits." Priscilla had been wrong. She had believed that Zach had spoken glibly, that he had no understanding of what she'd endured, but he did, for what he'd suffered at the hand of the guards was worse than her ordeal. The jailers had tried to destroy both his body and his spirit, but Zach had survived. More than that, he'd emerged a stronger man.

"Yes. John was right when he said forgiveness was the path to freedom. Our memories can imprison us more surely than the thickest walls."

Priscilla recognized the truth in Zach's words. It was the memories of what the Dunkler brothers had done that robbed her life of joy. She looked across the table and nodded slowly at Zach. "I'm not sure I can do it, but I'll try."

That night as she knelt next to her bed, Priscilla tried to form the words, but they would not come. Instead, images of Zach filled her mind. When he'd told her how he'd forgiven the jailers, his eyes had shone with peace, but soon afterwards, the pain that never seemed too distant returned. There was more to Zach's story than he'd told, more pain to be resolved.

"Dear Lord," she prayed, "heal Zach. Take away the pain he's feeling and give him peace."

11

Priscilla wakened to the sound of birds trilling, their songs so loud that for a moment she thought they were in the house, but the flap of wings against a hard surface told her one was simply sitting on the window ledge. She swung her legs off the bed and padded to the window, eager to see if she could identify it. Like the trees and flowers, many birds here differed from those in Boston, and this one had an unfamiliar song. As carefully as she could, Priscilla drew the curtain aside, but the motion was too much. The bird flew to a nearby tree, then faced the house and squawked, as if scolding her for disturbing it. Priscilla couldn't help smiling. Though it had interrupted her sleep, birdsong was a pleasant way to begin the day.

Her smile broadened when she spotted half a dozen dandelions blooming. Yesterday, there'd been nothing more than heavy, yellow-green heads on the plants. This morning, the flowers had emerged, unmistakable proof of spring's arrival. Priscilla gazed at the yard for a long moment, savoring the feeling of well-being that swept through her. Spring had always been her favorite season, for it brought with it Easter and the promise of new beginnings. What a joyous thought!

She touched her abdomen. Though it was too soon to feel the baby stirring, she knew there was life inside her. Each morning's queasiness was proof of that. Priscilla's smile turned into a grin as she realized that her stomach was settled. It had happened! Granny Menger had promised it would, and it had. Her morning sickness was gone. Priscilla thrust her arms into her dressing gown, unwilling to wait another minute to tell Zach the news. He would be as pleased as she. When she reached the doorway, Priscilla's smile faded as she remembered that Zach had already left. Last night he'd said he had to visit the far end of the ranch and, rather than be gone overnight, he'd decided to leave before dawn. It was silly to feel so disappointed. Zach would return for supper, and she could tell him then. In the meantime, she had Isabelle and Yvonne's visit to look forward to.

When the two women arrived, Priscilla was waiting for them on the porch. Both were smiling as they climbed down from the wagon, but though Yvonne was bubbling with happiness, Isabelle's smile appeared strained.

"I can't wait. I can't wait to tell you." Yvonne sounded younger than her twenty-two years as she giggled. She looked from one woman to the other, then took a deep breath. When Priscilla did that, it was to calm herself. If that was the goal, it had failed Yvonne, for when she spoke, her words came out in a rush. "I know I told you I suspected it, but I wanted you two to be the first to know—after Neville, of course. I told him last night. I couldn't even wait until he'd had dinner, and once he heard, he was so excited, I could hardly get him to eat. All he wanted to do was tell the world. There's no doubt about it. Granny Menger confirmed that Neville and I are going to have a baby. Oh, ladies, I'm so happy!"

Priscilla hugged her friend. "I'm happy for you." Though not unexpected, the news was as welcome as the bird's trilling and the sight of spring flowers.

"Me too." It wasn't Priscilla's imagination. Something was bothering Isabelle. Though her words were delivered with a smile, her eyes lacked their normal sparkle. "When's the blessed event?" Isabelle asked.

As Priscilla escorted her guests into the parlor, Yvonne continued her explanation. "Early September. Granny Menger warned me, though, that first babies arrive on their own schedule. Mine might be two weeks early or late. Oh, I hope it's not late. I don't think I'll be able to wait."

Though Priscilla wondered whether the baby would be as talkative as its mother, she asked only, "Are you feeling all right?"

"Oh yes." Yvonne patted her slightly rounded stomach, as though she were caressing her unborn child. Priscilla tried not to smile at the gesture, even though the reason for the plumpness was a fondness for bread. "Fortunately, so far I haven't been sick at all. I heard some ladies are not so lucky."

Priscilla nodded. Though she was close to admitting that she, too, was expecting a child, she would not do that today. Today was Yvonne's day. Priscilla would do nothing to spoil it or to detract from her friend's joyous announcement. "You are fortunate. My sister was ill every morning for several months."

Though Yvonne grimaced, Isabelle did not. Other than her initial congratulations, she had been uncharacteristically

208

quiet, her eyebrows furrowed, as if her thoughts were elsewhere. When she caught Isabelle's eye, Priscilla raised one of her brows in a silent question. Isabelle gave an almost imperceptible shake of her head. Whatever was wrong, she did not want to discuss it.

"Our meal is almost ready," Priscilla told her friends. "If you just relax, I'll get the food."

She was in the kitchen, pulling the tray of rolls from the oven, when she heard footsteps. Priscilla looked up, surprised to see Isabelle. "Where's Yvonne?"

"Visiting the necessary. All that talk of morning sickness made her a little green." Isabelle leaned against the table. "I shouldn't be glad, but I am, because I wanted to talk to you without her hearing." The way Isabelle twisted her hands told Priscilla the topic was not a pleasant one. If she was right, she would soon know why Isabelle seemed so preoccupied. The petite brunette's eyes were serious as she added, "I know what Yvonne would say, but I'm not sure how you'll feel."

"Is something wrong?" It was almost a rhetorical question.

"According to my parents, yes, but I don't think so." Isabelle's face crumpled, and Priscilla saw that she was struggling not to weep. "I'm confused. I love my parents and I want to obey them, but I don't think what we're doing is wrong."

"We?" Though Priscilla thought she knew what was coming, she needed to be sure.

"Gunther and me." Isabelle's words confirmed Priscilla's fears. "You know he asked me to help his daughter. How could I refuse? Eva's the sweetest child in Ladreville. She deserves a good life, and if I can help by teaching her to embroider and crochet and speak a few words of French, what's wrong with that?"

Priscilla covered the dinner rolls with a towel to keep them warm while she listened to Isabelle. "Nothing's wrong with that." How could she claim otherwise, when it was her idea? "It seems to me you're being a good neighbor. Surely your parents don't disapprove of that."

"Not exactly. They like Eva. It's Gunther they don't like."

"Everyone likes Gunther." Zach had told her that Gunther was one of the most popular men in Ladreville, and not simply because he was a first-rate miller. Even the town's curmudgeon had nothing bad to say about him.

"Not my parents. They don't like Gunther anymore. You see, when Eva's lesson is over, he comes to the store and we . . ." Isabelle's face flushed, though whether from remembered pleasure or embarrassment wasn't clear. "We talk," she said at last.

Priscilla removed the potatoes from the stove. "And you enjoy those conversations."

"Oh yes." The sparkle returned to Isabelle's eyes, and her lips curved in a sweet smile. "I could talk to him night and day and never run out of things to say. Gunther's got an opinion on everything. We don't always agree, but it's always fun."

"But your parents disapprove." Priscilla wasn't surprised. The older Rousseaus had not seemed pleased by Gunther's attention to their daughter at Priscilla and Zach's wedding supper.

"They think he's courting me. They think all he wants is a new mother for Eva."

"What do you think?" Sarah claimed that the looks Gunther

gave Isabelle were not those of a man thinking only of his daughter's well-being.

"I think Gunther wants a friend."

According to Sarah, Gunther wanted more than that, and so did Isabelle. "What if your parents are right? If he were courting you, how would you feel?"

Once again the color rose to Isabelle's cheeks. "I don't know."

"I think you do."

Isabelle bit her lip, as if considering what to say. "I like Gunther," she admitted. "He's the most handsome, most exciting man I've ever met, but . . ."

Priscilla schooled her face to show no emotion. Handsome and exciting were not words she would have applied to Gunther Lehman. However, if that was how Isabelle viewed him, Sarah was right to encourage this match.

Isabelle's smile faded as she finished her sentence, "Everyone knows that if you're a Frenchwoman, you marry a Frenchman."

Just as everyone knew that if you were a woman, you couldn't be a doctor. Priscilla took a deep breath. Her one-time dream might not have come true, but that didn't mean Isabelle should abandon hers. "You're an American now."

The look Isabelle gave Priscilla said she was naïve. "That's not the way my parents see it. Gunther's German, and that means they'd never accept him as a son-in-law, no matter how much I love him."

They'd reached the crux of the matter. "Do you love him?"

Isabelle nodded. "I do, but I love my parents too, and I don't want to hurt them. Maman looks sad, and Papa reminds me of what the Bible says."

At least Priscilla's parents had not quoted Scripture to her. "The commandment tells us we should honor our parents. It seems to me you are honoring them. You're considering their feelings. That's important, but it doesn't mean you have to obey every command they issue. You're a grown woman, Isabelle. You can make your own decisions."

Isabelle bit her lip, and once again Priscilla sensed she was trying to hold back her tears. "I wish that were true, but how can I marry Gunther, knowing it'll make my parents unhappy?"

"Has he asked you to marry him?" Gunther did not have the reputation of being rash, and surely it would be rash to have proposed so quickly.

"Not yet, but . . ."

"Wait." Hadn't Mama always advocated patience? "If Gunther is the man God intends you to marry, he'll show you the way to satisfy your parents."

Isabelle managed a weak smile. "I hope so."

He was late. Her heart began to thud with worry, and she felt her palms grow moist as she stared out the window at the empty road. He'd never been so late. Though she hadn't looked at her watch, her heart told her he was overdue by an hour, maybe more. She'd been waiting for so long, and still there was no sign of him. Something must have happened. Something horrible. Her heartbeat accelerated, and she turned away from the window, unwilling to look at the empty road, proof that he wasn't coming.

She knew she should occupy herself with something else, perhaps her needlework. That was what ladies did in these circumstances. But she could not rest. Instead she paced from one end of the room to the other, and each time, though she told herself it was futile, she gazed out the window, hoping against hope that she would see his wagon. At last, in desperation, she opened her watch to check the time. It couldn't be. She stared at the face, not believing what she saw. The watch must have stopped. She unpinned it and held it to her ear. It was still ticking. Priscilla began to laugh. The evidence was clear. He wasn't late. There were still five minutes before he had said he would meet her. It was only she who, eager to see him, had been ready far too early.

She returned to the window, then gazed at the door. She ought to remain indoors. Mama had cautioned her not to appear eager for a man's attention. But the day was so lovely. Surely there was no harm in sitting on the porch.

A moment later she was settled in the swing, and still he had not come. She opened her watch again, shaking her head when she realized that only a minute had passed. He wasn't late. Not yet. And then she heard it, the sound of hoofbeats, the rattle of wagon wheels. Her heart began to beat faster, keeping time with the racing horses. It must be him. It was!

He jumped from the wagon and ran toward her. "I know I'm early," he said as he doffed his hat, "but I couldn't wait to see you."

Though Mama would frown, Priscilla saw no reason to lie. "Me too. I've been ready for an hour." As he grinned and took her hand between both of hers, she said softly, "Oh, Zach, I love you."

Priscilla wakened, her heart pounding when she remembered

the dream. Mama had believed that dreams were powerful portents and had reminded Patience and Priscilla how often God had used them to tell his people about the future. Normally Priscilla woke with little or no memory of having dreamed, but today was different. Today the memory lingered, almost as vivid as the dream itself, and that set her mind to whirling. Could it be possible? Was Granny Menger right in saying that Zach was the man God intended for Priscilla? Was what she felt for Zach more than gratitude or friendship? Was it love?

Priscilla lay back on the pillow, smiling.

⌇

"If you're here to tell me I'm crazy, you can walk right back out that door." To be certain there was no confusion, Gunther pointed at the door Zach had just entered.

Zach stared at his friend, who was pacing the mill floor with uncharacteristic anxiety. "Why would I say you're crazy?" If anyone was crazy, it was he, for he'd been acting like a schoolboy, so eager to see Priscilla that he rushed through his chores each day. He wasn't slacking his responsibilities, but he also wasn't giving them the full attention he had a few months ago. He wasn't the person whose sanity was in question, though. It was Gunther.

"Everyone else thinks I'm a fool to be spending time with Isabelle." Gunther halted in front of Zach, shaking his head as he corrected himself. "That's not true. Not everyone used the word *crazy*. Some told me I was desperate. Desperate, crazy, and it's your fault."

Zach suspected it was. The town had been buzzing with the news that Gunther had found a new candidate for the position of Eva's mother. While that was exactly what Priscilla and Sarah had hoped would happen, Zach wasn't proud of his role. Why had he ever let himself get involved in a matchmaking scheme?

"What happened? The last I heard, Isabelle was teaching your daughter to speak French. In my book, that's neither crazy nor desperate. It seems to me that it's a practical solution to your problem."

"That's not how everyone else sees it."

Zach pretended to ponder the situation. Though he tried not to listen to the rumor mill, he had heard enough to know that Isabelle was doing more than teaching Gunther's daughter. "Surely no one objects to Eva being tutored. Maybe there's something you haven't told me."

Though Gunther had been glaring at him, now he dropped his gaze to the floor. "They might be talking about the fact that I see Isabelle most every day, and sometimes we talk a bit."

"How much would 'a bit' be?" Zach had heard rumors, but rumors were notoriously inaccurate.

Gunther shifted his weight from one foot to the other, clearly unwilling to answer. At last he said, "Most days it's the better part of an hour."

Certainly enough to provoke gossip. "There's no law against that, is there?"

"*Nein.*"

"And friends can talk to friends, can't they?"

"*Ja, aber . . .*" Realizing he was speaking German, Gunther corrected himself, "but . . ." And then he fell silent, as if reluctant to reveal anything more.

"Spit it out."

Gunther raised his head and stared at Zach for a long moment. "Oh, all right. But you can't tell anyone."

"I'm good at keeping secrets." Including several of his own.

"The thing is, I care about Isabelle."

Priscilla would claim that was good news. Zach wasn't so certain. "She's your friend, right?"

"*Ja*, but . . ." There was another long pause. Zach couldn't blame the man. He would have been equally uncomfortable discussing his emotions. "What I feel for her is more than friendship," Gunther admitted. "I've never felt like this, not even with Frieda." Frieda, Zach knew, had been Gunther's first wife. "Maybe I am crazy, because I want to marry Isabelle." Gunther ran a hand through his hair. "You don't need to say anything. I know it's impossible."

This impossible marriage was the one Priscilla and Sarah were promoting. Zach wished he'd refused to become involved, but it was too late. He was involved in the crazy scheme, and since he was, it was his duty to help his friend. "I wouldn't say impossible. Difficult, perhaps, but not impossible." When Gunther's expression brightened, Zach cleared his throat. How could he ask the next question without seeming to pry? Deciding there was no easy way, he blurted it out. "Does she care for you—as more than a friend?"

Clearly uncomfortable, Gunther stared into the distance. "I think so. We haven't said the words, but sometimes when she looks at me, I think she feels the way I do." His voice had softened as he spoke of Isabelle. Now it turned harsh again. "It would never work. Her parents won't let her marry a German. Everyone knows a Frenchwoman can't do that."

And that, of course, was the problem both Zach and Clay

had foreseen when Priscilla and Sarah had hatched their idea. "Maybe not in the Old Country, but this is America. Things are different here." Zach hoped he wasn't simply spouting platitudes. "It's true you'd be the first, and being the first is always difficult." Hadn't he said the same thing to Priscilla when she'd spoken of her desire to become a physician? "But if this is something you want, isn't it worth the effort?" Why hadn't he said that to Priscilla? It wasn't too late for her. Oh, it was true that it would be difficult, particularly after the baby was born, but if practicing medicine would bring her happiness, surely she should pursue it.

A smile lit Gunther's face as he considered a future with Isabelle as his bride. "What must I do?"

Zach was struck by the irony that he, the man who thought he would never marry and whose marriage was unconventional, was counseling a friend on the route to marital bliss. "I imagine she would like to be wooed. Most women do." Gunther nodded, as if he'd heard that before. "One word of advice. Everyone knows you're looking for a new mother for Eva."

"It's more than that."

Gunther's interruption told Zach what he'd hoped to hear. "If you love Isabelle, make sure she knows that's why you're courting her—for herself, not for Eva's sake."

"*Ja. Sehr gut.*" Gunther nodded in agreement. "But how do I do that?"

Zach frowned. What a hypocrite he was, giving advice that he hadn't followed. He hadn't wooed Priscilla, and he certainly hadn't given her any reason to believe he cared for her. As far as Priscilla knew, the only reason Zach had married her was to protect her unborn child. Though that might

217

have been true then, things had changed. The problem was, Zach had no idea how to tell Priscilla that he felt differently. His parents had insisted it was more important to show than to tell, but how did a man do that?

He looked at Gunther and shrugged his shoulders. "I wish I knew."

~

Another dead end. Lawrence drained his glass and plunked it onto the table. Men fitting the description of the Dunkler brothers had been seen approaching Seguin, and so he had followed them, only to discover that they were simply two tall, dark-haired farmers, not the notorious outlaws he sought.

"One more," he agreed when the waitress offered to fill his glass. It wasn't as if he needed his wits about him tonight. The Dunkler brothers were not here, and neither was Jean-Michel Ladre.

Lawrence frowned as he thought of the apparently wily son of Ladreville's founding family. The young whippersnapper was in a heap of trouble. It was bad enough that he'd stolen Albert Monroe's money. The empresario might have agreed to a minor jail sentence for that crime had Jean-Michel not taken the horse. But he had, and Texans were mighty particular about their horses. Still, a healthy number of his father's gold coins might have convinced Monroe that Jean-Michel should not hang. But now there was no chance of clemency. The day the young fool decided to end the peddler's life was the day he signed his own death warrant. One way or another, Jean-Michel Ladre would die.

Lawrence took a swig of his drink. It was odd how it had lost its flavor, almost as odd as the way his life had suddenly seemed devoid of pleasure. A year ago he'd believed there was nothing more rewarding than being a Texas Ranger, but now . . . He tipped the glass and swallowed the last drops. There was no point in wasting good whiskey.

"What else can I get you?" The waitress appeared at his side so quickly that Lawrence suspected she'd been watching him. The way she just happened to brush against his arm and the sultry tone of her voice told him she was offering more than another drink.

"Nothing else." Disappointment dimmed her smile. Lawrence shook his head as he rose. She couldn't help it that her hair was brown, not strawberry blonde. She couldn't help it that she was short and rounded, not tall and slim. She couldn't help it that she wasn't Priscilla. There was only one Priscilla, and she was another man's wife.

His mood decidedly worse than it had been a minute before, Lawrence stalked out of the saloon.

✒

"I bought something for us today."

Priscilla turned and laid the paring knife on the sink. The potatoes could wait. Zach's voice said whatever he had purchased was important. "I didn't know we needed anything."

His lips curved into a smile that made his face even more handsome than normal. "We may not *need* this, but I thought we could use it." Zach stepped outside for a second, returning with his purchase.

"A basket." Constructed of thin slats that had been bent and woven and boasting a sturdy handle, the container was both attractive and practical. It was also the only thing Zach had bought for Priscilla other than her wedding ring. What was the occasion?

"Not just a basket," he said with another smile. "It's a picnic basket. I thought we might go for a picnic after church on Sunday."

A gift and an outing. Priscilla almost clapped her hands with glee. "Thank you, Zach. I haven't been on a picnic since I was a child."

"Then you're overdue."

Though she had worried that rain might spoil the picnic, Sunday dawned clear and sunny. Priscilla had the chicken fried, the biscuits and the dried apple pie baked. All that remained was to pack the basket when they returned from church. She was humming softly as she dressed, wondering what today's sermon would be. Like Sarah and Clay, Priscilla and Zach alternated churches, and this was their week to worship with the Germans. Priscilla knew that for the past four weeks Pastor Sempert had followed his Lenten tradition of preaching about the events that led to Good Friday and Easter Sunday. Which would he choose today?

She and Zach slid into one of the back pews, where they were soon joined by Gunther and Eva. When the little girl nestled close to Priscilla, whispering, "You smell pretty," Priscilla resolved to buy a bottle of toilet water for the child. Perhaps, if everything went the way Sarah hoped, Eva would be able to wear it for her father's wedding to Isabelle.

All thoughts of Gunther and Isabelle fled when the minister climbed into the pulpit. "The Scripture reading for today is Matthew 19, verses 13 through 15." Priscilla blinked. For some reason, Pastor Sempert had deviated from custom, for this passage did not relate to Christ's death. The minister opened his Bible and began to read, "'Then were there brought unto him little children, that he should put his hands on them, and pray; and the disciples rebuked them. But Jesus said, Suffer little children, and forbid them not, to come unto me: for of such is the kingdom of heaven. And he laid his hands on them, and departed thence.'" Pastor Sempert looked out at his congregation. "Today, as we enjoy the beauty of spring and the rebirth of all living things, let us reflect on the blessings our Lord has given us, including the blessing of children."

Priscilla lowered her eyes, unable to meet his gaze. Did he know? Was the message for her? Sarah had told her how one of Pastor Sempert's sermons had led her back to her Savior. Had he somehow guessed that Priscilla was still struggling with the memory of how her child was conceived, and was this his way of comforting her? Whether or not the sermon was directed at her, Priscilla drank in his words, feeling like a flower that had been struggling to survive in parched earth as it received the first drops of spring rain.

"Good sermon." Though she and Zach normally discussed the sermon on their ride home, today he said nothing more. Instead, he changed the subject abruptly, suggesting she wear older clothing for the picnic.

Half an hour later, they were back in the wagon, heading north. When they reached the end of the road, instead of turning right to cross the river, Zach continued on a barely visible track. Though Priscilla knew the ranch extended past the road, she'd never been this far.

"Where are we going?"

"It's supposed to be a surprise," he said as he feigned a frown. "I'm beginning to realize your parents were right in not naming you Patience."

221

She laughed. "It's true. Patience and I were very different. My sister inherited all of our father's patience."

"And what did you get?"

"I'm not sure. Neither of my parents craved adventure the way I do."

Zach slowed the horses as the track worsened. "It appears to me, Mrs. Webster," he said, giving the formal address a joking tone, "that you're on an adventure right now. You're headed for parts unknown."

"Thank you kindly, Mr. Webster, for indulging my fancy."

"I hope you like where we're going." A serious note crept into his voice, as if he were uncertain of her reaction. They'd entered a heavily wooded section of the ranch. Though she found the shade and the cool air refreshing, Pricilla was thankful she was not driving the team. It was clear only a skilled driver could maneuver a wagon between the trees.

"Should we walk?" she suggested.

"Patience, Mrs. Webster. Patience. We're almost there."

A minute later the wagon emerged into a meadow so carpeted with flowers that it appeared blue.

Priscilla caught her breath. "Oh, Zach. It's beautiful!"

He grinned. "They're bluebonnets. You can find patches almost everywhere this time of the year, but this is the biggest one I've seen."

"It's magnificent." When he stopped the wagon, Priscilla climbed out and touched the delicate flowers. "Look. From a distance, I thought they were solid blue, but there are bits of white and yellow on the petals too. And look." She knelt on the ground and pointed to a vibrant red flower. "What's this?"

"Indian paintbrush. I can never decide which one is prettier."

"Luckily you don't need to decide. They're both here, and they're both beautiful." Though Priscilla had seen magnificent gardens in Boston, their beauty paled against this.

Zach nodded as if he'd heard her thoughts. "Sarah and Mrs. Bramble made pretty gardens, but to my mind, nothing compares to this. This is God's garden. And now, Mrs. Webster, it's time for the picnic you promised me." He pulled an old quilt and the basket from the back of the wagon.

Priscilla eyed the quilt and the masses of wildflowers. "I don't want to spread it on the ground. We might hurt the flowers. Maybe we should eat in the wagon."

Zach shook his head. "That's not a picnic. Don't worry. The flowers are sturdier than you think. Besides, the way I figure it, God put them here for us to enjoy."

She couldn't argue with that, and so she helped Zach spread the quilt. As she served the food, Priscilla watched the man she'd married. Perhaps it was the setting, but today he seemed happier than she'd ever seen him. Though his eyes still held sorrow, it seemed to have diminished. "This is a wonderful place," Priscilla said softly. "It's so peaceful here." The only sounds were their breathing, a bird's trilling, and a rodent scurrying through the grass.

"I saw it for the first time last fall when Clay took over the Lazy B. It may sound strange, but I felt at home here."

Priscilla looked around and smiled. "That doesn't sound strange to me. This would be the perfect location for a house." She wondered why the Brambles hadn't chosen it. The meadow was large enough to hold a house, a few outbuildings, and a garden, and if the house were located near the trees, they'd provide shade from the summer sun.

"That's what I thought. At the time I didn't think I'd be staying in Ladreville, but I told myself that if I ever did settle down, it would be in a place like this."

"And now you're going to own it."

A smile creased Zach's face. "God has a way of working things out for us, doesn't he? If he hadn't sent you here, I wouldn't have a house of my own and a family to make that house a home."

He was venturing into dangerous waters. Though they'd spoken of many things, they had not revisited the reason for their marriage. Priscilla knew that she had changed, that her feelings had altered. Had his? There was only one way to know. "Then you're content with our arrangement?"

"Yes." He answered without hesitation, but his eyes darkened and his expression was solemn as he turned to her. "And you?"

Priscilla nodded. She had sought reassurance, and so, it appeared, did Zach. "Four months ago I would not have dreamt that I'd be saying this, but yes, I am content. I've come to love Ladreville. Somehow it feels more like home than Boston ever did." She paused, then laid her hand on her stomach. It was time to tell Zach how she felt. She wouldn't embarrass him with words like love, for she wasn't certain that was what she felt, but she could talk to him about the baby. "Thank you for marrying me and accepting my child. If it weren't for you, I know I wouldn't be able to say this, but I'm looking forward to the baby . . . our baby."

12

If there was one thing Isabelle did not like, it was rainy days. There were fewer customers when it rained, and those who came were almost invariably grumpy, acting as if she were somehow to blame for the inclement weather. To make things worse, Karl Friedrich, the farmer who had hired her brother Léon to help with his crops, had no work for Léon today, and so her brother was stomping around the store, muttering that the shelves weren't stocked properly and that she hadn't displayed the ribbons to their advantage. As if he knew anything about ribbons. He was simply grousing because he hated being indoors. Today, so did she.

"What you need is to do something useful."

"Just what would you suggest?" Léon spat the words at her.

"You can mind the store while I go out." Isabelle reached for her umbrella.

Her brother stared at her as if she had suddenly lost her mind. "Are you crazy? It's raining."

"I am well aware of that." Maman would fuss about damp shoes and skirts, which she claimed led to the grippe. She would probably echo Léon's words and claim that Isabelle was crazy to walk in the rain, but at least she wouldn't be complaining about Gunther. Though Maman had had nothing but kind words for him last summer when he was courting Sarah, now not a meal passed without at least one disparaging comment.

"You'll catch your death out there."

Ignoring her brother's dire predictions, Isabelle opened the door and unfurled her umbrella. The rain, though still a steady downpour, was less intense than it had been half an hour before. Admittedly, it was not the ideal day for a stroll, but she'd be sheltered once she reached her destination: the town's open air market. All the vendors had tents over their tables. In the summer, the tents provided shade from the hot Texas sun. Today they'd keep the rain off customers as well as their merchandise.

Though water seeped inside her shoes, Isabelle smiled, thinking of the first table she would visit. Frau Bauer's unique jewelry, consisting of natural materials, had long intrigued her. When she'd come into the mercantile earlier that week, the German matron had mentioned the new style of jewelry she had made. Instead of using pinecones, as she usually did, these were fashioned from dried seeds. "Some of them look almost like pearls," she had explained. Isabelle smiled again. Admiring Frau Bauer's craftsmanship and perhaps buying a piece would surely lift her spirits.

As her feet squished and rain sluiced off her umbrella, Isabelle turned onto rue de la Seine, quickly covering the short block to rue du Marché. Though the market that had given the street its name was located directly behind her family's store, a tall wooden fence separated the lots. As she turned into the market grounds, Isabelle stopped abruptly, astonished by the sight of the man who was striding toward her. Why was he here?

"Isabelle!" Gunther sounded as surprised as she. "What are you doing out in this weather?" Unlike her brother's, Gunther's voice held no disdain. Instead, he grinned and his eyes sparkled as he juggled a package and his umbrella so he could doff his hat for her. No man could be more courtly than Gunther Lehman. That was one of the things she loved—she *liked*, Isabelle corrected herself quickly—about him.

"I could ask you the same question." Though she tried to keep her voice level, Isabelle's heart was racing, and she could feel blood rush to her face at the silly direction her mind had taken. This was Gunther, her friend, she reminded herself. No matter what hopes she might harbor, he had never crossed the boundaries of friendship.

If he noticed her discomfiture, Gunther gave no sign. Instead, he shrugged and answered her question. "No one wants grain milled today."

"No one wants to shop at the mercantile, either." Isabelle looked around the market. Though several of the tents were empty, the majority of tables were as filled with merchandise as on a sunny day. "I'm surprised to see so many vendors." The weather seemed to have discouraged all but a dozen customers. If she hadn't been restless, Isabelle would not have come. As for Gunther, she could not imagine what had brought him to the market today. The package he had tucked underneath his arm was too small to be bread or other foodstuffs.

He shrugged again as he looked at the tables laden with

227

goods. "I suppose a few sales are better than none at all." He paused, as if unsure what to do. Isabelle shared the feeling. Gunther had been headed in the opposite direction, probably going home, when she had arrived. She could hardly expect him to prolong his time in the rain. And yet, though the weather was less than conducive to conversation, she didn't want him to leave. They had so few opportunities to talk without every word being overheard. Despite the rain and the discomfort it brought, she and Gunther had a modicum of privacy here.

Gunther's eyes seemed to reflect some of the same ambivalence. "May I accompany you?"

Though her heart leapt with pleasure, Isabelle had to caution him. "You may find it boring." Léon and her father certainly would. "I came to see Frau Bauer's new designs."

Gunther reddened and glanced at his package. "Oh . . . well . . . um . . ." He stared at the ground as if he expected to see the words that eluded him written on it. At last he raised his eyes to meet Isabelle's. "Perhaps you shouldn't go there."

"Why ever not?"

"Because . . . um . . ." Gunther took a deep breath, then looked around. Was he worried that they would be overheard? Though the ten or so vendors who'd brought their wares to the marketplace had undoubtedly noticed Gunther and Isabelle's arrival, no one was close enough to hear them. Gunther shook his head slowly. "This isn't the place I would have chosen, but . . ." He pulled out the package that he'd been cradling next to his body and handed it to Isabelle, his face reddening again as he said, "I thought you might like this."

For a second Isabelle was speechless. "A gift? For me?"

It was embarrassing the way her voice squeaked. Gunther would surely realize this was the first time a gentleman had offered her a present.

He nodded solemnly, though his lips quivered as if he were trying not to smile. "That's what I said. You needn't worry, though. It's not a hog."

"I can see that." Isabelle smiled as she recalled Gunther's telling her that when he'd courted his wife, he'd given her a hog. Courting? Is that what he was doing? Isabelle's heart skipped a beat, then sank. Gunther couldn't be courting her, for he hadn't asked Papa's permission. Not that that would have accomplished anything, for Papa would have refused, just as she ought to refuse Gunther's gift. It wasn't seemly to accept a present from a man unless he was courting, and even then society dictated which gifts a lady could accept. Isabelle looked at the package, knowing she should not open it. And yet . . .

"Let's sit down." Gunther led the way to one of the empty tents and pulled out a bench. "There. That's better than standing, isn't it?"

It was. No longer separated by the expanse of their umbrellas, Isabelle could feel the warmth of Gunther's body as he sat next to her. Perhaps it was only chance, although Isabelle doubted that, for Gunther did nothing by chance, but he'd seated them so their backs were to the vendors. Though everyone in Ladreville would soon know that she and Gunther had been seen together, the details of their meeting were hidden.

Gunther cleared his throat and gestured toward the package she held. "I hope you like it. I told the person who sold it to me that it was a thank-you for teaching Eva, but that was a lie.

This has nothing to do with Eva. This is for you, because . . ." Gunther's voice faltered, and he stared at the ground again. When he raised his eyes to meet hers, color flooded his cheeks. "I like you," he said. "That's why I bought this for you."

"I like you too." With fingers that refused her command not to tremble, Isabelle untied the twine and spread the paper, gasping when she saw what was inside. "Oh, Gunther, it's beautiful!" No wonder he had not wanted her to visit Frau Bauer's tent. He had given her an exquisitely formed necklace made of seeds glued onto bits of pinecone. It could only be Frau Bauer's work.

Isabelle's heart sank. Maman would never allow her to keep this. It was a personal item, a gift only a husband should offer. She started to refuse it, then shook herself mentally. Gunther would be hurt, deeply hurt, if she did not accept his gift. No matter what Maman said, Isabelle would not hurt Gunther. She fingered the delicate necklace, then looked up at the wonderful man who'd chosen it for her. "How did you know I like these?"

"I remembered you gave Sarah one for her birthday, but I've never seen you wearing one."

Isabelle blinked in astonishment that Gunther had noticed her jewelry. Men, she thought, were oblivious to things like that. "This must be the prettiest necklace Frau Bauer has ever made."

"She said you'd like it."

"Oh, I do." It wasn't simply the necklace. What warmed Isabelle's heart even more than the beautiful creation were the words Gunther had spoken. He liked her! She smiled at him, hoping he could read the happiness in her eyes. "Thank you for such a wonderful gift. I'll wear it on Easter."

As she returned to the mercantile, Isabelle knew she would never again hate rainy days.

⮜⮞

"Are you ready?" Zach's voice was so close that Priscilla guessed he was standing outside her door.

"Almost." She straightened her hat again, wanting everything to be perfect this morning. Though she had let out some seams, her clothing fit a bit more snugly than it had in January, but she doubted anyone would guess that she was with child, especially when she wore this hat. The leghorn was trimmed with a veil and multi-colored ribbons in a style Isabelle had found in Frank Leslie's *Gazette of Fashion*. According to Isabelle, it was the latest style and perfectly suited for the occasion. Priscilla thought so too, for it would keep everyone's attention focused on her head.

"I've never celebrated Easter like this," she told Zach as they crossed the river. This was the first time she'd left home in darkness.

"That's because you've never lived in a small town before."

Though Priscilla suspected that Ladreville, with its mixture of settlers, was different from other small Texas towns, that mattered not a whit. What mattered was that she was looking forward to the day. Easter had always been her favorite holiday, and this day was extra special, for this was her first Easter as a married woman, a Texan, and—most importantly—a mother-to be. The message of rebirth that was such a vital part of Easter held more poignancy than normal as Priscilla reflected on God's gift to her. He had known how she had dreamt of holding a child of her own, even when she had been

231

convinced she would never find the man God had intended for her husband. Despite the circumstances of the baby's conception, God was making her dream come true.

"You'll like our celebration," Zach had predicted when he had explained that a sunrise service and breakfast for the entire community would be held in the open field where the Independence Day celebrations took place each July. Following that, the townspeople would enter their individual churches for another hour of worship. While Sarah and Clay went to the German church, Priscilla and Zach would attend the French service. Afterwards, they were invited to the Bar C for dinner and what Sarah apologetically called an afternoon of Thea's antics.

Though the sun had not yet risen when they reached the field, the pre-dawn sky was light enough for Priscilla to identify people. The scene was almost eerie, with hundreds of people gathered in silence. Even the children seemed to understand and stood quietly at their parents' side. While the congregation of Priscilla's church in Boston had greeted each other with the traditional "He is risen" on Easter morning, Zach explained that the people of Ladreville did not speak until after the sunrise service. They came together in quiet contemplation, remembering the sorrow that had brought Mary and the other women to the tomb that first Easter Sunday. It was only after the minister proclaimed the angel's words that they would speak.

Priscilla looked around. Though she knew few of the townspeople by name, she recognized many faces from the times she and Zach had attended church. Yvonne and Neville were on the opposite side of the field, flanked by Granny Menger and Frau Bauer. It appeared that Zach was right and the town's differences were forgotten, at least momentarily.

Isabelle and her family stood a few feet away from Priscilla and Zach, their posture announcing that something was wrong, something that Priscilla suspected had nothing to do with the holy day. Isabelle's face seemed strained, and her parents' mouths were pursed in disapproval. The reason for the disapproval wasn't difficult to find, for both of the elder Rousseaus glared at Gunther when he and Eva made their way to Isabelle's side. Priscilla was certain it was only the tradition of silence that prevented angry words from being exchanged. A moment later, Gunther and Eva moved on, settling on the opposite side. Zach had been wrong. Not all differences were resolved by Easter joy.

"Dearly beloved, we gather here to celebrate the most wonderful gift we or anyone have ever received." The two ministers took their place on a small platform and addressed the townspeople. "Today we shall read from the gospel according to Mark." Alternating verses, the men recounted the story of the first Easter morning, ending with, "And he saith unto them, Be not affrighted: Ye seek Jesus of Nazareth, which was crucified: he is risen; he is not here."

As with a single voice, the congregation shouted, "He is risen!" The wondrous words that filled her heart with joy each time she heard them washed over Priscilla, sending shivers down her spine. This truly was a day of miracles.

The early service concluded with a hymn and a final prayer, leaving the townspeople to make their way to the long tables now laden with breakfast. Perhaps it was in reaction to the silence, but the crowd seemed louder than normal, and they jostled each other in their eagerness to reach the food. Priscilla flinched at the unwanted touches and edged her way to the perimeter.

"I'm sorry, Zach," she said as he made a path for her. It had been months since she'd been attacked. Surely by now she should have recovered, and yet she had not. Just the thought of a man's touch made her cringe, and actual contact caused her stomach to roil.

Zach's smile was reassuring. "I understand." He must, for somehow he managed to part the crowds without touching her. Was this how Moses parted the Red Sea?

They were nearing the edge of the crowd when Priscilla saw Gunther approach Isabelle. His determined gait made Priscilla realize he would not be discouraged by the Rousseaus' disapproval.

"You wore it." The miller's face was wreathed with happiness, and though Isabelle's parents were close by, he appeared oblivious to them.

Isabelle fingered her necklace, a lovely combination of pinecones and seeds. This must be the "it" that had caused Gunther's happiness. "I promised you I would." Isabelle returned his smile, but it faded an instant later as her mother grabbed her arm.

"Isabelle, come here." Madame Rousseau's normally pleasant voice was tinged with anger. "Your place is with your family."

"Yes, Maman."

When they were far enough away that their words would not be overheard, Priscilla looked up at Zach. "It doesn't sound as if Isabelle's parents are happy with Gunther's courtship."

Zach shook his head and gestured toward Gunther, who was now surrounded by a group of men. "Looks like Gunther is being subjected to a harangue."

Priscilla's attention was drawn to his daughter, who stood at his side, her eyes closed as if she were trying not to cry. "Poor Eva. Those men are spoiling what should be the most joyous day of the year."

Zach frowned. "I'll see what I can do."

As he strode toward the men, Priscilla made her way to Isabelle. "Are you all right?" she asked, turning so that Madame Rousseau could not read her lips.

Isabelle shook her head. "No. Maman is angry because I'm wearing this necklace." Once again she fingered the offending piece of jewelry. "She hates it because Gunther gave it to me."

Isabelle's motion triggered memories of the hundreds of times Priscilla had touched her locket. Never again. Like so much else, that was lost. She swallowed deeply, resolving not to let her own dismay affect her friend. The locket wasn't important. Isabelle's happiness was. "I wish I could help you."

Isabelle shook her head. "It's what I was afraid of. No one can help."

That evening when she and Zach were back at the Lazy B, Priscilla broached the subject. "There must be something we can do. Isabelle's parents are making her miserable."

Zach's blue eyes darkened as he accepted the glass of buttermilk Priscilla had poured. "Gunther's friends are just as bad."

Priscilla took her seat across the table from Zach. "You and Sarah warned me about the town's divisions, but I never thought people would be so cruel. Especially on Easter." Somehow the fact that the unpleasantness had occurred on this holy day made it seem worse. "Even Yvonne made a nasty comment, and she's one of Isabelle's closest friends."

Zach emptied his glass before he spoke. "The town's prejudices are deep-seated. According to Clay, things are improving, but I'm afraid the distrust won't disappear completely for a long time. It was one thing to allow the children to attend school together, but it's quite another to sanction a marriage."

That might be true, but seeing the way Gunther and Isabelle had looked at each other convinced Priscilla they loved each other. "I still want to help them," she told Zach.

"So do I. Let's pray that God shows us the way."

The morning mist had evaporated; the sun was shining; it was a perfect April day. Though Easter Monday, as she'd heard it called, was a holiday in some countries, it was work as usual on the Lazy B. Priscilla smiled and began to hum as she pulled out the ingredients for gingerbread. Supper today would be simple: scalloped potatoes with leftover ham that Martina had sent home with her. But with the still-warm gingerbread, it would be a meal Zach could enjoy. The first time Priscilla had made gingerbread, he'd admitted it was a childhood favorite. That was one of the reasons she was serving it today. If Zach's stomach was content, perhaps his mind would find a way to help Isabelle and Gunther.

Priscilla had spent the day pondering the problem and had resolved nothing, yet she knew there must be a way to convince the town—and, more importantly, Isabelle's parents—to approve the marriage. It should be obvious to anyone who knew them that they belonged together. Priscilla had seen the sparks that flew between them. Furthermore, Sarah claimed that Gunther looked different when he was with Isabelle. She said the smiles he gave her were unlike those he had offered to either her or Olga Kaltheimer. The reason, according to Sarah, was that this time Gunther was in love. He now sought a wife, not simply a mother for Eva.

Priscilla continued humming, her mind whirling with ideas, as she reached for the molasses. She was measuring the thick sweetener when the pain struck. Gasping at the cramp that literally stole her breath, she doubled over and clutched her stomach. *Oh no! Please, God, no!* The pain was sharper than anything she had ever experienced, so intense that stars danced before her eyes. *No!* she cried as another cramp, far stronger than the last, clawed at her insides. *Help me!* And then she felt it. At first it was a trickle, but as she looked down and saw the pool of red at her feet, it increased. *Oh no! The baby!* Something was desperately wrong with her baby.

Trembling with fear, Priscilla staggered to a chair. What could she do? The bleeding was faster now, a steady stream. She needed help, but there was no one nearby, no one she could call. Granny Menger or Clay would know what to do, but she had no way to reach them. Priscilla's legs no longer supported her, her arms were shaking so badly she could not control a horse, and still the bleeding continued.

Come home, Zach. Come home. She whispered the words as she crawled toward the bedroom. Perhaps if she lay down, the bleeding would stop. Her mind moved as sluggishly as her arms and legs. There was something else, something Papa had told her. What was it? Elevation. The word drifted into her brain. That was it. Papa had said it was important to raise a woman's legs if she was bleeding. How could she do that?

Priscilla touched her forehead, wondering why she was unable to find the answer to a simple question. Had the morning fog returned? Was that the reason everything looked so strange? And why wouldn't her legs move? She was trying to crawl, but her arms and legs remained limp. Priscilla felt tears trickle down her cheeks. Where was Zach? He could help her.

"Priscilla, what's wrong?"

From a distance she heard a man's voice. Zach. He'd come home. Why was he here, and why was the room so cold?

"Priscilla." She heard his voice again. Priscilla knew she ought to open her eyes, but she couldn't, for her eyelids were too heavy, and she was cold, so very cold.

"Priscilla, look at me." His voice was stronger now. Surely she could do what he asked. Though it took every ounce of strength she possessed, Priscilla forced her eyes open.

"What's wrong?"

His words echoed inside her head, and for a moment she could not answer. Something was wrong, but what? Then memory slammed through her. Pain. Blood. Cold. "I lost the baby."

Zach muttered something under his breath. Then he slipped an arm around her. Priscilla moved instinctively, pressing closer to the warmth. "You need a doctor." Zach was speaking again. "I'll take you to Clay."

She shook her head. "Can't move. Too much bleeding."

"Then I'll summon Clay."

He was leaving. She couldn't let him leave. He was warm. He could help her. "Don't go. It's so dark. Oh, Zach, I'm afraid."

"One minute. You can hold on for one more minute. I'll be right back."

She heard heavy footsteps and Zach's voice yelling for their hired hand. A moment later, he was at her side. "Myron will get Clay. He'll help you. You'll be fine, Priscilla."

But his words were fading, and the darkness was growing thicker. "It's too late." Darkness overtook her.

⁓

"Wake up, Priscilla. Wake up." Zach stared at the woman who lay sprawled on the floor, her skirts bloodied, her face deathly pale. If he lived to be a hundred, he knew he would never forget the way his heart had stopped when he'd entered the house and seen her lying there. Nothing, not even the horrors of Perote or the nightmares that continued to plague him, had prepared him for the sheer terror of seeing his wife on the floor, her lifeblood ebbing away.

"Priscilla, wake up." But she wasn't sleeping. Zach knew that, just as he knew his life would be irrevocably changed if she died. "You can't leave me. You can't." Though he wanted to lift her onto the bed in hopes that she would be more comfortable, he dared not, lest the movement increase her bleeding. Priscilla had said she could not move, and so he would do nothing until Clay arrived. Still, she looked pale and cold, even colder than he was when in the nightmare's grip. Zach clenched his fists. How he hated being powerless! There must be something he could do to help Priscilla.

He looked around, his eyes lighting on the bed. Yanking the coverlet off it, he wrapped it around her. It wasn't much, but it might retain what little warmth she still possessed. There had to be more. As Zach folded his hands to pray, he nodded. There was something he could do. Priscilla hadn't pulled away in fear when he'd touched her before. Instead,

239

she had snuggled closer to him as if seeking his warmth. He could give her that. Zach lowered himself to the floor and lay next to Priscilla, gathering her into his arms. Perhaps his body heat would help her. It was all he had.

He closed his eyes, not wanting to think that Clay might be too late. *Dear Lord,* he prayed, *keep her safe.*

Heavy footsteps signaled Clay's arrival. Zach rose to greet his friend, wincing when he saw Clay's expression. If he'd had any doubt of the seriousness of Priscilla's condition, Clay's frown would have banished it. "I need to examine her." Clay opened his bag. "I'll call you when I'm done."

Though his watch claimed that only a few minutes had passed before Clay summoned him, Zach felt as if he'd waited for hours. When he returned to the bedroom, he found Clay had placed Priscilla on the bed, covering all but her face. Though she was breathing, Zach didn't need to be a doctor to know that the breathing was not normal. It was slow and so thin that each time, he feared it was the last.

"She's lost the baby."

Zach nodded. "That's what she thought."

"She's also lost a lot of blood."

"But she'll be all right, won't she?"

Clay's lips thinned as he laid a hand on Zach's shoulder. "I wish I could promise that, but the truth is, I don't know. I've done everything I can. It's up to God now."

This was what Zach had feared from the moment he'd found Priscilla crumpled on the floor. The woman who had brought joy back into his life was facing death. He lowered his eyes, lest his friend see his anguish. "I'd like to be alone with her."

Clay seemed to understand. "I'll wait in the parlor." Gently, he closed the door behind him, leaving Zach alone with his wife.

"Oh, Priscilla." Zach knelt next to the bed and reached under the coverlet for her hand. Though he couldn't explain it, he felt compelled to touch the woman who had once shied from his touch. His heart thudded with dread as he looked at her hand. It was so fragile, the ring he'd placed on it seeming to weigh it down. Poor Priscilla. She'd lost so much. First her sister, then her parents, now the baby. Could it be time for her suffering to end?

Zach bit the inside of his cheek, trying to control his emotions as he considered the possibility. He knew that death was not the end but the beginning, the ultimate healing. God would heal Priscilla. She would be reunited with her loved ones. How could he not want that for her? It was only he who would suffer. His life would be empty if Priscilla were no longer part of it. Zach stared at her face. Never, not even the first day when she'd arrived at the Bar C, had it been so pale. And now . . . now it looked drained of blood, drained of life.

Tears welled in his eyes as he thought of the day they were married and how brave Priscilla had been, allowing him to slip the ring on her finger. They'd promised to love and honor until death parted them. Surely it was too soon for that. Zach brushed the tears away. He wouldn't waste precious minutes weeping. If all he had were a few more hours with Priscilla, he would spend them remembering the times she had laughed. He drew her hand to his lips and pressed a kiss on it.

Was this part of God's plan? He had brought Priscilla into Zach's life for a reason. Zach was certain of that. In the few months that he'd known her, Priscilla had become the most important part of his life. He cared for her. He wanted her to be happy. Zach inhaled sharply as another thought assailed him. *I love her.* The vows he'd taken hadn't been empty words. He loved, honored, and cherished this woman. And, though it might be selfish, he did not want to lose her.

Keeping her hand between both of his, Zach bowed his head in prayer. "Dear Lord, you know what's in my heart. You know what I'm about to ask. I know that Priscilla is a gift from you. I beg you, let her live." Zach felt Priscilla's hand move. It was the slightest of movements, and yet it felt as if she wanted to clasp his hand but lacked the strength. "I'm not worthy of her love, but you know that I do love her." The tears were streaming down Zach's face unchecked. "I know that you have plans for us, and that your plans are good. If you take her, I will try to understand, but I pray that you will heal Priscilla so that I can give her the love you've put inside me. Please, Lord, spare the woman I love."

There was no answer, no change in Priscilla's condition, but the anguish Zach felt began to subside, replaced with the greatest calm he had ever felt. Whatever happened, he knew he'd been given the strength to bear it.

13

It was cheap whiskey. Jean-Michel scowled as the liquid burned his throat. He was accustomed to far better, but this rotgut was all the saloon offered, or so the proprietor claimed. He looked around the smoky room. He'd chosen this establishment over its four competitors because it had the air of a place where questions were neither asked nor answered. Though he doubted anyone in the state of Texas was smart enough to connect him with the peddler's death, Jean-Michel was taking no chances. No, sirree. He couldn't afford to run into a lawman.

There were none of them in sight. A couple white-haired men bellied up to the bar, but other than Jean-Michel, no one sat at a table the way a lawman would. Jean-Michel had chosen a table in the far corner where he could watch everyone. That was what a smart man did, and he was the smartest of the smart. That was why he was heading back to Ladreville to marry the prettiest gal in town.

He took another swallow as his thoughts turned to his

destination and his bride-to-be. They wouldn't stay there. One rainy day when he'd been holed up in a stable, he'd realized there was no reason to remain in his parents' town. He and Isabelle deserved more than life in a small Texas town. A man of his stature, particularly one with a beautiful wife, ought to live in a city, surrounded by the accoutrements of wealth. New York, Philadelphia, Boston. Why, he and Isabelle might even go to Paris. Of course. Paris. That was where they belonged.

"Another." Jean-Michel had lost count of the number of glasses the bartender had put in front of him. Maybe this one would taste better than the rest.

As the door opened and a gust of wind cleared the air, he blinked. It couldn't be. What was Zach Webster doing here? Jean-Michel blinked again and rubbed his eyes. Two? Why was he seeing two of Zach? How was he going to kill two of him?

"This way, Chet."

Jean-Michel took a deep breath and started to relax when he realized that he wasn't seeing double. There were two men, and neither one was Zach Webster, though to Jean-Michel's eyes, they looked enough like Zach to be his brothers.

"Hey, pardner, what you drinkin'?" the man called Chet asked as he and the other dark-haired man pulled out chairs. Though they had the whole room to choose from, they'd picked the table next to him. It wasn't hard to figure out the reason. They knew a man of quality when they saw him.

"Whiskey." Jean-Michel considered giving the men his opinion of the vile liquid but thought the better of it. There was no point in riling the proprietor and giving him a reason to remember the man who maligned his liquor.

"Well, Jake," Chet said to his companion, "it looks like we're drinkin' whiskey tonight."

They might not be Zach's brothers, but these two men were brothers. Jean-Michel would stake a pretty sum on that. "Where you heading?" he asked.

"Who wants to know?"

"Jean-Michel Ladre." Now, where did that come from? Hadn't he told himself he couldn't let anyone know his name?

"Well, Jean-Michel Ladre," the brother named Chet said, "what do you say we share a bottle?" Without waiting for an answer, the two men dragged their chairs to Jean-Michel's table. "I'm Chet, and this here's my brother Jake. Dunkler," he added.

The man acted as if Jean-Michel should recognize the name. Though he didn't, he nodded. A smart man didn't disagree with anyone, leastwise not men who looked as tough as these two did.

"Them's mighty fine boots you got," Jake said with an odd look at his brother.

"You got a saddle to match them?" Chet asked.

Jean-Michel nodded and puffed out his chest. It was clear the Dunkler brothers recognized him for what he was: a man of consequence. He felt inside his shirt for the sack of gold. "Let me show you what else I've got."

⁓

"Clay says it's a miracle you're alive." Sarah's eyes were serious as she urged Priscilla to take a spoonful of chicken broth.

Four days had passed since Priscilla had lost the baby, four days in which Sarah had come to the Lazy B before and after school, bringing food and doing her best to cheer Priscilla. Her efforts, though well-intentioned, had failed. Not even the vibrant blue of the Texas sky and the sight of puffy cumulus clouds which had always brought joy to Priscilla's heart had penetrated the miasma of despair.

"I wish I had died." Life here on the Lazy B, the future she had planned, her marriage to Zach—none of it made any sense now that there would be no child.

Sarah shook her head and drew a chair next to the bed. "I thank God you didn't. You're my friend, and I don't want to lose you." She patted Priscilla's hand in a gesture that was meant to comfort. Like her cheerful words and chicken soup, it failed. Sarah's eyes were somber as she said, "I believe God has a plan for all of us. I don't know why he took your baby, but maybe he will give you another one, one that's Zach's as well as yours."

"No!" The word came out with more force than Priscilla had intended. There would be no second baby. Never, ever. She would die before she'd endure what her mother had referred to as the marriage act. Priscilla closed her eyes as the memories she had tried so desperately to repress rushed through her. The pain, the shame, the horrible, horrible feeling of being unclean. It didn't matter that Zach was not Zeke. It didn't matter that she harbored gentle feelings for him, that she might even love him. Nothing mattered but the fact that Priscilla would never let a man touch her that way. This had been her one chance at motherhood, and she'd lost it. God had ended her dream of a child to love and nurture just as he'd taken Patience and her parents. Thanks to him, the future looked bleak. There was no reason left to live, but still she lived. Endured was more like it.

"Zach's a good man. He cares for you." Sarah reached behind her for the tray she'd placed on the table and handed Priscilla a glass of milk. "Drink this."

It was easier to obey than to argue with Sarah. Priscilla took a sip. "I know Zach's a good man," she said as she wrapped both hands around the glass, lest, in her weakness, she drop it. She cared about Zach; she wanted him to have a life filled with love. That was why she had to release him from this charade of a marriage. Unbidden, tears began to spill down Priscilla's cheeks.

Sarah wrapped an arm around her shoulders. "It's all right to cry," she said softly. "Tears can help."

Nothing would fill the emptiness deep inside her.

๛

Zach was not enjoying his ride, and Charcoal sensed it. The stallion was restive and balked more than usual when they reached the river. "C'mon, boy. Charlotte's waiting for her money." It was time for him to send her the monthly package. Normally, a trip into Ladreville was a treat for Zach, but today was different. Today worries about Priscilla over-shadowed everything, even the fact that there'd probably be a letter from Charlotte Tallman, telling him of Joshua's latest exploits.

Though it sounded as if the boy was a bit of a scamp, Charlotte invariably excused his hijinks, claiming they were nothing more than mischief and exuberance. A man didn't have to read between the lines to know Charlotte loved her son. Each word she penned made that evident. She was born to be a mother, just as Priscilla was. But now Priscilla's child was gone, and she was suffering.

Clay claimed sorrow was normal, and Zach wouldn't dispute that. Anyone would mourn the loss of a child. He did. But Priscilla's mourning wasn't normal. She was in a funk, unable to find pleasure in anything. This was far worse than when she first came to Ladreville. He'd seen her despair then, and it had been mild compared to this. Then she had at least pretended to have a normal life. She'd dressed, eaten meals, spoken with others. Now she would not leave her bed, and that worried Zach.

He feared that Priscilla's current mood was dangerous. Clay was a talented physician, but he had no experience with suffering and despair so deep that they made life untenable. Zach did. He'd known those dark moments of the soul when nothing seemed worthwhile. He'd reached the bottom of the pit in Perote and, had it not been for Clay's father, Zach would have taken his own life and spent eternity in hell. Somehow, someway he had to keep Priscilla from reaching that point. But first he had to send Charlotte her money.

Zach dismounted and tied Charcoal to a hitching post. If he did not tarry, he could be home within an hour.

"You look as miserable as I feel." Gunther crossed the street and joined Zach in front of the post office. "What's wrong with you?"

Despite his reluctance to prolong his time in town, Zach would not ignore his friend. "Priscilla's ill."

Gunther scuffed his boot on the ground, clearly uneasy with a discussion of female ailments. "I heard about the baby." He raised his head and looked at Zach. "Was it yours?"

Zach took a deep breath, trying to control his anger. Though he'd told Priscilla the townspeople would not openly speculate about the baby's father, it appeared he had been wrong. Or perhaps it was only because Gunther was a friend that he felt free to pose the question. Still, the fact that he had asked rankled.

There was only one possible response. "Yes, it was mine." In every way that mattered.

"Then it's a pity she lost it."

As Gunther's words registered, the anger Zach had tried to tamp down flared. How dare Gunther say that? How dare he insinuate that the child would have been less worthy of life if it had been fathered by a bandit? Zach fisted his hands and took a step forward. There was nothing he wanted more than to plant a fist on Gunther's face. He stopped abruptly and forced his hands to relax. Hitting Gunther would solve nothing. It would only confirm the town's speculation and make Priscilla's situation more difficult. The simple fact was, the baby's parentage was of no importance. All that mattered was Priscilla.

"I'm worried about her," he said, ignoring Gunther's last statement.

"Women are funny creatures. After Eva was born, Frieda spent days crying. She couldn't explain it, and I sure couldn't understand what was wrong. There we were with a beautiful, healthy baby and she had turned into a watering pot."

Zach wondered if there was something in the female constitution that made them prone to tears. Although he supposed that was possible, Priscilla wasn't given to fits of weeping. In fact, the only time he'd seen her cry had been over the loss of her locket. But she was grieving now. "What ended it?"

Gunther tipped his hat as a woman left the post office. When she was out of earshot, he said, "I wish I knew. One day Frieda woke up happy. The tears were gone. Mark my words. You'll soon have your cheerful wife back."

"I hope so." But in the meantime, he had to find a way to comfort Priscilla.

"At least you have a wife." Gunther glanced down the street as he had at least a dozen times before. Though Zach doubted he'd admit it, his friend was watching the mercantile, perhaps looking for Isabelle. "I tell you, Zach, this courting business is harder than I imagined."

"You making any progress?"

Gunther scowled, then looked back at the mercantile. "Only if you count going backwards progress. I talked to Isabelle's father last night. I figured that when I told him I loved his daughter, he'd forget I was German and agree that I could marry her." Gunther's scowl darkened. "I was wrong. Dead wrong. Monsieur Rousseau told me I wasn't worthy of Isabelle and never would be." Gunther kicked a pebble, waiting until it had stopped rolling before he spoke. "I don't know what to do next."

Though he was anxious to finish his errands and return home, Zach couldn't abandon his friend without suggesting one last course of action. "You could marry without her father's approval."

Gunther shook his head, confirming Zach's belief that he wouldn't like the final resort. "I can't do that to Isabelle. She loves her parents. If we married without their blessing, I'd be putting a barrier between her and them. I can't do that."

"Then what are you going to do?"

"I don't know."

That made two of them.

❦

Priscilla clasped her hands, trying to hide their trembling.

Today had been the first day she'd remained out of bed all day. Now that her strength was returning, she could delay no more. She knew what had to be done and had been rehearsing her words all day, hoping to deliver them without betraying her true feelings. The time had come.

"Zach, we need to talk." She'd waited until supper was over to broach the subject. With the dishes stacked, ready for the woman who'd been hired to cook until Priscilla regained her strength, she was as ready as she'd ever be. She closed the front door behind her and took a step toward her husband, who was sitting on the steps, staring into the distance. At her words, he rose.

"What did I do wrong this time?"

"You?" Priscilla blinked in confusion. "You did nothing wrong. Why would you think that?"

Zach gestured toward the swing and waited until she was seated before he perched on the railing opposite her. "You were so serious. When my mother sounded like that, usually she'd discovered one of my misdeeds. I soon learned that tone of voice was not good news."

"What I have to say is." For him. One of the things Priscilla had decided as she'd lain in bed trying to accept the loss of her child was that she wouldn't think about her future. What mattered was Zach's. "I want you to know that I appreciate everything you've done for me." Was that really her voice? It was like a stranger's, the phrases stilted. Surely she hadn't sounded so awful when she'd practiced.

"There's no need for thanks." Zach did not share her problem. His voice was normal, warm and filled with the kindness that was one of his finest characteristics. "You're my wife. I've only done what any husband would."

"That's what we need to talk about." Priscilla saw a question in his eyes and held up her hand to forestall him. "Please don't interrupt. This is difficult enough as it is." She took a deep breath, then let it out. "I've had a lot of time to think." That had been one of the worst parts of her recuperation, the endless hours with nothing but thoughts for company. She took another breath, preparing to deliver the speech. Once she started, she would not pause for fear that she would be unable to continue. This was what was best for Zach, she reminded herself. It was what he deserved.

Priscilla opened her mouth and let the words tumble out. "Everything has changed. With the baby gone, there's no reason for our marriage. You no longer need to protect me. Since ours was never a real marriage, it can be annulled. I think that's what you should do."

As she pronounced the final word, Priscilla stared at the man she'd married, the man who had been unfailingly kind to her. While she'd been speaking, the blood had drained from his face, leaving it gaunt and gray. "Is that what you want?" Zach's voice cracked as he spoke the words, and he sounded like an old man.

Priscilla wouldn't lie. She wouldn't pretend an annulment was what she wanted. "It would be best for you," she countered. "That way you'd be free to have a real marriage with a woman you loved." Zach deserved to have children, and that was something she could not give him.

As color began to return to his face, he narrowed his eyes and gave her a piercing look. "What about you? What would you do?"

"I don't know." Once again she would not lie. In her thoughts, the future loomed before her, dark and empty. She couldn't admit that, for Zach—kind, considerate Zach—would seize on it as a reason to remain in their sham of a marriage. He would insist on protecting her from an unhappy future just as he'd sought to protect her and the baby from shame. "It's not important. What is important is setting you free."

His lips thinned, and Priscilla sensed that Zach was trying to control his temper. Why would he be angry? She was offering him his freedom. Surely that was what he wanted.

"What if I don't want to be 'set free,' as you put it?"

Priscilla noticed that he did not say he had no wish for freedom; he'd simply posed a rhetorical question. "You don't need to spare my feelings, Zach. I know why you married me."

"Do you?" There was no mistake. Anger tinged his words. "It wasn't only to protect you. I wanted a home and a family. Those reasons are still valid."

She couldn't let him entertain hopes that she could not fulfill. "There won't be a family. I can't . . . I won't . . ." This was more difficult than she'd expected. He was supposed to be grateful and agree to her suggestion of an annulment. Why was he making her put her failure into words? Priscilla swallowed deeply before she blurted out, "I can't be a real wife. I can't give you children."

The pain she'd seen in his eyes returned. "We don't need children to be a family."

"But, Zach . . ." Why wouldn't he understand? Surely he didn't want to remain locked in a marriage that gave him nothing more than a house and a mealtime companion.

"Let's not be hasty." He spoke deliberately, as if he'd taken his own admonition to heart. "I'm in no hurry to be a

253

bachelor again. The way I see it, our arrangement is working out fine."

"But, Zach . . ."

He held up a hand, mimicking her earlier gesture. "Let me continue. I suggest we try it a bit longer—say another six months. Then if either one of us wants to end the marriage, we can. Does that sound fair to you?"

It was more than fair, more than she'd dared hope for. Though another six months with the man who brought sunshine to the grayest of days would make their parting even more painful, Priscilla could not refuse. She wanted to stay—oh! how she wanted to stay—and he'd given her the opportunity.

She had been wrong. God had not taken everything from her. He had left her with this wonderful man.

It felt odd, like being a guest in her own home, but Yvonne would allow nothing less. She had arrived at the Lazy B an hour before, announcing that she had brought dinner for both of them and that Priscilla was to prop her feet on a hassock while Yvonne prepared the food. As was her wont, Yvonne chattered constantly while she unpacked the dishes she'd brought. The only time she seemed at a loss for words was when Priscilla asked why Isabelle had not accompanied her.

"She was busy," Yvonne said shortly, then proceeded to entertain Priscilla with a tale of Neville's attempt to make breakfast. "The poor dear thought he would pamper me," she said with a fond smile, "but he wound up creating more work than if I'd done it myself. Men are wonderful, but they should not be allowed in the kitchen. Now, come try my *coq au vin*."

The chicken was delicious, as were the onions and carrots that had simmered in the same wine sauce. It was only when Priscilla had eaten the last bite that Yvonne turned to her, her expression serious.

"I'm sorry about what happened to you. I can't imagine what I'd do if I lost my baby. I don't think I could bear it."

Though most women worried that something might happen to their unborn children, Priscilla wondered whether Yvonne had a particular reason for her concern. "Didn't Granny Menger say you were healthy?"

Yvonne nodded. "She said I was like a mule."

"I thought they were known for being stubborn, not healthy."

"Granny said that too," Yvonne admitted. "That I was stubborn."

Priscilla didn't know the midwife well, but it sounded like a strange comment for her to have made. "Why would she say something like that?"

Yvonne raised her shoulders in a classic shrug. "She was giving me a piece of her mind. She told me I was like a mule because I wasn't speaking to Isabelle."

And that, Priscilla suspected, was the reason Isabelle had not joined them today. It wasn't that she was too busy but rather that she hadn't been invited. "Isabelle's your friend. Why aren't you two speaking?"

Yvonne's flush said she did not like being questioned about her actions. "Because of Gunther, of course. How could she consider marrying that man? I'd never do it."

"I imagine Neville is glad to hear that." Priscilla tried to turn Yvonne's obvious anger into a joke. "I don't think bigamy is allowed in Texas."

Her friend glared at her. "You know what I mean."

"No, I don't."

⌒୨

"Ow." Jean-Michel cradled his head in his hands, not daring to open his eyes. He could see sun trying to sneak its way under his eyelids, and experience told him that if he opened them, the pain would worsen. The best thing was to stay in bed until the pain and nausea subsided.

He turned over, then yelped. What was that? It felt like a rock. What was a rock doing in his bed? Grudgingly, Jean-Michel opened his eyes, cursing when he realized that he was sleeping in a field. How on earth had he gotten here? He started to rise, cursing again when he discovered his feet were bare. He never removed his boots when he slept outdoors. Never. And where was the horse? Though some infernal insects were buzzing loud enough to wake the dead, he heard nothing that sounded like a horse.

Struggling to a sitting position, Jean-Michel cursed again as dim memories of the previous night made their way into his brain. Two men. Talk of boots and saddles and . . . He felt inside his shirt. Nothing. The bag was gone. He redoubled his curses, punctuating them with loud shouts. How dare they do that? Those Dunkler brothers had taken everything—his money, his horse, his boots. They'd left him with nothing but a rock.

Jean-Michel reached for the rock, intending to hurl it away, but his eyes narrowed when he saw that it was covering a piece of paper. He smiled. Those fellows had been all right,

256

after all. The missing boots, horse, and money were one of those practical jokes folks in this country seemed to enjoy. He grabbed the paper, knowing it would be a note telling him where he could reclaim his belongings. This might not be the kind of joke he liked, but he wouldn't argue with the men. A smart man left when he was ahead.

As Jean-Michel unfolded the piece of paper and scanned the contents, his stomach began to heave. The likeness was good, amazingly good. What made him want to retch wasn't his picture. It was the words that bracketed it: Wanted Dead or Alive. Zach Webster was going to pay for this.

❧

"You're healing well, my child." Granny Menger nodded as she completed her examination. "Another week and you'll be able to go into town." She led the way to the parlor and settled into the rocking chair. "A bit of advice, though. You might want to avoid Yvonne for a while. She's riled at you."

Priscilla wasn't surprised, since Yvonne had left in a huff. "I only told her the truth: that I like Gunther and think he'd be a good husband for Isabelle."

"I happen to agree with you, but you and I are in the minority." Granny began to rock. Though her foot set a vigorous pace for the old rocker, Granny's coronet of braids did not so much as wiggle. "I haven't seen the town this divided since everyone thought Léon Rousseau was stealing their valuables. If I weren't the only midwife for miles, I doubt the French women would come to me."

That seemed like an extreme measure. "I know the history of Alsace, but I don't understand why things haven't changed now that everyone is an American."

Granny's foot stopped rocking, and she shifted in the chair, as if uncomfortable with the conversation. "Folks have long memories. The French can't forget that they were once conquered by Germans, and we Germans have the same memories of the French. It's hard to imagine marrying someone you view as the enemy."

"That doesn't make it right."

"I didn't say it did. I simply told you why folks act the way they do. Now, tell me what you're planning to do once you're better."

"I don't know." Priscilla's days had been empty before, but she'd consoled herself with the knowledge that they'd be filled once the baby was born. Now the future seemed bleak.

"I've been praying for you," Granny said. She gave Priscilla a smile as she added, "And for me. The Lord gave me an answer. He knows that I'm slowing down and need help, and he knows you need something to fill your life. I think he means you to be my assistant."

Priscilla blanched. A month ago, she would have been thrilled by the invitation, but that was then. "I can't."

"Why not? I know you're not afraid of blood, and you told me that you used to help your father on his rounds. This seems the perfect solution."

"I can't." Priscilla clenched the chair arms as she repeated her words. "Don't you see? Each time I helped a woman deliver her baby, it would remind me of my child and all that I lost. It would be like ripping the scab off a wound. I'll never get better that way."

"Maybe. Maybe not." Granny began to rock again. "This might be exactly what you need to heal. Think about it. That's all I ask."

Zach patted Charcoal as he let him into the corral. "Do you think she'll like it?" he asked his horse. When Charcoal snorted, Zach chuckled. It was silly to be asking a horse a question like that, just as it was silly to be so nervous. He was acting like a schoolboy, trying to impress his sweetheart. Zach shook his head slightly. The analogy wasn't far off the mark. He was trying to impress Priscilla, or at least bring a bit of happiness into her life.

Zach reached for the gift and held it behind his back. Would she like it? That was the question. He hoped so, but he was no expert on women. Perhaps he should have bought a bauble at the mercantile. That might have been better. Perhaps he should discard these and try again on another day. But then how would he explain coming home early? Zach straightened his shoulders and strode forward. The only way he'd learn whether Priscilla liked the gift was to present it to her.

As his feet covered the distance to the house, Zach's mind whirled with memories of the night Priscilla had suggested they end their marriage. She had claimed it would be good for him, but how could it be when the very thought wrenched his heart? An annulment was not what Zach wanted; it was not what he'd promised God he'd do. What he wanted was a life with Priscilla, a life where somehow, someway he could show her she was loved. That was why he was here, gift in hand.

He tugged the door open and looked around. The kitchen was empty. Had Priscilla gone into town? How foolish of him! He should have checked the barn to see whether the wagon was there. "Priscilla?"

When soft footsteps told him she was in the house, Zach's heartbeat returned to normal. "You're home early," she said

259

as she entered the kitchen. Perhaps it was his imagination, but she looked particularly pretty today. The green dress made her eyes look greener than usual, and she'd done something to her hair. Zach couldn't pinpoint the difference, but it looked softer.

Furrows formed between Priscilla's eyes as she looked at him. "Is something wrong?"

"No." Now that he knew she was here, nothing was wrong. Zach kept the arm that bore the gift behind his back. "I thought I'd spend more time with you." The widening of her eyes told him she had not expected that. If that surprised her, how would she react when she saw the gift? There was only one way to find out.

"I brought something for you." He extended his arm, handing Priscilla the bouquet of wildflowers he'd picked. As he released the flowers, the petals began to fall off. Zach stared at the brightly colored petals that now lay on the floor. *Oh no!* He had to be the dumbest person on Earth, bringing a present that disintegrated the instant it was indoors.

"I'm sorry. I didn't know that would happen." His gift, what was supposed to be a loving gesture, had failed. No doubt about it. He should have gone to the mercantile and bought something. His sentimental idea had been stupid.

To Zach's amazement, Priscilla laid the remaining flowers on the table, then knelt on the floor and began to gather the petals into her hand. A broom would have made short work of it, but she was picking up each petal as if it were a pearl. When she'd retrieved them all, she rose and faced him. "Thank you, Zach. These are beautiful." Ignoring the bouquet on the table, Priscilla smiled at the flower bits she had cupped in one palm.

"There's no need to spare my feelings. It was a dumb idea. What do I know about flowers?" When he'd started out this morning, he'd been thinking about how much Priscilla had enjoyed their picnic among the bluebonnets. The gift was supposed to remind her of that day. Now it would remind her of what an ignorant man she'd married.

Priscilla raised her hand to her nose, as if checking the petals' scent. There wasn't much. Zach knew that. "They're beautiful," she repeated. "It's a lovely gift. Thank you."

"But they're dead."

"Not to me, they're not." Priscilla opened a cabinet and chose a shallow bowl. Placing the petals in it, she held the bowl out for his inspection. "See how pretty they look?"

"It just looks like scattered petals to me."

Her smile was radiant. "Exactly. They'll turn into pot-pourri." Priscilla placed the bowl in the center of the table, acting as if he'd given her the most precious of gifts, when all it was were a few flowers that couldn't hold onto their petals. She was being nice. Zach knew that. She'd seen his disap-pointment and didn't want to hurt him further. That's why she was pretending to care about those miserable petals.

But when Priscilla looked up at him, Zach saw happiness shining from her eyes. Genuine happiness. Her voice was soft as she said, "When I was a child, my mother used to take a single flower to my grandmother's grave. You can imagine how proud I was when she let me carry a rose one time. I don't remember exactly what happened, but somehow I dropped it, and the petals fell off." Priscilla's smile was wry as she continued. "I was devastated as only a child can be, convinced that I had done something unforgivable, but Mama told me everything would be all right. We took the petals home and she put them in a bowl, explaining that they would change color and dry and become potpourri."

When Priscilla's eyes sparkled with unshed tears, Zach knew her memories were bittersweet. "I kept the bowl in my bedroom. Mama told me that whenever I looked at them, I should remember how beautiful the flower once was and know that nothing is completely gone so long as we have memories. I've loved potpourri ever since." Priscilla smiled again as she looked at the bowl on the table. "Thank you, Zach. You've given me back part of my childhood."

He blinked. Maybe he wasn't a failure, after all.

14

Priscilla ran her finger through the petals. Though they weren't as fragrant as roses, it was still a pleasurable experience to touch them, which was one of the reasons she had placed the bowl in the parlor rather than keeping it in her room. This way, whenever she passed through the front room, she could take a short detour and stir the potpourri. Each time she did, her thoughts turned to Zach. It had been so very kind of him to give her flowers. Though the petals were now dried and shriveled, they reminded Priscilla not just of her childhood but of the picnic she and Zach had shared in the field of bluebonnets, and that made her smile.

She touched the petals again. So many things made her smile these days, and most of them were connected to Zach. It was odd how everything worked out. Six months ago Priscilla had not met him, and now he was an important part of her life, perhaps the most important part. Six months ago she had not dreamt that the journey to Texas for Clay's wedding would result in another wedding, hers and Zach's. Six months ago love had been an abstract concept, something that others experienced. Now thoughts of love filled Priscilla's days and nights, for though she'd once been uncertain, she now believed that what she felt for Zach was nothing less than love.

At the sound of hoofbeats, Priscilla's pulse began to race, and she hurried onto the porch, hoping Zach had come home early. He did that occasionally now, acting as if he were eager to see her, and each time her heart threatened to overflow with happiness. Those extra hours together formed a chain of precious memories that she clutched to herself when she wakened in the night, shaking as the nightmare invaded her mind and rendered sleep impossible. It was then that she would force the evil thoughts away, replacing them with images of Zach's smile and memories of the kindness he showered on her. Thanks to Zach, the nightmares had diminished in both intensity and frequency.

Her smile so broad it was almost a grin, Pricilla shaded her eyes with her hand and looked down the lane. A second later she tried to school her expression not to reveal her disappointment. The horse was a palomino, not Zach's black stallion. The rider was blond, not black-haired. Instead of Zach, it was the Ranger, Lawrence Wood, who had entered the Lazy B.

Priscilla's pulse slowed, thudding with apprehension rather than anticipation. Had the Ranger come to tell her that he'd found the Dunkler brothers? Though for months she had prayed they would be captured and hanged, now that the nightmares came less often, she went whole days without thinking of the bandits and, because of what she had learned from Zach, she no longer desired their deaths.

She wasn't certain how she'd feel if the Ranger told her he'd shot them.

"Good afternoon, ma'am." He doffed his hat as he approached the porch. "You're looking well." The Ranger's blue eyes were serious as they moved from her face down to her feet. Surely it was Priscilla's imagination that they lingered on her stomach, as if searching for signs of the baby.

"Thank you. I'm feeling well." There was no need to tell him what had happened, that she'd lost a large quantity of blood along with the baby. Mindful of her continuing weakness, Priscilla settled into one of the chairs and gestured toward the other, encouraging him to sit. "I'm surprised to see you again." Despite everyone's assurances that the Rangers always found their quarry, she hadn't believed it nor had she expected him to take the time to report back to her.

"I wish I could tell you my job was done, but I can't." He stared into the distance as he said, "Unfortunately, I've had no luck in finding Jean-Michel Ladre. He's a wily one and more dangerous than I thought at first. But I feel like I'm close to the Dunkler brothers. They're getting careless, probably because they figure I've given up hunting them." The Ranger's lips thinned. "I won't do that. I promise you, I will not stop until they're brought to justice."

Priscilla nodded. "I'll rest easier knowing they're in jail and can't hurt anyone else." For the first few weeks, all Priscilla could think of was punishing the men who'd killed her parents. An eye for an eye, or in this case, a life for a life. It had been Zach who'd spoken to her of the futility of revenge, telling her how, as a result of his time in Perote, he'd vowed to never again kill a man.

Though she'd been disbelieving at first, gradually Priscilla's anger had subsided, replaced by the knowledge that Zach was right. Nothing could undo the damage that had been wrought. Whether Jake and Chet Dunkler lived or died, she had to live with the memories of her parents' deaths and Zeke's attack. If she was fortunate, those memories would continue to fade. While it was still important that the Ranger capture the bandits, the reason had changed. No longer did Priscilla seek vengeance. Instead, she wanted the assurance that no one else would suffer as she had.

"They're scoundrels, no better than the varmints every rancher kills. They deserve to be hunted down and shot like coyotes." Though the Ranger's voice was filled with anger, Priscilla saw something in his eyes, something that—if she had to describe it—she would have called a haunted look. "Part of me wants to shoot them on sight, but the other part knows that no matter how vile their crimes were, they deserve a fair trial, not like . . ."

He bit off whatever he was going to say, and Priscilla sensed his discomfort. As strange as it seemed, his expression reminded her of Zach when he spoke of his time in Perote. Surely the Ranger had experienced nothing so horrible. Trying to allay his discomfort, Priscilla gave him a small smile. "It seems to me that one of the best things about being a Ranger is that you have a life of adventure. That's what I always longed for. Although it didn't turn out the way I had planned, adventure was one of the reasons I wanted to come West."

The Ranger shrugged, as if dismissing her sentiments. "You may not believe me, but adventure loses its appeal after a while. At least that's what's happened to me. I'm thinking about leaving the Rangers once I bring the Dunkler brothers in."

Priscilla didn't try to hide her surprise. Though she knew he had a name, whenever she thought of the man who had rescued her, he was simply "The Ranger." That was his identity. How could he give it up? "What will you do?"

His lips quirked in an ironic smile. "That's the problem. I don't know. I can't picture myself as a rancher, and I sure as shootin' can't imagine being cooped up in a store all day. I tell myself there has to be something I can do, but at this point, I'm not sure what it is."

A mockingbird squawked from a nearby tree, its raucous call suggesting it had an opinion to share. Though Priscilla managed a small smile for the bird, which was hopping from one branch to another, her smile faded as she considered the Ranger's dilemma. "I know what you mean. I keep wondering what purpose my life serves." Both Mama and Papa had stressed that God had placed everyone on Earth for a reason.

"I'm surprised you'd say that." The Ranger's eyes moved toward her waist. "Soon you'll be a mother. No matter how this baby got started, raising a child is a mighty fine purpose for a life."

Priscilla bit her lip, trying to decide what to do. Though she hadn't planned to tell him what had happened, there was no point in lying. Besides, if he went into Ladreville, someone might tell him. The Ranger might as well hear it from her. "There won't be a baby. Not anymore."

Blood rushed to his face, and he dropped his gaze, clearly embarrassed by the mention of such a personal matter. "Then there's no reason . . ." He stopped abruptly, his face coloring again. When he spoke, he said only, "I'm sorry for your loss." Though the words seemed perfunctory, there was no mistaking the speculative look in the Ranger's eyes. What, Priscilla wondered, had he meant to say? There was no reason for *what*?

Zach was whistling as he rode into Ladreville. Today was a good day. If truth be told, most days had been good ones, starting with the afternoon he'd given Priscilla those silly wildflowers. Who would have believed that a few well-past-their-peak Indian blankets and verbenas would have made her so happy? All he'd hoped for was to add a bit of pleasure to her life. Instead, it appeared that the flowers had been a turning point. She had been visibly happier since that day, and he . . . he was happier too.

Zach looked up at the sky. It was another of those beautiful May mornings that made a man glad he was alive. Far from marring the scene, the puffy clouds that drifted slowly across the sky served to highlight the faultless blue. It was a day to celebrate life, and Zach did, though his heart was still saddened by the loss of the baby.

Though he had said little to Priscilla, not wanting to increase her sorrow, Zach had mourned the death more deeply than he'd thought possible. He didn't know when or how it had happened, but the prospect of raising a child had changed from a duty he had assumed into something he had anticipated with great joy. Like Clay, who found immense happiness in being a father to Thea, Zach had looked forward to being a father to Priscilla's child. This time, he had resolved, he would not repeat his youthful mistakes. He would be a father, a good father. But the chance had been taken from him, and he knew it would not be repeated.

268

Though Zach wanted nothing more than to make Priscilla his wife in deed as well as word, that would not happen. The damage the bandits had wrought was too extensive. Even though she was more comfortable around him, Priscilla was always careful to keep a distance between them. It would take a miracle for her to welcome his touch and a double miracle for her to willingly touch him.

Zach frowned, then forced his lips to curve upward. There was no point in railing at something he could not change. Instead, he would rejoice in Priscilla's recovery and the knowledge that her spirit was healing as well as her body.

Michel Ladre was not smiling. Though Zach greeted him amicably when he met him on the street in front of the post office, the mayor scowled. "What do you mean it's a good day? I've seen better." Michel gestured toward the building that held his office and the town's one jail cell on the first floor, his residence on the second. "Might as well come in. I trust you not to gossip, but I can't say that about the rest of Ladreville."

Zach remained silent until they were both seated, knowing from experience that Michel did not like to be interrupted. "I wish that Ranger would mind his own business," the town's founder muttered as he took the chair next to Zach.

Zach tried to mask his surprise. Though he'd been in this office numerous times, this was the first time the mayor had sat anywhere other than behind his desk. Still, the seating arrangement was trivial compared to Michel's words. "Lawrence Wood was here?" Zach's spirits soared when he remembered that the Ranger had promised to return after he'd captured the Dunkler brothers. The news that they were behind bars would reassure Priscilla and accelerate her healing.

Michel nodded. "He was here, all right, poking around, asking questions about my son. He never finds anything, because there's nothing to find, but he sure does worry my wife."

Zach did not share the mayor's belief in his son's innocence. The night he and Clay had caught Jean-Michel robbing a house had convinced Zach that Jean-Michel was not a petty thief but a dangerously disturbed young man.

"Horse thievery is a serious accusation in Texas."

Michel pounded the desk. "That's not all that confounded Ranger is accusing my son of." He glared at Zach. "And, no, I won't tell you what he said today. It's all lies. But thanks to his lies, Jeannette is heartbroken. She says she can't hold her head up in public. She thinks everyone will point fingers."

It appeared the mayor's wife felt the way Priscilla had a few months ago and feared that she would be shunned for something she had not done. Zach gave Michel the same counsel he'd shared with Priscilla. "I can't believe the townspeople would be so cruel." When Michel looked dubious, Zach added, "They respect you."

"Do they, or do they simply fear me?" The question surprised Zach. Introspection was not something he'd ever associated with the town's mayor. Michel was charismatic, opinionated, occasionally domineering, but introspective? Not that Zach had seen.

"I've been doing a lot of thinking recently," Michel admitted, "and I'm not proud of what I learned. I've made a lot of mistakes."

"We all have." Zach certainly had. "That's the unfortunate part of being human."

270

Michel stared at the wall where his prized maps of the Old Country hung. "Jeannette thinks we need to leave Ladreville. I'm beginning to agree with her."

Though he'd mentioned that once before, Zach had thought it nothing more than a passing fancy. "If you left, we wouldn't have a mayor, or a sheriff, for that matter."

Michel's shrug telegraphed his lack of concern. "The town will find someone." He turned to look at Zach. "Why not you? You'd make a good mayor."

It was a morning for surprises. "Me? Never. Two ranches are enough for me."

"Two ranches and a wife." Michel nodded slowly. "Looks like you're wiser than I was. You're sensible enough that your wife won't feel neglected."

"I hope not."

As he headed back to the Lazy B, Zach thought about Michel's words. He didn't want Priscilla to feel neglected. Though he came home early whenever he could, managing both ranches took a lot of time, and more days than not, he was late returning to the Lazy B. His one day of rest was Sunday. Zach smiled. That was the answer. Even though he couldn't change the weekdays, he would make Sunday a special day for Priscilla. Zach's smile turned to a grin as he remembered their picnic among the bluebonnets. The flowers were gone, but the spot was still beautiful. That's what he'd do. He'd arrange a Sunday picnic.

Zach was still grinning when he crossed the river and saw a rider approaching. Recognizing the Ranger's palomino, he reined in Charcoal and greeted the man.

"I just left your ranch," Lawrence said. "I wanted to tell Miss Morton . . . er, Mrs. Webster . . . that even though I haven't caught them yet, I'm getting closer to the Dunkler brothers."

You haven't caught them? Then why are you hanging around here instead of chasing them? Zach bit back the angry words. The Ranger was a good man; he knew that. From all that he'd heard, Lawrence Wood was one of the best of that elite group known as the Texas Rangers. If he was in Ladreville, he had a reason. There was no cause for Zach to bristle, even though he hadn't liked the man's tone when he'd spoken Priscilla's name. The fact that the Ranger's voice changed, that it sounded almost tender when he'd pronounced her name, shouldn't bother Zach any more than the fact that the man appeared to have forgotten, at least momentarily, that Priscilla was married. "Where are the bandits?" Zach demanded.

"They were last spotted near New Braunfels. Folks there said they heard Chet say something about the Hill Country. I wanted to head them off. No point in letting them get too close to Miss . . . Mrs. Webster." There it was again, that hesitation. Zach clenched his fists. "I haven't seen any signs, though." Lawrence concluded his explanation.

"Does Priscilla know you thought they were coming this way?"

"No." Lawrence shook his head. "I didn't see any reason to alarm her, especially since it appears it was a red herring."

"That's good. I don't need to tell you that my wife has already suffered too much." Zach didn't miss the way the Ranger flinched when he referred to Priscilla as his wife. It was the first time Zach had called her that in Lawrence's hearing. He liked the way it sounded. What he didn't like was the Ranger's reaction. It appeared Zach's instincts had been correct and the man harbored tender feelings for Priscilla. Zach couldn't blame him. His wife was a beautiful, loveable woman. A man would have to be blind not to see that. The question was, how did Priscilla feel? Though she almost never spoke of the Ranger, it was possible she regarded with favor the man who'd saved her from Zeke Dunkler. Zach tried to dislodge the lump that settled in his throat when he considered that that might be the reason Priscilla had suggested they annul their marriage.

"I hope you'll send us a message when you do capture the Dunklers." Zach picked up the reins, signaling the end of the conversation.

"That's one message I'll deliver in person."

And that was exactly what Zach feared.

❧

"I'm so glad you suggested this." Priscilla arranged her skirts as she settled on the quilt. Though the bluebonnets had faded, the small clearing where she and Zach had picnicked the first time was still beautiful. Today, mindful of the sun's warmth, they'd spread the quilt under the trees. Zach sat on the opposite corner, his back against a large oak.

"It was a wonderful idea, coming back here, but I could have cooked." Priscilla opened the basket and pulled out the food Martina had prepared. Despite her protest, she had been touched by the fact that Zach had gone to so much trouble to plan the day, even asking Clay and Sarah's housekeeper to provide food. Like the wildflower bouquet Zach had given her, today's picnic warmed Priscilla's heart with the realization that he thought of her when they were apart. That was just one of the reasons she smiled so often.

273

Zach shrugged as he accepted a plate of cold ham and beans. "You can cook next time."

Next time. Priscilla liked the sound of that. She knew that every time he came home early, though it was the highlight of her day, something was not getting done on the ranch. That could not continue indefinitely. She also could not expect Zach to spend all day Sunday with her. After church and dinner with the family, Papa had retired to his study, declaring he needed time alone. Zach probably longed for solitude too, but it appeared that he was willing to forego it for her. Priscilla smiled again.

Zach reached for the bowl of potato salad. "I want to be certain you're completely recovered."

She was getting better, and that was part of the problem, for with the renewal of her strength came boredom. "I feel better every day. I'm stronger now, just empty."

Zach's eyes were serious as he nodded. "I imagine that's normal. What you need is something to occupy your time."

He'd given her the perfect opportunity to broach a subject that had occupied her thoughts. "Granny Menger suggested I become her assistant." Ever since the midwife had suggested it, Priscilla had been mulling the idea. Though she still feared that watching another woman give birth might arouse painful memories, those fears were fading. Granny was right; helping others might help Priscilla, but she didn't want to make the decision without consulting Zach, for it was not only her life that would be altered.

Zach took a swallow of buttermilk to wash down the potato salad before he spoke. When he did, his voice rang with enthusiasm. "That's a great idea. I know it's not exactly what

274

you dreamed of, but it seems to me being a midwife is almost like being a doctor."

It was, and being a woman would be an advantage, not a barrier. That was the good part. "If I did agree, I'd be gone at odd times." That was the bad part. "Babies come on their own schedule, so I wouldn't always be home to cook supper."

Zach looked down at his plate and grinned. "Just keep some cans of beans in the cupboard. I've lived on less."

"Then you wouldn't mind?" It certainly didn't seem as if he did, but Priscilla had to be certain. Even if they shared a house for only a few more months, she wanted those months to be as happy as possible for Zach.

He shook his head. "Why would I mind? I want you to be happy. If working with Granny Menger brings you happiness, I won't complain about an occasional evening without my wife."

Priscilla felt the blood rush to her face. It was silly to be blushing, but she couldn't help it. Every time Zach had referred to her as his wife, it took her by surprise. "Thank you. I'll talk to Granny tomorrow." She offered Zach another piece of ham as she changed the subject. "Have you spoken to Gunther recently?"

"No. Why?"

"I wondered how his courtship of Isabelle was progressing. The last time she visited, Isabelle was miserable. She's still tutoring Eva, but she said she hasn't seen Gunther in weeks. He used to come every day; then he stopped. She doesn't know why."

Zach frowned. "I was afraid of that. The reason is simple. When Gunther asked for permission to court her, Isabelle's father refused, and he's too honorable a man to flout Monsieur Rousseau's wishes."

"So both he and Isabelle are unhappy." It wasn't fair. Priscilla twisted her napkin as she recalled Isabelle's red-rimmed eyes. "Oh, Zach, there must be a way to help them."

"The only thing I can think of is to try to knock some sense into Monsieur Rousseau's head." To illustrate his plan, Zach turned and thumped his fist against the tree.

Priscilla chuckled. "I would suggest a less belligerent approach." She was silent for a moment, considering the alternatives. "Maybe if you and I spoke—" She put an ironic twist to the word as she glanced at the trée Zach had punched "—to both of her parents, we might be able to convince them."

"Let's try it."

Priscilla and Zach waited until after supper the next evening, when the mercantile was closed for the day, before they climbed the outside stairs and knocked on the Rousseaus' door.

"Priscilla!" Isabelle smiled with pleasure as she opened the door. "I didn't expect you." Her eyes widened when she saw the man at Priscilla's side. "Is something wrong?"

Priscilla shook her head. "We wanted to speak to your parents. Alone. Perhaps you and Léon could take a walk. It's a lovely evening."

Isabelle's eyes narrowed with speculation. "Why do you want to see Maman and Papa?"

Before Priscilla could reply, Zach said, "It's personal business."

"Oh, all right. Léon's out for the evening. I'll go downstairs. I can arrange the new shipment of calico."

"Who's at the door, Isabelle?" Madame Rousseau called from the parlor. "It had better not be that man."

276

Priscilla flinched as she shooed her friend away. This was not an auspicious beginning. Though Priscilla had hoped that Isabelle's mother would be less opposed to Gunther's suit, the angry note in her voice when she pronounced the words *that man* made the possibility seem unlikely. "It's Priscilla Webster, Madame Rousseau. Zach and I thought we'd pay a brief call."

"Come in, come in." Her voice once more cordial, the older woman entered the kitchen and led Priscilla and Zach into the parlor. More formal than the rooms at either the Lazy B or the Bar C, the Rousseaus' sitting room boasted furniture with spindly carved legs, a floral patterned rug, and velvet draperies.

"It's good to see you again," Monsieur Rousseau said as he shook Zach's hand. "I'm looking forward to buying another one of your steers this year. Nothing compares to Texas beef."

His wife nodded her agreement. "It's true. It's more tender and has a different flavor from the meat we had in the Old Country."

Perhaps this was the opening they needed. Priscilla smiled. "I imagine you find many things different here. Texas seems different to me, and I only came from Boston." Though no one spoke, neither of the Rousseaus' expressions was forbidding. Priscilla took that as an invitation to continue. "I've been surprised at how free people are here. Things are allowed that would not have been permitted in Boston."

"What kind of things?" Isabelle's father appeared interested.

"For one thing, people are valued for themselves, not how much money they've accumulated, so a woman can consider a man's inner worth, not just the size of his fortune." Priscilla and Zach had agreed that they would try to turn the subject to marriage as quickly as possible.

Zach flashed her a look that said he appreciated her effort, then turned to Isabelle's parents and chuckled. "That's lucky for me, or Priscilla would never have married me."

Both of the Rousseaus joined in the laughter. "It's good to see you two happy together." Madame Rousseau patted Priscilla's hand. "I know your parents would be glad that you have such a fine husband. When you're a mother, you'll know what it's like. We want only the best for our children."

Zach nodded slowly. "Sometimes it's hard to know what's best for them. The best man may not look—or sound—the way you think he should."

Priscilla heard a hissing sound as Madame Rousseau breathed through clenched teeth. Though she said nothing, Isabelle's father glared at Zach. "Are you referring to Gunther Lehman?"

"Yes, sir, I am. He's an honest, hard-working, God-fearing man who loves your daughter very much."

"He's a German." Monsieur Rousseau pronounced the word the same way he might have "murderer."

Priscilla turned to Isabelle's mother. "Isn't love more important than a person's last name?" Though the woman remained silent, her eyes reflected confusion. It was obvious she loved her husband and wanted her daughter to have the same kind of loving marriage, but her prejudices were deep-seated.

Monsieur Rousseau shook his head vehemently. "You don't understand, either of you. How could you? You were born in this country. You don't know what it's like to fight the

Germans and lose. You don't know how vicious a conquering people can be." His frown deepened. "You don't know how difficult it is to come to a new place, to struggle to build a home from nothing, and to fear that your children will forget their past. You don't even know how important tradition is." He shook his head again, as if in dismay at Priscilla and Zach's ignorance. "In the Old Country, parents arranged their children's marriages. That was a good plan. Parents know what is best for their children."

Monsieur Rousseau turned to Zach, his expression regretful. "You probably meant well. I know Gunther is your friend. He's a good miller, and he may be a good man, but he is not a man I would allow to marry my daughter. She is a Frenchwoman, and she will not marry a German. Not today, not next year, not ever."

15

Priscilla's hands were shaking so badly that she doubted Zach would be able to read her note. *Stay calm*, she admonished herself. *Leah needs you*. She had been peeling carrots when Granny Menger's message arrived, telling her Leah Dunn's time had come. Though Priscilla had assisted Granny for close to a month now, Leah was the first of their patients to go into labor.

Setting the knife aside, Priscilla had grabbed her supplies and harnessed the buggy, then ran back into the house to leave a note for Zach. While he'd claimed he would not worry if he found her gone, this was the first time Priscilla would miss supper, and she didn't want to cause him any unnecessary concern. It was bad enough that he'd have to resort to eating beans. If Leah's baby had waited another hour, the stew would have been simmering, but babies, as Priscilla had warned Zach, paid no heed to schedules.

She looked down at her trembling hands. *Take a deep breath*. Hadn't Papa claimed that was the best way to settle nerves? As she turned the horse and buggy toward the river, Priscilla inhaled, holding her breath to the count of five, then released it slowly. When she'd repeated the process several times, she found that her hands were no longer shaking. Good. Excellent. Perhaps now when she reached the Dunn household, she'd appear to be calm, at least on the outside. Inwardly, she was still shaking with fear that she'd do something wrong.

It's normal to be nervous about your first patient. Priscilla recalled the day Papa had said those words to Clay. She probably would have worried, no matter who the patient was, but Leah Dunn was special. The mother-to-be had almost died a year ago when her windpipe had been crushed. Though Clay's surgery had saved her life, the postmaster's wife would never again breathe normally. And, though Granny Menger had told Leah not to worry, privately she'd admitted her concerns. A difficult labor took its toll on every part of a woman's body. Granny had confided to Priscilla that she wasn't certain how Leah, who breathed through a tube in her throat, would handle the additional strain of childbirth. Priscilla wasn't certain how she would handle it, either. This would be the first test of her resolve to find joy rather than sorrow in the sight of another woman's newborn child.

When she entered the postmaster's home, Priscilla fixed a smile on her face. Papa had told her the primary rule of medicine was to help patients relax. Fisting her hands on her hips, Priscilla feigned indignation as she approached Leah's bed. The mother-to-be was paler than normal, but Priscilla saw no sign of respiratory distress. "Couldn't you tell this little one to wait until I got my carrots peeled?"

As she'd hoped, Leah managed a small smile before the

next contraction seized her. "I'm sorry, Priscilla," she said. "He has a mind of his own. All I want is for this to be over. I want to hold my son." Though both Granny and Priscilla had reminded Leah that babies came in two varieties, she was convinced hers was a boy.

Leah groaned as pain ripped through her. "Why is this taking so long?"

"You're doing fine." Granny's voice was warm and soothing. "It's harder now, because the baby's almost here. Look, Priscilla." The midwife beckoned her closer. When Priscilla saw what could only be the infant's head, she gasped, amazed that the labor had proceeded so quickly.

"What's wrong?" Leah demanded. "What's wrong with my baby?"

"Nothing." Once again Granny spoke. "He's just anxious to be born." She rose from the stool she'd placed at the foot of the bed and gestured toward Priscilla. "Go ahead. You know what to do."

Priscilla's eyes widened in shock. "You want me to deliver this child?" She had expected to watch Granny at least a few times before she attempted to bring a child into the world.

Granny nodded. "That's what I said, isn't it? I'll be right next to you if you need me. It will be easy."

"Easy, you say?" Leah's voice rose, and she groaned again. "Nothing about this is easy. It's the hardest work I've ever done."

Before she settled onto the stool, Priscilla looked at her patient. Though Leah was panting from exertion, her color remained healthy. "That's why they call it labor." Following Granny's instructions, Priscilla checked the baby's position and then waited for the next contraction to begin. "Push,

Leah, push." As the young woman did, the child's head began to emerge. "Again." A shoulder appeared.

"You're doing fine, child," Granny said. "One more push is all you need."

Seconds later, Priscilla held Leah Dunn's baby in her hands. Though wrinkled, red, and clearly unhappy, he was the most beautiful thing Priscilla had ever seen. "Oh, Leah, you were right. You have a son." Priscilla turned the baby, inspecting him the way Granny had taught her before she placed him in Leah's arms. "He's a perfect little boy." As she looked at the mother cradling her child, tears of joy filled Priscilla's eyes. How could she have ever doubted that this was what she was meant to do? *Thank you, God. Thank you for the gift of life.*

Léon claimed there was always one exception. Why did this have to be the one? Isabelle twisted the handkerchief between her fingers as she thought of the man who sat in the next room reading the newspaper. Both she and Léon knew that Papa normally deferred to Maman. Why hadn't he this time? When Priscilla and Zach had left the other night, Papa had summoned Isabelle to the parlor and had informed her that he did not take kindly to her friends—he had spat the word as if it were an epithet—interfering in family business. Though Maman's eyes were sorrowful, Papa's flashed only anger as he announced that Isabelle would marry the man he chose for her and that man would never be Gunther Lehman.

Her tears had accomplished nothing, not that night nor the next, but she had to try again. Somehow she had to make Papa understand how unhappy she was. Swallowing deeply, Isabelle entered the parlor.

"I love him." Her father frowned. That wasn't the way she had planned to begin, but the words she had rehearsed flew from her head, and all she could remember was the fact that she loved Gunther.

Papa tossed aside the newspaper he had been reading and rose, his face suffused with wrath. "You don't know what you're saying. You can't love a German."

"I don't care that he's a German, Papa. I love him, and I want to be his wife."

The cuckoo clock began to chime. Though normally Papa would have waited for it to stop, this time he shouted over the bird's silly chirping. "Nonsense. You don't know what's good for you. Your mother and I will choose a husband for you. That's how it's always been done. Love comes after the wedding. Look at your mother and me."

It was true that they loved each other. No one could dispute that, but Isabelle knew that not all arranged marriages were happy. "*Tante* Eloise and *Oncle* Charles don't love each other." They barely spoke to each other, and when they did, their words were laced with venom. "Surely you don't want me to be as unhappy as they are."

"You won't be. Your mother and I will choose more carefully. But one thing I can promise you, daughter, is that you will never marry a German."

"It's getting worse."

Priscilla looked at her husband. She knew his frown had nothing to do with the stew she'd ladled into his bowl. He'd already eaten one helping and had declared it delicious.

"I heard two Frenchmen say Monsieur Rousseau was right and they should run Gunther out of town," Zach continued.

"Surely they wouldn't do that." Priscilla had no illusions about the arbitrary nature of vigilante justice, but wasn't it exacted for serious crimes like murder and horse stealing? Gunther had committed no crimes. All he'd done was fall in love with a woman who spoke French.

Zach shrugged. "I'd like to think they were only idle threats, but I'm not sure." He frowned again, his eyes darkening. "I've seen how sensible people change when they're part of a crowd. It's as if they lose every semblance of reason. A tiny spark turns into a conflagration as hatred and anger fan the flames. After that, they're out of control. A crowd does things no sane person would ever consider."

He was speaking of the war. She was certain of that. It sounded awful, almost as if men turned into beasts. What she didn't know was whether the pain that never seemed to leave Zach's eyes was caused by memories of what he'd endured then. He had told her he'd forgiven his jailers and had found peace, and yet the haunted look never completely disappeared, not even when he seemed relaxed and happy as he did on their Sunday excursions.

"I must have lived a sheltered life," Priscilla said softly, "because I've never experienced a mob."

"I hope you never do." Zach took another spoonful of stew, chewing thoughtfully. "I don't like saying this, but I'm afraid there's little hope for Gunther and Isabelle."

She didn't want to believe that. "The Bible tells us all things are possible with God."

Though Zach nodded, he also raised one eyebrow. "It also tells us that God has plans for us. What if their marriage isn't part of his plan?"

Priscilla had no answer.

Someone was pounding on the door. Priscilla laid down the sock she'd been knitting for Zach. The dream had come again last night, the dream where she was waiting for him. In the past, it had always been the same. Last night had been different, disturbingly different, for when she'd told Zach she loved him, his eyes had filled with pain and he'd said simply, "I cannot love you. You're soiled goods."

Priscilla had wakened, trembling. *It was only a dream*, she told herself, but still she was unable to dismiss the fear that she'd discovered the source of Zach's pain. Perhaps if she'd seen him she could have convinced herself there was no reason to be alarmed, but today Zach had left the ranch before she'd wakened, and so she'd spent the morning wandering aimlessly, trying to ignore the dread that clenched her heart. In desperation, she had picked up her knitting, hoping the intricacies of turning a heel would occupy her thoughts.

But now someone was pounding on the door as if there were an emergency. Had something happened to Zach? Her heart beating a tattoo, Priscilla raced to the door. Though she knew instantly that Zach was safe, her alarm did not diminish at the sight of the stocky young farmer.

"You need to come." Neville Beauvais's normally ruddy face was pale, his eyes clouded with worry. "Yvonne needs you."

"What's wrong?"

Neville shook his head. "I don't know. When she woke this morning, she had horrible pains in her middle. They haven't gone away."

Though she knew there could be many causes, Priscilla did not like the sound of her friend's symptoms. They reminded her all too vividly of the day she'd lost her baby. *Please, God, don't let it be that.* Priscilla ushered Neville into the house while she gathered her bonnet and bag. "Did you call Granny Menger?" Granny was the one with all the experience. If anyone could save Yvonne's baby, it would be Granny.

Neville's voice carried into Priscilla's room. "She's with Frau Lamar, but she said she'd come as soon as she could."

Priscilla frowned. According to Granny, Frau Lamar's labors were always long and difficult. That meant Priscilla would be on her own. *Help me, Lord,* she prayed as Neville drove the buggy into town. *Show me what to do. Help me save Yvonne's baby.*

When they reached the house, Priscilla found Yvonne lying on her bed, writhing in pain. Neville took one look at his wife and grabbed the doorframe. "Oh, honey," he said, his voice so faint that Priscilla feared he would topple over, leaving her with two patients.

"I'm scared," Yvonne admitted when Neville had accepted Priscilla's suggestion that he would be of more use if he remained in the parlor. "I'm afraid something is wrong with the baby." It was a measure of Yvonne's distress that she did not elaborate. The normally garrulous woman was uncharacteristically silent.

"It may not be that at all." Perhaps something Yvonne had eaten wasn't agreeing with her. But as she described the symptoms and showed Priscilla where the pain was centered, Priscilla knew this was much more than an upset stomach. Though it was far too soon, Yvonne was in labor.

"It's the baby, isn't it?"

"I'm afraid so." Papa had told her that a five month baby had little hope of survival. It would take a miracle to save

Yvonne's child. *Help me be that miracle,* Priscilla prayed. *Let this baby live.*

Though Priscilla tried everything she knew, her prayer was not answered. *Why, Lord, why?* she asked when it became apparent that the labor would not cease. There was no answer. Yvonne's baby was tiny and perfect and stillborn.

Priscilla began to sob. It had been horrible, losing her baby, but somehow watching a friend endure the same pain was worse. *Why, Lord?* Though she did not expect an answer, deep inside her heart Priscilla heard a voice say, *Yvonne needs you.* She looked down and saw blood gushing. Brushing aside her tears, Priscilla began to work. Yvonne would not die. She would not spend weeks recovering from the loss of blood. Priscilla might not have been able to save the baby, but she could save her friend.

Half an hour later, when the bleeding had been staunched, she helped Yvonne into a clean nightdress. "Let me call Neville," she said when she'd brushed Yvonne's hair and rebraided it.

"No. I'm not ready to see him." Tears streamed down Yvonne's cheeks as she cradled her baby. "Why did God do this to me?"

Her words wrenched Priscilla's heart as they brought back memories of the first few days after she'd lost her baby. She had asked the same question over and over again. "I don't know, any more than I know why he let my baby die." If that had been part of his plan—and it seemed that it was—Priscilla doubted she'd ever understand why he'd let her suffer so. The Bible claimed that God will turn everything to good for his believers and that suffering has a purpose. What purpose could there possibly be for a child's death?

"How did you survive?" Yvonne asked. "I want to die so I

can be with my baby." She looked down at the tiny form that had never taken a breath on its own. "I want to die."

Priscilla closed her eyes. *Please, God, give me the words to comfort her.*

"Let me die."

"I know how you feel." In those first days, it had seemed there was no reason to continue living. One rainy morning when even the sun had deserted her, Priscilla had considered ending her life, but as she reached for the glass, intending to break it and use the sharp edge to cut her wrists, she remembered Zach saying there had been too much killing. He had struggled with despair and had conquered it. If he hadn't, there would have been no one to help Clay's father walk, no one to marry Priscilla when she needed protection. How could she make a mockery of Zach's gift?

"Death is not the answer." Priscilla shook her head and placed a hand on Yvonne's shoulder. "What would Neville do without you? He needs you."

"How could he need me?" Yvonne began to sob again. "I failed him. I lost our baby."

Gently Priscilla took the lifeless body from her friend. "You didn't fail Neville," she said softly. "This happened." She laid the child in the cradle Yvonne had prepared for it. "Bad things happen. I don't know why they do. All I know is that we cannot give up. We cannot throw away the gift of life."

"But what do I tell Neville?"

Priscilla was silent for a moment, searching for an answer that would help her friend. At last she said, "Tell him you love him and you need him."

Yvonne gripped Priscilla's hand. When she looked up, though her eyes were filled with sorrow, the despair was gone.

"You're right, Priscilla. I do love Neville, and I need him to help me bear this." Yvonne brushed the tears from her face and looked at the door, as if expecting her husband to step through it. "Please call Neville."

The danger had passed.

As Priscilla gathered her bag and prepared to leave, her heart was lighter than it had been in months. She mourned her baby; she always would, but for the first time since that horrible day, she realized that her suffering had not been in vain. More than Granny Menger, perhaps more than anyone in Ladreville, Priscilla knew what Yvonne was feeling, and that had given her the wisdom to help her friend. *Was this your plan, dear Lord?* There was no answer, nothing but the warmth inside her heart. That was all the answer she needed.

"Look, Zach." Michel Ladre didn't bother to hide his exasperation. "I know Gunther is your friend. I like the man myself. He's a mighty fine miller. I'd help him if I could, but the truth is, I've got my own problems to worry about."

If he could redo the last fifteen minutes, Zach would not have entered the mayor's office. Ever since their last encounter, he had been concerned about Michel, and that concern had only increased when he'd heard that neither Michel nor his wife had been seen for over a week. Today the normally friendly man was visibly distraught, pacing the floor rather than sitting behind the massive desk, and he'd spent the last quarter hour ranting about the lies that Ranger Lawrence Wood and others had spread. Though he had steadfastly refused to discuss the nature of those lies, at length Michel strode to his desk and picked up a stiff sheet of paper.

"How am I supposed to hang this in the post office?" he demanded. "I know it can't be true, but what will people think?" He tossed the poster to Zach.

Zach gulped, unsure what he could say. Even if he hadn't recognized the picture, the man's name was printed in large, bold letters. "Jean-Michel Ladre, wanted for murder, dead or alive." Unlike Michel, Zach harbored no illusions about Jean-Michel. He was a troubled young man who considered himself above the law. Indulged by both parents, he had turned to petty crime as a diversion. But murder? Zach read the fine print. According to it, in addition to stealing from the empresario, Jean-Michel had killed a man named Tom Fayette. That was a far more serious crime than he had expected.

Michel didn't appear to notice Zach's silence. "I can't do it." He grabbed the poster from Zach and crumpled it. "Jeannette would be humiliated if people thought our son killed a man. I can't do that to my wife."

"It could be a mistake."

"The mistake was sending him to Houston last year. I should have kept him right here. I could have locked him up here."

Zach's head swiveled toward the town's only jail cell. "Where everyone in town would know about it, and anyone who came inside could see him? How would that help your wife?"

Michel blanched. "You're right. That would have been worse. I tell you, Zach, don't ever have children. They bring nothing but heartache."

As he left the mayor's office, Zach told himself that children were not a subject he wanted to contemplate. It was more pleasant to think about Priscilla, for she seemed happier each day. There was no doubt that working with Granny Menger had been good for her. Zach had rejoiced with her when she'd recounted her role in the birth of Leah Dunn's son, and she'd brought tears to his eyes when she'd told him of her experience with Yvonne Beauvais. The healing that he'd prayed for was occurring, but still there was a sadness in Priscilla's eyes, a sadness he wanted to erase.

Zach greeted three men who were heading for the post office, but all the while that he listened to their tales of spring planting, part of his mind remained focused on Priscilla. There must be something he could do for her. When the men proceeded up the steps, Zach snapped his fingers. A present. That was the answer. He would give Priscilla something more than flowers that shed their petals the instant they were indoors.

Zach started toward the mercantile, then turned abruptly as he changed his mind. It was true he could buy something new and she'd be pleased, but perhaps he could do more than that. He hadn't been able to forget the day he'd found Priscilla crying about her lost locket. Though she'd admitted it was foolish to weep over a piece of jewelry, the locket obviously meant a great deal to her.

Zach's thoughts whirled. The Dunkler brothers wouldn't have had any reason to keep it. As far as Zach knew, neither Chet nor Jake had a wife or a sweetheart. In all likelihood, they had sold the locket along with Priscilla's parents' jewelry. And if they'd sold it, there must be a way to find it. Zach suspected it wouldn't be easy, but he'd long since realized that the best things were not. He had to try. But first there was one more thing he had to do. Resolutely, he entered the mercantile.

"Is your father available?" Though Isabelle smiled when Zach opened the door, the smile did not reach her eyes, and the shadows beneath them bore witness to sleepless nights. Zach took a deep breath as he tried to slow his pulse. No matter how his words were received, he was right to have come. He couldn't let the situation continue without trying to change it.

Following Isabelle's directions, Zach climbed the stairs and entered the Rousseau residence. The man he sought was sitting behind a small desk, apparently working on his accounts.

"Good afternoon, Mr. Rousseau." Zach chose the address carefully, wanting to remind Isabelle's father that he was in America now.

The Frenchman looked up, his dark eyes hostile. "If you've come about Gunther, don't waste your breath. Nothing will change my mind."

There had to be something. Though it had not been offered, Zach took the seat on the opposite side of the desk. "I know you love your daughter."

Mr. Rousseau inclined his head. "That is precisely the reason I will not permit her to ruin her life. She will marry the man I choose, or she will not marry at all." He placed his hands on the desk and steepled his fingers. "You have no children yet, so you cannot pretend to understand how I feel."

"That is true." Zach wouldn't deny that he was on shaky ground where parenthood was concerned, but he did know how adults felt. "There's been some ugly talk in town. People are threatening Gunther, and they're claiming you're behind it."

The older man's lips thinned. "A man does what he must to protect his family."

"Even when an innocent man might be harmed? Even when anyone can see that your daughter is miserable? I don't understand how you can call yourself a Christian and yet justify such acts."

His face flushed with anger, Isabelle's father rose. "Get out of here." He pointed at the door. "You have overstepped your bounds."

Zach picked up his hat. When he reached the door, he turned. "What will it take to change your mind?"

"A sign from God."

That was something Zach could not provide. Though his heart was heavy, thinking of Gunther and Isabelle's plight, he had done what little he could. Now it was time to help Priscilla.

That night at supper he said as casually as he could, "I've been putting it off, but I need to ride the range." That wasn't a lie. It simply wasn't what he was going to do for the next few days. "I'll be back as soon as I can, but it might take a week." A week of hard riding, long hours in the saddle, and only minutes of sleep. A wiser man would have planned a more leisurely journey, but Zach didn't want to leave Priscilla alone any longer than absolutely necessary, for he knew that she found life on the Lazy B lonely.

She looked at him, those pretty green eyes widening with surprise. "Oh!" For a few seconds, though she said nothing else, Zach sensed that she was going to ask him to remain. What would he do? The dilemma resolved itself, for she cleared her throat and asked what she could prepare for him. It was only the next morning when he was loading the saddlebags that Priscilla's smile faltered. "Stay safe, Zach," she said softly. "I'll miss you."

16

Jean-Michel punched the saddle. He did not care what anyone said. A saddle did not make a good pillow. Oh, it was better than a rock, but then, anything was better than a rock. He supposed some men—like those despicable Rangers—thought they were living well when they wrapped themselves in a horse blanket and laid their heads on their saddles. Jean-Michel did not. He knew what living well meant, and soon—very soon—he would be doing exactly that.

In three days he'd be there. If everything went as planned, by the end of the week all would be complete. Zach Webster would be dead, and Isabelle would be his bride. Jean-Michel grinned, thinking about his wedding day. Revenge and a beautiful wife. What more could a man want? But first he had to get to Ladreville.

He turned, trying to find a comfortable position. Curse those Rangers! They were the reason he was forced to sleep outside. He'd heard they were after him. They were probably the ones who'd put out that "Wanted" poster. So what?

They'd never catch him. He was smarter than all of them put together. They didn't have a chance of finding Jean-Michel Ladre. No, sirree.

He turned again, filling the air with curses as a rock dug into his shoulder. A man of his stature should not sleep on the ground. And he wouldn't, once he got to Ladreville. He had it all planned. The first thing to do was kill Zach. Though his finger itched to pull the trigger, he knew it wouldn't be that simple. He had to find the right time and place. That meant taking a couple days to watch Zach and learn his patterns. Only a stupid man would risk killing him when others were around. Jean-Michel was not a stupid man. He knew what he had to do, and when he'd done it, he'd have his prize: Isabelle. He'd whisk her away from Ladreville and give her the life they both deserved, a life that would never again include sleeping on the ground.

As a light drizzle began to fall, Jean-Michel cursed again. Hard ground, rocks, and rain. It wasn't fair. Once he reached Ladreville, he would find a place to hide out, and you could bet your last dollar that that place would have a soft bed. It was a pity he couldn't go home. He had a mighty comfortable bed there, and the food was a sight better than anything he'd had since he left Houston. Home would be good. His mother would hide him. Jean-Michel knew that. The problem was, he wasn't sure about his father. After all, Papa was the one who'd sent him to Houston. Nope, he couldn't trust him. But there had to be a warm, dry, comfortable place to stay. He'd find it.

Jean-Michel pulled the blanket over his head, and as he did, he recalled all that had happened the night he'd been caught. It hadn't been just his life that had changed. Though the reasons were different, one of his friends had also left Ladreville that night. Jean-Michel grinned. That was the answer. The Lazy B would be empty. Perfect!

It was not a good day in Ladreville. Cold drizzle was falling, fraying people's tempers, and two normally friendly women had practically snarled at her when she'd greeted them with a smile. Priscilla couldn't help smiling. She was so happy that she felt as if her joy would bubble over. What a wonderful day it had been! When she'd reached the Samourins' home, a quick examination had told her it would be a difficult morning, for the baby was in the wrong position. Though Granny Menger had explained what to do with a breech birth, Priscilla's hands had shaken throughout the delivery, and she'd murmured silent prayers for both the mother and the baby's safety. Her prayers had been answered, for Annette Samourin was now basking in her husband's smile as she cradled their newborn son.

Her work done, Priscilla had left the Samourins' house, eager to return home and share the news with Zach. He would understand. He would take pleasure in her success. But Zach wasn't there. Priscilla's smile faded slightly as she realized how much she missed him. The house felt empty, not just in the evenings, which he normally spent with her, but all the time. And it wasn't only the house. Somehow, her whole life seemed empty without him to share it. Though he figured in her dreams almost every night and was in her thoughts all day long, that wasn't the same as being able to talk to him. With Zach out riding the range, Priscilla's life lost much of its color, becoming as gray as this morning's sky, but not even that could quench the joy she felt over the Samourin baby's birth. There must be someone she could tell about Ladreville's newest resident.

Priscilla looked down the street, her eyes resting on the mercantile. Slowly, she shook her head. Though Isabelle was a dear friend, she was so caught up in her own problems that she wouldn't understand what Annette Samourin's safe delivery meant to Priscilla. Yvonne would understand, but it would be cruel to tell her, for she was still recovering from the loss of her baby. Sarah couldn't be disturbed while she was teaching. Granny Menger was attending a delivery of her own and wasn't expected back until tonight.

Priscilla tried to swallow her disappointment. She'd go home, fix herself a cup of hot tea, and tonight she'd ride to the Bar C to tell Sarah. Though it wouldn't be the same as sharing her elation now, it would have to do.

She was passing the French church when a black-robed figure hurried from the parsonage. He wore no hat, carried no umbrella, and seemed oblivious to the rain. Bemused, Priscilla wondered which of his parishioners had summoned Père Tellier. To her surprise, he stopped in front of her. "Good afternoon, Mrs. Webster." The minister's eyes flitted over her face, as if he were looking for something. "Were you seeking me?"

There was something so eager about his expression that Priscilla hated to disappoint him. Rather than lie, she said, "Not really."

He tipped his head to one side, reminding her of a bird studying the ground. "That's odd. I had the strongest feeling that you needed me." He gestured toward the parsonage. "Come inside where it's warm and dry. Madame LeBrun has made fresh coffee, and I'm certain I smelled pastries baking."

The rumbling of her stomach reminded Priscilla that she hadn't eaten since breakfast. Perhaps Père Tellier was right. Perhaps she had been seeking him, though not consciously. She had wanted to share her news with someone, and though he wasn't a close friend, Père Tellier would understand what she was about to tell him. "I just delivered Madame Samourin's baby," she said when she was seated in the parsonage's main room, a cup of steaming coffee and a freshly baked pastry in front of her.

As the minister had promised, the parsonage was warm and dry, although devoid of embellishments. No rug covered the wooden floor, and the chairs were mismatched. Remembering the elegance of the French church, Priscilla was surprised by the almost Spartan environment of Père Tellier's home.

"Are Madame Samourin and the child all right?" The young pastor's eyes sought Priscilla's for confirmation.

"Oh yes, Father. It was a difficult birth, but they're both healthy, and Monsieur Samourin is proud as can be."

Père Tellier bowed his head. "Thank you, Lord, for bringing us a new soul, and thank you for leading Mrs. Webster to us. The town is blessed to have her."

"It is I who am blessed to be here," Priscilla said when the pastor had completed his prayer. "I didn't expect it, but I feel more at home in Ladreville than I ever did in Boston. I have friends here, and helping Granny Menger is very fulfilling. My life would be perfect if only . . ." Rather than complete her sentence, Priscilla picked up her cup.

When her words trailed off, Père Tellier prompted her. "If only what?"

She hadn't meant to speak of Isabelle and Gunther, and yet she couldn't stop now. "If only the town weren't so divided."

He nodded. "I assume you're speaking of Mademoiselle Rousseau and Herr Lehman."

"Yes." Priscilla took another sip of the rich coffee. "I believe God means them to be together, but the town is keeping them apart."

Père Tellier chewed his pastry slowly, apparently lost in thought. "I know them both well. Isabelle, of course, is one of my parishioners, but I visit Gunther occasionally." The pastor looked at Priscilla, his eyes twinkling. Before he spoke again, he glanced down at the plate of pastries. "Madame LeBrun has already warned me that she will stop baking if he leaves Ladreville. She claims no one else could mill flour as well as he."

Priscilla smiled. Though she doubted the pastor's housekeeper would follow through on her threat, it was a positive sign that not all the French townspeople were opposed to Gunther. "Then we both have reasons for wanting him to stay. Gunther's a fine man, and he'd be a good husband to Isabelle if only he had a chance. Oh, Father, isn't there something you can do?"

He was silent for a long moment. "I doubt I would have much effect alone, but perhaps if Pastor Sempert and I joined forces, we could do something." Père Tellier picked up his coffee cup, then placed it back on the saucer. "That's it," he said with a smile. "We'll try."

༄

Lawrence Wood tried to bite back his disappointment. He'd traveled every street in Ladreville, talking to residents

300

and looking for clues, but there was no doubt about it. Jean-Michel Ladre was not here, and that was difficult to accept. Lawrence's instincts were rarely wrong, and those instincts had told him a man like Jean-Michel would return to his home. By all accounts, the man who'd turned from petty thievery to murder was a man who liked his creature comforts. Lawrence's lip curled as he thought of the places he'd tracked Jean-Michel. He certainly hadn't had many comforts there, but everyone agreed he had been pampered here. That's why it made sense that he would have returned. Unfortunately for Lawrence, it appeared that he had not. The trail, which had been absurdly easy to follow at the beginning, had ended twenty miles away. It was almost as if Jean-Michel had disappeared. Lawrence mounted his horse. People didn't disappear. They simply went into hiding. That's what Jean-Michel had done. The question was, where?

A chill ran down Lawrence's spine as he thought of the woman who lived on the opposite bank of the river. He gripped the reins, then forced himself to relax. Priscilla was not in danger, at least not from Jean-Michel. The man had never met her. Even if he was over there, he would have no reason to harm her. Besides, it made more sense for Jean-Michel to stay on this side of the river. After all, that's where his parents and their nice, comfortable life were. Logic said that Lawrence's quarry would be on this bank of the Medina. Lawrence trusted logic, just as he trusted his instincts. And yet, though he knew it was illogical, he could not dismiss his fear.

A minute later, he was fording the river, heading for the Lazy B. He had to be certain Priscilla was safe.

‍❧

Zach! Zach was home! The thought ricocheted through Priscilla's mind as she raced to the door. The sound of hoof-beats served as a siren song, drawing her outside to welcome her husband. She stepped onto the porch, her heart pounding with anticipation, her smile so wide she felt as if her face would split. It would be wonderful to see Zach again, to hear about his week and to tell him of hers. How grateful she was that the waiting was over! It had been less than a week, but it seemed that Zach had been gone far longer than that. And now he was home again.

She squinted, anxious for her first glimpse of her husband, and as she did the elation that had buoyed her drained away. The approaching rider was the Ranger, not Zach. Numb with disappointment, Priscilla took a step forward to greet her visitor.

"Good afternoon, Mrs. Webster." As he dismounted, the Ranger doffed his hat. "I'm sorry for bothering you, but I wanted to assure myself that you were all right."

The words surprised Priscilla. Why would he think something was wrong? Had the Dunkler brothers come this way, after all? Surely not. It had been more than six months since Zeke had been killed. If they blamed her for their brother's death, surely they would have sought revenge before now. There must be another reason the Ranger was here. Perhaps he'd heard that Zach was gone and was simply checking on her, the way a neighbor might.

"I'm fine," Priscilla said, "other than a bit lonely. You probably know Zach is riding the range."

As the lawman shook his head, his eyes moved quickly, looking around the ranch, searching for anything out of the ordinary. Priscilla had seen him do that on his previous visits.

This must be part of being a Ranger, having to be constantly vigilant. Perhaps he'd grown tired of it and that was one of the reasons he was considering leaving the Rangers.

"Might I trouble you for a glass of water?" he asked as he stepped onto the porch.

"It's no trouble at all." But it was the first time he'd accepted any form of hospitality. Something was different today. Though there was no wind, she shivered and wished Zach were home. Forcing a polite smile onto her face, Priscilla nodded at the Ranger. "I have fresh buttermilk if you'd prefer that."

When she returned with the buttermilk and found him pacing the porch, Priscilla's uneasiness grew. In the past, the Ranger had been calm, betraying no emotion and certainly not displaying any signs of anxiety. "Please have a seat." She gestured toward the chair opposite her. Though it would be rude to tell him that his pacing made her nervous, she wanted it to cease.

He sank into the chair and took a long swallow of milk, his eyes never leaving her face. Carefully placing the glass on the floor, he leaned forward. "I worry about you."

Priscilla tried to mask her surprise. Whatever she might have expected him to say, it was not that. "Why?"

"I know what you endured last year. That was more than any woman should have to go through. I worry that, because of the Dunkler brothers, you've been cheated out of the life you deserve."

As the hair on the back of her neck began to rise, Priscilla sought a way to end the conversation. The Ranger was touching on things she did not want to discuss, but it wasn't only his words that disturbed her. His eyes seemed unnaturally bright, as if he had a fever. Perhaps he was ill. Perhaps that was why he was saying such odd things. That would explain his asking for water. "I . . ."

He held up a hand. "Please let me continue. I know why you married Zach. It's my fault." If it wouldn't have been incredibly rude, Priscilla would have risen, putting an end to the Ranger's visit. But she could not be rude. Her mother had impressed on her the need to be polite, particularly to visitors. The Ranger was not just a visitor. He was the person who'd saved her life.

"You needed a man to protect you," the Ranger continued. "I should have realized that and offered to marry you that day."

"Mr. Wood . . ." This time Priscilla did rise. Rude or not, she was going inside the house.

"Call me Lawrence."

The emotion in his voice kept her from moving. She couldn't be cruel to this man. "Lawrence." The name sounded odd on her tongue. In her mind, he was simply The Ranger. "I wasn't in any condition to marry anyone that day." She hadn't been ready to marry in January, either, but her pregnancy had left her no choice.

"I know, but I hate the thought that I missed my chance." The Ranger looked down at the porch floor, as if trying to compose himself. When he raised his eyes to meet hers, she saw the same brightness that had alarmed her earlier. "What I'm trying to say is that I love you, Priscilla. I always will."

He was ill. That was the only explanation. But as Priscilla recalled the number of times he'd visited when there had been no real reason for him to be in Ladreville, she wondered if the illness was one of the mind, not the body. He had confused love with another emotion, perhaps sympathy, more likely pity. Whatever it was, it was not love. No one could love her, not after what had happened. Oh, it was true that Zach cared for her, but that was because he was a kind man. He didn't love her—not the way a man would love his wife. The dream that had turned into a nightmare reminded her of that on a regular basis. Zach did not love her.

The Ranger didn't, either. There had to be a way to make him understand that. Priscilla seized on the most obvious obstacle. "I'm married."

He nodded. "I'm painfully aware of that, but I don't believe it's a real marriage." She blanched. How had he guessed that? She hadn't told anyone that hers was a marriage in name only, and she doubted Zach had.

The Ranger appeared unaware of her distress, for he continued. "I'm not saying it isn't legal, but I don't think your marriage is based on love." Priscilla took a deep breath, relieved that he didn't know the truth of her arrangement with Zach. "If you ever decide to end it, I would be honored if you would become my wife."

Priscilla rose and took a step toward the door. This conversation had gone beyond the bounds of propriety. There was no reason to continue it. "I'm sorry, but . . ."

The Ranger rose and looked down at her, his blue eyes filled with pain. "I'm the one who's sorry. I took you by surprise. There's no need to answer now. Just know that if you ever need me, all you have to do is send for me."

As he mounted his horse, Priscilla gripped the porch railing, trying to calm herself. She wouldn't send for Lawrence. Even if Zach asked for an annulment, Priscilla knew she would not wed again. There would never be anyone like Zach, a man who knew her deepest secrets and cared for her despite them, a man who'd captured her heart and shown her what love could be. Zach was the only husband she would ever have, the only one she would ever want.

～⁓

When she heard the horse, Priscilla shuddered. Since Lawrence's visit yesterday, she'd been almost afraid to go outside. It was silly, of course, to be so skittish, but she couldn't help it. The memory of the Ranger's conversation haunted her. What had she done to make him think she would be interested in marrying him? She'd been polite, even friendly, each time he'd come to the ranch, but surely she hadn't done anything to encourage him or to make him think she harbored tender feelings for him. And why would he think she would want to end her marriage? It was true she'd offered Zach an annulment, but that was for his sake, not hers. If Zach decided he wanted to be free when the six months were over, Priscilla knew she would leave Ladreville, but she would not remarry. Why, then, had the Ranger asked her to marry him? It made no sense. But it also made no sense to remain inside the house, cowering just because a horse was approaching.

She stepped onto the porch, her fear disappearing as she realized that it was Zach who was only a few yards from the house. The smile she'd worn yesterday reappeared as she hurried down the stairs.

"It's good to be home." Zach covered the short distance between them in three long strides, then stood there, smiling down at Priscilla. "I missed you."

"I missed you too. There's so much to tell you." She wanted to share everything that had happened while Zach had been gone, everything except the Ranger's visit. "But first, were the cattle all right?"

Zach climbed the stairs and opened the door for Priscilla. "I don't know," he said as they entered the house.

Priscilla turned and stared at him. "What do you mean? I don't understand."

Zach gave her a sheepish grin. "I wasn't riding the range. I was looking for something for you."

"Me?" For the second time in as many days, Priscilla was at a loss for words. "What on earth were you looking for?" She led the way into the kitchen and sank onto one of the wooden chairs. Though the parlor was more comfortable, she knew Zach would not want to sit there until he'd bathed.

"Something special." His smile widened. "Does it surprise you that I want to give you a present?"

"It's not my birthday or Christmas."

"It wasn't either of those the day I gave you flowers, but you seemed to like them anyway."

"I did." She glanced toward the parlor where the china bowl with the dried petals sat. "I still do."

"I think you might like this even better." Zach reached into a pocket and handed her a small paper-wrapped item. When she stared at it, trying to imagine what might be inside, he said, "Go ahead. Open it."

She unwrapped it carefully, then gasped. "My locket!" Somehow, somewhere he had found her locket. Tears of joy filled Priscilla's eyes as she realized Zach had remembered the day when she'd wept over the loss of the necklace. Though another man might have dismissed her tears as female foolishness, Zach had done what he could to banish her sorrow. What a wonderful man she'd married. "Oh, Zach, where did you find it?"

"Near New Braunfels." He acted as if what he'd accomplished was trivial, that this was an ordinary present, not the restoration of something she had believed lost forever. Zach's lips curved in another smile. "I figured the Dunkler brothers would sell it, and they did. The biggest problem was figuring out where." Zach gestured toward his travel-stained clothing. "It took a bit longer than I'd hoped to find the man who'd bought the locket. He was saving it for his wife's birthday, but when he heard my story, he agreed to sell it to me."

Priscilla fingered the locket that she held in one palm, then looked up at the man who had brought it to her. "Oh, Zach, I don't know how to thank you. I never thought I'd see this again." Though she was eager to clasp it around her neck, there was something far more important to do first. Priscilla slid her fingernail between the two halves.

"Wait a minute." Zach spoke quickly. "I know what you're looking for, but the pictures are gone. The farmer said the locket was empty when he bought it. The bandits must have thrown the photographs away." Zach's eyes were serious as he said, "I'm sorry, Priscilla. I know how much you cherished them."

They were what had made the locket special, for they were her last link to her family. Priscilla stared at the necklace for a moment, preparing herself for the disappointment. Now that she knew the locket was empty, perhaps she should not open it. Nothing would be served by confirming Zach's words, and the sight of the plain metal would only revive unhappy memories.

Priscilla unhooked the chain, determined that once the locket was around her neck, it would never be removed. She reached behind her neck, but as she started to fasten the clasp, her hands refused to complete the simple task. No matter how painful it was, she needed to look inside. With trembling hands, Priscilla opened the delicate heart-shaped locket. As Zach had told her, the two halves that had once held her parents' and her sister's portraits were now nothing more than empty frames. But, though the locket was empty, Priscilla's heart was not. Instead of the pain she'd expected, she felt only joy at the realization of all Zach had done for her.

"I'm sorry the pictures are gone," he said again. "An empty locket doesn't seem right."

Priscilla rose. "It won't be empty for long." A moment later, she returned from the parlor, the china bowl filled with dried flower petals in one hand. When Zach raised an eyebrow, Priscilla explained. "I'm going to put petals in place of the pictures." She stirred the potpourri carefully before pulling out two of the larger pieces. As Zach watched, she slid them into the two halves of the locket, then closed it and clasped it around her neck. "It's perfect," she said, willing him to understand how much he had given her. "The locket was part of my past, but now it will be part of the present too. Don't you see, Zach? It's perfect that the gift from my parents should be filled with the first thing you gave me."

He appeared unconvinced, as if she made little sense. Priscilla smiled again as she said, "Thank you, Zach. There are no words to tell you how happy you've made me." That was the problem. Mama had always said actions were more powerful than words. She needed to show Zach, not just tell him. Priscilla took a step closer, then bent to press a kiss on his cheek. But as her lips approached him, memories of the bandit's rough skin and fetid breath assailed her.

Priscilla jumped back with an anguished cry. "I can't!"

17

It was Sunday. Jean-Michel kicked the ground in frustration when he heard the distant peal of bells. Somehow he'd lost track of the days, and now he'd have to wait another twenty-four hours. As unfortunate as the delay was, he couldn't risk going into Ladreville on a Sunday. Nothing was predictable on Sunday, and that increased the chances of being seen. He couldn't let that happen. He'd come too far and planned his revenge too carefully to do anything that would jeopardize his success.

Jean-Michel led the horse back into the trees, resigning himself to another boring day. As much as he hated the idea of another night spent outdoors, it couldn't be helped. Tomorrow would be different. Tomorrow he would be in Ladreville. Tomorrow he would sleep in comfort again. And then . . . Jean-Michel smiled as he thought of Zach Webster's lifeless body sprawled on the ground and Isabelle, sweet Isabelle, rushing into his arms. Soon everything would be perfect.

"Are you certain you won't sit with us?" Isabelle raised an impeccably groomed eyebrow as she darted a glance at the pew where her parents and Léon were seated.

Priscilla shook her head. "We'll be more comfortable in the back." Though she and Zach occasionally sat with the Rousseaus, today was one day Priscilla wanted to keep a distance. She had heard nothing from Père Tellier and did not know how he and Pastor Sempert planned to address the problem with Isabelle and Gunther, but if he used today's sermon to make a point, Priscilla did not want to be seated with the Rousseaus. If Monsieur Rousseau believed that she had meddled in his affairs again, he might grow angry, and the church was no place for a confrontation. "We'll sit with you next time," she told Isabelle.

"Good morning, Yvonne." Priscilla greeted her friend as she entered the church.

Though she murmured a response, Yvonne kept her eyes averted from Isabelle and quickly moved into one of the pews. When Isabelle flushed at the insult and hurried toward her parents, Priscilla sighed. The rift between two women who'd once been friends was senseless, and yet it persisted. Afraid that Père Tellier and Pastor Sempert would be unable to change anything, Priscilla said a silent prayer, asking God to soften the parishioners' hearts.

When Père Tellier moved to the pulpit for the sermon, the congregation settled back in their pews. Some of them, Priscilla knew from previous Sundays, would doze while he spoke, but the majority would listen. Like Pastor Sempert, Père Tellier was respected by the community, and his words bore far more weight than ordinary citizens'.

Priscilla looked at the man who'd raised her hopes for re-uniting the town. Was it her imagination that he stood there silently for longer than normal, as if he were assessing his parishioners' moods? But when he spoke, Priscilla tried to swallow her disappointment. It appeared she'd been mistaken in thinking he and Pastor Sempert would use their sermons to promote harmony.

"Today's sermon is based on the gospel of Matthew, chapter 7, verses 16 through 20." The minister paused, then began to read from his Bible. "'Ye shall know them by their fruits. Do men gather grapes of thorns, or figs of thistles? Even so every good tree bringeth forth good fruit; but a corrupt tree bringeth forth evil fruit. A good tree cannot bring forth evil fruit, neither can a corrupt tree bring forth good fruit. Every tree that bringeth not forth good fruit is hewn down, and cast into the fire. Wherefore by their fruits ye shall know them.'" Père Tellier paused, his eyes once again moving slowly from the first to the last pew.

Priscilla recognized the passage and wondered what his message would be. Though Pastor Sempert sometimes used obscure references, Père Tellier did not. Priscilla took a quick breath when she realized that Pastor Sempert might have chosen this, that it might have a connection to Isabelle and Gunther.

"Our Lord was speaking of false prophets," Père Tellier continued, "but his words apply to each one of us in our daily lives." Priscilla nodded. That sounded like something Pastor Sempert would have said. Père Tellier kept his eyes focused on his congregation. "How do we judge our fellow men? Do we consider their fruits, the things they have accomplished, the deeds they've done, or do we measure them by other standards?"

He paused again, letting his questions ring throughout the church. Priscilla saw several people fidget, as if they were uncomfortable with the minister's words. Her heart soared when she realized that Père Tellier was being a true shepherd, leading the flock in the direction he had chosen, using his words and the Lord's as a shepherd would his crook.

"Do we judge men as more or less worthy because of the color of their hair or the language they speak?" Père Tellier lifted his Bible and held it so all could see the pages. "You heard our Lord's words. I ask you, are hair color and language the fruits our Lord meant, or are they nothing more than outer trappings?" The fidgeting grew worse. Priscilla saw several people lower their heads, though whether in shame or prayer she did not know.

"My children, God has brought us here to a new country. He has blessed us with health and prosperity. How do we thank him? Do we follow his commandments? Do we seek to live a life that shows the world we are disciples of Christ? Or do we come here each Sunday and make promises that are no more than empty words?" Though Père Tellier's voice had risen, he lowered it to little more than a whisper as he said, "I ask you to look deep inside your hearts. Are you judging each other—even those who are not members of this congregation—by their fruits or by something else, something contrary to our Lord's commandments?"

He was silent for a long moment, letting his words penetrate his parishioners' hearts. "In the very same chapter of Matthew, verses 1 and 2, our Lord says, 'Judge not, that ye be not judged. For with what judgment ye judge, ye shall be judged: and with what measure ye mete, it shall be measured to you again.'" The minister folded his hands as he looked at his flock. "Search your hearts, and if you have wronged another through your judgment, today is the day to make amends. Today is the Lord's day. Let us use it to do his will."

The church was silent as Père Tellier ended his sermon. Instead of immediately announcing the final hymn, he said nothing, merely stood in the pulpit, his head bowed in prayer. Two rows in front of Priscilla, Yvonne turned to Neville, and there was no mistaking the tears that coursed down her cheeks. *Thank you, Lord, for opening her heart.* There was a rustle further forward. Priscilla's eyes widened as Isabelle's father stood and made his way to the front of the church. When he turned to face the congregation, he appeared to have aged a dozen years.

"In anger, I told Mr. Webster that only a sign from God could change my mind. I did not want such a sign, but today Père Tellier has given it. He is right." Monsieur Rousseau's voice was little more than a whisper. Clearing his throat, he spoke again, more loudly this time. "I have counted myself a righteous man. I come to church each Sunday. I read the Bible every day, but I have failed my Lord. I have judged a man—many men and women—by things that are unimportant. I've measured them by their surnames, the church they attend, the language they speak."

As Monsieur Rousseau's face contorted with pain, Priscilla heard Zach's intake of breath, and he whispered, "Thank you, Lord."

Isabelle's father straightened his shoulders as he looked out at the congregation. "I have been the worst of hypocrites. I was happy to have Ladreville's German citizens come into my store. Their money was as good as anyone's. But when a man—an honorable man—asked for my daughter's hand in marriage, I refused him for the simple reason that he was a German."

He closed his eyes for a second, perhaps in an attempt to fight back tears. When he regained his composure, he said, "I was wrong. I will ask his forgiveness as I will beg for my Lord's. Now I ask for yours. If my words and deeds have led you to consider our German brothers and sisters less worthy than us, I was wrong. Please forgive me." He looked at the pew where his wife, daughter, and son were seated. "Gunther Lehman is a good man. If he will forgive me, I will be honored to call him my son-in-law."

A second later, Isabelle was at her father's side. Though tears were streaming down her face as she wrapped her arms around him and led him back to their pew, everyone in the church heard her say, "I love you, Papa."

༄

"I won't call it a miracle," Clay said an hour later as Martina served Sunday dinner at the Bar C, "but it came close."

Priscilla laid down her fork. Though the roast chicken and sweet potatoes were delicious, what Clay was saying was more important than any food. He confirmed what Priscilla had surmised, that Pastor Sempert's sermon was similar to Père Tellier's.

"The men who'd been the most outspoken in their criticism of Gunther surrounded him when the service was over," Clay continued. "I saw some pretty sheepish faces."

"The same thing happened to Isabelle," Priscilla told her friends. "I was so happy when I saw Yvonne hug her that I wanted to shout 'hallelujah.'" Père Tellier's sermon had been the most powerful one Priscilla had ever heard, leaving no doubt that God had directed his words.

Sarah handed her sister another biscuit. "Today has been an answer to prayer."

Zach raised one of his brows as he looked from Priscilla to Sarah, his expression appraising. "I guess this means you ladies consider your matchmaking a success."

At the far end of the table, Clay's father made a sound that was suspiciously like a chuckle. When Sarah nodded, Clay's lips quirked in a grin. It appeared he shared his father's amusement. "Zach, my friend, I have some bad news for you. If you think they're retiring, you don't know women very well. Sarah and Priscilla will find another set of victims."

"Victims?" Priscilla feigned indignation. What joy it was, laughing with friends on a beautiful day. The sun was out in all its glory, and God had opened the townspeople's hearts. What more could anyone ask? "That's a horrible way to describe Gunther and Isabelle. They're not victims. Why, I doubt there's anyone in Ladreville who's happier than they are today."

Sarah looked up from the biscuit she was buttering, and her eyes sparkled. "Clay and I might challenge them for that honor." She gave her husband a smile of pure happiness before she said, "We have some good news. We're expecting a baby."

A baby. Priscilla pushed a stab of envy aside. If anyone deserved happiness it was Sarah and Clay. Besides, it wasn't their fault that she was childless. She could have a baby of her own, if only . . . Taking a deep breath, Priscilla tamped down the memories that even now had the power to roil her

316

stomach. "That's wonderful." She rose and hugged Sarah, then flashed Clay a bright smile. "When is the baby due?"

"October." It was Sarah who answered. "I expect you to deliver it."

Priscilla gave her another hug. "I'm so happy for you." And she was. Truly. She'd had her chance at motherhood. Now her mission was to help other women's babies be born.

"Me going to have baby to play with," Thea announced.

"You are, indeed." Priscilla nodded at the little girl who'd welcomed her into her heart the first day she'd come to Ladreville. "Sarah will need your help."

"Me know. Me and Papa Clay help with the baby." For the second time Clay's father chuckled.

As Priscilla took another bite of chicken, she watched Zach clap Clay on the shoulder. "Congratulations. You'll be a great father."

"So will you. Your turn is coming."

Though Zach looked away quickly, Priscilla saw the discomfort on his face. Had he lied when he said that he didn't need children? It appeared he had regrets, deep regrets.

He had intended to wait until dark to enter Ladreville, reasoning that fewer people would be outside, and that even those who were would have trouble seeing him. But then a new idea had popped into his brain. He was so smart! This plan was better. There was no reason to go through town. If he continued north, bypassing Ladreville, he could cross the river upstream where no one lived. All it meant was a couple miles more riding, but that was better than hanging around in the forest, waiting for the sun to set. Once he forded the river, he'd be on the west bank. Perfect. No houses and lots of trees. What a great plan! No one would see him, and he'd get to the ranch in time for dinner.

Jean-Michel spurred his horse as the thought of a good meal made him salivate. Even though the Brambles had been gone for months, he'd bet there was some food left. At a minimum he reasoned there'd be canned goods, and maybe if luck continued on his side, there'd be some smoked meat. Whatever else folks might say about the Widow Bramble, she was a fine cook. Jean-Michel's stomach growled at the memory of the pies she occasionally provided for their poker games. And then there were the jams she used to bring to the potluck suppers. Those were mighty delicious. Even if all he had was hardtack, it would be tasty with some of Widow Bramble's peach preserves on it. Yes, indeed, this was a good plan.

Two hours later, he reined in his horse as he approached the ranch house. There was no point in being foolhardy. A smart man took no chances, and Jean-Michel Ladre was a smart man. He looked around. The place was better cared for than he'd expected. There were even some flowers growing close to the porch. It was almost as if someone had planted them. A prickle of concern snaked down his back, but he dismissed it. Who would have planted posies? No one lived here. There was another explanation, a simpler one. Didn't his mother talk about flowers coming back year after year? That's what happened here.

He was grinning as he drew closer. Yes, sirree, that house looked downright appealing. He'd have a roof over his head and a soft bed under his back. Mighty fine.

Jean-Michel's grin faded abruptly when a strange woman

stepped onto the front porch. He drew his gun. It had been different in the Old Country, but Texas ladies could be just as dangerous as the men. He was taking no chances.

"Who are you?" he demanded. There wasn't supposed to be anyone here. The woman had reddish hair, and even from here he could see that her eyes were green. She was pretty enough, if you liked tall women and fiery hair. Jean-Michel didn't. He had his mind set on wedding a brunette who came no higher than his heart.

"I'm Priscilla Webster."

"Webster?" Was it possible? Had luck come his way? Jean-Michel narrowed his eyes. "Are you related to Zach Webster?"

The woman nodded. "I'm his wife."

Elation shot through him. Zach had a wife! Oh, what a perfect day! Coming here had been a stroke of pure genius. A dry bed, good food, and a double helping of revenge. What more could a man want?

Jean-Michel dismounted and gestured toward the door. "Let's go inside."

꒰Ꙩ꒱

The man was evil. She could see it in his eyes. Though his facial features were not the same, his eyes held the same gleam as Zeke Dunkler's. Priscilla started to shake as memories of the stagecoach holdup and its aftermath surged through her. *Help me, Lord*, she prayed silently. *Give me strength*. When her trembling subsided, she faced the stranger. "It appears you've lost your way." Perhaps if she pretended she didn't see the menace in his expression, he would leave.

He shook his head. "That's where you're wrong. I'm right where I'm meant to be." He walked toward her, swaggering

319

slightly as if he owned the ranch. "I've got a score to settle with your husband."

Why would anyone hold a grudge against Zach? He was a peace-loving man who had vowed never to hurt another. Still, there was no doubt about the stranger's feelings. Whether the cause was imaginary or not, he meant to hurt Zach. Priscilla blanched at the thought of the Dunkler brothers' rifles and her parents' lifeless bodies. She couldn't let that happen to Zach. Somehow she had to warn him and keep him away from the ranch until the stranger left. Oh, why did today have to be the day the ranch hands were helping at the Bar C?

"Who are you?" Though she was confident she had never met him, something about the stranger tugged at Priscilla's memory.

Keeping his gun trained on her, the man sneered. "I'm Jean-Michel Ladre." Priscilla nodded slightly. Now that she knew to look for it, there was a resemblance to the town's mayor. The name did not reassure her. This was the man who'd robbed his employer and killed an itinerant peddler.

"My mama taught me to always say 'at your service'," Jean-Michel continued, "but the truth is, you're at my service." He waved his gun toward the front door. "Inside. We'll wait for Zach there. I can think of some mighty pleasant ways to pass the time."

The smile he gave her sent another shiver of dread through her. Jean-Michel wore the same expression as Zeke Dunkler just before he had attacked her. Priscilla clenched her fists. She would not be a victim. Never again. She had to get away from him. Her eyes moved quickly, measuring the distances. She had no chance of reaching Jean-Michel's horse. That left only the house. She was closer than he, for he still had to climb the stairs. Priscilla spun around and raced into the house, sliding the lock behind her.

"Let me in!" It was only an instant before he pounded on the door. "Let me in!" His words were followed by a burst of gunfire.

Priscilla dropped to the floor, covering her head as bullets entered the house. When the shots ceased, she took a deep breath, then shuddered. The kitchen. She'd forgotten there was another door. Scrambling to her feet, she ran into the kitchen, but she was too late.

As she entered the room, she felt his presence. Somehow he'd moved more quickly than she. It was almost as if he knew the house. Of course he did. Hadn't Sarah said that Jean-Michel was one of the men who'd played poker here every week? The thoughts tumbled through Priscilla's mind in the instant it took for him to reach out from behind the door and drag her against him. She gagged at the smell of his body and the pressure of his arm around her. *Help me, Lord*, she prayed. *Show me what to do.*

"Not so smart are you, little lady?" Jean-Michel chuckled as he pressed his gun into the small of her back. "You just learned a lesson. No one's smarter than me."

There had to be a way to stop him. Though her heart was beating faster than a hummingbird's wings, Priscilla willed her voice to remain even. "What do you want?"

"Your husband." To Priscilla's relief, Jean-Michel pushed her into one of the chairs, then perched on the edge of the table, keeping the gun pointed at her. Her first prayer had been answered, for it appeared that he had no intention of harming her. *Keep Zach safe*, she prayed. *Take away this man's anger.*

Jean-Michel's eyes were cold with fury as he glared at her.

"It's thanks to your husband"—he spat the word as if it were an epithet—"that my father sold me into slavery. If it hadn't been for Zach Webster, I would never have been banished. But, no, he had to interfere. He had to tell my father all those lies. Now he's going to pay."

Priscilla thought quickly. Somehow she had to warn Zach, and to do that, she had to distract Jean-Michel long enough to escape. "You must have traveled a long distance," she said as calmly as she could. "I imagine you're tired and hungry. Would you like something to eat?" She gestured toward the stove. "It will be hours before Zach comes home."

"You think I'm stupid? That's some kind of trick."

"You think common hospitality is a trick?"

His stomach growled. "All right," he said at last, "but don't try anything funny." He tugged her to her feet. "I'll be watching every move."

"I could heat some pot roast and fry some potatoes. How does that sound?" Priscilla kept her tone matter-of-fact as she took a step toward the stove. Then, before he could react, she whirled around, knocking the gun from his hand and jabbing her fingers into his eyes. As Jean-Michel yowled with pain, she ran outdoors and raced toward his horse.

Just another few steps, and she'd be there. Just another few steps, and she'd be on her way to find Zach. Just another . . . Priscilla's heart was pounding so hard that she did not hear the footsteps behind her. All she knew was that one instant she was running, the next she was face first on the ground with a heavy body atop her.

No! Memories flooded her brain. Not again! *Help me, Lord,* she prayed. *Help me.*

Jean-Michel yanked her arms behind her and pulled

Priscilla to her feet. "You shouldn't have done that." His lips curled with contempt. "Now I've got no choice. I have to kill you."

⟊

The dream came again last night. The dream, not the horrible nightmare that had disturbed his sleep for so many years. Zach slid off Charcoal and began to inspect the fence. Thank goodness the wire was only bent and not cut. He wiped the sweat from his face as he recalled the dream. In it, he'd been riding home. As was true of dreams, while some of the details were vivid, others were not. He knew he'd been gone a long time, but whether it was weeks or months or even years was not clear. All he knew was that he was filled with an urgency to be home. He'd ridden through the thicket. Somehow, the trees had seemed taller and closer together than he remembered, as if they'd grown while he was gone. It should have taken only a few minutes to traverse the forest, but in his dream, it seemed endless. In desperation, he'd slid off Charcoal and made his way on foot, but that was worse, for he felt as if he were caught in quicksand, struggling with all his might, unable to make any forward progress.

And then at last he reached the clearing. There it was, the house he'd dreamt of for so long. He stood for a moment, smiling, though he knew others would not understand the way he felt about it. After all, it was nothing more than a simple farmhouse with a wraparound porch, steep gables, and flowers in front. Compared to the Bar C or even the Lazy B, it was nothing to brag about. And yet it was home. His home and hers.

As he approached the house, anticipation turned to disappointment. He'd thought she'd be on the porch waiting for him, but the porch was empty. Only the plume of smoke rising from the chimney told him someone still lived here. He climbed the steps, more slowly than normal, his hand hesitating for a second before he opened the door. And then he saw her standing just inside the door, beckoning him to enter. Her smile was so full of love that he wondered how he could have doubted anything. This was where he was meant to be. This was the woman he was meant to love.

She smiled again, then spoke so softly he had to strain to hear her. "Welcome home, Zach. I have something to show you." She turned and led the way to a small room he hadn't remembered being there. Gently, she turned the knob and swung the door open. There might have been other furniture. Zach wasn't certain, for his eyes focused on the rocking chair and what stood next to it. For a second, he couldn't identify the small wooden object, but when he did, his eyes widened.

One instant she was standing next to him. The next she was bending over to reach into the cradle. When she stood, a tiny form nestled in her arms, Priscilla smiled again. "Do you want to hold your son?"

That was when he woke. It was when he always woke, before he had a chance to cradle his child, to gaze at the baby's face and touch the miniature features. The aftermath was predictable. Each time he had the dream, he would waken filled with an intense longing. It was only a dream, he would tell himself. It would never come true. And yet, though he knew he and Priscilla would never have a child, every fiber of his being wished that this dream would come true.

Think of all that is good, Zach admonished himself as he mounted Charcoal. Priscilla was healing. Though he doubted she would ever fully recover from the bandit's attack, he took comfort from the fact that she no longer shied from him. Theirs might not be a conventional marriage, but it brought Zach more happiness than he'd thought possible. He would have to be content with that.

"C'mon, Charcoal." Perhaps it was recalling the dream that made him anxious to be home. Perhaps it was simply thinking of Priscilla. Zach didn't try to explain it. Instead, he leaned forward and urged Charcoal to gallop. The day was beautiful. Perhaps he and Priscilla could ride to the clearing after supper. Perhaps that was why he remembered the dream. Perhaps it was the clearing that was important, not the baby he'd never hold.

When he reached the Lazy B, Zach's hackles rose. Why was a strange horse tethered to the front porch? This wasn't the Ranger's palomino, and no one in Ladreville would have such a poorly groomed animal. Itinerants came to town, but they would have no reason to be on this side of the river and even less reason to venture onto the Lazy B.

A shiver of dread passed through Zach as he recalled Lawrence Wood's words. The Dunkler brothers. Had they come to exact revenge? Zach's heart pounded at the thought of one of the men who'd killed Priscilla's parents being inside the house with the woman he loved. He pulled his gun, then moved with the stealth he'd learned in prison. Silently Zach lifted the latch and entered the kitchen.

No! Blood drained from his face, and for an instant the world turned black. Though his heart shrieked denial, Zach knew he was not imagining the scene before him. This was worse than Perote, worse than any nightmare he'd ever had, for it was Priscilla's worst fears come true. She hated to be touched, but she had obviously been touched, because there

325

she was, tied to a chair. It was bad enough that her feet were roped together. Even worse, her hands were bound behind her. Zach knew how she hated to have her hands restrained in any way, for Zeke Dunkler had tied her hands before he attacked her. To complete the nightmare, a dark-haired man stood before her, his knife at her throat.

"Zach!" As Priscilla cried out his name, the man turned, and Zach's blood turned cold. Not even in Perote had he seen such hatred on a man's face.

"Hello, Zach." Jean-Michel Ladre's smile was little more than a sneer. "I'm glad you could join our party."

"What are you doing here?" The man was evil. That was clear. He intended to harm Priscilla. That was equally clear. What wasn't clear was why.

Jean-Michel smiled again. "I thought that was obvious. I've been waiting for you."

Revenge. Zach remembered Jean-Michel's threats the night he had been apprehended. At the time Zach had dismissed them as nothing more than an angry man's ranting. Though it appeared he'd been wrong to underestimate Jean-Michel, that was unimportant now. What mattered was keeping Priscilla safe. Though he looked at Zach, Jean-Michel kept the knife so close to Priscilla's throat that Zach feared even a twitch would slice the tender skin.

"You thought you were smart, turning me in to my father. Your lies were the reason he sent me to Houston to work as a common laborer. You're the one who kept me from marrying the woman I wanted." Jean-Michel's lip curled in contempt. "You thought you were smart. Well, look at you now. You're not so smart. You're going to watch your wife die, and then it'll be your turn."

Zach stared at the handsome young man who had thrown away his chance at a normal life. If Isabelle Rousseau had ever cared about him, it was only as a friend, but Jean-Michel had taken a simple neighborly smile and invented a grand romance. If the situation had not been so serious, Zach might have pitied Jean-Michel, but there was no time for pity.

He tightened his finger on the trigger. "You're wrong. I can kill you before you have a chance to hurt Priscilla." As he pronounced the words, Zach's mind replayed the image of John Tallman's body and he heard Margaret's shrill cry. *If you leave, I'll kill your baby.* Zach shuddered. Never again. He had sworn that he would never again be the cause of a death. And now . . .

"Don't do it, Zach." Though Priscilla's eyes were filled with fear, Zach sensed the fear was for him, not herself.

Jean-Michel sneered again. "Listen to your wife, Zach. She's smarter than you are. Besides, everyone in Ladreville knows you'd never kill a man. We all heard you say there'd been too much killing."

There had been. Zach took a deep breath, keeping his gun trained on Jean-Michel. He didn't want to kill him, but if he didn't do something, another innocent person would die. *Lord, give me strength. Show me the way to save Priscilla.* "Let her go. Your quarrel is with me."

"Why should I let her go? Thanks to you, I learned a lot of lessons. One of those lessons was that killing is easy. There are no regrets."

Zach steeled himself to show no emotion. As he had feared, Jean-Michel was like several of the jailers, a man with no conscience. There was no reasoning with someone like that. *Lord, open his heart. Let him see how wrong he is.*

"Leave, Zach. Leave while you can." The blood had drained from Priscilla's face, making her three freckles stand out in relief.

"That's right, Zach," Jean-Michel taunted him. "Show your wife what a coward you are. Leave her here to die alone."

There was no choice. Zach raised his gun slightly, aiming it at Jean-Michel's arm. "Drop the knife, Jean-Michel. You know it's no match for a six-shooter."

"No match? What do you think of this?" He pressed the knife into Priscilla's throat.

As Zach watched, beads of blood began to form on the blade. Jean-Michel wouldn't stop. Zach knew that. Unless he acted, Priscilla would be dead. *Help me, Lord*. He pulled the trigger.

"You won't . . ." As he pronounced the words, Jean-Michel wheeled around, and the bullet that had been aimed at his shoulder slammed into his chest. A second later, he lay crumpled on the floor, an expression of surprise on his lifeless face.

Zach's stomach heaved. Priscilla. He had to help Priscilla. There was nothing he could do for Jean-Michel. Zach grabbed the knife and slit the ropes, releasing both her hands and feet. As she shook her hands, trying to restore the feeling, he fished a handkerchief from his pocket and pressed it to her throat to staunch the bleeding.

"Are you all right?"

Priscilla examined the handkerchief. "The bleeding is stopping. Thanks to you, I'm fine." Her eyes darkened. "What about you? Are you okay?"

Zach looked at the lifeless body on the floor. "I don't know."

18

He'd vowed never to kill again, and yet he had. Tears welled in Zach's eyes as he stared at Jean-Michel's body. Zach's finger had pulled the trigger, and because of that, a man was dead. Regardless of the circumstances, he had broken his vow. *Thou shalt not kill.* The commandment echoed inside his head, followed by the memory of Robert Canfield's words. *There has been too much killing.* Zach had not heeded his mentor, and—far worse—he had disobeyed his God. He dropped to his knees and bowed his head. "Dear Lord, forgive me." The words came out as little more than a whisper, but he knew his heavenly Father heard him.

So, too, did Priscilla. She knelt beside him and offered her own prayer. "Thank you, Lord, for answering my prayers. Thank you for sparing my life and keeping Zach safe. And thank you for making him the instrument of your will."

Astonished by the direction her prayer had taken, Zach turned to stare at her. "Do you think it was God's will that I kill Jean-Michel?" God did not condone killing; he forbade it.

Priscilla's eyes were clear and filled with conviction as she said, "I believe he sent you to save me. I also know you are not a murderer. I saw what you tried to do. You were aiming for Jean-Michel's arm. If he hadn't turned, you would have only wounded him and forced him to drop the knife. It was Jean-Michel's action, not yours, that killed him."

Though he wanted to accept her words, Zach could not. The presence of the still form was proof that he had failed. Another being had died because of him. Zach bowed his head again and closed his eyes. *Listen to her*, the voice deep inside him said. As he nodded, peace flowed through Zach. *Thank you, Lord*. He remained in silent prayer for another minute before he rose.

"Even though I didn't plan to kill him, the result is the same. Jean-Michel is dead. How can I tell his parents?" Zach thought of the conversations he'd had with Michel and how much both Ladres had worried about their son. Now the worries were ended, but not in a way anyone would have chosen.

Priscilla touched her throat. Zach wasn't certain whether she was checking to see if the wound had reopened or whether the action was a simple reflex. Her gaze met his as she said, "We'll tell them together."

They waited until dark. Though Priscilla had been ready to go immediately, Zach remembered Jeannette Ladre's humiliation when the town had learned of her son's actions last year. It would only add to her sorrow if someone saw the body in the back of the wagon and started to gossip. Even with the blanket covering Jean-Michel, a curious onlooker would readily identify the form in Zach's wagon as a human body, and if they saw the wagon near the mayor's house, speculation would commence. The least Zach could do was spare the Ladres that pain.

Though his face turned gray and he seemed to age ten years in the space of as many minutes, Michel listened in silence as Zach recounted what had happened. When he finished, Jeannette jumped to her feet. The beautiful Frenchwoman's face was contorted with anger, and in that moment the resemblance to the man who had held Priscilla hostage was striking.

"You killed my baby!" Jeannette clenched her fists and began to pound on Zach's chest. "You're a murderer! You killed my son!"

Zach let her shriek. Her anger and sorrow needed an outlet. Though she'd regarded Priscilla with suspicion when they'd first arrived at the house, Jeannette had blanched at the sight of the angry red line where Jean-Michel's knife had slit Priscilla's skin. Madame Ladre couldn't direct her anger at Priscilla, when it was obvious she had been as much a victim as she believed her son to be. That left Zach, the man who had pulled the trigger.

"I hate you," she screamed.

When Jeannette's venom was expelled, Zach looked at Michel before returning his gaze to Jean-Michel's mother. "I ask your forgiveness for my part in your son's death." Zach included both parents in his plea, though he doubted Michel would say anything. The news of Jean-Michel's attack on Priscilla and his plan to kill Zach appeared to have silenced the mayor.

"I will never forgive you." Jeannette spat the words. "Do

you hear me, Zach Webster? I will never forgive you." She turned to her husband, her lips curled in anger. "It's just as much your fault as his. All you care about is this town. Ever since we came here, you've had no time for Jean-Michel or me. Look what it's gotten you. Our son is dead."

The next morning the town was buzzing with the news that the Ladres were gone. No one knew why they'd chosen to leave their home in the middle of the night. No one knew where they were headed, but by noon, everyone in Ladreville knew that Michel had left a note, saying he could be of no further use and that he and Jeannette would not return to the town that bore their name.

❦

"Oh, Priscilla, I'm so happy!" Isabelle slid off her stool and ran around the counter to hug Priscilla. "It's only sixty-seven days until Gunther and I are wed."

Priscilla smiled at her friend. In the two weeks that had passed since Jean-Michel's death, she had made daily trips to the mercantile to help Isabelle with wedding plans. That was better than remaining in the house and remembering what had happened there. Though Zach did not speak of it, Priscilla knew that Jean-Michel's death weighed heavily on his heart. Her own heart ached at the price Zach had paid to save her.

Here at least there were no reminders of the young man whose life had gone so wrong. Without fail, each day Isabelle greeted Priscilla with the number of days until her wedding. Priscilla wagged her finger as she said, "You'll need every one of those days if you don't decide on the pattern for your dress."

"But I did!" Isabelle gave her a radiant smile and opened a copy of *Godey's Lady's Book*. "What do you think?" She pointed to a sketch.

Priscilla studied the gown, not surprised that Isabelle, who had a reputation for being the most fashion-conscious woman in Ladreville after Jeannette Ladre, had chosen a style that would flatter her. "You'll be a beautiful bride," Priscilla told her friend. "Of course, you're beautiful no matter what you wear."

Isabelle flushed. "Jean-Michel used to say the same thing, but I never believed him."

Priscilla dropped her eyes to the sketch, lest her expression betray her. She and Zach had agreed that no one in Ladreville needed to know that Jean-Michel was dead. They would tell Lawrence Wood the next time he came to town so the Ranger could stop his search, but as far as everyone else was concerned, Jean-Michel was still in Houston. With his parents gone from Ladreville, no one would expect him to return.

"Silly Jean-Michel. He was always saying things like that."

Isabelle's words triggered a memory. "That sounds like a man who's courting." Though Isabelle had never mentioned Jean-Michel's name in that context, Priscilla wondered if her friend might be the woman he had wanted to marry.

"I didn't encourage him, but I could tell he was interested."

Priscilla schooled her face to remain impassive. It was indeed Isabelle that Jean-Michel had wanted. Although, judging from the fact that he'd used the word *want* rather than *love*, Isabelle was fortunate his courting hadn't progressed. "Gunther is the perfect man for you."

"I agree." As she showed Priscilla the lace she was considering as trim for her wedding dress, Isabelle raised an eyebrow. "What do you think the town will do now? We need a mayor, a sheriff, and a schoolmarm. That's more change than we've had in years."

"At least the citizens seem to have resolved their differences."

Isabelle gave Priscilla an appraising look. "It was quite a coincidence that both ministers chose the same Scripture reading that Sunday, wasn't it?"

"A happy coincidence." Though Priscilla nodded, she had no intention of mentioning her role in the sermons. God had simply used her to help resolve a problem.

Isabelle's eyes narrowed. "Right." She knew.

❦

Zach handed his package to Steven Dunn and waited for the postmaster to weigh it. It made no sense. He was mailing money to Charlotte Tallman, and yet he was thinking of Margaret. Ever since the day he'd shot Jean-Michel, Margaret had been in his thoughts far more often than normal, and that was unnerving. She was a part of the past that he wanted to forget.

The postmaster accepted Zach's coins and turned to the cubbyholes behind him. Pulling out an envelope, he said, "I've got a letter here for Mrs. Webster. I reckon I can trust you to take it to her." Steven accompanied his words with a wry smile.

Thankful for the reprieve from thoughts of his past, Zach grinned. "I won't let it get too wet." Everyone in Ladreville had chuckled when they heard how Thea, who had insisted on carrying a letter home for Sarah, had dropped it into the river, leaving Clay to wade through waist-deep water to retrieve it, only to discover that the ink had run, making the letter practically illegible. Fortunately they'd been able to make out the signature, but Thea's career as a mail carrier had ended.

Steven feigned solemnity. "Dry is better than wet."

༈

"I brought you a letter," Zach announced as he entered the kitchen. This was the earliest he'd come home in weeks, but he didn't want his wife to have to wait for her mail. His wife. It was amazing how good it felt to pronounce those words or even to think them.

Priscilla turned, her face flushed from the heat of the stove. Judging from the two loaves of bread that filled the room with their mouth-watering aroma, she had spent the day baking. "Thanks. It's probably from my parents' attorney." Zach knew she'd been waiting for him to report the sale of the family home. Priscilla wiped her hands on her apron and accepted the envelope. Slitting it open, she pulled out the paper and began to read, and as she did, the blood drained from her face.

"What is it?"

She stared at the sheet of paper as if it were a venomous reptile. "It's from Lawrence." A flush stained her cheeks, returning some much-needed color. "The Ranger," she said, correcting herself. "He caught Jake and Chet Dunkler. He said it didn't take the judge long to decide that they should hang."

"That's good news. Now you know they won't hurt you

or anyone else." For a moment she did not reply, and Zach sensed that Priscilla's thoughts were miles away. How could she possibly regret the bandits' capture? There must be something else in the letter that caused her distraction. He waited for her to explain, but all Priscilla said was, "It is good news." She refolded the letter and placed it in her pocket, then turned back to the stove.

As he curried Charcoal, Zach considered his wife's strange behavior. Normally she let him read her mail, saying she appreciated another person's opinion, but she had been almost secretive about this one. And then there was the way she referred to the Ranger by his first name. Priscilla was a proper Bostonian, steeped in the rules of etiquette, but she'd called the Ranger Lawrence. When had that informality started?

Charcoal whinnied, as if he sensed his master's discomfort and wanted to help him. It was a nice try, but the only thing that would help was answers, and Zach wasn't sure he wanted them. Unless he was greatly mistaken, there was more in that letter than a report of the Dunkler brothers' capture. The flush on Priscilla's cheeks made him think that the Ranger had included a personal note.

Zach tightened his grip on the currycomb. He didn't doubt that Lawrence Wood harbored tender feelings for Priscilla. He'd heard it in his voice and seen it on his face when he'd spoken of her. Zach couldn't fault the Ranger for that. Any man with an ounce of sense would find Priscilla attractive. Not only was she a beautiful woman on the outside, but she had a beautiful inside too. It was no wonder the Ranger cared for her. The question was, did Priscilla care for him? Were her flushes and her almost furtive handling of the letter caused by embarrassment that Zach had been watching? There was only one way to know, and that was to ask her.

Straightening, Zach stared into the distance, trying to calm his roiling thoughts. Though his heart ached at the prospect, he knew what he must do if Priscilla loved the Ranger. He must grant her the annulment. The night he had prayed for her life, Zach had promised God he would show Priscilla the face of love. No matter how empty his future might loom, he would do everything he could to ensure Priscilla's happiness. He loved her. He could do no less.

Priscilla fluffed the pillow. Perhaps that would help her sleep. Nothing else seemed to be working. Each time she closed her eyes, she pictured Lawrence's letter. His handwriting was surprisingly well-formed, as if he'd spent many years practicing penmanship. But it wasn't the appearance of the carefully formed loops that was engraved on Priscilla's mind. It was the words themselves. Though he'd pronounced the same words on his last visit, it was different seeing them committed to paper. Spoken words could be colored by expressions. There were no such nuances with the written word. Lawrence's letter left no room for misunderstanding.

Priscilla turned again, trying to find a comfortable position, wishing he hadn't written what he did. Sarah had spoken of the poetic epistles she'd received, letters she'd called her paper roses. According to Sarah, the letters had wooed her, and she'd fallen in love with their author before she met him. There was nothing poetic about Lawrence's missive. His prose was as precise as his penmanship, direct and unembellished.

Some words needed no embellishment. *I'll always love you.* If only it had been Zach who'd written them.

When she finally fell asleep, Priscilla's dreams were troubled. In them she was running, not knowing where she was going, not knowing why she was fleeing, simply knowing she had to escape. She'd almost reached safety when the man began to scream. On and on and on it went, a sound so horrible it defied description. *Stop!* she pleaded. *Stop!* But the cries continued. Priscilla's eyes flew open as she realized this was no dream. It was Zach who was yelling. Someone was hurting him.

She raced into his room, her heartbeat slowing ever so slightly when she saw that he was alone. Whatever was wrong, it was only a nightmare.

"Wake up, Zach." Priscilla stood at the side of the bed, speaking as firmly as she could. Moonlight spilled onto the bed, showing the tangled sheets and the sheen of perspiration on his face. "It's all right. You were dreaming."

Though his eyes were open, they refused to focus, and his body continued to tremble. Zach might be awake, but his mind was still caught in the snares of the dream. The only thing that had changed was that his screams had ceased.

"It's all right, Zach." If he heard her, he gave no sign. His body shook uncontrollably, and, though the night was warm, his teeth chattered as if from cold. Priscilla grabbed a quilt from the foot of the bed and laid it over him. An instant later, he had thrown it off. "You need that." But when she replaced the quilt, just as quickly, he tossed it away.

He needed warmth. Papa had told her how important it was to regulate a patient's temperature. Papa had also warned her that diseases of the mind could be as dangerous as those that affected the body and that one way to alleviate them was to return the patient to a state of normalcy. For Zach, that meant warmth. He needed more than the room's warmth if he was going to escape the nightmare.

Priscilla bit her lip as she realized there was only one course of action. She had to share her body's heat with Zach. Closing her eyes for a second, she forced away the memories of another man's body close to hers. This wasn't the same. Nothing was the same. This was Zach, not the bandit. This time she was doing the touching; she wasn't being touched. She could do it. She had to. The man she loved needed her.

Though her limbs were trembling almost as violently as Zach's, Priscilla climbed onto the bed and lay down next to him, slipping her arms around him, drawing the quilt over both of them. "It's all right, Zach." She pressed herself against his side. "Everything will be fine."

For what seemed like forever, she kept her body next to his, praying that her warmth and her words would soothe him. "Everything will be fine," she repeated. At length the shudders subsided and Zach turned. The vacant look that had frightened her was gone, and his eyes focused on her.

If Zach was surprised to find Priscilla in his bed, he said nothing. "It won't be all right," he muttered. "I can't ever make it right."

Though his voice was filled with anguish, Priscilla took comfort from the fact that his body seemed to be warming. "You had no choice," she said softly. "You shot Jean-Michel to save me."

Zach shook his head. "Not Jean-Michel."

If it hadn't been Jean-Michel's death that triggered it, the nightmare must have been caused by the time Zach had spent in prison and the atrocities he'd witnessed and endured there. That was probably why he was so cold. Since it had been winter when he'd been incarcerated in Perote, his mind must have imagined frigid weather.

"The war's over, Zach. You're safe now."

Disentangling himself from her arms, he sat up and braced himself against the headboard. Though his eyes were alert, the pain that radiated from them made Priscilla cringe. "I'm sorry you had to see this. I thought the nightmares had ended, or I'd never have slept inside the house."

"It's all right, Zach. I know about nightmares." Fortunately, she had not had one in months. Priscilla had thought that meant she was cured, but Zach's experience seemed to indicate that they could return at any time. "Perote was horrible," she said softly. "It's no wonder you still dream of it."

Zach shook his head. "It's not the war I dream about. It's worse. I used to think that hell was hot, but now I know it's cold. Horribly cold."

As he shivered, Priscilla rose to retrieve another quilt and wrapped it around his shoulders. "What could be worse than the war?" she asked as she dragged a chair next to the bed and settled on it. What made him think he was in hell?

Zach was silent for a moment, gazing at the window. The moon shone; the stars sparkled. It was a scene of ineffable beauty, and yet the shudders that wracked his body told Priscilla Zach was seeing none of God's creation. Instead, he was locked in some unspeakable memory. At length he turned to look at her, his eyes still filled with pain. "What's worse is what I did to Margaret. It was only cool that night, not cold, but somehow in my nightmares, it's always terribly cold."

Involuntarily, Priscilla shivered, then chided herself for the picture her mind had invoked. Zach was not like the bandits. He would never, ever have forced himself on a woman. And yet she could not ignore the anguish in his voice. That told her that, whatever had happened between him and a woman named Margaret, it still haunted him. Priscilla reached for a candle, then stopped. Darkness might be better for what she was about to propose.

"Sometimes it helps to talk." Mama had claimed that talking was like lancing a boil, a painful but necessary step if healing was to begin.

Zach shook his head. "It's been fifteen years, and I haven't told anyone what I did, not even John Tallman or Clay's father."

Priscilla did a quick subtraction. "Fifteen years ago you were still a boy." Surely whatever had happened wasn't what she had imagined. Surely he had not raped Margaret.

Zach shook his head again. "I was old enough to know better. I should never have drunk all that whiskey, and I should never have taken her down to the river that night."

Priscilla's heart began to thud. Whiskey and a boy on the verge of manhood were a dangerous combination. "What happened?" The words came out as little more than a whisper.

"You don't want to know."

That was probably true, but her imagination would fill in missing pieces, creating a whole that might bear no resemblance to the truth. Surely it was better to know the truth. Without that, she had no chance of helping Zach. "I want to help you."

Zach tugged the quilt tighter. "Margaret was the prettiest

girl in Haven, Texas." When Priscilla said nothing, he added, "That's where I grew up." His voice was neutral, almost as if he were telling someone else's story. "Every boy wanted to be Margaret's beau, but I was the one she favored. I never could figure out why."

Priscilla could.

"We planned to get married when we were older, but then that night happened." He swallowed deeply, and Priscilla saw his hands tighten on the quilt. "We both had too much to drink. When Margaret suggested a walk by the river, it seemed like a good idea. We knew we'd be alone there, and that was what we wanted." The shaft of moonlight that spilled through the window revealed the anguish on Zach's face. "It was going to be only one kiss, but one kiss led to another, and then we weren't just kissing."

Priscilla shuddered as, unbidden, images flashed before her. She was lying on the ground, staring up at the stagecoach, the memory of gunshots reverberating through her mind. And then there was a man, a man with Zach's face. *Stop it!* she cried. What happened that night in Haven wasn't the same. Both Margaret and Zach had chosen to walk by the river, knowing how the evening might end. No one had been forced. Zach had not attacked Margaret.

He looked directly at Priscilla as he said, "Six weeks later, Margaret told me I was going to be a father."

Zach had a child! Priscilla dropped her eyes in confusion. Why had she never heard about this? She knew he sent John Tallman's widow money each month, but she was unaware of anything going to Margaret. "What did you do?"

He waited until she met his gaze again before he said, "I ran away." Regret shone from Zach's blue eyes. "I was such a coward that I thought it would be better to fight the Mexicans than accept my responsibility, so I joined the army. When I drew that black bean at Perote, I figured it was God's way of punishing me." Zach looked out the window, then back at Priscilla. "You know what happened next. I didn't die, and I tried to change my life. When I got back to Texas, I sent a letter to Margaret, offering to marry her. I figured she'd be happy that I was showing some signs of responsibility, but she wasn't. She said I'd made my choices, and so had she. As far as Margaret was concerned, I was dead. She didn't want to see me or ever hear from me again." Zach stared into the distance again, his voice as bleak as his expression as he said, "I don't even know whether I have a son or a daughter or nothing at all. You see, when I told her I was leaving, Margaret threatened to kill the baby."

"Oh, Zach." Priscilla longed to put her arms around him and comfort him as she would have a child, but the look he gave her could have frozen boiling water.

"I don't want your pity, Priscilla. I was wrong, and I know it. I was a coward."

And he'd lived the rest of his life regretting that. Perhaps he'd also spent the past fifteen years seeking a way to atone his sin. At the time she had thought it was Christian kindness that led Zach to offer her his name, but now that she knew about Margaret's pregnancy, Priscilla knew that was the reason he'd married her. Regardless of his motivation, Zach had rescued her when she was desperate and, though it had meant breaking a vow, he had saved her life. There must be a way she could help him.

"You may have been a coward." Or simply a scared boy. "But so was Margaret."

Zach's head swiveled, and his eyes widened in amazement. "What do you mean?"

"It's true you ran away, but so did she." When he started to shake his head, Priscilla continued. "Oh, not literally, but in her heart, Margaret ran away from her responsibility too. Even if she no longer wanted to marry you, when she heard from you, she should have told you about your child. That was the right thing to do."

The cleft in Zach's chin deepened. "Maybe, but it's over now."

"No, it isn't. The fact that you still have nightmares says it's not over."

Zach swung his legs off the bed. "I don't know what to do. I've tried everything—working until I'm beyond exhaustion, patent remedies, hours of prayer. Nothing worked." He shook his head slowly. "This is the first one I've had since we were married. I thought they had ended, that I'd finally put the past to rest, but I was wrong. I don't know how to make the nightmares stop."

His words confirmed Priscilla's suspicions at the same time that they encouraged her. Though it was reassuring to know that Zach had gained something from their marriage, what mattered now was breaking the nightmares' grip on him. Priscilla shook her head. "You do know how to stop them. The answer is forgiveness."

Zach rose, wrapping the quilt around himself, and walked to the window. "God has forgiven me. I know he has."

Though she wouldn't touch Zach again, she didn't want him to be alone. Priscilla moved to stand beside him. "Have you forgiven yourself?"

"I . . ." He hesitated, then said, "Of course I have."

Priscilla looked at the man she loved, a man who was caught in a living nightmare. "I don't think so. I believe you're still clinging to your sins." When he started to protest, Priscilla held up her hand, forestalling him. "I may be wrong, but it seems to me that the only way you'll heal is to talk to Margaret and learn what happened. You probably should have done that when you were released from prison rather than writing a letter, but that can't be undone. It's time to face her and ask for her forgiveness so you can forgive yourself."

The way Zach clenched his fists told Priscilla he did not like the idea. "Margaret doesn't want to see me."

He was clinging to the excuse like a frightened child to his mother's hand. "That's what Margaret said fifteen years ago. You've changed. She may have too. The only way you'll know is to go to Haven." Zach had said that Haven was in southeastern Texas, only a day's journey from the Gulf of Mexico. Though it would take close to a week to get there, it was something he needed to do. Zach clenched and un-clenched his fists as he stared out the window. *Open his heart,* Priscilla prayed. *Let him heal.* "You may be right," he said at last. "I'll leave tomorrow."

Thank you. Priscilla nodded briskly. "We'll leave the day after tomorrow."

Though he'd started to stride across the room, the plural pronoun caught Zach's attention, and he turned to stare at her. "We? You're not going."

"Yes, I am. I'm your wife. If nothing else convinces Margaret that you've changed, the fact that you married me to protect my unborn child should be proof that you're not the same Zach Webster who abandoned her half a lifetime ago."

345

Zach's eyes narrowed, and Priscilla guessed he was searching for an argument to dissuade her. "It'll be a long, hard ride."

She gave him a little smile. "Didn't I tell you I wanted adventure in my life?"

"Yes, but . . ."

"I'm going."

19

"Ready for dinner?"

Priscilla nodded. The truth was, she was ready to get off Dancer and never mount another horse. It wasn't Dancer's fault. The mare was gentle and seemed as tireless as Zach. It was Priscilla herself who was the problem. Here they were on only the second day of what would be at least a five day journey to Haven, and she was exhausted.

Traveling was far more grueling than she'd expected. It wasn't merely the long hours in the saddle, although those took their toll on her body. Added to them was the difficulty of cooking over an open fire and the seemingly impossible challenge of finding a comfortable position to sleep when your bed was a blanket spread on the sun-baked ground. And then there was the sun itself. Texas in June was hotter than anything Priscilla had experienced. But, regardless of the hardships, she would not complain. Zach had tried to dissuade her, warning that the trip would not be easy, but Priscilla had ignored his advice. She'd sought adventure, and she had found it. If it was more difficult than she'd expected, that was her problem, not Zach's.

She looked around, wondering where Zach planned to stop. The hills and plains of Texas bore little resemblance to the groomed trails that had been her childhood haunts. There were more hazards here: the spines of the prickly pear cactus, poisonous snakes, the relentless sun. Yet, despite the rigors and the undeniable fatigue, Priscilla loved this land, which was as different from Ladreville as it was from Boston.

The route Zach had chosen was farther south than the one the stagecoach had taken, the terrain dotted with more brush than trees, the towns smaller and farther apart. Though some might call it inhospitable, Priscilla found it beautiful. She simply wished for the opportunity to explore it at a more leisurely pace. A decidedly more leisurely pace.

When she spotted a small stand of trees, she nodded, knowing that was Zach's destination. "Indeed, I'm ready for dinner," Priscilla said as she gave him a wry smile. "I'm afraid my stomach's been growling for the better part of an hour."

He met her smile with a frown as he turned Charcoal toward the river and the welcoming grove of pecan trees. "You should have told me. We could have stopped earlier."

"But then we wouldn't have found shade." Since they'd left the Hill Country and its trees, they'd been traversing open plains. This was ideal land for farming and grazing, but the absence of anything resembling a forest meant that travelers were as sun-baked as the grass. Priscilla slid to the ground, thankful for the opportunity to stretch her legs as well as a chance to rest in the shade. "This is wonderful."

"The shade or being off the horse?"

It was as if he'd read her mind. "Both," she admitted.

"We can slow our pace."

Priscilla reached for the sack of food that would become their noon meal. She had known Zach would offer to rest more often if he realized how tired she was. That was the reason she kept a smile fixed on her face. "I told you I wouldn't hold you back, and I won't. Besides, I'm anxious to see Haven." That was no lie. As they'd ridden, Priscilla had found herself wondering about the town where Zach was born and raised and where—had it not been for one mistake—he would have spent his whole life. There was something poetic about the fact that they left for Zach's birthplace the day after she'd received a letter from her attorney containing the proceeds from the sale of her parents' home and her father's medical practice. Priscilla's past was settled; it was time to confront Zach's. "What's Haven like?"

Zach leaned against one of the trees, stretching his legs in front of him, as he accepted the biscuit she'd split and filled with ham. "I can't tell you what it's like today, but fifteen years ago, it was a small town—maybe 150 people, most of them farmers. We had a school, a general store, and a church. That's all."

The way Zach smiled told Priscilla his memories were happy ones. "The postmaster was also the town's barber and lawman. When the blacksmith wasn't shoeing horses or making barrel staves, he served as the mayor." Zach gave Priscilla another smile, warming her heart and making her forget how tired and sore she was. "You may have noticed that I didn't mention medical care." She nodded. Trust Zach to realize that she, more than most people, would think about that. "Haven was so small it didn't have a doctor, not even a midwife. Occasionally peddlers would come through, and folks would buy their remedies. Somehow, most of us survived."

Mama would have been appalled. She had insisted Papa give her a tincture of something whenever she felt the least bit ill. The thought of living without a physician would have made Priscilla's mother swoon. Papa's reaction would have differed. Though it might be seen as denigrating his own profession, he would have said that Haven's survival despite the absence of a doctor only proved how strong humans were.

"You liked living there."

Priscilla watched the play of emotions on Zach's face. "Yes, I did." He took a bite of the biscuit and chewed thoughtfully. After he'd swallowed, he said, "Part of me is eager to see Haven. The other part dreads the thought. What I do know is that, no matter what happens, it's no longer my home. Ladreville is."

Priscilla nodded, realizing that she had said the same thing more than once. Though her childhood home held many happy memories, it was part of the past. Until the day she had received the money from its sale, she had had no firm plan, but that day everything became clear. Somehow she would convince Zach to let her help pay for the Lazy B. Even if he chose to end their marriage, she wanted him to have the home he longed for.

Zach tossed a biscuit crumb onto the ground, grinning when two black birds squabbled over it. "I'd venture to say Haven is not much like Boston."

"That's probably true," Priscilla agreed. "I didn't expect it to be. It's not simply that Boston is so much larger. Texas is very different from the East. It's younger, still taking shape. I think that's one of the reasons I love living here. It's exciting."

He gave her a wry smile. "An adventure."

"Yes." Though the trip to Texas had taken turns Priscilla could never have envisioned, it had brought her what she had once sought: adventure.

Reaching for another ham-filled biscuit, Zach asked, "What will you do when the adventure loses its appeal?"

Priscilla blinked at the unexpected question. "What makes you think it will?"

"It always does." Zach's eyes darkened, and she wondered whether he was thinking of the way his escape from Haven to the army had turned from exciting to terrifying, or whether it was something else—perhaps life in Ladreville or their marriage—that had disillusioned him. Priscilla hoped it wasn't the latter.

"You sound like Lawrence."

This time there was no question about his feelings. Zach's lips twisted in annoyance, and when he tossed crumbs to the two birds, he practically hurled them. "What did he say?"

Though she regretted having mentioned Lawrence's name, since it appeared to have bothered Zach, Priscilla owed her husband an answer. "He said that he was thinking about leaving the Rangers."

Zach took a swig from his canteen, rising to refill it from the river. When he returned, his eyes had lost their warmth and were steely blue. "I'm not surprised."

"Really? I was."

"It's difficult for a man to combine life as a Ranger with marriage." The look he gave her made Priscilla think Zach was aware of Lawrence's proposal. But how could he be? She had burned the Ranger's letter the night she had received it, believing that the best course. There was no reason to trouble Zach when she had no desire to marry Lawrence, or so Priscilla had thought. But it appeared that her good intentions were unsuccessful, for the expression on Zach's face said he knew of and had been disturbed by Lawrence's declaration of love. Why did he care? Though she hated seeing pain reflecting from Zach's eyes, Priscilla's heart leapt at the thought that his feelings for her might be deeper than she'd believed. Was it possible that he loved her, even though she was not a true wife to him?

Priscilla did not ask the question, reasoning that they were discussing Lawrence's feelings, not Zach's. "How did you know?"

"That Lawrence wanted to marry you?" When Priscilla nodded, Zach shrugged. "I heard it in his voice whenever he spoke of you. A man can tell."

She wouldn't lie. "He did ask me to marry him. Twice. Once when he visited and again in his letter." Something that looked like doubt filled Zach's eyes, causing Priscilla to add quickly, "I refused."

Zach plucked a strand of grass and studied it, as if it contained the answers to the mysteries of the universe. "You wouldn't have had to wait the full six months. I would have given you an annulment right away," he said softly, keeping his gaze fixed on the ground. "I still will, if that's what you want."

"It's not." When Zach looked up, Priscilla shook her head vehemently. Perhaps the gesture would convince him if her words did not. "Lawrence is a good man, but he's not the man God intended for me."

The furrows between Zach's eyes disappeared. "Are you sure?"

"Yes."

Zach scanned the horizon, searching for a place to stop for the night. This would be their final rest before they reached Haven, and he wanted to make it as pleasant as possible for Priscilla. It was certain that the trip had not been easy for her. As Zach darted a glance at the woman who rode at his side, his heart swelled with admiration. She had not complained once, even though they'd maintained a pace that had to be difficult for her. He'd seen the way she walked gingerly, as if her muscles were sore, and yet she'd said not a word. To the contrary, when he had suggested they go more slowly, Priscilla had refused, and when he'd slackened the pace, thinking she would not notice, she'd told him there was no need.

Zach smiled as he looked at the woman whose face was now lightly tanned. This was a far different woman from the one who'd ridden to the Bar C with the Ranger. That woman had been broken, defeated. This woman was strong and resilient, able to find humor in almost everything. No wonder her family had nicknamed her Sunny Cilla.

Only one thing had not changed: her fear of men. Though he doubted she would bolt if he touched her, Zach was careful to keep a distance between them. Admittedly, the distance was less than it had once been, but it was still there, a buffer designed to comfort her. Though he longed to stroke her hair, to clasp her hand in his, to press his lips to hers, he did not. Even the slightest contact was dangerous, for it might cause Priscilla to retreat into her shell.

The one exception had been the night she had interrupted his nightmare. That night she lay beside him, her arms wrapped around him, giving him her warmth. For a few moments when his tremors had subsided and the horror of

353

the dream began to fade, they could have been any husband and wife, sharing a bed. But that was an illusion. Zach knew it had been Priscilla, the healer, not Priscilla, the woman, who had climbed into his bed, and so he had not dared to mention what had happened then. Thanks to Zeke Dunkler, Priscilla might never again view men as anything more than brutal animals. And that, he suspected, played a large role in her refusal of Lawrence Wood's proposal. Zach could not regret that. Though he did not wish the Ranger ill, he knew Lawrence could not love Priscilla the way he did. No one could.

Forcing those thoughts from his mind, Zach turned toward his wife. "As I recall, there's a bend in the river in about half an hour." Though it meant traveling a few extra miles, he'd kept their course near rivers, first the Medina, then the San Antonio, knowing that the water and the shade that frequently accompanied the water were essential for both horses and humans. "If it hasn't changed, it would be a good place for us to stop."

Priscilla looked at the sky, measuring the sun's height and calculating the time. "If you're stopping early for me, there's no need. I can keep riding."

"I know you can." Zach knew better than to challenge her. His wife would not back down from anything she considered a challenge. "I thought you might like a chance to clean up a bit." The little he knew about women included their need to look their best when meeting other women. Though she had asked few questions about Margaret, Zach was certain tomorrow's encounter weighed almost as heavily on Priscilla as it did on him.

Her smile confirmed his assumption. "Thank you. I've got

some soap I've been saving, and I can use some extra time." Priscilla touched her hair and made a moue. "I don't want you to be ashamed of me."

"I could never be ashamed of you." For as long as she was willing, this was his wife, the woman who filled his heart with admiration, not shame.

Zach turned his eyes back to the road, scanning the road itself for obstacles, the sides for possible predators. He'd always done that. He suspected he always would. While his vigilance had not changed, other things had. No matter what happened in Haven, he could not regret that they'd made the journey. For the first time, he and Priscilla had been together almost constantly, and that time together had given him a chance to discover the depths of the woman he'd married. They'd spoken of family and friends, of dreams and disappointments, of surprises and sorrows. Even when they were silent, he'd uncovered new aspects of his wife. Zach knew he would remember these days for the rest of his life, for these were the days when he'd discovered how deeply he loved Priscilla and how much he wished she was truly his wife.

He knew that wouldn't happen. There were too many barriers to overcome before that particular dream became reality. It wasn't simply what Zeke Dunkler had done to her. Zach knew there was also the hurdle—the huge hurdle—of his past with Margaret. Though he wished it were otherwise, he could not forget Priscilla's face when he'd told her what had happened that night by the river. She'd looked at him as if he were no better than the bandits and had recoiled with horror. Zach couldn't blame her. How could he, when he still blamed himself? If only he hadn't drunk the whiskey. If only he'd had more self-control. If only . . .

Zach averted his head, fearing his expression would betray him. While one portion of his brain was on the alert for danger, the other continued to think about the two women in his life. Though Margaret was part of his past, he could not ignore her importance. She was what John Tallman had called "unfinished business."

There was no undoing the sins he had committed or the pain he had caused Margaret, though tomorrow, if God was with him, he might atone for them. Tomorrow Zach might be able to put his past behind him, and then perhaps the nightmares would end. Unfortunately, that would not help his future.

No matter how much he loved her, no matter how much he longed for her, he could never make Priscilla his true wife. As wonderful as these days of traveling together had been, they had also provided constant torment. It had been difficult enough, riding next to her, sharing three meals a day, wanting to touch her. The days were bad; the nights were worse. Though he'd kept a decorous distance between their bed rolls, Zach could hear her breathing, and he lay awake, listening to the soft sounds she made. Each time Priscilla sighed, he remembered how wonderful it had felt to have her arms around him. As he closed his eyes, he recalled the comfort she had given him, and he ached, knowing that would not be repeated.

Perhaps this was his punishment for that long-ago sin. Now that he was approaching Haven, prepared to ask forgiveness from the woman he had wronged, he had discovered what true love was. Zach loved his wife with every fiber of his being. He loved her; he would do anything for her, but he knew she would never love him. How could she when he was not worthy of her love? This sham of a marriage was all Zach would ever have.

༫

Priscilla knelt next to the river, hesitating only a moment before she dunked her head into the water. It was the first time she'd washed her hair anywhere other than at home, and it felt strange. Being outdoors was only part of the reason. What bothered Priscilla more was knowing that Zach could watch her perform such an intimate task. He wouldn't, of course. He'd told her he would remain at their campsite, far enough away that he could not see her but close enough that he could come if she needed help. There was, he reminded her, always the threat of snakes and what many Texans considered more fearsome, a particularly ferocious animal called a javelina. The wild boar had been known to attack settlers without provocation. That prospect had been almost enough to dissuade Priscilla from washing her hair. Almost, but not enough.

She raised her head, squeezing the excess water from her hair before she began to soap it. It felt so good to be doing this. Thanks to Zach's decision to follow rivers, she'd been able to wash her face and hands and sponge the worst dirt off her clothing each evening, but there hadn't been time to do more than brush her hair. Now she would be more presentable when they reached Haven.

Perhaps it would make no difference. He claimed it would not. But Priscilla wanted everything to be as perfect as possible for Zach. Tomorrow he would face his past. If Margaret had not hardened her heart, Zach might find peace. But if she had . . . Priscilla frowned, considering the possibility the woman Zach had once planned to marry might not forgive him. If that happened, she didn't know what he would do.

Lord, show me the way to help him. There must be something I can do. Priscilla dunked her head once more, rinsing the soap from her hair. As she began to comb it with her fingers, removing the largest tangles before she reached for her comb, she remembered Zach's expression when she had spoken of her parents.

"You were lucky to have their love." Though his voice was steady, for some reason he had refused to meet her gaze. "You deserve love." And then he'd quickly changed the subject.

Priscilla's hand moved instinctively, pulling the comb through her hair, as her thoughts whirled. Was that the answer? Was that the reason Zach's eyes were so haunted? Was it possible he believed he was unworthy of a woman's love? Surely he knew that love was a gift, not something to be earned, but perhaps he did not. Priscilla stared into the distance, trying to recall everything he'd told her, especially the night they'd spoken of Margaret.

What if he thought that the night he and Margaret had spent at the river had made him repulsive to a woman, just as she feared that the bandit's attack had sullied her forever?

Priscilla winced as she thought of her own behavior. She loved Zach, but she had never said the words. The day they'd spoken of Lawrence would have been the perfect opportunity to tell Zach he was the man she loved, but she had remained silent. Worse, she had given him no signs—no special smiles, no kisses, no loving touches. How was Zach supposed to know that she loved him when she shied away each time he came close?

Priscilla closed her eyes and bowed her head. *Dear Lord,*

I believe Zach is the man you chose for me. I know he needs me. I know he needs my love, but I'm afraid to give him that love. Please, Lord, grant me the strength to show Zach how much I love him. She knelt silently, waiting for her Lord's answer, and he gave it. Filled with peace and a sense of purpose, Priscilla rose and returned to the camp.

Though normally she braided her hair as soon as she brushed it, today she left it loose. Though normally she sat several feet away from Zach as they ate, today she left only a few inches between them. Though normally she kept supper conversation simmering, today she was largely silent, all too aware of the man who was now so close to her, the man who was giving her surreptitious glances, the man whose eyes held something she wanted to believe was love. He would never speak the words; Priscilla knew that, for to tell her he loved her would make him vulnerable. He would not risk rejection, for that would only confirm his belief that he was unworthy of love. As difficult as it would be, Priscilla had to take the first step.

When the meal was over and the pans once more stored in their saddle bags, Zach started to walk away. That was the routine. He would leave her alone. She would climb into her bedroll. He would return only when she was settled and possibly asleep. It was time to break the routine.

Priscilla watched as he turned. Now. She had to do it now, before she lost the tiny bit of courage that still remained. She stretched her hand out, as if to stop him, but he didn't see her.

"Don't go." Was that her voice, that pitifully weak croak?

Zach turned back and gave her a reassuring smile. "I won't be far away. You'll be safe."

"I'm not afraid." It was a lie. She *was* afraid, but not of snakes or javelinas or other marauding predators. She was afraid of him. No, that wasn't true. She was afraid of herself, that she would fail, that at the last moment she would pull back in fear as she had the day he'd given her the locket. She could not let that happen, for Zach needed her, and this was her only chance to help him.

"I don't want you to leave." This time her voice sounded almost normal, though there was no disguising the tremor.

Zach said nothing, but his eyes held a question. He deserved an answer. Priscilla took a deep breath, searching for the words to make him understand. A few yards away the river flowed silently, its surface dappled with sunlight and shadows. Her heart expanded with a sense of rightness. It was not by chance that God had led them here. An encounter by a river had caused Zach's nightmares. Perhaps another encounter, this one sanctified by holy vows, would exorcise them.

She exhaled slowly, then willed her voice to remain steady. "When we talked about Lawrence the other day, I told you he wasn't the man God had chosen for me."

"Did you lie?" Zach demanded, his voice harsher than normal.

"No, but I told you only part of the story." Priscilla took a step toward him, then another and a third, stopping when they were no more than a foot apart. "I should have told you everything then, but I was a coward."

"You? A coward?" Zach's voice rose in surprise. "You're the strongest woman I know."

He was wrong. "If I'd been strong, I would have told you the truth. The truth is, Lawrence is not the man God chose for me. You are." Priscilla stretched out her hand, hoping

Zach would take it in his. Though she wanted to show him that she did not fear his touch, Mama had impressed on her the fact that a lady could do no more than extend her hand. She must never be so brazen as to actually initiate a touch.

To Priscilla's disappointment, Zach did not grasp her hand, but his eyes lit with something that she believed was hope. "What do you mean?"

"God meant us to be together. That's why he brought both of us to the Bar C." Slowly, Priscilla lowered her hand to her side. Zach wasn't ready for a gesture. He needed more words to break down the barriers he'd constructed over half a lifetime. Priscilla kept her eyes on his face, searching for signs that he understood. "I believe God wants us to help each other. We both have parts of our past that are painful, but they're over."

Furrows appeared between Zach's eyes. Was it possible that he did not know how much he'd helped her? He'd saved her life, but that was only the last of many, many things Zach had done for her. "I don't know how I would have survived these past six months if it hadn't been for you. You were always there, every time I needed someone." Priscilla touched the locket he'd brought back to her. "You even found this for me. There's no way I can repay you for all you've done."

"There's no need. I wanted to help you."

As I want to help you. But she wouldn't say that, for she sensed that Zach would consider accepting help a sign of weakness. "Our past is behind us," she said, "but we have the future. I believe it can be a good one."

Zach nodded. "I want us to be together."

"So do I." *Oh, so do I!* Priscilla swallowed. Zach had given her the opening she needed. It was up to her to take the next step and walk through that opening. Though she wanted to smile, Priscilla could not force her lips to turn upward. Mustering every ounce of strength she possessed, she said, "I love you, Zach." His eyes widened, and she sensed that, though he wanted to believe her, he did not. "I love you, and I want ours to be a real marriage."

Blood drained from his face. "You mean . . . ?"

"Yes, Zach." It was time. No matter what Mama had taught in her deportment lessons, Priscilla could not wait for Zach. She had to be the one to act, the one to prove beyond any doubt that she loved him. She closed the distance, putting her arms around his neck and pressing her lips to his. "I want to be your wife in every way."

Zach pulled away so that he could see her face. "Are you certain?"

"More certain than I've been of anything." The smile that had remained frozen deep inside Priscilla blossomed as she nodded.

Joy filled Zach's eyes, and he wrapped his arms around her, drawing her closer. "Oh, my darling," he whispered, his voice husky with emotion. And then there was no need for words.

20

The chirping of birds wakened her. For the briefest of moments, Priscilla wasn't certain where she was; then as memories flooded through her, she smiled. Patience had been right. She had told Priscilla that the love a man and a woman shared was pleasurable. But Patience had understated reality. It was more than pleasurable; it was wonderful.

For so long, Priscilla had feared a man's touch, certain that anyone, even Zach, would bring back unbearable memories. That had not happened. To the contrary, Zach's gentle touch and his sweet words had banished the horrors of the bandit's attack. She had believed that no man would want her, that Zeke Dunkler's act had destroyed her hope of a normal life. She had thought that she would feel unclean for the rest of her life, that a good man would consider her used goods. She had been wrong. Zach's kisses had washed away the shame, making her feel beautiful and clean, inside and out. Priscilla smiled again. This was a new day, and she was a new woman—Zach's wife.

She sat up and looked around. Where was he? When her mind registered the soft plunk as something fell into the river, she bit her lip. Though the night had been wonderful for her, perhaps she had been wrong in believing God had brought her and Zach to this spot. Perhaps she, in her effort to help Zach, had reopened wounds. Was he reliving the hours he and Margaret had spent by a river? If so, that might make today's meeting more painful. Oh, why hadn't she considered that? Priscilla scrambled into her clothes. Not bothering to braid her hair, she hurried toward the river. As she feared, Zach was there, kneeling on its bank. When a twig crunched beneath her feet, he turned.

"I'm sorry. I didn't mean to interrupt you." His posture and the expression on his face told Priscilla he had been praying. For forgiveness?

Zach shook his head, as if he'd heard her thoughts. "You weren't interrupting. I had just said 'amen' when I heard you. I know the Lord won't mind my sharing my prayers with you." Zach smiled as he rose to his feet. "I was thanking him for giving you to me."

The worry that had filled Priscilla's heart disappeared, melted by the warmth of Zach's smile. Last night had not been a mistake, for Zach's smile was the brightest she had ever seen, and his eyes sparkled more than newly fallen snow. Even his posture seemed different, as if he had sloughed off a weight. When he opened his arms, she ran into them, letting him enfold her in his embrace.

"I love you, Priscilla," he murmured as he stroked her hair. "No matter what happens today, don't ever doubt that."

She smiled and raised her face for his kiss. "I love you too."

Though never a garrulous man, Zach was quieter than normal as they rode toward Haven. The reason, Priscilla was certain, was apprehension. She tried but failed to imagine how she would feel if she were in his boots, if today was the day she might come face to face with someone she had loved but wronged and a child she had abandoned before it was born. Though Zach had spoken primarily of Margaret, the anguish she had heard in his voice told Priscilla that he had spent half his life wondering about the child. Today he would learn whether he had a son or a daughter or whether Margaret had followed through on her threats.

"If I calculated correctly, we should be there in less than an hour." When Zach had suggested they stop for a midday meal, Priscilla had suggested they eat while riding. Now that they were on the final leg of their journey, she did not want to waste any time, for each hour increased Zach's anxiety.

"Where do you want to go first?" she asked.

"I'm not sure. I've been praying, but God hasn't given me any answers."

"Maybe he's waiting until we arrive."

"Maybe." Zach said nothing more until they topped a small rise. Reining in his horse, he pointed to the settlement in the valley. "That's it. That's Haven."

Priscilla looked down. The community was even smaller than she'd expected, no more than thirty or forty buildings clustered around one main street.

"I wonder if my house has changed." There was a pensive note to Zach's voice.

She smiled. "That's your answer. That's where we'll go first." It made sense. Seeing the place where he'd grown up and the changes time had made would ease him into the

365

meeting with Margaret. When she learned that the Webster home was on the outskirts of town, Priscilla realized the wisdom of starting there. Zach's entry into Haven would be observed by few.

His former home proved to be a simple white frame house, considerably smaller than the Lazy B. Though the house was freshly painted and obviously well cared for, the yard boasted only a few flowers. The reason, Priscilla suspected, was the two young children playing catch with a large hound. Between two active boys and the dog, flowers would have little chance of survival.

Zach smiled at the boys' exuberance. They were so caught up in their game that they paid no attention to the strangers on horseback, although Priscilla suspected that strangers were rare in Haven. "It's a good place to raise children." Zach looked around, his eyes moving slowly as he studied the house and the outbuildings. "It didn't change much."

That, Priscilla suspected, was good. "Where did Margaret live?" she asked when Zach seemed ready to move on.

"At the other end of town. We might as well try there. Even if she's moved out, whoever lives there now ought to know where she is."

Priscilla and Zach rode slowly through the middle of town. Haven was, as Zach had said, smaller than Ladreville and, judging from the condition of many of the buildings, less prosperous. Its stores had been built with an eye to utility rather than boasting the fanciful European architecture of Ladreville's commercial establishments. Though the towns differed, their residents had at least one thing in common: curiosity. As Priscilla and Zach rode down Main Street, curtains parted and people emerged from the buildings.

Zach seemed oblivious to the stares. Instead, he appeared intent on studying the town. Perhaps that was the reason for his leisurely pace. But Priscilla suspected the slow walk that frustrated both Charcoal and Dancer was more likely a wish to delay reaching Margaret's childhood home.

"This is it," Zach said as he reined in Charcoal. The house was similar to Zach's former home, a simple frame building, but there were differences. Besides being a bit larger and having two stories, this one was painted pale gray and surrounded by a swath of brightly colored flowers. No children played on the grass here; no dog tumbled against the picket fence. Priscilla guessed that only adults lived here now. Even if Margaret had remained, her child would be close to fourteen—almost an adult.

"The addition is new." Zach nodded toward what appeared to be one or two rooms awkwardly grafted to the side.

"Ready?" When Priscilla nodded, Zach slid from his horse and helped her dismount. Saying nothing, but keeping her hand clasped in his, he led the way up the front steps and knocked on the door.

"I'll get it, Mama." As Zach tightened his grip on her hand, Priscilla realized he recognized the woman's voice. Margaret still lived here, and so, it seemed, did her mother.

A moment later, a brown-haired woman perhaps an inch or two shorter than Priscilla opened the door, her pleasant expression fading as she stared at Zach.

"What are you doing here?" she demanded.

She had changed. She was plumper now, and lines had begun to form at the corners of her eyes and her mouth. Her hair was different too, coiled in a knot at the base of her neck rather than being plaited. Despite the changes, Zach knew he would have recognized Margaret anywhere.

"I've come to see you," he said, pleased that his voice betrayed none of his nervousness. He had Priscilla to thank for that. The night she had spent in his arms had banished the worst of his doubts, disproving his deepest fears and showing him that one woman—the woman he loved—loved him. This woman was another story. Zach looked steadily at Margaret. "We have unfinished business."

Her lips thinned, and the brown eyes that had once sparkled when she looked at him were cold. "You're not welcome here."

Though her reaction was what he had expected based on the one letter he had received, Zach had hoped that the years would have changed Margaret as much as they had him. But it appeared that hope would not be realized.

"We won't stay long." Zach tugged on Priscilla's hand, drawing her closer to him. The affection he had once felt for Margaret was nothing compared to the love that blazed inside him for Priscilla. She was the woman he wanted to spend the rest of his life with. She was the one whose love would help him through this afternoon.

"Margaret, I'd like you to meet my wife. Priscilla, this is Margaret Early."

Margaret's eyes narrowed as she studied Priscilla. Did she see a tall, beautiful strawberry blonde with emerald green eyes, or was Priscilla nothing more than another unwanted visitor? Margaret looked down from the front stoop, her expression openly hostile. "I'm Margaret Morgan now. Hank and I married soon after you left." As if recalling her manners, she stepped back into the house and nodded briefly. "You might as well come in. No point in giving the town anything more to gossip about."

"Who is it, Margaret?" The older woman's voice came from a distance, sounding slightly querulous, as if she resented her daughter's absence, no matter how brief. Mrs. Early had been friendlier fifteen years ago, but there was no telling what the years had wrought.

Margaret turned and raised her voice so it would carry clearly through the house. "It's just some people passing through. They needed directions," she lied. "I'll be with you in a minute." Though Margaret had closed the door behind them, she did not offer Priscilla a chair or even a glass of water.

"Is your mother well?" Zach wondered if Mrs. Early's health was the reason for the addition to the house. Her voice had sounded as if it came from that direction. Perhaps she could no longer climb the stairs.

Margaret shook her head. "She hasn't been the same since Pa died."

Though the last time he'd seen Mr. Early had been decidedly unpleasant, Zach had always liked Margaret's father. "I'm sorry to hear that."

A scowl crossed Margaret's face. "There's no point in pretending, Zach. You don't care about me or my family or my son."

Zach felt as if the breath had been knocked from him. A son! Margaret had borne a boy, and he had lived. The child he'd dreamt about existed. "We have a boy?" He wanted to hear her say the words.

Margaret shook her head. "*We* have no children. Hank and I have a son."

The joy that had surged inside him vanished. He had been wrong. The child he had fathered had not been born. Zach shuddered as he remembered the pools of blood that had ended Priscilla's pregnancy. Had Margaret suffered as his wife had? He hoped not. Priscilla squeezed Zach's hand, as if she knew the direction his thoughts had taken and wanted to comfort him.

"Congratulations." Somehow, he forced the word out.

Margaret stared at him for a long moment, indecision apparent in the way she moved her lips without forming words. When she spoke, he suspected it was involuntarily. "Hank's the only father Paul has ever known. Don't try to change that."

As the import of Margaret's words registered, Zach felt himself grow light-headed. Priscilla slipped an arm around his waist and drew him closer, as if she feared he would fall. He wouldn't. He was simply giddy with the knowledge that the child was his. Zach closed his eyes for a second, letting relief wash over him. His nightmare had not come true. Despite her threats, Margaret had not rejected their child and had not chosen to end its life before it had been born. *Thank you, Lord.*

The child, his son, Paul. What had once been a nebulous concept—a child—was now a reality. Zach took a deep breath, thinking of all that he'd learned today. He knew that his child had been born, that it was a boy and that his name was Paul. If that was all that he had learned, he would have been satisfied, but Zach also knew that Paul had had a father in his life, a man who had raised him as if he were his own child, a man who had done what Zach had been afraid to do. That was more than he had dared hope. God had blessed Paul.

Zach raised his eyes to meet Margaret's. There was only one more thing he wanted. "I won't interfere. I came here to ask your forgiveness, not to claim my son, but I would like to see him."

Her eyes were cold, her expression wary. "Why should I trust you? Go back wherever you came from, Zach. I don't need you, and neither does Paul."

∽

"I'm sorry you had to witness that."

Priscilla tightened her grip on Zach's hand, hoping to provide a bit of comfort. So much had changed in less than a day. Twenty-four hours ago he would not touch her hand; now it was firmly clasped in his. Twenty-four hours ago she had believed a man's touch was something to be avoided; now she welcomed the feel of Zach's skin next to hers. Twenty-four hours ago Zach had not been certain he had a child; now he knew. But that knowledge did not appear to bring him the comfort it should.

"She hates me." Zach muttered the words as he helped Priscilla mount her horse.

Priscilla waited to answer until they were riding slowly through Haven, retracing the route they'd followed. She needed the time to collect her thoughts, to find the way to make Zach understand how a mother might feel. "I don't think Margaret hates you. I think she was frightened."

Zach's head swiveled and he stared at Priscilla. "Frightened of me? Why?"

Before she could reply, Priscilla heard the sound of boys' laughter and turned to see what had caused such mirth. She smiled at the sight. There were three boys, each carrying a fishing pole. Though she saw no sign of fish, they appeared not to mind. Instead, they were joking, slapping each other on the back, digging their toes into the dirt as if they had not a care in the world. If only Zach were so carefree!

Priscilla turned to look at her husband. For some reason, he had averted his eyes. She could not, for something about the trio drew her. She watched them, her eyes widening as the boys neared. It wasn't her imagination. She knew it wasn't. "Zach," Priscilla said, slowing Dancer so she could be certain. "The one in the middle looks like you. I think that's Paul." Though the boy's hair was lighter than Zach's, he had the same square chin with a cleft in it, and the way he swaggered reminded her of Zach on a good day.

Priscilla heard the intake of breath and turned toward Zach. His face bore an expression of disbelief mingled with wonder. "He looks happy."

She nodded. "He should be. He has friends and parents who love him."

One of the boys nudged Paul and pointed toward Priscilla and Zach. "You folks need help?" Paul called out.

Zach shook his head. "Just passing through." More softly, so only Priscilla could hear him, he said, "We'd better leave."

Though she heard the regret in his voice, she knew he was keeping his word. No matter how much he wanted to meet the boy, he respected Margaret's wishes. Zach would not interfere in his son's life.

"Why do you think she fears me?" he asked when they were outside the town.

Priscilla reached over and laid a hand on Zach's arm, hoping her touch would comfort him. "Because you are Paul's father. Margaret protected him all these years. She created

372

a new life for both of them. Now she's afraid you'll disrupt everything she's worked so hard to build."

"But I wouldn't. I told her that."

"She didn't believe you." That had been clear to Priscilla. Margaret was both fearful and distrustful. In her place, Priscilla might have felt the same. "She needs time to get used to the idea of you meeting Paul."

"Another fifteen years?"

Priscilla heard the pain in Zach's voice and wanted to assuage it. "You knew this might not be easy. We've come all this way, and there's no reason we have to rush back. Why don't we stay in the area for another day? That'll give Margaret time to think. God may soften her heart."

"Judging from the way she acted today, it would take one of his miracles to do that." Zach was silent for a moment, his eyes fixed on the town they'd just left. "Let's find Hank. His father used to be the blacksmith. I imagine he is too."

He was. The stocky man with medium brown hair and dark brown eyes looked up from the horse shoe he'd been hammering, and Priscilla saw confusion cloud his eyes. "Zach? Is that you?"

When Hank Morgan approached them, keeping the hammer firmly gripped in his hand, Priscilla cringed. Zach did not. Instead, he took a step toward the man who had raised his son. "Yeah, it's me. I came to see Margaret, but when I heard you were married, I thought I'd deliver my congratulations in person—especially after she said you two have a son."

Perhaps it was the words. Perhaps it was the conciliatory tone of Zach's voice. Priscilla didn't know. All she knew was that Hank relaxed. He did not, however, relinquish his grip on the hammer.

Zach took another step toward the blacksmith. "I think my wife would appreciate it if you'd put that hammer down." This time, Zach's words were laced with amusement.

"Sorry, ma'am," Hank said as he laid the hammer on a shelf. He gave her a long, appraising look, then turned to Zach. "So you found yourself a wife who's almost as pretty as mine." The blacksmith nodded. "Pleased to meet you, Mrs. Webster." His grin revealed uneven teeth and a missing incisor. Hank Morgan might be friendly, but he was far from handsome.

"It's my pleasure. I'm happy to meet one of Zach's childhood friends."

The man shook his head. "Make no mistake, Mrs. Webster. Zach and I were never friends. He was the one the rest of us envied. Without even trying, he had all the girls flocking to him."

"But the prettiest girl in town married you."

Hank appeared to consider Priscilla's words. "That she did." He turned to Zach. "How long you fixin' to stay in Haven?"

"We'll be heading out tomorrow morning."

Priscilla tried not to show her disappointment. She had hoped Zach would agree to give Margaret at least a day to change her mind.

Hank tipped his head to one side in the way he seemed to do when he was contemplating something. "Well, then," he said at last, "I reckon you better come to supper tonight."

"That's mighty generous of you, Hank," Zach said, "but Margaret was pretty clear that she didn't want to see me again."

"You'll be welcome for supper." Hank pulled out his watch

and checked the time. "I reckon I better go home now and let Margaret know we're expecting company."

Despite Hank's promise that they'd be welcome, the meal was strained. Though she insisted she was feeling well, Margaret's mother seemed reluctant to eat. Instead, she kept her gaze fixed on Zach, as if worried he would steal her daughter or perhaps her grandson. Margaret said very little, and though Hank tried to initiate conversation, it was stilted. Only Paul appeared relaxed.

"You're the folks I saw this afternoon," he said as Hank performed the introductions. When Paul grinned at Zach, the resemblance was noticeable, though Priscilla doubted the boy recognized it. Why would he, when he believed Zach to be nothing more than an old friend of his parents? Still, for Margaret's sake, Priscilla knew it was best that she and Zach leave Haven in the morning. There was no need for others to spot the resemblance and begin to speculate.

Like many boys his age, Paul's primary concern was eating as much as he could in the shortest amount of time. It was only when dessert was served that he slowed down enough to talk. As he shoveled a piece of apple cobbler into his mouth, he turned toward Zach. "That's a mighty fine horse you've got."

"You've got a good eye for horseflesh. Charcoal cost more than I wanted to pay, but I've never regretted the money. He and I've been together ever since I got out of the army."

Paul's eyes widened, and Priscilla sensed that he was impressed with something Zach had said. "You fought the Mexicans? Were you scared?"

"Every day."

It was clear from Paul's expression that that was not the

response he wanted. "My pa wouldn't have been scared. He ain't scared of nothing."

Hank tried to suppress a smile. "Now, son, that's a bit of an exaggeration."

"Is not. Everybody knows you're the bravest man in town."

"Maybe so," his mother said sternly, "but no one likes a braggart. You may be excused if you take Grandma back to her room. Your father and I are going to have coffee with our guests."

As the boy raised an eyebrow, Priscilla imagined Zach had worn the same expression when he was Paul's age. "Grown-up talk, huh?"

"That's right." Hank nodded toward the door. "Close it behind you."

When Margaret had poured the coffee, she sat down and placed her folded hands on the table. She gave Priscilla a quick glance before turning her attention to Zach. "I owe you an apology." Though Margaret's voice was low, it rang with sincerity. "I was unkind this afternoon."

Zach shook his head at the woman he had once considered marrying, the woman who had borne his child. "I deserved it. When I left, it was the act of a coward. I should never have abandoned you, but I did. I deserve for you to hate me."

Though Hank took a sip of the coffee, no one else seemed to have any appetite for the fragrant beverage. Priscilla wished she and Hank were not here. Surely this was a matter for Zach and Margaret alone, and yet Margaret had specifically requested that all four of them remain in the kitchen.

"I won't lie," Margaret said, her expression solemn. "I did hate you for a long time. It took a good man"—she looked at

Hank, her eyes filled with love—"a better man than I deserve, to show me that hatred hurt me."

Priscilla nodded slowly. She had learned the same lesson.

"What we did was wrong." Margaret emphasized the plural pronoun, and as she did, Priscilla watched Zach's expression lighten. "We were wrong, Zach, but God turned our sin into something good. Paul is a wonderful child, and because you left me, I have the best husband any woman could want."

Hank reached across the table and clasped Margaret's hands in his. "You know I always loved Margaret, but she didn't even notice me when you were around."

Margaret's face flushed. "I was foolish. I was attracted by Zach's good looks; that was all. I liked the idea of a handsome man squiring me around."

"And no one would ever call me handsome." Hank chuckled as he pronounced the words.

Margaret continued the story. "When Hank offered to marry me, I was desperate. I married Hank to protect my child."

Priscilla's eyes filled with tears as she realized how much she and this woman shared. "So did I. I was unwed and expecting a child." There was no reason to tell Margaret and Hank the details. "That's why I married Zach. Now I know it was part of God's plan. I'm sorry Zach hurt you, Margaret, but I can't be sorry that he didn't marry you. If he had, I would never have met him, and I might have spent my whole life not knowing what it was like to love and be loved."

The look Margaret gave Priscilla said she understood and that she, too, was thankful Zach had left Haven. "God has a plan for all of us," she said softly as she looked at Zach. "I'm glad you came back."

"I came for a reason. I wronged you, Margaret. Can you forgive me?"

Margaret exchanged a look with her husband. "I forgave you years ago. The first time Paul called Hank 'Pa,' I knew I had been wrong to hate you and to blame you for what happened. Can you forgive me for being so hard-hearted?"

"Of course."

Though Margaret and Hank offered them a bed for the night, Priscilla was glad that Zach refused. While it would have been pleasant to sleep on a bed rather than the ground, she wanted to be alone with him. They rode in silence until they reached a spot along the river that Zach claimed would be a good camping site. It was far enough outside town that Priscilla was certain this was not where Zach and Margaret had come that fateful night fifteen years ago.

When he helped her dismount, Zach kept his arms around Priscilla, his eyes dark with emotion. "You were right when you told me I needed to come back."

Priscilla studied the face that she loved so dearly. Though familiar, it looked different than it had this morning. The features were the same—the straight nose, the firm lips, the cleft in the chin—but the tension that had always marked those features was gone. In its place, Priscilla saw peace. *Thank you, Lord*. Her prayers had been answered.

"Are you sorry Paul will never know you're his father?"

Zach shook his head. "It was strange, sitting at the table and seeing a younger version of myself on the other side," he admitted. "I have no doubt that Paul is my son, but I realized I wasn't his father."

Priscilla's face must have registered her confusion, for Zach continued his explanation. "When I left, I gave up that claim.

Fortunately, God provided Margaret with a husband and Paul with a father. I hope Margaret will write occasionally and tell me how he's doing, but if she doesn't, I can live with that. No matter what, I won't return to Haven. It wouldn't be fair to anyone."

Zach stared into the distance for a moment, and Priscilla wondered whether he was regretting the fact that he would not see his son again. When he spoke, a smile colored his voice. "As we rode by my old house, I thought about something my mother used to say. She claimed life was a journey and that we all follow a road." Zach chuckled at the memory. "I think I was about eight when she told me the story, so you can imagine how little I listened. Now I wish I could tell her that she was right. According to her, at first the road seems straight, but there will always be bends. Like the river."

Perhaps it was not coincidence that Zach had chosen a spot where the river made a lazy bend to the left. He smiled again. "Ma said that even though the turns take us in new directions, they're easy. All we do is stay on the path. It's the forks that are difficult, because we have to make a choice each time we come to one." His eyes darkened as he added, "She warned me to choose carefully, because there's no turning around. Once we've taken a step, it's done."

A lump lodged in Priscilla's throat when she thought of the forks she had chosen and the times she had wished she could undo the past. Zach's mother was right; no one could turn back. All that was possible was to make the best of the chosen direction. As if he read her thoughts, Zach touched Priscilla's lips, urging the corners to tilt up. "There've been more twists in the road than I expected, and I've stumbled more times than I can count, but I can't regret a single moment, because they've all led me here."

He understood. This man who was so dear to her understood what she was feeling, for his words echoed her thoughts. "God has blessed me," Zach continued. "Though I did nothing to deserve it, he's brought me to you." Zach touched her lips again, this time letting his finger trace their outline. "I love you, Priscilla. I always will."

A bird twittered; the breeze rustled the oak's leaves, and a few yards away Charcoal and Dancer whickered. Though Priscilla was dimly aware of the sounds, nothing mattered but the love that shone from Zach's eyes. It dissolved the lump in her throat and sent warmth surging through her. He was right. Everything that had happened had been part of God's plan. The losses she had endured had made her stronger. Her suffering had given her the ability to help others. And through it all, God had been guiding her. This was where she was meant to be. This was the man he meant for her.

"Oh, Zach, I love you so much." Priscilla placed her hands on his cheeks, savoring the feel of his skin, reveling in the smile that lit his face. "I never dreamt I could be so happy." She swallowed deeply, then touched the cleft in his chin, smiling as she said, "Isn't it amazing the way it all turned out? When I left Boston, I was looking for adventure. I never thought I'd find love."

Zach was grinning as he pulled her closer. "Now we both know the truth. Love is an adventure." He lowered his lips to hers and murmured, "Isn't it grand?"

Author's Letter

Dear Reader,

I hope you enjoyed Priscilla and Zach's story. In some respects, it was the most difficult book I've written. Although I have always believed in the healing power of love, never before have I written a story where the characters needed so much healing. And though I normally enjoy research, the only way to describe some of the reading I did for *Scattered Petals* is "painful." I cringed and cried as I read other women's accounts of rape and its aftermath, but I knew that I had to learn what they'd experienced if I was to make Priscilla come to life. I hope that I succeeded.

One of my greatest pleasures as a writer is hearing from readers, and so I encourage you to visit my website (www.amandacabot.com). It includes an email link, my snail mail address, and information about my books. It also has discussion guides for readers' groups. Please let me know what you've enjoyed about my stories and what you'd like to see next.

If this is your first Texas Dreams book, I hope you'll read *Paper Roses*, the first of the trilogy, which tells the story of Sarah's arrival in Ladreville. Though you know that she and Clay have a happy ending, I assure you it wasn't always certain. And if you're wondering what happens to Lawrence, you'll find the answer in the third Texas Dreams book, which will be available in March 2011.

Until we meet again, I send you blessings and remind you of Joshua 1:9. "Be strong and of a good courage; be not afraid, neither be thou dismayed: for the LORD thy God is with thee whithersoever thou goest."

Amanda Cabot